James P. Sumner
CRY HAVOC

BOOKS

By James P. Sumner

GlobaTech Series

D.E.A.D. Till I Die
Crossfire
Danger Close
Cry Havoc

Vinci Books

vinci-books.com

Published by Vinci Books Ltd in 2025

1

Copyright © James P. Sumner 2022

The author has asserted their moral right to be identified as the author of this work in accordance with the Copyright, Designs and Patents Act 1988. This work is a work of fiction. Names, characters, places and incidents are the product of the author's imagination or are used fictitiously. Any resemblance to actual persons, living or dead, places and incidents is entirely coincidental.
All rights reserved. No part of this publication may be copied, reproduced, distributed, stored in any retrieval system, or transmitted in any form or by any means, including photocopying, recording, or other electronic or mechanical methods, nor used as a source for any form of machine learning including AI datasets, without the prior written permission of the publisher.
The publisher and the author have made every effort to obtain permissions for any third party material used in this book and to comply with copyright law. Any queries in this respect should be brought to the attention of the publisher and any omissions will be corrected in future editions.
A CIP catalogue record for this book is available from the British Library.
Paperback ISBN: 9781036701178

Foreword

Six months ago, after years of secret planning, Quincy Hall, the CEO of Orion International, launched an attack on the United States and seized control of the government. Using Tristar Security's significant private army to maintain order, he ran the country like a dictatorship, intent on establishing his own long-lasting regime.

The remaining GlobaTech forces led a rebellion against the Orion occupation and ultimately won, rescuing President Schultz and reinstalling him as the true leader of the country. But despite this victory, Adrian Hell still felt lost. His world crumbled around him when he discovered the wife he thought long-dead was actually Jay, the Tristar assassin responsible for numerous atrocities over the last twelve months. Ignoring the pleas of both GlobaTech and Blackstar, he embarked on a crusade of violence to discover the truth behind his wife's reappearance.

Julie Fisher, Ray Collins, and Jericho Stone began their own investigation and discovered a hidden enemy. The

Foreword

Nemesis program, a privately funded project based on old CIA experiments, was producing dangerous assets, conditioned through subliminal manipulation to become unstoppable mercenaries.

Jay was the program's first success story.

With Blackstar's assistance, the GlobaTech team learned more about this new enemy, but they were always one step behind Adrian Hell's trail of destruction. Despite intervening to save both the assassin and Jay from a Tristar hit squad, they were destined to collide with their former ally. Adrian Hell, in a fit of desperate rage as he began to see enemies everywhere, beat Ray Collins almost to death.

Angered by the assault on his brother-in-arms, Jericho attacked Adrian. Although a surprise attack by a team of Nemesis assets reunited them, the damage was done. GlobaTech lost a valuable piece of technology, and Blackstar lost a key member of its team, leaving the remaining allies feeling broken and defeated.

Julie negotiated with Jay, offering her freedom in exchange for her help in the upcoming fight. Held together by a fragile alliance, GlobaTech, Blackstar, Adrian, and Jay came together to mount a final assault on the location believed to be where the Nemesis program began.

After a hard-fought skirmish, the group cornered the head of the program, Benjamin Marshall. But just when they believed they had won, the world came tumbling down around them once again.

Quincy Hall reappeared, revealing himself to be the mastermind behind the Nemesis program. It was time for him to finally reveal his true endgame. Hall had a sleeper agent in play, who had been working with Adrian and GlobaTech the entire time. With a defiant, evil grin on his face, he activated his secret Nemesis asset: Adam Rayne. He shot and killed Adrian Hell, then kidnapped Jay and escaped with Quincy Hall in the confusion.

Now, those who remain must face their bleak new reality, overcome their grief, and stop Orion once and for all, before it's too late…

Prologue

His footsteps crunched in the snow like bones breaking. The cold wrapped around his dominating frame like a spiteful blanket, but Jericho Stone navigated the Baltimore streets regardless; his focus and inherent anger toward the world warmed him against winter's relentless assault.

He was a week removed from having buried his friends. A week removed from the day everything once again changed. A week removed from the day his next fight began.

Jericho wore a short, insulated jacket with the Globa-Tech logo stitched over the left breast. His face was etched into a permanent scowl. Thick gristle coated his jawline and throat. His eyes blinked at abnormally long intervals. With his hands shoved down into his pockets, he walked as casually as he could along the sidewalk. His imposing stature effortlessly carved a path through the hundreds of people around him.

His target was Stephen Cook, a Tristar mercenary who was in the room the day Adrian Hell died. The day they found out Adam Rayne was a Nemesis asset. The day Quincy Hall escaped with Jay and GlobaTech's soul drive.

It was the day they lost.

Jericho's jaw tensed so hard, he feared his own teeth would shatter. That day was on a loop in his head, torturing his every waking moment, reminding him of his failure. It enraged him.

He was about to put the fear of God into Stephen Cook.

Leads were increasingly hard to come by, and locating Cook was a lucky break. Jericho had waited in the cold and dark outside Cook's apartment, hoping he would do something useful.

Cook emerged a half-hour ago. He was walking thirty feet ahead of Jericho, moving at an easy pace and talking animatedly into his cell phone. Jericho followed him.

He turned a corner, cutting down an alleyway between a small hardware store and a bakery. Jericho slowed before turning in after him. It was narrow, with barely enough room for him to squeeze past the large dumpster on his right. A pile of trash was strewn next to it. As Jericho walked past it, a cardboard box tumbled down it, landing at his feet. The frozen corpse of a rat rolled out. Jericho grimaced and knocked it away with his foot mid-stride.

Cook was almost at the other end of the alley, which opened up into a courtyard formed by the surrounding buildings. He turned right at the end.

Jericho quickened his pace to catch up. As he stepped out and headed right, he was met with a stiff blow to his face. Unprepared, Jericho stumbled backward but remained upright, despite almost losing his footing on the thin, slippery snow on the ground. He took a moment to recover and shake off the sting of the punch. He looked up to see Cook standing there, clearly waiting for him.

"You're literally the *worst* choice to follow someone, do you know that?" said Cook.

Jericho took a deep breath. A cloud of steam drifted in front of his face.

"Y'know, I said the same thing," he replied. "But they insisted on sending me anyway. Probably something to do with my incredibly effective interrogation techniques."

Cook wavered for a heartbeat. "You picked the wrong guy, asshole. I don't know anything, and I wouldn't tell you if I did."

"Yes, you would."

Jericho cracked his neck and took a step forward. He stood squarely in front of Cook, hands by his side, balled into fists that looked like wrecking balls.

Cook swallowed hard. "You think I'm scared of you?"

Jericho didn't move. "Yes."

Cook smiled. "You're in the wrong part of town to play the tough guy."

The light crunching of multiple footsteps faded into earshot behind Jericho. He glanced over his shoulder to see three men exiting one of the buildings.

He looked back at Cook and took a loud, impatient breath. "Let me guess: that's who you were talking to on your phone?"

Cook nodded. "Dude, I've known you were following me since I left my apartment. Now, before the streets run red, you're gonna tell me why."

Jericho paused and looked around. The five of them were surrounded on all sides by buildings at least two stories tall. Only one other alley led into the courtyard, and that was directly opposite the one he followed Cook down moments earlier. The snow wasn't thick underfoot, but it still coated the ground completely. Ice-cold wind whipped around the buildings. Jericho felt it tear through him, but his body was too tense to let a shiver escape.

He turned his attention back to Cook. "Okay. Word is, you were in the room last week when shit went sideways for GlobaTech."

Cook hesitated, then a crooked smile crept onto his face. "I thought I recognized you! Only so many guys your size, right? Yeah, yeah... I was there. I was standing next to Mr. Hall when your little assassin buddy got dropped. Never thought I'd see the day. That bastard was Tristar's public enemy number one for months. Good times."

"Uh-huh. I'm gonna need you to tell me where Hall is. And the Nemesis asset who killed the assassin."

Cook laughed. The men behind Jericho joined in. He glanced back at them again.

"Are you deaf?" asked Cook. "I told you, I ain't saying shit. That's not how we work."

"No one's working for Tristar anymore. That company's been shut down."

Cook shook his head. "Not shut down. Just... restructured."

"That's a fancy term for shut down."

"You should read the business section more."

"I'm too busy populating the obituaries."

Cook smiled. "Big talk."

Jericho shrugged. "I'm a big guy."

"You're a dead guy."

Jericho shook his head. "Not today."

He reached into his pocket and retrieved a small device, no larger than a key fob. It had a blinking red light on it. He held it toward Cook, so he could see it, then tossed it casually at his feet.

"What's that?" asked Cook, frowning.

"A tracking device."

"So, what? You've been tracking me?"

"No. Someone's been tracking me."

A pitch-black whirlwind appeared from the alley to Jericho's right at a furious speed. The figure wore dark combat pants, boots, and a dark hoodie stretched over a large frame and tied up around their face. The new arrival charged the line of men behind Jericho, who sidestepped so he could watch without obscuring Cook's view.

The figure carved through the men like a hot knife through butter. Each fist and elbow they threw was devastatingly accurate. The first two men dropped like a stone from blows to their heads. The figure spun around for added momentum and launched an uppercut at the third man's jaw, which connected and lifted him clear off the ground. He landed a few feet away, his jaw hanging off its hinge.

Jericho turned to Cook, who was rooted to the spot with fear. His mouth hung open and his eyes had begun to water. Jericho paced over to him and placed a large hand around his throat. He pushed him back against the wall with enough force to knock the wind from him.

"Please, wait! Look, I... I don't know anything. I don't, I swear!" Cook pleaded, gasping for air.

The hooded figure strode over to Jericho's side. He was a similar size and build. Cook looked back and forth between them, as if unable to comprehend the two behemoths.

The man unfastened the drawstrings and pulled them apart. He lowered the hood and revealed his smooth, ebony skin.

"Hey, Link," said Jericho.

"Jericho." His voice was like a bear's growl.

"Find me okay?"

Link nodded. "Tracker worked like a charm. So, this guy refusing to talk?"

"Says he doesn't know anything."

"Huh. That's a shame. The chance of him knowing something is the only thing keeping his head on his shoulders."

Cook waved his hands in front of him. "No, no, wait! I *do* know something. I do. I... I just remembered."

Jericho raised an eyebrow. "Well, that's convenient."

Cook glanced beyond the two men, staring at his friends.

Link noticed and smiled. "If you're hoping they're gonna wake up and miraculously be better fighters than they were two minutes ago, you'll be here a while, asshole."

Cook exhaled and lowered his gaze. His shoulders slumped forward with defeat. Jericho tensed his arm to keep him upright against the wall.

"Tell me where Hall is," demanded Jericho.

"I... I don't know, I swear," said Cook. "But I know who might."

"Enlighten me."

"Like I told you, Tristar ain't gone, man. They just have a new boss. Word is, she was hand-picked by Mr. Hall to rebrand the company. He... he knows what people think of Tristar after everything that's happened. They're no use to him now, but... but it's too valuable an asset to just throw away, right? So, there's this whole PR thing going on. Guys like me, we were told to go home, lie low, and wait to be told if we still have jobs."

Link looked over at Jericho. "You buying this?"

Jericho shrugged. "Sounds plausible, I guess." He pulled Cook away from the wall, then slammed him back against it. "Who's running Tristar now?"

Cook winced from the impact. "Some hotshot Wall Street type called Parker. Gwen Parker. That's it. That's all I know."

Jericho glanced to his right. "Link?"

"On it," he muttered. He took out his cell phone and began tapping the screen. After a few moments, he looked up. "Got it. There was a press conference yesterday, apparently. Says it right here: Gwen Parker announced she was the new CEO of Tristar Security. It was a real low-key thing. Didn't even make it into the mainstream news cycle."

Jericho nodded. "No doubt what's left of Hall's influence, burying it like that. No wonder we didn't pick up on it before now. But I doubt anyone will buy that so soon after Orion's occupation ended. What's the timeframe?"

"Doesn't say. Just that they expect more details about the company's restructuring in the coming weeks."

Cook quickly looked back and forth between them. "See? See! I told you. And that's it. That's all I know. If anyone knows where Mr. Hall is, it'll be Gwen Parker."

Jericho took a deep breath. "Okay."

"Okay? So, what? I can go?" Cook laughed to himself. "I can go?"

Jericho shrugged and let him go. Cook blew a sigh of relief, but his reprieve was short-lived. Jericho had moved only three paces away before Link lunged for Cook. His giant hands wrapped around Cook's head and face, and with a sudden and powerful twitch of his arms, Link broke his neck. He let go, watching Cook's lifeless body crumple to the ground.

Jericho looked down at the body, then at Link, furrowing his brow with silent disapproval.

Link shrugged. "Like the boss man said: it's time we do things the wrong way."

Jericho let out a taut breath and walked away, slowing to scoop up the tracking device as he passed. Link pulled his hood back up over his head and followed, stepping unceremoniously over the three bodies he left in the snow as he followed Jericho down the alley.

Chapter One

December 8, 2020

Julie Fisher stood outside the boardroom door, staring blankly at the handle. She felt nervous. It was a mindset that didn't really have a place in her line of work. At least, not until a week ago.

After the assault on the Nemesis compound in New York, Julie was informed by more lawyers than she knew existed that Moses Buchanan had named her his replacement. It wasn't something she wanted or expected, and it had turned her world upside-down. She needed a mission. She needed an enemy she could shoot. She wasn't built for having meetings about meetings, in which something may or may not be agreed on.

She wriggled on the spot, trying to adjust to the pantsuit she was wearing. She was uncomfortable and self-conscious. Her hair was tied back, and she was wearing the least amount of makeup she could get away with to hide the dark rings beneath her eyes.

In her hand was a thick folder containing the agenda for the meeting. *Her* agenda. *Her* meeting. She reached for the handle and saw her hand shaking. She closed her eyes and balled her hand into a fist. She took a deep breath, opened her eyes again, and stared at her hand as she flattened it out, daring it to shake again.

It didn't.

Damn right, she thought.

Julie cracked her neck and opened the door, walking inside with all the confidence she could muster. Facing her was an oblong, beechwood table. In the middle of it, resting on a silver tray, was a large jug of water and several upturned glasses.

Sitting around it were ten men. The youngest looked to be in his mid-sixties. Four lined each side, with two at the far end. All eyes turned to her as she entered. The muted conversations stopped. Julie made eye contact with each one of them, then slammed the door closed behind her and took her seat at the head of the table. She placed the folder down in front of her and clasped her hands on top of it.

As she opened her mouth to speak, a man's hand shot up to stop her.

"Miss Fisher, if I may?"

Silently, she sat back in her chair and gestured for the man to speak.

"We… we understand the protocols that are in place for CEOs of this company. It's a unique position, and we agreed a long time ago that CEOs should have sole discretion to name their successor."

Julie rested an elbow on the arm of the chair and placed her cheek against her fist. She stared at him, knowing exactly where this conversation was heading. She had expected it. That didn't make it any easier to hear. Or any less insulting.

The man continued. "We all liked and respected Mr. Buchanan for what he did for this company. Like you, we're all committed to rebuilding this company and moving forward. But we all feel that your... inexperience in this type of role would be detrimental to GlobaTech's future. Everyone here knows what you did for this country, Miss Fisher..."

His words faded away. Julie's vision blurred as she stared at the surface of the table. Very few people except for Buchanan ever unironically called her Miss Fisher. She never expected to hear it again. She wasn't ready to hear it again.

"...I would ask you to consider relinquishing your position so that we, the board, can—"

Julie held up her hand. "I'm gonna stop you right there, Mr... Hobbs, is it?"

Hobbs nodded. "That's right, ma'am. Gerald Hobbs. I'm the Head of Finance."

She couldn't tell if he was being polite or condescending, but she was in no mood to figure it out.

"Okay, well, I'm sorry, Gerald. I hung in there as long as I could, but this is my meeting, not yours." She looked around the room at the stunned faces of GlobaTech's board of directors. "You're right. I have no qualifications or experience that would prepare me for this job. But I'm a damn good soldier. I led the rebellion against Orion and won. So, to put your minds at ease about what kind of head for business I have, understand that if I can handle an invasion of this country, I can hold my own in a boardroom debate."

She got to her feet, pushing her chair away from her slightly with her legs. She felt her confidence returning. She walked around the table, stopping level with the jug of water. She leaned over between two board members and poured herself a glass. She took a sip, then walked back to her place, put the glass down gently, and turned her attention back to the directors.

"Before we get started, I'm going to say this one time, and one time only." She turned her attention to Hobbs. "As you said, Gerald, the CEO position comes with certain provisions. The first of which is that we can choose our own replacement. Moses Buchanan chose me."

She opened the folder in front of her to the first page, pointing to it for reference. "Another provision is that the CEO owns fifty-one percent of GlobaTech's shares. That means whoever sits in the chair is both technically rich *and* has a controlling interest in the company. The boss literally runs the show."

She closed the folder and sat back down, then took another sip of water from the glass in front of her. "The ten of you are here because you collectively own the vast majority of the remaining forty-nine percent. You all hold high-ranking positions in the company. Some are important. Some are mostly symbolic. And that's okay. Ultimately, your contributions and insights into this company's success were invaluable to my predecessors, as I'm sure they will be to me. But I'm not Moses Buchanan. I'm not Josh Winters. I'm not Ryan Schultz. My vision for GlobaTech may differ from theirs… and from yours. My experience comes from being on the front lines, not from being in the boardroom. I have experience and insights no one before me had, and I think that could be invaluable too."

Hobbs moved to speak, but Julie stopped him.

"Gerald, please. I haven't finished." She looked at everyone sitting around the table again in turn. "I will come to you for advice. I will ask your opinions. I will tell you what I want to do, and I will listen to you as you help me try to make the necessary decisions. However..."

She stood slowly and leaned forward, spreading her palms across the smooth surface of the table. Each man leaned back in his chair.

"It would be wise to not mistake my politeness and diplomacy for weakness. I'm not a scared little girl looking for acceptance into the old man's club. This is the twenty-first century, and I have as much right to be here as you do. Please also understand that while the last few months have been difficult for all of us, the last couple of weeks have been particularly difficult for me. GlobaTech has powerful enemies. I know... I've fought them. I got my ass kicked, and I lost good people. That means I'm more motivated to see this company succeed than you could ever hope to be. So, if you disagree with me, or if you have a problem with me, I ask that you bring it to my attention in a timely and professional manner, so we can sit down together and discuss it. If you don't show me the respect that I or this position deserve... or if you continue muttering behind my back to try and undermine my newfound authority... understand I will not hesitate to fucking shoot you."

The color drained from the men's faces, making them look older and whiter than they already were. Julie took a deep breath, managing the gentle rush of adrenaline she just got. Her face remained neutral, giving nothing away to her board of directors except the confidence they now knew she had.

The men exchanged glances of fear and surprise. Then they relaxed. They settled back into their chairs, composed themselves, and focused their attention on her, patiently waiting for her next words.

Julie took a calming breath, then took her seat and turned the page in her folder. "Now, to business. For years, GlobaTech has been the market leader in pretty much every industry that matters. But for everything we've done to help this world, we've inadvertently bred the next thing to defend it from. I want to change that. That means no more weapons. No more high-end technology. No more satellites. No more leading the fight against domestic threats. We should leave all that to the military and let them do their job of defending this country."

The room was deathly silent. Every board member stared intently at Julie, focused with a mix of intrigue and disbelief.

Julie continued. "I want to streamline what we do here and focus on helping as many people as we can. I believe we should focus on our contract with the United Nations and earn back their faith in our ability to be their peacekeepers around the world. So, I'm proposing we sell off every division in the company except pharmaceuticals and private security. And I want you all to help me figure out how to do it."

Chapter Two

Kim Mitchell's apartment overlooked Central Park. It was one of five on the twentieth floor of the exclusive building that helped dominate the crowded skyline of the busiest city in the world. Large glass windows bathed her bedroom in natural light, providing a panoramic view of the trees below. It looked majestic in winter, with the treetops coated in white.

She sat on the bed, her long legs stretched out in front of her, protruding from her short, pink bathrobe and crossed at her ankles. She was reading a magazine, occasionally glancing over the top of it to gaze out of the window.

Both of her former bosses had paid her incredibly well, which meant she owned the luxurious apartment and had enough savings to live comfortably without ever having to work again. She was probably the highest paid secretary in the country.

The bedroom door led to the living area, which was spacious yet cozy, with high ceilings and a similar view. She could hear the dull murmur of conversation floating through, but it was muted enough that she couldn't make out the words. She didn't want to anyway. He needed his privacy.

She leaned to the side, peering through the open doorway. She could just about see Ray Collins's back. He was sitting on the L-shaped sofa, talking into the laptop camera.

She smiled to herself, partly out of love and admiration and partly out of sympathy. That man had been through so much. She just wanted him to be okay.

Collins stared at the screen, his fingers toying absently with one of the strings of his hoodie. He hadn't shaved in a couple of weeks. He hadn't slept much in that time either. He looked a lifetime away from the smooth, confident man he used to be.

So much had changed for him.

On the screen, speaking from an office somewhere in the Middle East, was his therapist, Dr. Moss. It was only his second session, and he was still getting used to talking to a therapist. It was hard enough for him to talk with someone he knew, let alone a stranger who was only listening because she was being paid. However, both Kim and Julie had insisted he needed the help, and he had neither the strength nor the justification to argue with them.

Dr. Moss was friendly and professional, and Collins had taken an instant liking to her. As uncomfortable as he was, she put him at ease during their sessions, and he appreciated that.

"And how have the headaches been, Ray? Getting any easier?"

Collins shrugged, discarding the hoodie string and

resting back into the soft cushions of the sofa. "Aye, a little bit, I guess. At this stage, I'm honestly not sure why I'm still getting them—the lack of sleep, the concussions, or the…" He paused to tap his temple with his finger. "Ya know… crazy stuff."

Dr. Moss smiled, patient and understanding. "Ray, you're not crazy. You're dealing with a serious trauma, both mentally and physically. That's perfectly normal. And while I appreciate that you're probably joking around when you say that, it's not healthy to sit in that mindset of self-deprecation. Long-term, it doesn't help, okay?"

He held his hands up. "Sorry, Doc. Force of habit, ya know. I've been taking the pills they gave me for the pain. I'm managing."

"Good. Now, in our last session, we set goals for what we want to achieve here, but we also began to look at what happened to you. How do you feel about looking at that a little more?"

Collins shrugged again. "Sure, Doc. Whatever ya want."

"It's not about what I want, Ray. It's about what you're comfortable with. I know it isn't easy for you. Our sessions go at your pace, not mine."

"Aye, I know. Sorry. I mean… sure. I can talk about it with ya. It's okay."

"Okay, then. Now, you told me briefly what happened and what led up to it, but I want to talk about *why* you think it all happened the way that it did."

Collins frowned, confused. He sat forward, rested his forearms on his knees, and clasped his hands. "How do ya mean, Doc? It went down the way it did because Adri… *he* was a bloody psychopath. I always figured we were friends, but I guess not. Not really. If we were, he wouldn't have been able to push that to the side so easily and beat the hell outta me, right?"

Dr. Moss pursed her lips and tilted her head slightly. "Hmm... not necessarily. Take yourself out of this for the moment. Take GlobaTech out of it. Just look at... him. If I could ask him what happened and why, what do you think he would tell me?"

"Not much. He's dead."

The response was sharp and cruel, which took her by surprise. She watched Collins for a minute, letting him sit in the silence and process how he felt. She shuffled in her seat to get comfortable.

"Ray, I know it might sometimes look like I'm playing Devil's advocate, or even like I'm taking someone else's side, but that's not what this is. I'm on no one's side. I'm simply trying to help you process what you went through, so you can begin to heal from it. I asked you to tell me what he would say because I want you to try and see this from his perspective. If you can understand why he acted the way he did, it will help you forgive him."

Collins looked away, his gaze suddenly drawn to the thick carpet, then the table, then the window... anywhere except the screen. He closed his eyes and took a deep breath, eventually nodding to himself.

"Sorry, Doc. I didn't mean... I'm not trying to be unhelpful, ya know."

"I know. It's okay. You have nothing to apologize for. You're entitled to feel how you feel."

"I just... I don't know how to see it from his point of view. There was no part of what he did that was right. Way I hear it, he said as much himself afterward."

Dr. Moss nodded along, listening patiently, letting him speak.

Collins sat back again, relaxing into the conversation. "Everywhere he looked, he saw enemies. He was so... messed up from seeing his wife again, he wasn't thinking clearly. He pushed people away who wanted to help him. Ruby, his lady friend, she had it worse than anyone, seeing the fella self-destruct like that. Must've been hard to love him."

"Yes. It must have been."

"But why me, Doc? Out of everyone, why come at me the way he did? I always had his back. Back in the day, I helped sneak him into Pripyat to rescue his girl."

"This... Ruby?"

Collins shook his head. "No, this was before her. This was Tori. She... she was in Texas when..."

Dr. Moss nodded. "I see."

"But then, only last year, I flew out to Tokyo to help him with some shit he'd got himself into with the Yakuza. I was always happy to help because..."

"Because... what?"

"Because he and I are cut from the same cloth, ya know. I related to him. I understood him. Hell, I admired him. Don't get me wrong, he did some wicked shit. We all have in this line of work. But he was... honest. Never shied away from who he was or what he did. I respected that."

"And that's why what happened hurt you beyond the physical distress you endured? You felt betrayed by him?"

Collins nodded slowly. "Aye. Aye, I guess I did."

"Sounds a lot like how *you* said *he* felt."

He smiled to himself. "Aye. I guess it kinda does."

"If you consider yourself similar to him, you shouldn't find it difficult to put yourself in his shoes. I think you know that, and I think it scares you that you could be similar to someone who was capable of doing what he did to you."

Collins raised his eyebrow. "Well, someone's a smartass, ain't ya?"

Dr. Moss smiled. "I have a lot of certificates that say so, yes."

He smiled back, then glanced away, shaking his head to himself silently, as if cursing himself for not arriving to her conclusion on his own.

"Ray, with him gone, you can't confront him to get closure," continued Dr. Moss. "So, you need to look for a way to get it yourself. One way that can be achieved is by admitting to yourself what happened and trying to understand why he did it."

"I've admitted what he did…" he said defensively.

"Not really, no. I don't know if you've noticed, Ray, but you can't even say his name. You're still in denial over what happened. You've acknowledged your wounds, and you can talk about what you endured, but you can't tell me who did it."

"Ya know who did it…"

"Then tell me his name."

Collins went to speak but froze. His words caught in his throat, choking him. His gaze misted over as he stared at the screen. The world disappeared around him.

…

…

…

"Ray? Ray?"

The sound of Dr. Moss's voice broke through into his mind. He shook his head to clear the cobwebs. The room faded back into existence.

"Come back, Ray. Follow my voice."

His vision refocused on the screen. He looked into the doctor's eyes. She smiled back at him.

"Are you with me, Ray?"

"Huh? Yeah. Yeah, I'm listening. Sorry."

Dr. Moss watched him with patience and sympathy. "This process is a marathon, Ray. Not a sprint. It will take time, and it won't be easy."

Collins stared at the floor between his feet. His eyes began to glisten. "I just... I don't want to feel this way anymore, Doc. I feel like I'm trapped in my own body. I feel helpless. I've had my ass whooped plenty of times before. I always bounce back. But this time, I can't. This time..."

"This time, you knew the person who attacked you. And this time, you were close to death. When we are forced to face our own mortality, it changes us. We're never the same after it. Not one of us."

"But I do that every day of my life. Ya know how many times I walked into a gunfight, Doc? If I only have one a day, I feel like I'm on vacation."

She couldn't help but smile. "But that's different, isn't it? That's a choice. And I've worked with plenty of soldiers and fighters before. Your minds are wired differently than the rest of ours. You have an unwavering belief that you will survive. In every conflict, you simply *know* you will be around for the next one. You can't live the life you have any other way."

Collins shrugged humbly. "Aye, I guess."

"But this wasn't one of those times. You didn't choose this fight, and from what you told me yesterday, there was a point when you genuinely thought you were going to die. That experience has muted the part of your mind that believes it will always survive, and part of this process is about helping you hear it again."

"Aye."

"But it all starts with saying his name, Ray. Until you

admit to yourself who did this to you, it will always be this anonymous ordeal you can't take control of. Which means you'll stay in this cycle of guilt and suffering."

Collins ran a hand over his face, discreetly trying to remove the tears from his eyes. Dr. Moss watched the internal struggle on his face.

Finally, he took a deep breath. "It was... Adrian. Adrian Hell. Or Adrian Hughes. Whatever. That's who did this to me." He looked at the screen, staring into her kind eyes. "Adrian Hell was going to kill me."

"Yes, he was. But he didn't." Dr. Moss sat forward in her chair. "Ray, that was incredibly brave, what you just did. That showed real strength. Strength you've always had. Do you understand that? Your feet are on the road to recovery now. From here, we can only go forward. Well done."

He smiled, which forced new tears to trickle down his cheek. "Thanks, Doc."

She sat back again. "This is probably a good place to end our session today. Tell me, how are you sleeping?"

Collins gestured to his own face. "Do ya really have to ask, Doc? I look like the star of a George Romero movie. Come on."

She rolled her eyes. "I wouldn't go that far, Ray. But are you still having the nightmares?"

He nodded. "Every bastard night. It's always the same. I wake to the sound of my skull splitting open in a car door."

"I can prescribe you something to help you sleep, if you want?"

He shook his head. "Nah, I'm good, Doc. Honestly, I'm all for painkillers and whatnot, but I don't like the idea of taking pills that mess with my head. I'll figure it out."

"Okay. The option is there for you if you change your mind."

"Appreciate it, Doc. Thanks."

"Let's book our next session for the day after tomorrow. I think you've earned a little break after today."

"Aye. Sounds good, Doc."

"Take care, Ray."

He smiled at the screen as the call ended. He closed the lid and flopped back into the sofa, staring up at the ceiling for a moment. He wiped his eyes with his sleeve, then got wearily to his feet. He was wearing long pajama pants and nothing under his thin hoodie. He glanced out of the window on his way past, padding into the bedroom.

Kim looked up as he entered, immediately placing her magazine on the nightstand. She pushed herself up onto her knees and patted the bed beside her. Collins sat down and stretched out. She shuffled to his side and linked his arm.

"How did it go?" she asked.

"Aye, it was all right, as these things go," he replied. "Wasn't easy, but the doc thinks I made progress today, so who I am to argue?"

Kim smiled. "That's great. I'm proud of you."

He looked at her, staring into her wide, blue eyes. "I really appreciate ya looking after me, love. And for letting me stay with ya. I know we... ya know... always had... anyway, I'm just saying, I appreciate it, but ya don't have to. I'll be okay on my own. I know ya probably have stuff ya should be doing."

She leaned up and kissed his forehead. "Ray, there's nowhere I'd rather be, and nothing I'd rather be doing, okay?"

"But what about GlobaTech?"

Kim shook her head. "There's nothing for me there anymore. I've lost two bosses to that place, both of whom I loved. I can't let that company take anything else from me. So, I'm here making sure I don't lose you."

"You're a real diamond, love. Ya really are."

He slid down on the bed and turned on his side, cuddling into her. She put her arm around him and held him tight. She felt him take a deep breath and relax. She stared out of the windows ahead as she held him, letting her mind wander.

GlobaTech had taken as much as it had given her, true. But she wasn't done with that place just yet. Buchanan had left her instructions in the event of his death. His team needed things that only she could give them.

She took a deep breath.

She wasn't done yet.

Chapter Three

The convoy of Humvees tore through the Nevada desert, kicking up dust clouds along the sides of the dirty road. The temperature stubbornly pushed back against winter's grip. It wasn't hot, but it wasn't freezing like most places were, either.

Quincy Hall sat comfortably in the back of the middle vehicle, staring absently out of the window like he was on vacation. His left arm was resting next to the glass; his right lay across his lap, a cigar hanging between two fingers. His beige suit was freshly pressed, and his thinning gray hair was smartly styled.

It had been an eventful week for him. After dealing a killing blow to GlobaTech, he had set his sights on the future. The final stage of his plans could finally move forward without interruption.

Sitting beside him, rigid and upright in his seat, was Rayne. Hall glanced at him and smiled. The ace he had been waiting to play for over two years. That was the beauty of the Nemesis program: Adam Rayne had no idea he was even a part of it. He was chosen because of his potential. He was accepted into the SEALs on his own. His involvement in Blackstar was subtly orchestrated so that Hall would have that silver bullet, should it be needed.

One week ago, it was.

Hall turned back to gaze at the mountainous landscape rushing past outside.

"Has our guest been any trouble?" he asked.

Rayne stared ahead. "Not really. She hasn't spoken in days."

"She will," he replied with a smile. He looked over at Rayne. "We need to make sure we're prepared for what comes next. We have a lot of moving parts to coordinate if this is to go off without a hitch. If I've learned one thing about GlobaTech, they're relentless sonsofbitches. Killing the assassin was necessary... and rather enjoyable to watch... but the negative effect on their morale will only last so long. Defeat will turn to inspiration. Buchanan's little pet project will come at us with everything they have. I won't be caught out again."

Rayne turned his head slowly to face Hall. "Just tell me who I need to kill."

A wicked smile crept across Hall's face. "Soon enough."

The convoy drove on. After a few minutes, the first buildings began to appear against the skyline. Eventually, the entire compound bloomed before them. A previously disused military base was converted to suit Orion's needs over the last few years. A sprawling collection of buildings, tall and flat, wide and narrow, was encased by a high, chain-link fence topped with razor wire.

The sight of it never failed to fill Hall with a sense of childhood excitement. This was his Santa Clarita, and from here he would change the world.

The entry checkpoint let them through without delay, and the vehicles circled to a stop in the large open area formed naturally by the layout of the buildings.

The driver of the Humvee opened Hall's door for him. He stepped out and looked around, marveling at the scope of what he created. The noise of bodies hustling with his purpose was deafening, yet offered a level of bizarre comfort.

As he turned away from the vehicle, Hall's eyes lingered on his greatest creation. A towering monster looked down at the world like a king surveying his kingdom. Despite being a half-mile away, it still dominated the sky, such was its size.

Hall took a deep breath, his chest swelling with pride. Each time he saw it was like the first time. It was a feeling he knew would never go away.

He strode across the dirt-covered expanse toward one of the buildings to his right, flanked by Rayne and three men dressed in the familiar dark attire of Tristar Security. It was a low, single-story facility that looked like it had been chiseled into one large, single block of smooth concrete.

As the group approached, the tinted glass doors hissed open. Hall and his entourage walked across the short lobby and stopped by a bank of elevators. One of the Tristar guards hit the button, and a moment later, the group stepped inside.

They descended three levels. The doors opened, presenting them with a single, wide corridor. People in black uniforms and white lab coats moved along it with purpose, entering and leaving the rooms on either side.

Hall walked the full length of the corridor and turned right, then left, navigating the simple maze until he reached a large, metal door that looked old and out of place compared to the rest of the compound. A guard stood to attention outside.

"Open it," said Hall sharply.

The guard did without hesitation. Hall and Rayne headed inside, leaving their security detail in the corridor. The room was spacious and mostly empty, save for three large, connected holding cells built into the right wall, the fronts of which were made of thick glass.

Only the middle one was occupied.

Hall stopped in front of it and stared inside. Rayne lingered a couple of steps behind him, over his left shoulder.

"So, how are you?" asked Hall calmly.

Jay was sitting on the edge of the bed, upright and motionless, staring at the cold floor in an almost trance-like state. Upon hearing Hall's voice, she turned her head to stare at him, glaring with muted venom.

Hall chuckled. "Wow. If looks could kill, eh? Tell me, Madam Butterfly, who am I talking to right now? The killer I paid for, or the helpless, grieving widow?"

Jay didn't reply. She took a deep breath and turned her attention back to the floor between her feet.

Hall watched her curiously for a moment. "You know, I could deactivate you any time I want. What do you think would happen if I did, hmm? The mind-bending pain is a given, but do you think it would kill you? Or maybe nothing would happen at all, and you would simply be a confused and scared little housewife again. No one really knows. Marshall's team had their theories, of course, but there weren't any solid facts."

Jay remained silent, concentrating on her breathing. Occasionally, her jaw muscles pulsed with tension.

Hall smiled. "Listen to me, sweetheart. You're going to tell me everything you know about GlobaTech, one way or the other. I want to be ready for them. That interfering bitch, Fisher, is relentless. She will no doubt be highly motivated by the fact that I killed that pathetic cotton-picker she called a mentor. I won't be caught unprepared again."

Jay's emotions betrayed her. She cast a sideways glance to her left, staring at Hall with her dark eyes. The hatred was obvious. His words were getting to her.

Hall grinned like a shark sensing blood in the water. "Look, I know you're dangerous. Hell, you goddamn should be. Enough money was spent on training you. But understand you're nothing but a defective asset to me. You're all alone here, Jay... Janine... whatever you want to call yourself today. No one's coming for you. I'm not even sure there's anyone left. Let's see, shall we? You clung to Brandon Crow's side like a needy puppy—he's dead. Benjamin Marshall trained you—he's dead. You found out you had a husband... my colleague here buried that sonofabitch like he was nothing. Seems like every man in your life winds up dead. And there's no way GlobaTech gives two shits about you, so they won't be coming to your rescue. No... you're going to rot here unless you help me."

Jay got to her feet and paced across the cell. She stopped directly in front of Hall. He stepped closer, so only a few inches of glass separated them. The two of them stood in silence for a long moment, like a zookeeper watching a wild animal trapped in a cage.

"Get your shit together," said Hall finally. "Maybe there'll be a place for you by my side in the new world I'm about to create."

In a sudden flash of movement, Jay slammed her palm against the glass, making Hall jump backward with shock. The corner of her mouth twitched with satisfaction as her gaze locked onto him, looking at the zookeeper like he was lunch.

Rayne stepped calmly forward, squaring up to Jay and putting his body between her and Hall. Her attention turned to him. The muted smile faded, replaced by a sneer of primal rage.

Hall moved to Rayne's side, his confidence and swagger returning.

"Y'know, it's funny... the way I hear it, you're probably standing exactly where he did," he said cryptically.

Jay frowned. Her eyes narrowed at him.

Hall smiled. "You tell me what I want to know, and maybe I'll tell you all about the poetic irony of your current situation. Wouldn't that be nice, hmm? You... me... together. Maybe a few drinks." He made a show of looking her up and down with a lecherous smirk. "Marshall told me you were a real specimen under all that violence. Maybe I'll find out for myself."

Jay recoiled at the comment, glancing away as her jaw once again pulsed with emotion. She screwed her eyes shut. In her mind, a whirlwind of pain and confusion ripped through her. The conflict between her activated and deactivated personalities continued to war with one another, and it took genuine effort to quiet the noise. Flashes of memories she couldn't guarantee were real swirled behind her eyes. Screaming. Tears. Shame. A shadow that laughed as she suffered.

And then it was gone.

She opened her eyes, returning to the comfortable anger she felt before. She stepped back to the glass and stared at Hall.

"I think I'll kill you last," she said, speaking for the first time in days.

Hall raised his eyebrows and laughed. "Is that so?"

"Yes. That way, you can watch me dissect *him*." She turned her attention to Rayne, who matched her gaze without backing down. Then she looked back at Hall. "Give you a real good look at what I'm gonna do to you."

Hall shook his head slowly, like a disappointed parent. "So, you really have gone native? Such a shame…"

Jay frowned. Her face contorted into disbelief. "I don't give a shit about GlobaTech, you fat moron. Or anyone else, for that matter. I don't care what you're trying to do. I don't care if Fisher and her band of merry men stop you or not. I just want to disappear. I want to forget everything that's happened, and I want everyone involved to forget me… and I'll kill anyone I have to on my way to the exit."

She turned back to Rayne and tilted her head with a disturbing curiosity. "Except you. You, I *want* to kill."

Rayne's eyebrow twitched with the smallest of movements. He remained quiet.

Hall turned to him. "Come on. I think our guest needs some time to cool off. Besides, it's time you sent another message to our friends at GlobaTech. One they will hear loud and clear."

Hall turned and headed for the door. Rayne lingered in front of Jay a moment longer before following.

Jay watched them leave, then moved back over to the bed. She sat down heavily, rested her forearms on her thighs, and went back to staring at the floor.

Chapter Four

December 9, 2020

Julie wasn't sure when morning had happened. Her office looked out over the busy streets of downtown D.C., and the faint sound of traffic drifting up from below had suddenly become noticeable.

The room wasn't as big as her predecessors' office, which suited her fine. She didn't like being the only person in a huge room. She also didn't like how big rooms tended to invite people to fill them.

She felt tired and overwhelmed. She caught herself missing the brutal simplicity of being out in the field, following orders and dodging bullets, as she always had.

A loud ping rang out, startling her. Yet another e-mail arriving. She sat with her head resting in her hands, staring at the sea of paperwork scattered across her desk with a furrowed brow.

There was a laptop under there somewhere.

Julie let out a loud, exaggerated groan of frustration. Then a knock on the door interrupted her. She looked up as Jericho appeared, blocking the doorway with his huge frame.

"This a bad time?" he asked with a smile.

She shook her head slightly with disbelief and resignation. "Isn't it always?"

He stepped inside and shut the door gently behind him. He strode over to the desk, falling into the seat opposite Julie wearily. His thin sweater clung to his impressive torso as if it was painted onto his skin.

"If it helps, you look cute when you're stressed," he offered.

She stared at him, unimpressed. "Bite me."

He smiled. She relented and smiled back.

Julie sat back in her chair and let her head loll back against the headrest. Having Jericho back was a comfort to her. He had left two days ago to get into position for his mission in Baltimore. They hadn't seen each other or spoken since.

"How did your meeting go yesterday?" asked Jericho.

She shrugged. "It was fine. I expected my plans to be met with resistance and skepticism."

Jericho nodded. "Yeah. So, how long before you threatened to shoot someone?"

Julie narrowed her eyes and pulled a face, feigning offense, then glanced away sheepishly. "Six minutes."

Jericho smiled. "That's my girl."

"How did it go for you? Did you find Stephen Cook?"

"I did."

"And?"

"And... we didn't get much. As I feared, he made me

almost instantly. Tried setting me up for an ambush with three of his friends."

"I'm guessing that didn't go so well for him?"

Jericho smiled. "Not so much. To be fair, I didn't do anything. Link tore them up like they were paper."

"Yeah. I reckon he's still working through some stuff. So, did you get anything useful from Cook?"

"Nothing that wasn't already in the papers."

Julie frowned. "What do you mean?"

"It was announced the day before that Tristar Security was taken over by a new owner, who was eager to rebrand them and put some distance between them and any association with Orion. It seems like they're trying to go legit."

"And are they?"

Jericho shrugged. "Who knows? The article seemed genuine, at least. But we all know the media rarely knows the full story. And this big announcement was buried so far down the news cycle, it was in the sports section. Personally, I think that reeks of Hall's influence. Keep it under the radar, don't draw too much attention… position themselves to make a move no one will see coming. Same old, same old."

"You're probably right. Christ… we're all too busy to have even noticed that. Who's this new CEO?"

"A woman called Gwen Parker."

Julie shook her head. "Don't know her. I'll add her to the list. So, how was Link? Really."

Jericho sighed. "He's… focused. Perhaps a little too much. When we were done, I was preparing to lay Cook out when he stepped in and snapped his neck. Damn near ripped the guy's head clean off. He said we gotta do things the wrong way. Part of me thought it was overkill. But another part of me agrees with him. I think we'll need a little bit of the wrong way in the days and weeks to come."

Julie rubbed the bridge of her nose between her finger and thumb and blinked hard. "Yeah, you're probably right. I also think Link needs us as much as we need him right now. He was close to Jessie. Then his best friend turned evil and killed his boss. He's dealing with a lot."

"Agreed. I'll keep an eye on him. Reel him in if I have to."

"Thanks."

She fell silent and stared at the paperwork again. Her shoulders slumped forward a little.

Jericho shifted in his seat, searching for comfort. "You okay?"

"Yeah."

"Uh-huh. So, are you okay?"

She looked up at him and smiled. "Between me and you, I feel like I'm in over my head. When I'm doing the job, I just kinda get on with it. But when I stop and actually look at it all, I feel like I'm drowning. I've been in this chair a week, and it feels like a decade. I can't tell you how many times I've silently wished for another invasion, just so I can get out of this goddamn office and shoot something."

Jericho couldn't help but smile. "You're doing great, honestly. You've taken to this more naturally than anyone else would have. No one here is a stranger to following your orders. Just remember who the hell you are, and you'll be fine."

"Thanks, but that's easier said than done sometimes. Josh and Moses took this role under similar circumstances—as strangers to the position. They did amazing work. I don't know how the hell they managed it."

The door opened.

"They had me."

Jericho and Julie looked around to see Kim standing in the doorway, smiling. She wore a long, fur-lined overcoat that rested just above her ankles. A thick, white scarf was wrapped around her neck. She looked as if she had stepped straight out of fifties Hollywood.

Relief washed over Julie. She got to her feet and walked over to Kim, embracing her like a long-lost sister.

"I'm glad to see you," she said with a smile.

Kim looked around the room. "You've got a nice office."

"Well... it's no Santa Clarita, but I can't complain."

Kim smiled and moved toward Jericho. He stood and extended his hand, which she shook firmly.

"How are you doing, Kim?" he asked.

She nodded slowly. "I'm... okay. Thank you."

Julie sat back behind her desk. Jericho side-stepped and offered his seat to Kim, who politely waved the offer away.

"I'm not staying," she said.

Julie's relief gave way to disappointment. "Kim, please. I need your help navigating all... *this*." She gestured to the covered desk. "We need your experience, now more than ever."

Kim smiled sympathetically. "I appreciate you holding me in such high regard, but I... I just can't. I'm sorry. I've given everything I have to GlobaTech, and I'm tired. You don't need me to rebuild this place. I'm just a secretary."

Julie rolled her eyes. "We all know you're way more than that. You're... Kim! I'm pretty sure it's in my contract that you come with this office."

Kim laughed. "Thanks. I think. But no, I can't. I have things I need to do. Starting with this..."

She reached inside the pocket of her coat and retrieved

a flash drive. She stepped toward the desk and held it out for Julie, who took it curiously.

"What's this?" she asked.

"You're not the only one who inherited something from Moses," replied Kim.

"What do you mean?" asked Jericho.

Kim looked at him. "Moses had measures in place, should anything happen to him. He left me with instructions to carry out. This is one of them." She turned back to Julie. "About a year ago, he came to me with this and said I was to give it to his eventual replacement, no matter the circumstances."

Julie swallowed hard and sniffed back a wave of emotion. She began rummaging through the paperwork, trying to find the laptop she was sure she left there.

Jericho looked at Kim and gestured to the door. "Come on. I'll... ah... I'll walk you out."

Kim nodded. "Sure."

Leaving Julie to the contents of the drive, the two of them stepped out into the corridor and closed the door behind them.

"I didn't want to ask in front of Julie. She has enough to worry about," said Jericho. "But how's Ray doing?"

Kim's expression softened. "He's... getting there. It's going to be a long road for him, but he's taking things one day at a time. He's making progress. I'll tell him you asked."

Jericho nodded. "Thanks. Listen, we all know Julie is one of the most capable women we've ever met, but all jokes aside, she could really use your help. Is there no way you would consider coming back for a little while?"

Kim shook her head. "I know she has a lot on her plate, but I can't. My place is with Ray now. He needs me more than anyone here does."

Jericho sighed. "Yeah, I get that. I'm glad he has you. I wish I could do more to help him, but with everything going on…"

"It's fine. He understands there's still a fight to be had. Don't worry. And look, just because I'm not on the payroll doesn't mean I'm not still here for the three of you. Josh chose you. Moses loved you. You, Julie, and Ray are a family, and you're the heart and soul of GlobaTech, whether people know it or not. I'll always be around to talk to if you need me."

"I appreciate that. Thank you." He took a deep breath and glanced back at the door. "Listen, I'd best get back in there. I think she might need some moral support looking at that drive, y'know."

As he turned away, Kim reached out, placing a hand on his forearm. He looked back at her and raised a questioning eyebrow.

"I mean it, Jericho," she said. "If you ever need to talk…"

She rubbed her thumb over the material of his sweater, feeling the rough scars mapped onto his arm beneath. Jericho winced slightly, then tensed his jaw in frustration with himself for betraying the discomfort it caused.

"Julie needs you, not me," she continued. "Now more than ever, and definitely more than she'll ever admit to either one of us. But you can't pour from an empty glass. You need to look after yourself too. Take time to process everything that's happened, okay? You don't have to be G.I. Joe twenty-four hours a day."

Jericho held her gaze for a few seconds. His expression was hard and cold, but he wasn't really staring at her. He was staring absently ahead, processing her words, and she just happened to be standing in his line of sight.

Kim let go of his arm, which pulled him back into the moment. He adjusted his sleeve. A subconscious gesture to make sure it covered his arm. Then he simply nodded to her and headed back inside the office.

Kim watched the door close and signed heavily.

Moses was right, she thought to herself. *He'll always be too proud to accept help.*

Chapter Five

Jericho closed the door behind him and looked over at Julie. She was staring blankly over the lid of the laptop, her gaze distant and her eyes misted with tears. Jericho took a deep breath and walked over to the desk.

"You okay?" he asked.

Julie said nothing. She simply shuffled to the left, silently inviting him to look at the screen. He stepped in front of it and used the trackpad to play the video file still highlighted.

Moses Buchanan's face filled the screen. He was sitting in his office at the old Santa Clarita compound. He was smiling slightly, but it couldn't hide the fact that he looked awkward and uncomfortable in front of the camera.

Jericho leaned forward on the desk and watched.

"Julie, if you're watching this, it means I've retired as CEO of GlobaTech, either voluntarily or otherwise. As my replacement, there are a few things I want you to know before you get started."

Jericho swallowed hard and glanced away for a moment. Hearing Buchanan's deep, growling voice again was difficult. He couldn't help but wish he was still around. Buchanan would know exactly what they should do right now.

He looked back at the screen.

"First of all, do whatever you can to keep Kim around! I don't know how she does it, but she's incredibly adept at keeping people in our position sane." He chuckled to himself. "Trust your instincts. This company is unlike any other. Running it doesn't require business degrees or sales tactics or marketing strategies. It requires your gut. We are in a unique position to do some genuine good in this world. That should always remain our priority. We stopped selling our weapons and technology, but we still develop and use it to give us the edge. That's a necessary evil. Perhaps it's time we found a way to make it less necessary."

He paused to take a deep breath and glanced down at the surface of his desk. Jericho figured he was looking at the notes he had made prior to recording.

"The relationship we have with the White House can be a pain in the ass sometimes," continued Buchanan. "But it's invaluable. President Schultz helped build what you're now in charge of. He's an asshole, and he's a politician, but he's a good man. He can navigate the political minefield better than anyone. Trust him. And if he asks for your help, always answer the call. If you're watching this and someone else is in the hot seat, well... that's for you to figure out, I guess.

"There are an increasing number of things going wrong in this world that no one besides GlobaTech is equipped to deal with... even now. To borrow one of *my* predecessor's pop culture references: with great power comes great responsibility. We fight because we can."

Jericho looked over at Julie, who hadn't moved. He placed a comforting hand on her shoulder and squeezed gently. In an almost trance-like state, she moved her hand to rest on top of his.

"Finally, speaking of my predecessor... Josh Winters was the most intelligent human being I've ever met. His understanding of this world was, and will likely remain, unparalleled. I've already told you about the soul drive. Not the name I would've chosen for it, I confess. But the whole thing was Josh's idea. He created it in the aftermath of 4/17 to ensure GlobaTech will always have what it needed to rebuild itself." Buchanan hesitated, as if ashamed that he hadn't said this to them sooner. "And... that wasn't the only thing. He had something else too. A database he began compiling when he first started working here. He was very protective of it. This database was basically his cheat sheet for the world. The details of where he kept it are on the flash drive. Maybe you'll find a use for it."

Buchanan took a deep breath, like a weight had been lifted off his shoulders. He rested back against his chair and stared directly into the camera.

"You're like a daughter to me, Miss Fisher," he said. "You might think I'm out of my mind for giving you this job, but there's honestly no one in the world I trust more to carry GlobaTech forward. I have every faith in you that you'll do what's best. Goodbye... Julie. And good luck."

Buchanan's face froze as the video ended.

Jericho took a deep breath and straightened. He turned to face Julie, looking at her with sympathy. That was hard for him to see and hear. It must have been almost impossible for her.

Julie got to her feet and stepped toward him. She wrapped her arms around his body and held him tightly. Jericho kissed the top of her head and embraced her. The two of them stood together for a few minutes in a comfortable, yet heartbreaking silence.

Words weren't needed.

When they finally parted, Julie took her seat again. Jericho stepped back and perched on the edge of the desk beside her, giving her room to move back in front of the laptop.

"How are you doing?" he asked her.

She shook her head. "I just... I don't understand it. Why would he do this to me? Why would he put me in this position? I never once said I wanted this." She grabbed a handful of papers and waved them before throwing them across the desk. "All *this*... it isn't me. He was like a father to me, Jericho. How could he put this burden on me? It makes no sense."

Jericho folded his arms across his chest and shook his head. "I think you're wrong."

She looked up at him. "Oh, really? You've seen me drowning here every day since I took over."

Jericho leaned over to the laptop and clicked on the video file, hoping his hunch would be correct. He opened the submenu that showed its properties and pointed to the date the file was created.

"Look," he said, quietly relieved.

She does, frowning. "What?"

He sighed patiently. "Julie, Buchanan recorded this on September twenty-sixth last year."

"Right..."

"That was the day he found out Roach's Tristar unit killed our guys in Cambodia and stole all that tech. We were in Canada at the time, remember? That was before we knew about Orion and what Quincy Hall was planning. But that was the day Buchanan realized a fight was coming, and we needed to be ready for it. In hindsight, if you think about it, that attack in Cambodia was the catalyst for everything bad that has happened to the world in the last twelve months. And that day, he recorded this video. Julie, your promotion wasn't a snap decision. He put you in charge of our unit. Not me. Not Ray. You. Don't you get it? He's been grooming you from the start to be his replacement. You spent a lot of time with him. You saw him deal with all the bullshit that comes with this job, which you can't just aim a gun at. Buchanan was a smart guy. I think you're far better equipped to deal with this job than you realize."

Julie scoffed defiantly. "It doesn't feel like it."

"Maybe not. But it will. Like he said: trust your gut. Your plan is for GlobaTech to focus solely on our contract with the U.N. That is one hundred percent the right thing to do. Buchanan thought so too. GlobaTech has fought plenty of battles, but there's only so much good we can do by waging war. There's no denying we have a fight ahead of us. Probably the biggest one we've ever faced. But once that's over, we should change how we do things around here. Through your vision, we can help so many more people. And what makes it even more impressive is that you're a soldier. It's in your nature to fight. Yet you're the one spearheading this plan for a peaceful future. People are gonna respect the hell out of you for that, and they *will* follow you."

Julie looked up at him. She went to speak but stopped herself when she realized she had no valid argument. She sat silently, thinking back to all the times Buchanan asked her to accompany him to meetings. Especially during the aftermath of the Palugan crisis. He always said he needed her expertise as someone who had been out in the field.

Someone who could explain that side of things to a room full of suits who otherwise would never understand it.

Maybe Jericho was right.

She resigned to simply nod and look away.

Jericho let slip a small smile to himself.

"What has the board said about everything so far?" he asked.

Julie sighed. She sat back in her chair and turned slightly to face him. Her hands were clasped in front of her. "They had concerns, as you would expect. Mostly financial, which I had considered. I'm not naïve enough to dismiss them, obviously. I told them my reasons for wanting to make these changes, and I asked them to help me find a way to implement them without GlobaTech imploding."

Jericho nodded. "That's fair. What did they say?"

"Not much, at this stage. But we scheduled a series of strategy meetings that will help plan to gradually withdraw from certain areas and industries. We'll probably sell off assets and contracts, then use the money to rebuild and invest in the few areas we want to stay relevant in. It was pointed out to me that we run the risk of creating a power struggle in the marketplace that could do more harm than good."

"How so?" asked Jericho, frowning.

"Well, first, we have to make sure we do all this gently enough that it doesn't impact our stock prices too much. We're big enough that we could crash the stock market if we so much as sneeze at the wrong time. We also need to be extremely careful who we work with. We don't want to hand the keys to a bunch of kingdoms over to the next Orion, y'know?"

Jericho nodded.

Julie continued. "I've also got a few meetings booked in

with the U.N. Security Council—the prospect of which honestly scares the shit out of me. But I think they should know what we're planning to do. They need to understand we're committed to investing in our training and resources, so we can strengthen and grow the peacekeeping force they're paying us to provide. We have a lot of ground to make up with that after Paluga. And we need to rebuild now that the Orion occupation is over and…"

Her words trailed off as she saw the smug smile on Jericho's face.

She narrowed her eyes. "What?"

"Listening to you talk… it's like you've been CEO for years. It suits you. Looks to me like Buchanan made the right choice."

Julie rolled her eyes and smiled. "Thanks. I still don't see what you and Buchanan do, but I'm getting there. I couldn't do it without you, Jericho."

He waved his hand dismissively. "Of course, you could. But I'm not going anywhere."

She straightened in her chair, pulling herself closer to the desk. "I guess I should get back to it. What are you doing now?"

Jericho got to his feet and moved around the desk to stand in front of her. The time for being her boyfriend was over. It was time to be her asset again.

"We have reports of renewed activity at a Tristar weapons cache in Richmond," he said. "I'm gonna take a team and check it out."

"Sounds good. You taking Link?"

Jericho shook his head. "No. He said he had some things to take care of. He'll be in touch when he's ready."

"Okay. Watch your back out there."

"Always." He nodded toward the laptop. "What are you

going to do about that database Buchanan mentioned? It sounds like something we should get."

"Well, I'm too busy to go looking for it myself." Julie glanced at her watch. "I'm already late for another meeting."

"We should send someone we trust."

"I agree." She reached for the desk phone. "And I know just who to ask."

Chapter Six

The New York City streets teemed with life. A near-constant flow of people hurrying about their days swept back and forth along the sidewalk. The sun was shining behind thin, gray clouds, giving its light without the benefit of its heat.

The woman's heels scraped and clacked on the ground as she walked purposefully to work. She wore a navy dress suit with pinstripes, which was immaculately pressed. In one smooth, manicured hand, she carried a brown leather briefcase. In the other, she held a fresh coffee, double-cupped against the heat and still steaming through the hole in the lid. Despite the crowds, she navigated the streets with effortless expertise, twisting through gaps and timing her stride to avoid delivery men crossing her path.

Her short, blonde hair was slicked back with product until it shined. Her features were attractive and sharp. She looked naturally confident and completely at ease with herself. She barely noticed the world around her as she talked animatedly into the earpiece she wore.

"Yes… yes…" She sighed heavily. "Kevin, I don't care

how much they say it will cost, okay? Tell them they have a schedule that is vastly more important than their budget."

She took a careful sip of her coffee while Kevin continued to debate his point. She swallowed it and momentarily closed her eyes, relishing the caffeine hitting the soul she never let people know she had.

"Kevin, Kevin... *Kevin!* I'm going to stop you right there." She rolled her eyes. "Please don't think there is any chance whatsoever of you making a difference. They will continue to do as they've been instructed. If they go over budget, I'll find them more money. That's not an issue here. But they don't... stop... working. Is that crystal-clear?" She smiled to herself. "Thank you."

She ended the call and sighed.

I'm surrounded by goddamn amateurs, she thought.

She walked on, glancing at her watch to see she was running late for a meeting. She crossed the street, ignoring the horns of disgruntled drivers who were forced to brake hard so as not to run her over. The other side wasn't any less busy. She threaded her way through the tide of people, growing increasingly impatient.

As she passed by a newspaper stand, a man fell in step beside her.

"Excuse me, miss," he said. "Do you have the time?"

She glanced at him. His long, scraggly beard matched the dirt etched onto his skin and the stench emanating from his clothes.

She groaned and rolled her eyes again. "I can't tell you how much I don't have the time right now."

She quickened her pace, but the man stayed level with her, his eyes never leaving her.

She turned to look at him, frowning with frustration. "Are you good?"

They drew level with a narrow, dark alleyway between two stores. It was empty and enveloped in warm, musty steam blasting up from the grates in the ground. The man skipped ahead and spun to stand in front of her, blocking her path.

She shuffled to a sudden stop, glaring at him. She was about to unleash a tirade of abuse at him, but then she saw his hand was in the pocket of his long, dirty coat. Something inside was pointing out at her. The man moved it to the side, gesturing toward the alley.

"Quit screwing around, lady," he ordered. "Let's go. Come on."

The woman recoiled in disgust. "You want me to go down a smelly, secluded, dark alleyway with you at…" She checked her watch. "…not even nine a.m.? Are you serious?"

The man shook his head and grabbed her elbow with a firm grip. He shoved her toward the alley, then moved close to her, ushering her alongside him as discreetly as possible. He knew the chances of anyone noticing were slim. People are always far too busy with their own lives to notice a homeless man walking into an alleyway.

The woman stumbled on the uneven ground in her heels, dropping her coffee as she was forced against the nearby wall.

"Hey! Watch it, asshole!" she protested.

The man stepped away from her, still pointing his pocket at her. "Shut it, bitch. Hand it all over. Necklace. Watch. Phone. Briefcase. Come on, come on. Let's go!"

Once more, she frowned, contorting her face into a look of disbelief and disgust. "Are you kidding me? No!"

The man was confused. "What?"

"I said no. Are you deaf?"

"But…" He nodded toward his pocket. "I have a gun."

"I don't care! First, you spill my coffee. That was my special morning drink—a double-shot mocha with low-fat milk, chocolate sprinkles, and three drops of vanilla CBD oil. That was eight bucks. Then you drag me down here." She looked around, wrinkling her nose and grimacing at her surroundings. "It smells like a freakin' sewer and—oh my God, is that a rat? Ew!" She paused to shudder. "And now, you're demanding I give you all of my things, which, let's be honest, collectively are probably worth more money than you've seen in your entire life. And I'm supposed to, what? Just go along with it like it's all okay? Well, no. I won't."

The man stared blankly at her.

"You talk a lot, lady," he said. He stepped closer to her and finally took his hand out of his pocket, revealing a switchblade. "Maybe I should shut your mouth for you first…"

The woman's shoulders relaxed. She rolled her eyes and her head in one exaggerated movement. "Oh, it's a *knife*. I thought it was a gun in there. Or something even more gross. Oh, thank God. I was starting to worry."

The man stared at his knife, confused. He looked back at her, about to say something, but he never got the chance. The woman delivered a pinpoint-accurate headbutt to the bridge of his nose. The sound of bone and cartilage breaking under the impact was audible over the gentle roar of the nearby steam vent.

The man dropped the knife, clutching his face with both hands as he staggered backward. Blood seeped through his fingers. His eyes popped wide with surprise.

The woman calmly placed her briefcase on the ground beside her, careful to avoid any damp patches. It was expensive leather, after all. She then began to circle around to the side, stalking the man like a lion in the Serengeti watching its next meal.

"You know, you're making me late for a meeting," she said coldly.

She stepped toward him and delivered a powerful right hook to his body. The technique was flawless. Hips, shoulder, elbow... then clench the fist right before impact for maximum effect.

The guy keeled over, dropping to one knee. His arms twitched and danced in the air, moving between his face and body. His brain was unsure which blow it wanted to comfort. He settled for one hand on each.

He grimaced through gritted teeth, sucking in air that hurt to inhale. He looked up at her through watering eyes. "Look, I'm... I'm sorry, lady. I shouldn't have... just leave me alone, okay? You'll never see me again, I swear."

She rolled her eyes. "Well, *obviously*..."

She clicked her heels together, and a small blade snapped out of the rounded toe on her right shoe with a sharp swish. The man saw it. His eyes bulged in their sockets, wide with fear.

The woman didn't hesitate. She kicked his stomach like she was clearing a field goal. The blade pierced his clothing and flesh with devastating ease. He groaned as he doubled over in pain, blood dripping out onto the ground in front of him. As he leaned forward, the woman lashed out again, delivering another front kick that buried the blade into the thin flesh at the top of his throat, just below the jawline. The man gasped, but his scream never got the chance to leave his lips. With eyes locked wide, he fell forward, flattening out on the cold, damp ground. Blood gushed from his throat, pooling around him.

The woman clicked her heels again to retract the blade.

She straightened her jacket and skirt, cracked her neck, then paced calmly back over to her briefcase. She crouched elegantly to retrieve it, then headed for the street. As she passed her now empty cup of coffee on the ground, she huffed with frustration. Then she turned left and stepped out onto the sidewalk, instantly merging with the flow of human traffic and disappearing in the crowd.

Inside her jacket, her phone began to ring again. Remaining focused on weaving through the people ahead, she tapped the earpiece still clipped to her right ear to answer it.

"This is Gwen Parker."

Chapter Seven

President Schultz sat behind his desk in the Oval Office, signing the last page of a large stack of forms. He gathered them together neatly and placed the pile on the edge of the desk.

He sat back in his chair and glanced at the wooden cane resting next to him. It was made of smooth, dark wood, with the top shaped into a detailed horse's head. He reached out and ran his thumb over it, allowing his mind to wander.

The job wasn't as enjoyable as Schultz remembered it being before Orion took over. Sure, it was stressful, and the circumstances surrounding his promotion into office were far from ideal, but he firmly believed in the honor and tradition of his position. He worked hard to be the best man he could be while sitting in this chair.

Despite being a prisoner for the last six months, it was the last couple of weeks that had changed him. He wasn't sleeping. He was barely eating—not that anyone would notice, given how his suit jacket still stretched over his large frame. He resented every moment he had to spend in this office. He was probably the most powerful man in the world, yet he had never felt more powerless.

A knock on the door disturbed his musings.

"Yes?" he called out.

The door opened to reveal his secretary standing there, smiling politely.

"She's here," she announced.

Schultz nodded. "Send her in. No calls for the next hour, okay?"

"Yes, sir."

The secretary stepped back, and a moment later, Julie Fisher walked in. She closed the door behind her, then took a deep breath and rested her gaze on the president.

"Everything okay, Miss Fisher?" asked Schultz.

She smiled awkwardly. "A little nervous, if I'm honest, sir."

He frowned. "Why? It's not like you haven't been here before. You've dragged my sorry ass to safety more than once, and I'm pretty sure you were standing right over there..." He pointed to a space on the opposite side of the room. "...when you screamed at me and told me to go to hell. At this point, we're practically family."

Julie's cheeks flushed with color, and she glanced away in a failed attempt to hide it. "Yeah... sorry about that, sir."

Schultz smiled to himself. "Water under the bridge, Miss Fisher. Now, sit, will you? Makes me nervous when people loiter by that door."

She paced over toward the desk and took a seat in front of the president.

"I understand you're still settling into your new role, Miss Fisher," he said. "Hell, I know the circumstances aren't ideal for any of us right now. But we ain't got the time for first day nerves, okay?"

Julie nodded. "Of course. Sorry, sir."

She took a deep breath.

Schultz rested back in his chair and placed his palms flat on the desk in front of him. "Now, where are we at?"

She cleared her throat. "Well, I've already had a couple of board meetings in which I outlined my vision for GlobaTech's future."

"Yes, I saw the report you sent me. How did the Rich, Old, White Man Brigade take it?"

Julie let slip a small smile. "About as well as expected. But they're on board and committed to making the transition work while protecting GlobaTech's legacy."

"That's good to hear. I think it's a damn fine idea, Miss Fisher. Moses would be proud of you."

"Thank you, sir."

She glanced away again, looking to her left and inadvertently finding herself staring at the patch of navy blue carpet she knew had recently been replaced.

"Now, onto the real business," continued Schultz. "Where's the sonofabitch who stole my country?"

Julie took a deep breath. "We haven't seen or heard anything from Quincy Hall since he disappeared last week with... with Rayne and Jay. However, I suspect it's only a matter of time before we do."

"I see. So, we have no idea where they're keeping her?"

Julie shook her head. "Not yet, sir, no. But we're using every resource we have to find out. Jericho tracked down one of the Tristar operatives who was in the room last week when... everything happened. He didn't give us much, but we got a name: Gwen Parker."

"Should I know who that is?"

"Probably not, sir. We didn't. But apparently, she's the next Brandon Crow. She released a low-key statement to the press a couple of days ago, saying she's working to rebuild Tristar Security and rebrand it to be a market leader now that all ties to Orion have been publicly severed. I doubt people are buying that, but that's the official line."

"You think she's working with Hall?"

"I'd bet the house on it, sir. The fact it was buried in the news cycle so as not to draw attention to it screams of Hall's influence. I think we're beginning a new game of chess, and this is Hall's first move."

Schultz thought for a moment, then nodded. "I think you're right. What are you doing about it?"

"We've got a team of analysts poring over the data we already have, looking for any clue as to what Hall could be planning."

"Good. The last thing we need is a sequel to his goddamn hostile takeover. I'm not sure we could win a fight like that again."

"Me neither, sir. But I don't think it'll come to that."

Schultz sat forward a little. "You don't?"

Julie shook her head. "No. Hall tried that already and failed. Tristar's manpower is heavily reduced, but so is Hall's social standing and influence. From what I understand, you've seen to it personally that many of his assets are frozen. Orion International is completely offline pending more investigations and hearings than we can count. While he may still have some control over the media, it's nothing like as effective as it used to be. My guess is Hall installed Gwen Parker at Tristar to publicly distance their association with Orion. That suggests he wants to reset the secret link he has with them, but it'll be a long time before the public can be fooled by that again."

Schultz nodded. "A fair assessment. So, what's the bastard actually doing?"

"I honestly don't know, sir. Best guess, he's holding Jay somewhere and trying to extract any information from her about GlobaTech that he can. Then he'll come after us, using Nemesis assets."

"I agree. You're the face of his defeat, Miss Fisher. Consequently, you're the face of hope for this country. Taking GlobaTech out of commission permanently is the only message he can send now that people will listen to. You'd best watch your back out there, you hear me? I'm done losing people."

"Me too, sir. Me too. We're reopening multiple facilities every day. More and more of our security force is returning to the United States by the hour now that the borders are open again. We're almost up to full strength on domestic soil now."

Schultz frowned. "You ordered a full recall of overseas deployment?"

"Mostly," she confirmed. "Right now, the rest of the world doesn't need us as much as America does. If we can kill Orion once and for all, maybe we can get back to helping the United Nations keep everyone else together. But we're no use to anyone until we get our own house in order."

He nodded. "Well, you're not wrong there, I guess. I have all branches of the U.S. Armed Forces ramping back up to full service. All federal agencies too. They're not quite there yet. Still some confusion and uncertainty about leadership and responsibilities after Orion, but the FBI, CIA, and the NSA are all ready to help bury Hall for good."

"I'd happily leave that to you if I could, sir. GlobaTech

will always help this office, but once Orion has been dealt with, I hope we simply won't need to, going forward."

Schultz scoffed. "Yeah, if we can ever keep up with you, I'd take that scenario any day. That's what Moses and I started trying to do with Blackstar…"

He trailed off, and the room fell silent for a moment. Neither of them made eye contact.

"Thank you for helping arrange a new head office for us here in D.C.," said Julie eventually. "We've felt like squatters ever since Santa Clarita fell."

Schultz shrugged modestly. "Well, you folks need a permanent base of operations. That building was emptied during the invasion, so I just put a word in and earmarked it for you. Honestly, it's nice to know I still have some pull in this town…"

Julie smiled. "We're putting it to good use, I promise. We have a team coordinating all sites across the country as we regroup. Our satellite network is almost back to full strength, so our analysts are back in business. Manufacturing has started back up at key locations, which will maximize production of technology and weaponry in the short term."

"I thought you were stepping away from all the R and D programs?" asked Schultz.

"We are. We're just making enough equipment to replace what we lost during Orion's takeover, so our people can do their jobs. We're not looking to reinvent the wheel or sell anything to anyone."

"Okay. And what about this… soul drive of yours? Any progress tracking that down?"

Julie pursed her lips. "No. Nothing yet. We think Hall has it with him. We'll find him, take the drive back, shut down Orion and maybe even the Nemesis program entirely."

Schultz nodded. "It sounds like you have everything under control. That's good."

"Just about, yes, sir."

"Tell me, Miss Fisher... how have you found it delegating everything and not doing it all yourself?"

He smiled knowingly, which Julie reciprocated.

"I'm... managing," she said with a shrug. "Hard not to do it all myself, but at the same time, I couldn't if I wanted to. GlobaTech is a hell of a resource. We'll get there."

"Excellent. Thank you for your time, Miss Fisher. I'd best let you get back to it."

"Thank you, sir." She got to her feet but lingered by her chair. "Sir, I wanted to ask..."

Schultz looked up at her. "Hmm?"

"How are you doing, sir?"

He took a deep breath, then sat back in his chair and smiled. "I'm getting there. I don't exactly have a job that allows time off, but I'm off the IVs now. I have my cane to help me walk around. I thought it made me look old and weak, but my advisors tell me all the great presidents had one."

Julie smiled. "I mean, they're not wrong, sir."

He shrugged. "I know. FDR had a cane. But he also had polio."

Julie failed to suppress a laugh. She held a hand up in apology. "Sorry, sir. I didn't mean to—"

He waved the comment away. "They're paid to make me feel better. But like my daddy used to say: you can't bullshit a bullshitter."

"Well, sir, if you ever need a quote for the dust jacket of your autobiography, I think that's the one."

Schultz chuckled. The sound was deep, coming from his belly. "Get back to work, Miss Fisher. You have enough to worry about without concerning yourself with me. That's an order."

Julie smiled and nodded. "Yes, sir."

She left the office, closing the door gently behind her. Schultz watched her go, then went back to admiring his cane.

Chapter Eight

The four men sat quietly in the SUV. Outside, the dull afternoon sky was transitioning into darkness. The temperature was dropping with the sun.

Jericho drummed his fingers on the wheel as he stared out across the street at the laundromat. Traffic was steady around them. Sidewalks were the same. It looked like a normal street in Richmond.

But everyone in the SUV knew different.

Jericho had handpicked his team. Men he either knew personally or by reputation. All experienced, with many years at GlobaTech under their belts. All competent. All business.

"Sir, are you sure this is the place?" asked Nixon, a bulky, grizzled man sitting beside Jericho in the front. "We've been here for hours and seen nothing."

Jericho didn't take his eyes off the building. "I'm sure."

"You think maybe we missed them? That they've already cleared out of here?"

"They haven't."

In the back, the other two members of the unit, Frederickson and Owens, shifted uncomfortably. Both men were stocky and bearded.

"It's a bit cliched, isn't it?" asked Owens. Everyone turned to look at him. He shrugged. "I'm just saying. I mean, a laundromat? What, do they have an illegal poker game in the back or something?"

Frederickson let slip a small smile. Nixon rolled his eyes and went back to watching the building.

Jericho took a deep breath. His jaw muscles twitched with impatience. "Six months ago, this place served as one of Tristar's main supply hubs for delivering weapons to their forces up and down the eastern seaboard. If they're playing poker in there, it's only to kill time while they're planning a second invasion. Now, stay focused and shut your mouths. We have work to do."

Immediate and absolute silence blanketed the vehicle's interior. Fifteen minutes passed without so much as a loud breath. Then a mid-sized van pulled up outside the laundromat. Three men got out, all dressed in street clothes. They huddled together on the sidewalk and looked around them. They appeared skittish and out of place. Their movements were tense and rapid, as if nervous or unsure of themselves. Seemingly satisfied, they unlocked the door of the laundromat and disappeared inside.

Jericho looked around the SUV, meeting each man's eyes with his own. "We're up."

The four men climbed out of the vehicle in unison. They were all dressed in the signature GlobaTech uniforms —black with red trim. They picked a gap in the flow of traffic and crossed the street, watching for any signs that their targets weren't alone. Pedestrians all around began to navigate around the building like it was toxic, or simply turned around and walked away at the sight of the four men.

Jericho paused at the rear of the van. He tapped the screen of the Tech Sleeve strapped to his left forearm, waking it up. It beeped and flashed as the interface loaded. Despite not being an advocate of too much technology on the battlefield, Jericho had missed having this device at his disposal. The Tech Sleeve was invaluable, but it had been made redundant when GlobaTech's satellite network was taken offline by Orion. Now that they were back up and running, his arsenal was once again complete.

Jericho tapped the license plate of the van into it and searched. Just a few seconds later, the screen showed it was registered to a holding company owned by Orion International.

He turned to face his men. "These are definitely our guys. Owens, you stay outside. Guard the door and watch our six. Nixon, Frederickson, you're with me. We move in, secure the building, and question the targets. When we're done, we leave them for the authorities to pick up. Questions?"

Everyone shook their heads.

Jericho nodded. "Let's go."

They all moved for the door. Jericho opened it and stepped inside, immediately drawing his *Negotiator*. Frederickson and Nixon followed and did the same. Owens let the door close, then turned his back to it, standing with a hand hovering over his own handgun as he watched the streets.

The air was stale. It smelled damp, with the faint stench of detergent mixed with it. The white tiles underfoot were dirty. Four rows of washing machines stood dormant, forming two walkways through the main area.

Jericho and his team continued forward, walking past a

raised counter with a cash register and through a single open door. It led to a small vestibule with three doors coming off it. The left one was closed. The right one was slightly ajar. Jericho could see a mop and bucket resting against some metal shelving. He assumed that was a maintenance closet.

Directly ahead, fluorescent light flooded through the open door. Rows upon rows of storage lined the walls in front of them, filled with boxes. The trio formed a triangle, with Jericho at the point, then moved quietly inside. The room stretched away to the right. The large space was wider than it was long, and the storage on the other walls was packed with the same sized boxes as the first.

In the middle of the room, the three targets were stacking boxes into a large square. They worked quickly and in silence.

Jericho raised his gun. His finger rested against the outside of the trigger guard. "All of you, stop what you're doing right now. Turn around and put your hands in the air."

Each man twitched and jumped on the spot, then did as they were instructed before turning around slowly to see the new arrivals.

Without needing to be told, Frederickson and Nixon circled left and right respectively, flanking the men and forming a wide triangle around them. Happy the men were covered and seeing no visible weapons, Jericho relaxed his aim a little. He studied the men. They were all Caucasian, probably in their mid-thirties. Their frames were unimposing. Their eyes were fearful. Whoever they were, they weren't soldiers.

"Tell me where these weapons are going," demanded Jericho.

The group exchanged a nervous look. One of them shook his head at Jericho. "Wh-what weapons?"

Jericho stared at him with unblinking eyes, slightly arching his brow. "What's your name?"

The man shifted awkwardly on the spot. "Gus. Gus Weaver."

"Okay, Gus. Now isn't the time to be funny, understand? GlobaTech is back to full strength, and we've been tracking this place. We know Tristar ships weaponry out of here. I want to know where you're taking these guns and what Hall is planning next."

Gus swallowed hard. "Um... who?"

Jericho sighed. "Seriously? You're gonna pretend you don't know the man who just invaded this country for six months?"

Another man, the shortest in the group, shuffled forward half a step. "Wait, you mean Quincy Hall? No... no way, man. You got this all wrong. We don't work for Orion. We work for Tristar."

Jericho narrowed his eyes. "Are you being this stupid on purpose?"

He tightened his aim again, forcing the short man to backtrack. He began waving his hands, panicking as he stepped back to huddle with his friends. "Wait, wait, wait! Don't kill us, man. Please. This is our first gig. We all started working for Tristar, like, three days ago. This is a delivery job, okay? We were just told to come here and pick up some boxes."

Jericho studied him. The man was sweating profusely, despite the low temperature. His hands were shaking. His breathing was rapid. The man was afraid. He also wasn't lying.

Jericho nodded. "And where are you supposed to take them?"

Gus took a deep breath. "To the freight terminal at Richmond International."

"Where are they flying to?"

"I don't know, man, I swear. A crew there is supposed to unload this stuff and transfer it to the plane. We were just told to drop it off. We don't know anything else."

Jericho stood tall and cracked his shoulders. He holstered his gun and folded his arms across his chest. "You really don't know what Tristar did, do you?"

Gus shrugged. "I mean, I heard they have nothing to do with Orion now. They've been bought out. They're—"

"Rebranding?"

Gus nodded excitedly. "Yeah, exactly."

Jericho rolled his eyes. "Christ. Okay. Nixon, check that box next to you."

Nixon moved to one of the boxes on his left and pulled at the tape fastening it closed.

Jericho looked at the three men in turn. "Ignorance isn't an excuse. You're all transporting weaponry for an organization responsible for the greatest act of domestic terrorism in this country's history. You're going to—"

"Um, boss?" Nixon called out.

Jericho looked over at him. He was stood straight, holding a bulky wad of cash in his hand.

"These boxes ain't got guns in them," he said. "This is a big-ass stash of hundreds."

Jericho was confused. "How much?"

Nixon blew out a heavy sigh. "I reckon there's ten grand in this bundle. The box maybe holds… six deep and five square, so that's… a hundred and fifty bundles, which is about a mil-five in each box."

Every man in the room looked around the shelving surrounding them. Jericho's eyes widened.

"There's at least a hundred boxes in here," he observed. "Are you telling me Orion has one hundred and fifty million dollars sitting in the back room of a laundromat?"

Nixon let out a low whistle. "Goddamn…"

Jericho looked at Gus. "Why are you moving cash around?"

Gus shook his head. "Hey, man, I didn't know we were."

Jericho glanced at Frederickson, who was staring at one of the boxes nearby in disbelief. "What the hell is going on here?"

"That's none of your business."

The voice from behind startled him. Jericho turned around to see Adam Rayne standing there, flanked by two men wearing Tristar's uniform. All three of them had weapons drawn and raised.

Jericho locked eyes with Rayne. The surprise had worn off. He started laughing.

"Man, I'm gonna enjoy this…" he said.

Rayne smiled. "Oh, I doubt that."

He stepped to the side, and Owens's limp body flew through the door, landing unceremoniously on the floor between them. Jericho stared blankly at his dead colleague, then over at the door in time to see a third Tristar operative casually stroll in.

"What the hell is going on here?" asked Jericho, trying to quell the rising anger inside him.

"I'm delivering a message," said Rayne, still smiling.

"Don't think I won't rip you in half, you piece of shit. I don't care if you're activated or not. You'll pay for what you did."

Rayne shrugged. "Whatever you say. But you can't fight us all."

Jericho scoffed. "You Nemesis assholes think you're

unbeatable, but you're really not. You're still human. You still bleed, just like me. You forget I've fought alongside you. I know you, Adam. You'll need more than a couple of Tristar lackies to take me down."

Rayne tilted his head to the side and narrowed his gaze. "Who's Adam?"

The comment caught Jericho off-guard. The initial wave of anger he felt over Owens's death had subsided, replaced by an unfamiliar uncertainty. He quickly looked at the three Tristar operatives standing around him, noting their positions before refocusing on Rayne. The man who betrayed them all and killed Adrian Hell. Except he wasn't, and Jericho had momentarily forgotten that. The man before him wasn't the man who he had fought beside in the past. He had no idea who he really was. Only who the activation process made him. Right now, he was his enemy. But he was also an ally.

Jericho tensed his jaw muscles.

Rayne watched him impassively. "But you're right, Jericho. Tristar personnel isn't enough…"

Behind him, more men filed into the back room, stepping over Owens's body and forming a circle around Jericho and his team.

They all had visible tattoos on their necks.

Jericho couldn't recall a time in his life when he had ever felt afraid. But as he looked around the room, seeing six Nemesis assets staring back at him, he figured this was probably close.

Rayne cleared his throat. "Drop them."

In a flash of movement, guns were raised and bullets were fired. Jericho dropped a knee and brought his hands up to his head in an instinctive attempt to protect himself. The deafening sound of gunfire died away as quickly as it had blasted out, replaced by a loud thud.

Jericho lowered his hands and looked around, confused by the fact that he was still breathing. The bloodied bodies of Frederickson and Nixon lay on the ground. Gus and his two friends were also down, surrounded by an expanding pool of blood.

Jericho slowly stood straight. The five assets stood in a circle around him. Ahead of him, the three Tristar operatives formed a wide line behind Rayne, who stood alone, staring into Jericho's eyes with a frightening lack of emotion.

Jericho took a deep breath. He had no way out of there. Even he knew he couldn't take on more than one Nemesis asset, let alone six of them. He let his gun hang from his finger by the trigger guard and held it out. One of the assets stepped forward and took it from him.

He looked at Rayne. "Okay. You got me. So, what's the message?"

Rayne stepped forward and raised his gun. The barrel was dead level with Jericho's forehead. He smiled. "You are."

Chapter Nine

Quincy Hall stood before Jay's cell, watching her with bemusement. His hands rested casually inside his pants pockets. His suit jacket was open. His shirt was unfastened at the collar with no tie.

He had been there a little over fifteen minutes. He was alone, although two Tristar guards were stationed outside the holding room. He had some time and wanted another attempt at encouraging Jay to work with him.

So far, it had proven fruitless.

Jay sat calmly on her bed, resting back against the wall with a thin pillow behind her. One leg was stretched out in front of her. The other was bent, and she rested an arm on her knee. She looked tired. Without makeup, the lack of comfortable sleep was difficult to hide.

She was permitted one shower and one bathroom break a day. She was given fresh clothing each day, which consisted of matching olive-green jogging pants and a sweater, with black canvas sneakers.

She had never served time in a prison before, but she figured this is what it felt like.

Jay stared blankly ahead, ignoring Hall's presence as best she could.

Hall smiled at the increasingly futile attempt at defiance.

"This isn't doing you any favors," said Hall. "You know that, right?"

No reaction. No response.

Hall sighed. "I have all the time in the world. You're not in a penitentiary. No one knows you're here... or even where *here* is. You have no rights. You have no friends. You have no chance... no chance *at all* of leaving here alive unless you come back into the fold and stand beside me. You do understand that, right?"

Jay didn't move, but her eyes flicked slightly to rest her gaze on him. "Then kill me already. Get it over with."

Hall laughed. "Oh, you don't mean that. Too much of your original personality has pushed itself through the programming to allow you to truly think like that, and we both know it."

Jay raised an eyebrow with the tiniest of movements. "Don't underestimate how truly irritating you are."

Again, he laughed out loud. "Stubborn until the last. I like that. I'm going to tell you a story, Jay. Consider it a courtesy. An... olive branch, of sorts. I want to show you I'm not the bad guy here."

"Jesus Christ..." she muttered. "You *are* the bad guy. Because *I'm* the bad guy, and you trained me and sent me to kill a whole bunch of people. At least I have the balls to admit it."

"Indeed. You do have more testicular fortitude than most people I know." His expression hardened, deleting his smile. His jaw tensed. His eyes narrowed. He took a step closer to the glass wall. "However, you would be wise to remember that since your groundbreaking efforts with the Nemesis program, we have created an army of assets who are superior to you. The longer you keep up this charade of defiance, the less valuable I'll consider you to be."

Jay held his gaze. Any humor in his expression, exaggerated or otherwise, had gone. His eyes were cold and emotionless. In that moment, she realized there was more to Hall than just the arrogance, power, racism, and misogyny. He was a goddamn monster.

"What's your story?" she asked, as genuinely as she could to distract him.

Hall relaxed. His lighthearted persona took over once more, and he smiled. "Oh, you'll love it. See, once upon a time, there was a group of terrorists. Russian extremists still bitter about the Cold War. They weren't particularly big, but they were well-funded and genius marketeers. Their plan was to attack the United States. They created a fake threat to sucker hundreds of soldiers into a conflict that didn't really exist, just so they could bury them. They would publicly claim responsibility in the name of the Motherland, which they hoped would force the U.S. to retaliate against Russia, thus causing a third world war."

Jay shrugged. "Okay..."

Hall began pacing slowly back and forth in front of the cell, staring at the floor as he continued. "It was a truly genius idea. Masterful, in fact. But they failed. The execution lacked... finesse. They didn't zero in on the details. They didn't factor in all the variables. They also didn't involve the people. See, no one knew about their plan. There was no buildup. No fear. No widespread panic. It was stopped before it even started because they focused only on the destination, not the journey."

"Sucks for them," mused Jay, who was quickly tiring of the tale.

"Indeed. Their biggest mistake was that they didn't consider the most common cause of failure in such things: plain bad luck. You see, their entire operation was ultimately toppled by one man, who happened to be in the right place at the wrong goddamn time." Hall stopped and stared at her, smiling. "Care to guess who that man was?"

Jay frowned. Then her face relaxed and her eyes widened. There could only be one reason Hall was telling her this.

"Adrian," she said.

Hall pointed his finger at her like a gameshow host. "Ten points to you. Yes, your ex-husband was in town on… business, and he stumbled into the middle of their plans. Being the kind of man he was, he got involved, because… well, who wouldn't, right? At one point, they captured him and held him prisoner in their base—an abandoned military compound in the middle of the Nevada desert, about twenty minutes outside Heaven's Valley."

Jay sat upright, swung her legs over the bed, and rested forward on her thighs.

Hall grinned. "You see where this is going now, yes? Now, these terrorists made the mistake of underestimating Adrian Hell—something I confess to being guilty of myself. They brought him into the nerve center of their entire operation and dropped their guard. He killed them all and destroyed the base before any innocent soldiers could get close. That man saved a lot of lives that day. He also reduced that base to a crater."

Jay huffed. "Good for him."

"Quite. Good for me, too. You see, that crater was a lot cheaper to buy than the base would've been. Especially in the financial climate seven years ago. So, I snapped it up. It might not have looked like much at the time, but the location was prime real estate. I needed somewhere secluded. Somewhere in the desert where no one would think to look. The problem is, most of the Nevada sandbox is spoken for and swarming with conspiracy theorists. Florida and California were taken too, and far too public. There's Texas, but… well, that was in no shape for what I wanted to do *before* it was blown halfway to hell. So, here we are. The way I hear it, based on the old blueprints for the base, you're sitting in about the same place he was. Poetic, no?"

Jay glanced around the room, momentarily distracted by the thought of Adrian sitting where she was. What *exactly* was he telling her? And why? He told her she was in the middle of the Nevada desert. He told her he built a base of operations on the site of an old military compound. He said Florida and California were too public. Why them, specifically? And conspiracy theorists? What the hell was he talking about?

Hall watched the expression on Jay's face change with each heartbeat, desperately trying to figure her situation out. He smiled to himself. He knew he could get to her. All that bravado was just masking her own fear. Take that away, give her something to think about, and she'd turn back to him in no time.

Jay suddenly snapped her gaze toward Hall. "You can't be serious?"

Hall raised his eyebrows, happy to play the game with her. "Hmm? Serious about what?"

She got to her feet and paced closer to the glass wall of the cell. "The states you mentioned. Nevada... Florida... California... Aside from being hotter than hell, there's only one thing they all have in common."

His smile grew wider. "And what do you think that is?"

"NASA. JPL. Area 51. They're all—"

"Launch sites. Yes."

"You're crazy. That's impossible."

Hall shook his head. "You won't have seen it, as you were unconscious when you arrived here, but about... twenty feet above you and maybe a quarter-mile to your left is a rather large and incredibly advanced rocket, standing tall, pointing to the heavens."

Jay scoffed. "What do you need a rocket for? Finally realized the moon is the only place left for you to hide from GlobaTech?"

Hall rolled his eyes. "Please! There's nothing of value on the moon."

"Why are you telling me this?" she asked.

"I wanted you to know the man who turned your life upside-down almost died here once, and if you don't tell me everything you know about GlobaTech, I'll make sure the family tradition continues."

Jay sighed. "I already told you, I don't know anything about GlobaTech that you don't. They told me the bare minimum, then you took me right after you... after you killed Adrian. I've been here ever since. What could I possibly know about what Julie and everyone is planning right now? You care so much about finding out, why not hack into that hard drive you took from them?"

Hall sighed patiently. "Because that isn't what it's for. The *soul drive* isn't about the people. It contains the technology they need to reboot all GlobaTech systems from scratch. Without it, no phoenix can rise from the ashes when I destroy them. They're gone forever. Maybe I'll use it to create my own GlobaTech, who knows. There's no denying their resources and their knowledge are second-to-none. But, no... that drive controls the machine. I want to know about the *people*. You fought alongside them long enough to get to know them... to see what makes them tick. I underestimated them once before, and I won't make the same mistake again. Now, I can imagine what they're thinking of doing... what they're prioritizing... but I think *you* know how they're likely to go about it. I want to understand my enemy, and I believe you can help me."

Jay held her nerve and shook her head. "I didn't pay attention to shit like that. I just wanted to make sure they would leave me alone if I went along with their little plan. I can't tell you anything that will help, and honestly, I wouldn't if I could."

Hall's eyes narrowed, focusing on Jay's face. "Oh? And why's that?"

She shrugged. "Because I don't want to. And because it's fun screwing with you. God knows I need to stay entertained somehow in this goddamn box you're keeping me—"

Hall slammed his palm against the glass, glowering through gritted teeth. Jay didn't flinch. She just smiled, which only enraged him more.

"Listen to me, you useless whore. I've been nice. I've been patient. Now, I'm just going to be honest. I own you! Do you understand that? You belong to me, and you will do what I say!"

His cheeks flushed with color. Veins in his neck bulged against the thin skin loosened by age.

Jay laughed in his face. "Or what? You'll kill me, right? I already told you I'd rather you do that than keep me here.

Listening to you go on with yourself day after day... it's inhumane."

"No, dearest *Janine*... I won't kill you. I'll *break* you. Maybe you have information I can use, maybe you don't. Ultimately, you're nothing but a defective asset, and I don't want one of my million-dollar machines running around malfunctioning. So, I'll beat you, I'll torture you, I'll keep you awake and let every man in a Tristar uniform run a train on you until you're *begging* me for death. But I won't kill you. Once you're completely dismantled, I'll simply rebuild you in the program. Or maybe I'll keep you as my own personal pet, just like Marshall did. He always spoke highly of your... enthusiasm."

His sick smile made Jay's flesh crawl, and she felt herself shrinking at his words. In that moment, the fear in the woman outweighed the strength of the warrior. She stepped backward until she reached the bed. She sat without breaking eye contact with Hall. She stared into his dark, soulless eyes and believed every single word he just said. The idea of being subjected to that left her shaken. It sapped the strength out of her.

In a single heartbeat, she was more afraid than she could ever remember being.

Hall's sickening grin grew wider. "I've given up trying to change the world. It's easier to just own it. You have two choices: you can help me, or you stay here and get violated until you want to kill yourself. Either way, you'll be standing by my side when all this is over. You have a day to think about how easy, or how difficult, you want to make this for yourself."

He stormed away and banged his fist on the door. It was opened from the outside. He disappeared through it, and it slammed shut again behind him.

Jay sat back against the wall and brought both her knees up to her chest, hugging them close. The color had drained from her face, leaving her feeling cold and vulnerable. She leaned forward and rested her forehead on her knees. A single tear escaped down her cheek.

Chapter Ten

Kim knocked lightly on the door before opening it, just enough to see if anyone was inside. Through the gap, she saw Julie sitting behind her desk, talking on the phone. She looked up and waved her inside.

Kim stood quietly by the door, keeping a respectful distance while Julie finished her call. She looked around the office. The window ran almost the full width of the opposite wall, stopping at waist height. Darkness had fallen outside, although it wasn't late in the evening. Just winter. In the distance, over to the left, she could see the White House, illuminated like a beacon.

She paced away to the right to admire the artwork hanging on the wall. It was a large, black-and-white landscape photograph of Santa Clarita, taken before Orion's invasion. Kim took a deep breath. She had many fond memories of working there. Some bad ones too. She swallowed against the swell of emotion. She missed Josh. She missed Moses. But she was glad she had decided to walk away.

She turned as she sensed the call coming to an end.

"Well, I really appreciate you helping us out," said Julie. "It means a lot, and I know it can't be easy." She paused. "I will. You too."

She ended the call and looked up at Kim, smiling. "Hey."

"Everything okay?" asked Kim.

Julie waved a dismissive hand at the desk phone. "Oh, yeah. Everything's fine. Just my… billionth phone call of the day? Trillionth? I don't know anymore…"

She laughed wearily.

Kim walked over to the desk and took a seat opposite her. "Yeah, I've seen *that* look a few times. No matter who sits in that chair, you get days like that."

"Well, right now, *every* day is like that."

Kim smiled patiently. "Julie, you've been here a week and a half. You're doing fine."

Julie leaned forward on the desk, reaching toward her with both hands. "And you're sure I can't tempt you back? I'll pay you more money than *I'm* earning to come and help me!"

"As tempting as that sounds… I'm good."

Julie sat back and huffed. "Fine."

"So, aside from the calls, how's it all going?"

"It's… going, I guess," replied Julie with a heavy sigh. "Plans to transition toward our new long-term goals are underway, but honestly, if I'd known how many meetings I'd have to endure, I'd probably have just kept my mouth shut."

Kim smiled. "Anything worth doing is rarely easy."

"Yeah, I know." Julie gestured to the three neat stacks of paperwork on her desk. "But I mean, look at this: budget reports, asset deployment, contract management… I started working here to make a difference, yeah, but I kinda liked it when I could just shoot people. I've never been a desk job kinda girl."

Kim shrugged. "You get used to it. I'd take a desk over being shot at any day. Although, with this place... the two are less separated than you would think."

"Ain't that the truth..."

The two women shared a smile and a moment of comfortable silence.

"How's Ray doing?" asked Julie. "I feel terrible for not going to see him. I keep meaning to, but then this place..."

Kim held up her hand. "It's okay. Jericho said the same thing earlier, and like I told him: Ray understands. He knows this job just as well as you do. He gets it. Besides, it's probably a good thing, him getting some distance for a little while, y'know?"

Julie nodded. "How's the therapy going?"

Kim paused, trying to decide how much to tell. She understood both Julie and Jericho were like family to Collins, but at the same time, she needed to protect his privacy.

"It seems to be going well," she said finally. "It's not always easy, but he's making progress. It's going to take time. Honestly, I think patience is what he's struggling with the most."

Julie smiled. "Sounds about right."

Kim raised an eyebrow. "Seems to be a prerequisite for working here..."

"Pretty much. Tell him I asked after him, will you? When all this shit is done with, I'm gonna take him to get drunk. If anyone's earned a few drinks lately, it's him."

Kim smiled. "I will. Thank you." She checked her watch. "It's after eight. Have you eaten yet?"

"Is it? Jesus. What day is it?"

"Wednesday."

"Seriously? I'm sure it was Friday an hour ago."

Kim shook her head and got to her feet. "Well, you sure are his protégé. Come on. I'm taking you for sushi."

"Thanks, Kim, but I can't. I gotta prepare for this meeting tomorrow, and I have to look at the most recent data from our analysts on—"

Kim leaned on the desk, spreading both palms on the surface. "Listen, Miss Tough Guy. I've had to practically force-feed two CEOs already, and they were a lot bigger than you. I swear to God, I will drag you out of here myself and shove an egg roll down your throat if I have to."

Julie held her gaze, half bemused, half genuinely concerned.

She sat back in her chair. "Damn. Never mind being my secretary... do you want a gun?"

Kim winked at her. "Just because I prefer the desk doesn't mean I can't kick some ass when I need to. Moses wasn't as bad. With a bit of training, he listened and did what he was told. Josh was a stubborn bastard, but I kept him fed and watered all the same. Hop to it, lady."

Julie stood, laughing.

Then the door burst open.

Both women turned to see a disheveled-looking guard, wearing the black and red uniform but without any armor or weapons.

Kim turned her body to face the door and folded her arms across her chest. "See, I thought being CEO meant everyone knocked..."

The man was out of breath. "I'm sorry, sir... ma'am..." He grimaced to himself. "Damn it... Miss Fisher, you gotta come with me right now."

Julie frowned, exchanging a worried glance with Kim. "What is it?"

"It's… it's Jericho."

Twenty minutes later, Julie and Kim were standing at the foot of Jericho's hospital bed in a secure ward at George Washington University Hospital. Julie's hands were clasped over her mouth as she stared, bewildered and distraught, at the sight before her.

Jericho was unconscious, hooked up to an array of machines which beeped with a worryingly infrequent regularity. His upper body was a patchwork of purple and yellow contusions. His face had some fresh wounds but nothing too prominent.

It wasn't the fact he had been severely beaten that concerned Julie. She had seen people get beat up before. But this was Jericho. He was an excellent soldier and a real force of nature. He dwarfed most men and had almost inhuman power to back up his fighting skills. She had never seen him lose so completely. She didn't think it was possible.

He looked… normal, and it sucked all the hope out of her.

The door opened and a doctor walked in, holding a clipboard. He wore an open white coat which rested just below his knees. He was fresh-faced with styled hair. She thought he looked younger than her. He probably was.

"What the hell happened?" she asked, trying to not to sound as shaken as she felt.

The doctor cleared his throat. "We found him lying on the ground outside. His I.D. was shoved inside his mouth. That's how we knew who to call. Although, in truth, many of us here knew who he was. We've carried out an immediate assessment, and he's in no real danger. His wounds might look bad, but they're mostly superficial, I promise. His right shoulder was dislocated, but we were able to pop that right back in there. I'm guessing it wasn't his first time. Despite how badly his torso is bruised, only one rib is broken. No sign of any head trauma."

"Why is he unconscious?" asked Kim.

The doctor looked at her. "We sedated him so we could tend his wounds. He was… agitated, and clearly in a lot of pain. He initially refused any medication. We gave him a shot of benzodiazepine so he would rest. He should come around in a couple of hours."

"Do you have any idea what happened to him?" asked Julie.

He shook his head. "He was beaten. If I were to guess, I would say by more than one person. He's a big guy. I doubt one or even two people could inflict this amount on punishment on him. It's a miracle he's not in a worse state."

Julie scoffed.

The doctor smiled politely. "Forgive me. I simply mean there are practically no broken bones, no signs of a concussion, no knife or gunshot wounds. That means whoever did this knew what they were doing. They beat him to the absolute limit without causing any long-term damage. Frankly, I've never seen anything quite like it. It's almost surgical."

Julie took a deep breath and momentarily closed her eyes. She knew that could only mean one thing: Nemesis.

The doctor looked at Kim. "I'll leave you two to it. I'll check back in on him in an hour or so. For now, the best thing for him is rest."

He nodded and left the room.

Julie couldn't tear her eyes away from Jericho. She couldn't shake the feeling of loss from her mind. She knew he was alive and would be okay. That wasn't it. Seeing him lying there like a victim gave her an overwhelming sense of defeat. If the Nemesis assets could dissect someone like Jericho to this extent, what hope did any of them have?

Kim turned to her and placed a hand on her shoulder. "Do you want me to stay?"

Julie snapped out of her trance and looked around at her. "Hmm? No, it's okay. Thank you. You'd best get back to Ray."

Kim nodded. "The Amtrak is over three hours to New York. I should really get going."

Julie stared back at Jericho for a moment. "You sure you wanna take the train? I can arrange transport for you."

"No, it's fine," Kim said. "I don't mind the train. You stay here."

"Okay."

"I'm not going to mention this to Ray. I don't think it will help him right now. But please keep me posted, okay?"

Julie nodded absently without looking at her. "Yeah. That make sense. I will. Thanks."

Kim took Julie's hand and squeezed it gently before leaving the room.

Julie moved to the side of the bed and knelt beside Jericho. She placed a hand on his arm, frowning as she noticed the row of short lines etched into the skin.

She simply sighed and ran her thumb over the wounds carefully.

"I won't let this stand, Jericho," she said defiantly. "This is a declaration of war, and I promise Hall's going to pay with his life."

Chapter Eleven

December 10, 2020

Collins sat on a stool at the kitchen counter, hunched against the cold that seeped into the apartment from outside, with his hand wrapped around a warm mug of coffee. He wore sweatpants and a hoodie, which had become something of a uniform for him, of late.

In front of him, the laptop stood open, and Dr. Moss's face filled the screen. She was smiling politely as Collins finished speaking. They were a little over twenty minutes into their session.

"It was a huge step forward, being able to say his name out loud," said Dr. Moss. "You made a lot of progress in our last session, and it's important to keep that momentum going, even if you find it difficult at first."

Collins sighed. "I know, Doc. I understand why I'm finding it hard to empathize with the fella, but I just… don't want to."

"Even if you know if it will help you?"

"Aye."

"And what's leading you to think about it like that?"

"Because..." He glanced away from the screen, suddenly fixated on a spot on the counter. "If I do, I'm giving what he did to me some validity. It feels like I'm justifying it, and I don't agree with that."

Dr. Moss nodded. "I understand that completely. It's hard to—and I'll borrow from a religious premise here—turn the other cheek when somebody wrongs you. But this process isn't about forgiveness, Ray. It's about understanding. If you *understand* why he did what he did, you can accept it. And if you can accept it, you can move on from it."

Collins took a sip of his coffee, relishing the warmth as it traveled through his body. He stared ahead for a moment, searching for the right words.

"Look, I don't want ya thinking I'm being awkward about this, Doc," he said finally. "I'm not, I swear. I just don't see a way that I can ever move past this. Not now that he's gone. Not now that I can't talk to him and... ya know... deal with it between us."

Dr. Moss smiled patiently. "Ray, when you first start doing anything new, the point where you're an expert at it always seems far away and unattainable. Did you ever think you would be where you are now on your first day of basic training?"

Collins huffed. "No, I guess not..."

"Exactly. This is your third session with me. We're just getting started. Of course, you won't be able to visualize a time when you're over this. My job is to get you there, no matter how long it takes. The first step is processing what happened to you."

"I got my ass kicked. That's what happened."

She nodded. "Yes, you did. But that's not processing it. That's not looking at *why* it happened."

Collins sighed heavily. "But how can I understand it if I can't ask him why he did it? I can't look him in the eyes and demand answers from him. I can't hear an apology. I can't put this behind me because the sonofabitch was selfish enough to die before I could talk to him and... and..."

He was breathing hard. His hands were trembling. Dr. Moss simply watched in silence as he caught himself losing control and tried to regain it.

Across the room, Kim appeared in the doorway leading to the bedroom. She was wearing a sports jersey that rested halfway down her thigh. She smiled faintly, offering silent support. He stared at her for a long moment, feeling his heartrate and his temperament calm. He returned the smile, nodding slightly. She blew him a kiss and disappeared back inside the bedroom.

Collins looked at the screen. "Sorry, Doc. I didn't mean..."

Dr. Moss held her hand up. "You don't need to apologize. But I do want you to listen. Your fixation on getting closure is preventing you from moving forward. Closure comes *after* you've healed, not before. A common misconception is that closure is something tangible—an apology, or information that helps you justify forgiveness. That's not it. Closure happens naturally. It's not a switch you can flick to make yourself instantly okay. It's a byproduct of the work you put into other things."

Collins nodded. "Aye, that makes sense, but..."

"Think of it this way, Ray. You can't confront Adrian about what happened and hear him say he's sorry, right?"

"Aye."

"Well, ask yourself: would you trust the person who hurt you to make you feel better?"

Collins sat back on his stool and folded his arms across his chest. His eyes narrowed as he stared ahead, thinking about it.

"Huh..." he said after a few moments.

"Ray, the reality is, even if you could talk to Adrian right now, there isn't anything he could say that would undo what he did to you. What you went through doesn't define who you are... but how you rebound from it does. Closure is a solitary thing. In your own time, you'll learn to accept what happened and move past it. You don't need Adrian for that. Right now, the only thing stopping you... is you."

He stared at the screen, smiling at Dr. Moss. Then he started laughing, shaking his head with embarrassment. "This is one of those situations where someone explains something to ya so clearly, it makes ya feel stupid for ever letting the problem be a problem in the first place."

"I'm glad it makes it sense, at least," she said. "But understand that PTSD isn't silly or insignificant. It's a real problem thousands of people just like you deal with every day, and it isn't treated anywhere near as seriously as it should be."

"Aye, ya not wrong there. Well, listen, I know I can be a stubborn bastard, but I appreciate all that ya doing for me, Doc. Ya nothing short of a magician!"

She smiled. "I don't know about that. You're facing a problem you've never encountered before, and I'm simply helping you find new tools to deal with it."

Collins finished his coffee and slid the mug away from him. "I gotta ask, Doc. What made you choose to work specifically with soldiers and vets dealing with this? It's admirable an' all, but it can't be easy for ya..."

Dr. Moss went to speak but hesitated. She shifted in her seat. "Ray, is Kim there with you?"

He frowned. "Aye, she's in the other room. Why?"

"Could you please call her in here?"

"Okay…" He looked over at the bedroom. "Kim, love, ya got a minute?"

Kim appeared again and padded barefoot across the room to stand beside him. She placed an arm around his shoulders and leaned forward to see the camera.

"Hey," she said with a smile.

"Hi, Kim. Thank you for stepping in," said Dr. Moss. "Ray has just asked me why I work with soldiers dealing with PTSD. I wasn't sure what I should tell him."

Kim tensed, which Collins felt. He looked up at her and noticed concern creeping across her face.

"What's wrong?" he asked her. He then looked back at the screen. "Listen, I didn't mean no offense. If it crosses a line, ya don't have to answer. I just wondered, seeing as you've helped me so much."

Kim relaxed and gently squeezed his shoulder. "I think it'll be okay, Kaitlyn. You can tell him."

Collins looked back and forth between them. "Tell me what?"

Dr. Moss smiled. "Up until 2017, I was a therapist in Abu Dhabi. My clients were either insanely rich or expats who were simply struggling with life in general. Obviously, it was a difficult time for everyone back then."

Collins shrugged. "Aye, ya not wrong there."

"Then, one day, I took on a client who changed my life. He was a former soldier, and the things he was dealing with truly altered my perception of the world. They also put my life in danger. He saved me more than once, and I was able to escape that situation unharmed."

"Jesus…"

"I never saw him again after I left Abu Dhabi, but from that moment on, I dedicated my career to helping people just like him—soldiers, vets, warriors, heroes… all struggling with the mental rigors of the life they led."

"That's crazy. I'm glad ya stayed safe an' all. But why was that such a big deal to tell me? Ya didn't breach the whole client confidentiality thing…"

Dr. Moss took a deep breath. "Because that client was Adrian Hell."

His eyes went wide. "What? That's… insane! Are ya serious?"

"I am."

He looked up at Kim, who had stepped to his side. "And ya knew?"

She nodded. "I did. Honestly, it's part of the reason I recommended GlobaTech hire her to help you. Not only is she incredibly experienced and qualified, but she can offer a unique perspective on your situation, which I thought might be useful." She paused. "Are you angry with me?"

She pursed her lips together, and her eyes started to mist with tears.

He frowned at her. "What? No. No, love. Of course, I'm not." He took her hand in his and kissed it softly. "I'm just a little… shocked, is all."

Silence fell around them.

Finally, Collins looked at the screen. "What was he like, Doc? Away from all this."

Dr. Moss thought for a moment. "He was… he was a good man. We grew closer than we perhaps should have, although the circumstances surrounding our time together weren't exactly typical. I often wondered how he was doing, and I was saddened to hear of his passing. As for what he was like, he... he thought of himself as the world's big brother. I think his abilities and skills scared him a little. He knew what he was capable of, and he spent most of his life trying to neuter himself for the sake of the rest of us. He understood that wasn't always possible, but he always tried to help as many people as he could. I think it helped him justify who he was to himself... as if balancing the scales of his soul. He also took it personally when he failed to help anyone."

Kim placed a hand on Collins's shoulder. He reached up to rest his on it.

"From everything you've told me about what happened," continued Dr. Moss, "he was at his lowest point, feeling helpless in the face of overwhelming adversity, and probably more scared of himself than he had ever been. My opinion, Ray, is that he acted the way he did because it was all he knew. It was the only thing that made sense to him at that time. That... primal instinct to defend himself against what he perceived to be his biggest threat."

Collins swallowed hard. "Me?"

She shook her head. "No. You were there at a bad time. It gave Adrian the chance to give his enemy an identity when he needed it the most—a single target he could direct his anger toward because that's easier than trying to fight everyone. You felt he betrayed your friendship by attacking you. If I were to guess, I would say that you becoming the face of his enemy led to him feeling betrayed too. When it was all over, you said he felt guilt for his actions. Honestly, all that sounds exactly like the man I knew."

"Damn..."

"Ray, please understand, I enter our sessions with no bias or preconceived notions about what you're dealing with. Nothing from my experiences with Adrian factors into the work we've been doing together. If anything, I better understand what you're going through, which means I can be more effective."

Collins shook his head. "I get it, Doc. Honestly. I'm not mad at either of ya. If anything, I reckon it probably helps me too."

"Really?" asked Kim, smiling.

"Aye. Knowing he was… human, just like the rest of us. Honestly, there have been times when I questioned it, ya know!" He chuckled to himself. "But you're right, Doc. This is about what happened to me, not who did it. Let me tell ya, I ain't been beaten like that in my entire life. So much of what we do relies on us believing we're invincible. It's a state of mind. Ya gotta think like that. Step onto a battlefield with anything less than complete certainty ya gonna be home for tea, and you're a dead man. Adrian showed me I wasn't, and I'm struggling with that. I guess I just need to focus on getting my mojo back."

Dr. Moss smiled, lighting up her eyes. "Exactly. I'm not taking anything away from what he did to you. It was horrible and wrong. I've been trying to help you see it from his perspective so you can see it wasn't personal. Adrian didn't do what he did because it was *you*… you just happened to be there. The state of mind he was in at that moment, he would've done the same thing to anyone. For you, the focus now should be on moving past what happened and, as you put it, getting your mojo back."

"I'll do my best, Doc."

She smiled again. "That's all we can ask. I think that's a good place to leave it for today, don't you?"

"Aye. Thanks for everything today. I really appreciate it."

"My pleasure." She looked at Kim. "Thank you."

Kim smiled back at the screen. "Take care, Kaitlyn."

The call ended. Collins closed the lid of the laptop and spun around on his stool to face Kim, resting back against the edge of the counter. She straddled him, wrapping her legs around his waist and her arms around his neck.

"Are you sure you're not mad at me?" she asked.

Collins held her waist. "Not at all, pet. I appreciate ya putting so much thought into this, honestly. But why didn't ya just tell me from the start?"

She sighed. "Everything was still so... raw for you. I was worried you wouldn't take it in the spirit it was intended."

"Aye. I get that. Did Jules and Jerry know about the doc?"

She nodded.

"Aye. Well, I honestly see it as a good thing. But I gotta ask, is there anything else I don't know that ya didn't think I would take well? Because I promise I'm doing okay, and I can handle it, okay?"

Kim swallowed, then glanced away.

Collins frowned. "What? What is it, love?"

She looked back at him, absently straightening his hair with her hands. She took a deep breath. "Jericho got hurt pretty bad yesterday. He's in the hospital."

"Are ya serious? What happened?"

"I don't know, honestly. When I left Washington last night, he was still unconscious. Julie was with him."

Collins stood, lifting her with him before gently lowering her to her feet. He walked away from the counter, heading for the bedroom. Kim ran after him, moving in front of him and placing her hands on his chest.

"Ray, there's nothing you can do," she said. "Please, you need to rest and get better. Julie can handle this. I'm sure Jericho will be fine. He's strong. He'll bounce back."

Collins shook his head and gently moved her to the side by her shoulders. "I don't care, love. This is Jerry. Understand? Something takes him out, we got a problem. Jules needs someone to watch her back. Who's gonna do it if I don't, hmm?"

"But you're not ready. Physically or mentally. Please, Ray, you need to take care of yourself."

"Sorry, love. They need me. I can walk. The rest of my shit can wait." He smiled at her. "Gotta go be a hero."

He marched into the bedroom with necessary purpose.

Kim let out a heavy sigh, then pursed her lips as she watched him go.

Chapter Twelve

The dark gray rental nosed into one of the many free spaces in the lot. There was no snow in Missouri, but that didn't change how cold it was. Ruby pulled her fur-lined hood up over her head, steeled herself with a deep breath, then slid out of the car. As soon as she shut the door behind her, she buried her hands in her pockets and hunched against the temperature. The wind howled all around, biting at any exposed flesh.

It had been a long drive. Plenty of time to think. Too much time for her liking. She had spent most of it trying to figure out if agreeing to help Julie was the wrong decision. Since losing Adrian, she had been drifting through each day, desperately looking for a way to process everything that had happened. She didn't want to fight anymore.

But how could she say no?

She sighed, causing a steam cloud to manifest and dissipate in front of her face, then focused on her surroundings. She turned a slow circle, looking around the near-deserted parking lot. She took her hand out of her pocket, clutching at a scrap of paper and a keychain, which she had collected from Julie the day before.

She unfolded the paper and stared at the name.

KC Storage Units.

Ruby looked over at the three enormous buildings that loomed over the lot in a wide horseshoe. A huge sign, yellow with a blue border and blue writing, hung above the roller doors on each one, stating the same name. Beneath it was a slogan: *Unbeatable Security. Unbeatable Prices.*

She set off walking toward the unit on her right, then finally stopped outside the second large roller door from the left. She stared up, craning her neck. It was easily twenty feet high, if not more. Perhaps half that again wide.

Ruby looked around again, checking that she was alone. There was no reason to think anyone would know she was there, but under the circumstances, paranoia was understandably high.

She reached behind her, allowing her fingertips to feel the comforting size and weight of the gun holstered at her back, beneath her coat. Then she moved in front of the numerical keypad next to the roller door and entered the six-digit code scrawled hurriedly at the bottom of the paper. A loud, metallic clang startled her. Somewhere inside, a long-dormant motor rumbled into life. After a moment, the shutters began to rise, creaking and grinding like stiff joints. She stepped back and watched as they ascended in front of her, slowly revealing the intimidating sight stored behind them.

The vehicle dwarfed her. Its modest, stylized hood protruded beneath a large windshield caked with grime. She leaned to her left and peered along the side. It stretched back quite a way.

"Holy crap," she whispered to herself.

She stepped inside the unit and stood by the doors to the state-of-the-art Winnebago. She stared at it for a moment, preparing herself for what she might find inside. She wasn't sure if she was ready. She hadn't really thought about how difficult she would find this when she agreed to help, and now that she was there, she was beginning to think she should have just said no.

Her shoulders twitched as she shivered involuntarily against the freezing temperature. She sighed and groaned loudly to herself.

"Fine," she huffed.

She pressed a button on the fob that was attached to the keychain. The alarm beeped as it deactivated, which echoed around the otherwise empty unit. A second later, the doors clicked as they unlocked. She pulled them open and climbed the steps.

The interior smelled musty and damp but was mostly clean. Many of the surfaces and pieces of equipment were covered with plastic sheeting. To her right was the cab, with two large armchairs fixed on a swivel, separated by a futuristic-looking center console. She traced a line through the dust with her finger before resting a hand on the back of the chair nearest to her. She stared at the wheel and smiled to herself, briefly distracted as she thought about the adventures the two men who sat here must have had, once upon a time.

Then she moved left, toward the spacious rear section. She paid no attention to everything laid out in front of her, beneath the covers. She was there for a reason.

Two tall, narrow cupboards were built into the small walkway linking the front to the back. She opened the one to her right and saw a large generator, nestled tightly into the deep space. Then she opened the left one. It was empty, save for a pair of shoes and an umbrella. She frowned and looked around it.

"That can't be right," she muttered.

After a few minutes looking back and forth between them both, she realized something.

The cupboard on the left wasn't as deep as the one opposite.

Ruby began examining the back wall, seeing how it was built and fitted. She moved her hand along it, pushing gently, feeling for anything that was out of the ordinary.

"Come on," she whispered. "Be as paranoid as I think you were…"

Eventually, she heard a click. A section in the middle sank into itself, then slid upward with a muted, mechanical hiss. Behind it was a safe.

"Bingo," she said.

She checked the paper again for the combination to the lock, then entered the second code, which was slightly longer and more complex than the first. A dull thunk from inside signaled that the safe was unlocked.

She took a deep breath to steady her nerves, then pulled the door open.

Inside was some cash, a USB flash drive, and a bunch of paper files, bound together by string.

Ruby took everything but the cash and shut the safe. She moved the panel back into place and made her way outside. She locked the Winnebago and entered the code on the keypad to lower the shutters. Then she hurriedly walked back to her car, eager to get out of the cold.

Once inside, she placed the contents of the safe on the seat beside her, started the engine, and cranked the heater up to max. She lowered her hood and rubbed her hands together for a moment, blowing into her palms to speed up the thawing process.

After a few minutes, when the feeling had returned to her fingers, she glanced at the files beside her. She reached for the top one.

"Okay, Josh," she said. "Let's see how smart you really were."

Chapter Thirteen

Gwen Parker paced around her office, listening to the conference call through a wireless headset. Her huge, expensive desk made from dark oak dominated the room, but she hated sitting behind it. She was an active person and felt most comfortable when she was on the move.

She lingered by the window and stared out at the busy New York streets below.

"Hal? Hal. Let me just step in here." She stepped away and leaned on the headrest of her chair. She idly moved her hands over the material of her suit jacket, which hung over the back of it. "It's great that we're already ramping up recruitment to the security division, but we need to focus on the PR. We have to spin this the right way, or people will simply think we're doing what this company always—"

She rolled her eyes.

"Linda? Honey. I'm talking, okay? That means you don't." She took a breath to calm herself. "So, Hal, like I was saying… I want you to plateau the security side for now. Focus on transport. Focus on advertisement. We need the media on our side if we're going to sell this rebrand. The official line is we have zero connection to Orion International anymore. If we want the world to believe us, we have to act like it's true. Jesus, people, try to keep up!"

Parker looked up, distracted by the sound of her door opening without a prior knock. Before she could launch into a tirade about protocol and common decency to the new arrival, Quincy Hall stepped through and slammed the door shut behind him. He lingered by the door and stared at her impatiently.

His unexpected arrival left her momentarily off-guard. She stared, noticing his gaze drawn unsubtly to the low-cut silk blouse she wore.

"I'm going to step away from the call," she said absently. She took off the headset and tossed it onto her desk. "Mr. Hall, what are... what are you doing here?"

"I've come to see how things are going, Gwen," he said calmly.

Hall walked over to the desk and sat down in one of the chairs facing hers. Parker hurriedly shrugged on her jacket and buttoned it, then took her own seat.

"It's going well," she said, recovering. "Recruitment is picking up, but I'm prioritizing the marketing strategies right now, as we discussed. They've started strong, but honestly, you walking in here in broad daylight is really stupid and potentially damaging, and you should know better."

Hall held her gaze. His expression betrayed nothing. "You've impressed me since taking over this company, Gwen."

"Thank you."

"In just under a week, you've accomplished more under your own initiative than Brandon Crow ever did. That man couldn't think for himself if his life depended on it. In fact, it did... and look how that turned out. Case and point."

Parker shifted uneasily in her seat. "Yes, sir."

Hall smiled without humor. "But just because I like you, that doesn't mean I will tolerate you forgetting your station and talking to me like I work for you."

His tone sharpened, and she took a deep breath to steel her nerves. Parker wasn't easily intimidated. She could look after herself, and she was ruthless in the business world. But she understood and respected the power Hall still had. She knew the risks with a job like this. The opportunity to be on the winning side in what was to come had been too great to ignore, but she wasn't blind to the dangers it presented.

His temper was one of them.

Hall leaned forward, jabbed her desk with his finger, then pointed at her. "I gave you this job. I can take it away again just as easily. Watch your tone with me."

"Of course. My apologies, Mr. Hall."

He sat back in his chair and relaxed. His demeanor softened in a heartbeat. He crossed his legs and gestured to her with a casual wave of his hand.

"Tell me how the cash distribution is going," he said.

She nodded. "Mostly fine. There was a slight issue yesterday at one of the storage units. Three of our drivers were—"

Hall held up a hand. "I know. That was me."

Parker frowned. "I'm sorry?"

"I arranged that. I sent a handful of Nemesis assets to intercept a GlobaTech unit surveilling the property."

She shook her head. "I don't understand. How did you—"

"They were acting on intel I made sure their little satellite network would find. I banked on them sending someone of consequence, and they did. Jericho Stone. Big bastard. A competent soldier, by all accounts. It was largely his efforts that turned the tide in Paluga. And now, he's in a hospital bed, regretting ever going up against me."

"Okay. Sir... I understand our primary threat is GlobaTech, but you tasked me with rebuilding Tristar and establishing them as a new, independent corporate entity in the eyes of the public. If you're going to use me and my company to set a trap for the enemy, that's something you should tell me. I could've spun this in a news cycle to say GlobaTech still have a vendetta, that they—"

"I don't have to tell you shit, Gwen. Right now, GlobaTech isn't your concern. You focus on doing your job and making Tristar great again."

"I *am* focused on that, sir. With all due respect, you hired me to this position because you and I both know I'm the best in the business at corporate restructuring."

Hall nodded, smiling slightly.

"You need to let me do what I need to do. Which means not showing up to the office to see me and not getting my new recruits killed in what is essentially friendly fire. It's a PR nightmare, and it's working against the job you hired me to do."

Hall shrugged. "I see your point, Gwen. I do. But if you can't deal with these little challenges when they arise—and they *will* arise from time to time—then perhaps you're not the best person for this role after all..."

Her jaw clenched as she sighed a taut breath. She smiled begrudgingly. "I can handle it, Mr. Hall. It's no issue."

"Excellent." He smiled as he stood. "Keep up the good work. I'll see myself out."

Parker watched him leave the office. He didn't shut the door behind him.

She let out a long sigh and relaxed in her chair, slumping slightly as she unbuttoned her jacket again.

"Sophie!" she yelled. "Get in here!"

A few seconds later, her assistant scurried into the office. She was wearing a dark pantsuit and held a folder in her hand. She was young and fresh-faced. Her makeup was borderline excessive but remained tasteful. It helped mask the state of perpetual fear that she wore like a mask. Her mousy brown hair was tied into a ponytail.

"Yes, Ms. Parker?" she said.

Parker looked at her as she massaged her temples. "I need coffee, a handful of Tylenol, and the newest intern we have."

Sophie frowned. "Okay. Um, why the intern? I'm sure I can help with whatever—"

Parker tilted her head. "Because I'm having a bad day, Sophie. Okay? I just got my ass chewed out by my boss—and not in a pleasant way. In this business, shit rolls downhill, so I need to fire someone to make myself feel better. Do you really want to help with that? Or do you want to go and get me an intern?"

Sophie swallowed hard. "Of course. Sorry, Ms. Parker. I'll go and... I'll go."

She disappeared, then popped her head back around the door a moment later.

"Do you have a... preference, or—"

Parker glared at her impatiently. "Sophie!"

"Okay. I'm going."

She disappeared again. Parker rested her head back and stared blankly at the high ceiling. The beginnings of a migraine gently gnawed at the base of her skull. She spun around in her chair and looked out the window, admiring the skyline.

There was a soft knock on her door.

She spun back around to see a tall, wiry young man wearing a cheap gray suit standing nervously in the doorway.

"Y-you wanted to see me, Ms. Parker?" he asked timidly.

Parker sat straight in her chair and smiled at him. She could feel her headache start to subside.

Chapter Fourteen

Julie stared absently at the far wall. Her hand rested on top of Jericho's, her thumb gently stroking the back of it. Occasionally, she glanced down at his exposed arm, at the short lines etched onto the skin. She was confused by them. Angered by them. Saddened by them. But they were a discussion for another time. All that mattered now was getting Jericho out of this hospital and back in the fight.

Her phone buzzed on the nightstand next to her. She reached for it and checked the screen, then dismissed it. She had been ignoring calls and messages and emails for most of the day. She knew she couldn't ignore her responsibilities, but she was where she needed to be. There were a lot of competent people she trusted to pick up the slack. She remembered a conversation she had had with Buchanan once, in which he said the hardest part of the job was delegating.

Today, she had really gotten the hang of it.

Julie glanced up at the clock and saw it was after ten. There were no windows in the room, but she didn't need them to know it had been dark for hours outside. She took a deep breath as her stomach rumbled in protest of the lack of food it had received.

The door opened. Julie looked up, expecting to see a doctor or a nurse standing there. But she didn't. She got to her feet and moved around the bed to greet Collins.

He shut the door behind him and walked gingerly across the room toward her. They embraced.

"Ray, what are you doing here?" asked Julie. "You should be resting."

Collins rolled his eyes. "Aye, well... shouldn't ya be running a multi-billion-dollar company?"

She glanced away. "Touché."

He walked slowly over to Jericho's bedside.

"How are you feeling?" she asked him. "You're walking like you're still in pain."

He waited for her to sit back in her chair, opposite him, then flashed an awkward and embarrassed smile. "I'm fine, mostly. I ache a lot. Still got a few bumps and bruises that aren't fully healed, but physically, I'm almost back to normal."

Julie frowned. "I mean, that's great. But you're walking like it's a struggle. I just thought..."

Collins shook his head. "It's fine, love. I'm just... I've not been outside much. I'm a bit... unsure of myself is all."

Julie nodded. "I see. Sorry... I didn't mean—"

He waved the comment away. "Honestly, it's fine. I'm fine. I'm here."

"I bet Kim didn't let you leave without a fight..."

Collins smiled. "Something like that. She's a good woman."

Julie raised an eyebrow. "So, are you two, like... together now, or what?"

He shook his head and laughed. "Ya really want the latest gossip at a time like this?"

"I need something right now."

"Aye." He sighed heavily. "Aye. I get that. Me and Kim... we're there for each other. That's all. Perhaps she's there a bit more for me at the moment, but we're... just dealing with shit together. No sense in being alone, right?"

Julie nodded. "Yeah. I get that. I'm happy for you, Ray. It's good to see you getting better."

"Thanks. But enough about me." He nodded toward Jericho. "What the hell happened, Jules?"

She sat back in her chair and clasped her hands behind her head. "He woke up a few hours ago. He managed to bullet point what went down before the doctors sedated him again."

"Ah, shit. Was he in too much pain?"

She smiled. 'No, he... ah... he tried to fight his way out of here, so he could go and butcher someone."

Collins smiled back. "Aye, that sounds about right. Same old Jerry. So, who did this to him?"

Julie's expression hardened. "Nemesis. More specifically, Adam Rayne... along with a whole team of assets."

Collins moved a hand to his mouth. "Sweet Jesus..."

"Doctor said the beating they gave him was almost surgical. They destroyed him as much as they possibly could without doing any lasting damage."

"So, this was a message? For us... or for you, I'm guessing? Being the boss lady now, an' all."

"Pretty much."

"Damn. How did they find him?"

Julie moved forward and took Jericho's hand in hers once more. "He was in Richmond, following up on a lead on an old Tristar weapons cache. Our intel showed recent activity there. But Jericho said they weren't storing weapons there... it was cash. Millions of dollars in boxes. High denomination. There were three Tristar delivery guys on-site. He questioned them, and they seemed to have no idea what was in the boxes, or even that Tristar was linked to Orion anymore."

Collins frowned. "Are ya serious?"

She nodded. "Jericho believed them. Tristar has a new CEO, a woman named Gwen Parker. They're on a big rebranding kick, apparently. Seemingly trying to go legit and distance themselves from their previous association to Hall."

"But that's all bullshit, right? I mean, whose money was it? Why was Tristar moving it if they're not up to some wicked shit?"

"That's what we're asking, yeah."

"Aye. Okay. So, that's when Rayne jumped him?"

"Yes. They came in, killed Jericho's team and the Tristar delivery guys, then set about delivering their message."

Collins backed away from the bed. His breathing grew slightly faster. He began flexing his hands as he felt pins and needles spread through his fingertips. Sweat formed on his brow.

Julie frowned. "Ray? Ray, are you okay?"

He nodded rapidly, trying to take deep breaths. Each one trembled through his body.

Julie stood and rushed to his side. She put an arm around his shoulder and guided him to her seat.

"Sit down," she said. "Take a minute. You're okay."

He didn't argue or resist. He sat and leaned forward, resting his elbows on his knees. He stared at his hands, watching them tremor uncontrollably. He couldn't feel his fingers. A cold shiver travelled along his spine.

Collins closed his eyes, trying to hide his embarrassment. He tuned out the noise of the room around him and focused on his breathing. After a minute or so, he felt his heart rate begin to slow. He felt the pulsing in his arms as the blood began to rush back into his extremities. After another minute, he opened his eyes and looked at Julie.

"Sorry, love. I just…"

She was standing at the foot of the bed, her arms folded across her chest. "You just had a panic attack, Ray."

He glanced at the floor, feeling ashamed. "Aye. Just a little one, though. My first in a few days. I'm getting better, I promise. Just a bit much, hearing what happened to Jerry."

Julie sighed. "You should go home, Ray. Spend time with Kim, focus on getting better, and come back when you're a hundred percent again."

He shook his head and got to his feet. "No way, Jules. That could take weeks… months, even. We both know we don't have that kinda time, and ya need all the help ya can get right now."

She went to speak but caught the words she knew even *she* wouldn't believe if spoken. Collins was right.

He paced away from the bed. He placed a hand on Julie's arm as he passed her, ushering her to follow, as if moving away from Jericho in case he could hear them.

"Look, we know Hall's been building the Nemesis program in secret, right?" said Collins in a hushed voice. "These folks don't seem to be as rare as they used to be. We can barely handle *one* of these guys, and he sent a bunch of them after Jerry. Rayne was a handy bastard when he was on our side, which makes him a pretty dangerous bad guy, right? I mean… he killed Adrian, for Christ's sake. No way Hall's gone quietly into the night and retired after taking our soul drive and wiping half of us out. He's planning something. I want back in the game, Jules."

She studied his face. She still saw fatigue and doubt in his eyes. He was grizzled and unshaven. He wasn't ready. But he *was* right. The fight was coming, and it wasn't going to wait until any of them felt better.

She nodded. "Okay. Get some rest. We'll meet at the office first thing tomorrow, and I'll debrief you."

Collins frowned. "Are ya gonna follow ya own orders?"

Julie smiled and rolled her eyes. "I'll be right behind you. I want to check in with the doctor one last time, then I'll leave Jericho to rest and head home to do the same. Promise."

Collins nodded, then the two of them embraced, parting with a kiss on the cheek.

"We got this, Jules," he said. "No matter what… we'll beat these bastards. We always do."

She smiled, grateful for the enthusiasm, then watched him leave. She let out a heavy breath and turned back to look at Jericho. His breathing was slow. Fifty-eight beats per minute, according to the machine he was connected to.

"I hope you're right, Ray," she whispered to herself. "I really do."

Chapter Fifteen

December 11, 2020

The sun did little to illuminate the dull, winter sky. Clouds were low and pale, threatening another snowfall. Collins watched the people below from the window of Julie's office. Everyone was dressed for a big freeze.

He had arrived a half-hour ago, looking like he hadn't slept much the night before. His eyes were dark and bloodshot. He wore a red hoodie beneath a thick, dark jacket, with dark jeans and boots. The hood was pulled up, with a few strands of unkempt hair poking out.

Julie had brought him up to speed on everything, from Jericho and Link's mission to Baltimore to her plans for GlobaTech, right up to the moment he walked into Jericho's hospital room last night.

It was a lot to process.

"So, we're assuming this Gwen Parker chick is in with the big bad, right?" said Collins. "Like, she isn't *really* rebuilding Tristar. That's just the bullshit she's telling the rest of us. She's really working with Hall, but we don't know why yet."

Julie sat behind her desk, looking equally strung out. She was dressed for combat—dark fatigues, thick boots, and a fitted jacket with the GlobaTech logo over the breast. She felt more comfortable. Her eyes were also tired, which she had tried hiding behind subtle makeup. Her hair was down, resting on her shoulders. It was a rare sight to see her without her signature ponytail.

"Basically," she agreed. "There's no way Hall isn't up to some shady shit. We know he didn't stop working after the invasion ended. We know he's been running the Nemesis program in secret this entire time. We also know he's too smart to try exactly what he did the first time. The public will see right through it. Tristar can't be a part of the buildup."

"But they could be a part of the endgame…"

"That's what I'm thinking, yeah."

Collins nodded, then turned to face her, resting back on the window frame. "So, what's ya plan, boss lady?"

"Our priority needs to be finding Jay," said Julie.

"Ya think she's still alive?"

She nodded. "I do. She's a valuable resource of knowledge about GlobaTech, and Hall will want to take advantage of her. She's still a prize Nemesis asset, regardless of any mental malfunctioning. But she's also a bargaining chip. It's not exactly a secret that we're running low on allies nowadays. Our security force is almost completely back Stateside now, but with the U.N. contract still up in the air, we can't be seen waging our own personal war so soon after the rebellion. We need someone like her on our side, and Hall will know that."

"Aye. But she could be anywhere. We have no clue

where Hall is, let alone what he's doing. How do we even start?"

Julie leaned back in her chair and blew a heavy sigh toward the ceiling. "Well, that's the million-dollar question, isn't it? Wherever Rayne took her is probably their main base of operations. There's nowhere else safe enough. Not with the feds almost back up to full strength and on a major Tristar hunt. Every outpost and safe house they had will be at risk."

Collins shrugged. "Maybe. If that's the case, then wherever she is, the soul drive is likely there too, right? We find her, we find that."

"That's what I think, yeah. I've got our analysts working around the clock, looking for any clue as to where Rayne went after... after last week." She grimaced to herself as a painfully vivid memory flashed into her mind. "Nothing yet, but it's only a matter of time."

"Not a luxury we have a lot of, sadly."

There was a knock on the door. The two of them looked over as it opened to see Ruby standing there.

"This a bad time?" she asked, flashing a tired smile.

"Never," replied Julie as she stood to greet her.

Ruby shut the door and walked over to the desk, embracing Julie like family.

"It's good to see you," said Julie. "Did everything go okay?"

Ruby nodded. "It did. It was a long drive, and I damn near froze my ass off, but it was fine."

She turned to face Collins. He smiled, pulled his hood down, and stepped toward her.

"How ya doin', love?" he asked with a smile.

Ruby paced toward him. She met him in the middle of

the room and threw her arms around him, holding him tight.

"I'm okay," she replied when they parted. Then she took a step back and eyed him up and down. "You look like shit, though."

She grinned. He laughed back.

"All part of the allure. Ya know that."

"Seriously… Kim lets you leave the house like that?"

He winked at her. "What can I say? She's better at undressing me."

Ruby rolled her eyes and smiled. "Yeah… you're fine."

Julie joined them in the middle of the room so that they formed a loose triangle in front of her desk. "So, what did you find?"

Ruby unfastened her long, white coat to reveal a thin bag hanging over her neck and shoulder. She reached inside and pulled out a thick folder, which she handed over to Julie. She followed it up a moment later by handing her a flash drive.

"That," she said, nodding to the contents of Josh's safe, "is the proverbial motherlode. On the surface, it's all about Adrian. Everything he's ever done since the day Josh met him, along with a comprehensive outline for the retirement plan Josh had in place for him. I think it actually would've worked too…"

Ruby's gaze drifted away and glazed over as she tried to suppress the sudden swell of emotion inside. Collins placed a comforting hand on her shoulder, and she flashed him a grateful smile.

"But that's only about ten percent of what his database contains," she continued.

Julie moved over to her desk, sat behind it, and spread

the contents of the folder out in front of her. "Okay. So, what's in the other ninety?"

Ruby turned to face her. "I haven't read it cover to cover, but from what I've seen, there's a lot about GlobaTech, Orion, Tristar, and a few other people and places... all of which made it onto Josh's paranoid radar. Seriously, those two were a match made in Heaven. He basically outlined different worst-case scenarios, along with several contingency plans to deal with them."

"Are ya serious?" asked Collins.

He walked over to stand behind Julie, and the two of them spent a few moments of silence poring over the information.

He pointed at a specific page. "This fella was like Nostradamus! Look, he says here about the growing impact of the news and social media." He leaned forward and started reading. "He said, 'Orion International can take over the country overnight using the kind of influence they have. In a few years, battles will be won or lost in a news cycle... we should be ready for that.'"

He looked up at Ruby, who was nodding.

"Yeah, he was a once-in-a-generation mind, for sure," she said. "I don't know how useful all of that will be to you, but if you're looking for any immediate solutions to your current problems, I would start with this stuff."

"I agree," said Julie, tearing her gaze away from the files to look up at Ruby. "This is... incredible. Thank you for helping us out."

Ruby shrugged. "It was nothing, really. Glad it's of some use." She paused. "Listen, Julie, I've given you everything I found, but when all this is over... assuming any of us are still alive... could I maybe get the stuff about Adrian back from you? I wouldn't mind keeping it, y'know."

Julie smiled warmly. "Of course. Whatever you want, it's yours."

"Thanks." She took one of the chairs in front of Julie and Collins, sat back wearily, and crossed her legs, resting her clasped hands gently across her stomach. "So, are you gonna fill me in on how badly everything's gone to shit in the last week, or what?"

Julie raised an eyebrow. "You looking to get back in the fight? Because we could sure as hell use you."

Ruby's expression contorted into an uncertain grimace. "I'm... just making conversation for now. I want to help if I can, but I'm not sure I'm ready to pick up the guns again."

"That's fair." Julie looked up at Collins. "You'd better get the coffee. You know how this conversation goes."

He smiled and headed for the door. Ruby looked over at him.

"Just water for me, thanks," she said. "I sleep like shit as it is... I don't need caffeine."

Collins flicked his eyebrows and half-smiled. "Aye. Lot of that going around."

He disappeared outside.

Ruby turned back to Julie. "So... lay it on me. How screwed are we this time?"

Julie sat back in her seat and let out a tired sigh. "In a word? Very."

Chapter Sixteen

The guard opened the door to the holding area. Rayne walked over the threshold, followed by another Tristar employee who was holding a tray of food. He paced across the clean, clinical dungeon, bathed in fluorescent light, and stopped in front of the glass-fronted cell.

Jay was sitting on her bed, staring blankly at the covers. She rhythmically tapped each fingertip onto the tip of her thumb with both hands, as if playing an invisible piano. She looked up as Rayne approached but didn't react. She wore a neutral, disinterested expression. Her dark eyes stung, aching from fatigue.

Without a word, the guard crouched by a large letterbox in the bottom of the glass wall and slid the tray of food through. It scraped lightly across the cold, smooth tiling. Jay leaned to her side and glanced down at it. She raised an eyebrow at the unidentifiable TV dinner, then went back to her fingers and thumbs.

The guard turned and left without a word. Rayne remained outside her cell, standing rigid and tall as he stared at her impassively. He felt nothing toward her. There was no hatred, resentment, or anger. She was a target. A mission. Nothing more.

In his mind, he read through her file, which he had memorized over the last few days. He knew who she was and what she had done for Orion and Tristar. He understood the theories behind what was happening to her right now. Her unraveling. He thought it made her weak.

Rayne had first laid eyes on Jay a little over a week ago. He woke to find himself standing in a room full of armed enemies. He instantly knew what his mission was. Without hesitation, he killed the assassin and took the defective asset away, just like Mr. Hall had ordered him to do. What he didn't understand was why she was still alive. But then, it wasn't his place to know everything Mr. Hall was planning. He was a weapon, and he went where he was told.

Unable to ignore his unblinking gaze any longer, Jay finally looked over at him. She stared back into his eyes, matching his lack of emotion.

"You have no idea the shit you've caused, do you?" she asked him.

Rayne shook his head slowly. "I did what I was ordered to do. At least one of us still can."

"You say that like it's a good thing." She got to her feet and moved to stand in front of him, separated only by three inches of bulletproof glass. "And believe me, before all this is over, you *will* care. You want to know about GlobaTech? They're like cops when one of their own is downed... only a million times worse. More relentless. Less merciful. Trust me, I know."

A slow, evil grin spread across his face like a forest fire. "I know all I need to know about GlobaTech. They're broken and weak. They're inferior to us. The Nemesis program is the future. We've already proven they're no threat. Whatever war Mr. Hall is waging with them will be short-lived."

Jay scoffed. "Yeah, he thought that last time."

"Last time, he didn't have me. Every single time we've gone up against GlobaTech, we've cut through them like a blade through paper. This will all be over in a few days."

Jay shrugged. "Okay. Say you're right. Say it is all over by the end of the week. Have you thought about what happens to you then?"

Rayne's eyes narrowed slightly, but he refrained from replying.

"They won't leave you activated," continued Jay. "I'm sure Hall has learned his lesson with me. That means you'll be turned off again. Cast aside without a second thought, and all that will be left is the man you actually are. The man who fought *with* GlobaTech. The man who *idolized* Adrian. If he doesn't kill himself with guilt when he finds out what you did... what *he* did... then GlobaTech will. What you've done will outweigh any moral debate about the fact that we're all human underneath the tattoo. Bottom line: as soon as this war is over, you're dead. One way or the other."

Rayne smirked. "Nice speech. But I was debriefed the moment we got back here. I know exactly what happened before I was activated, and it sounds to me like I did those sorry bastards a favor. The assassin took out one of their own to save you, from what I understand. That was after the woman who worked for him sacrificed herself to save him. And after the message I sent a couple of days ago, they're running out of people to hold a grudge."

Jay stepped forward, frowning. "What happened a couple of days ago?"

His grin widened. "I had orders from Mr. Hall to send a

message GlobaTech would be unable to ignore. We took out Jericho Stone. As I said... not many of them left now, is there?"

She failed to hide the look of surprise. Her eyes popped wide and her mouth fell open. "You went after Jericho? Is he... is he dead?"

Rayne shook his head. "No. But he might as well be. GlobaTech's in pieces, scattered across a battlefield they don't even know they're standing on. If you're not careful, *Butterfly*, you'll be scattered next to them."

He gave an almost imperceptible twitch of his eyebrow—a final, smug exclamation point—then walked away before Jay could respond.

She remained where she was, watching him leave the holding area. When she heard the locks click into place behind him, she sat on the edge of the bed and stared blankly at the TV dinner on the floor in front of her.

If Jericho was no longer in play, GlobaTech would be feeling hopeless right now. It worried her that Hall was somehow much stronger this time, despite not having Tristar anywhere near full strength. But it terrified her that Rayne was probably right; she was unlikely to see the end of this.

Jay wasn't sure how much time had elapsed since Rayne left. Maybe an hour. Maybe two. She had done her best to stop worrying about her current predicament. Thankfully, her hunger was beginning to overshadow her fear and stubbornness.

She reached down for the tray of food and placed it on her lap. She stared at it for a moment, willing herself to be hungry enough to eat it. There wasn't ever any cutlery, so she ate by hand. Usually, her meals consisted of sandwiches and salad, or boneless meat in some form. She lifted a sliver of… something and held it up in front of her, grimacing as she tried to identify it. The pink cut of meat could've been pork or an incredibly rare piece of steak.

Maybe Hall's trying to turn me vegan, thought Jay, *to properly crush my spirits*.

She sniffed it, then shoved it unceremoniously into her mouth. It was cold, tough, and rubbery, but food was food… even if it was coated in congealed gravy. The taste of it triggered her gag reflex, and she began coughing. At the same time, she inhaled, which made her choke. The half-chewed meat was sucked back into her throat. Her eyes went round with panic as she started gasping for air. Each breath was ragged and rasped. She launched the tray away from her and staggered toward the glass, slamming her palm against it. She heaved and choked and clutched at her throat, eventually dropping to her knees.

No one could hear her.

She rolled over to sit on the cold floor, resting back against the glass wall. She looked up at the camera fixed into the top left corner of the room and began waving wildly, hoping someone would see her.

Her stomach ached from heaving. Her throat was raw from coughing. Her eyes remained wide with surprise and fear. She reached inside her mouth, desperately trying to clear the food, but she couldn't without choking more.

She banged again on the glass. She waved again at the security camera. If someone didn't come to her aid soon, it looked like Hall's cooking might do his job for him.

A Tristar guard named Knox sat back in his chair, his feet resting up on the desk as he laughed at a video on his phone. He wore jet-black coveralls and a baseball cap, both unmarked. A handgun was holstered to his belt. To his right, the console of security feeds flickered with life. Multiple screens in full color showed almost every inch of the entire base.

He had been on shift almost three hours. There were still five left to go, and he was already struggling. Luckily, he still had some cell signal this far underground, so he could keep himself entertained.

The video he was watching on the small screen showed various instances of cats being frightened by cucumbers. One in particular jumped so high, it landed in the bath, which freaked it out even more, resulting in a mad scramble in the water.

Knox laughed hard, closing his eyes and looking away as he held his belly. After a few moments, he shook his head and opened his eyes again. He absently glanced at the security feeds, then turned back to his phone.

A moment passed, then he snapped his gaze back to the console. His attention was drawn to the feed coming from the holding area. The woman on the screen writhed around on the floor, banging on the glass as she clutched her throat. He saw the discarded dinner tray upturned on the floor beside her and quickly drew the obvious conclusion.

His eyes filled with panic. "Oh, shit!"

He leapt from his seat and bolted from the security room, waving urgently at the two guards stationed outside the holding area.

"Open the goddamn door!" yelled Knox. "Open it now!"

Both guards looked at him, then at each other, confused.

"What are you talking about, man?" asked Emerson, a tall, thin man who looked much younger than he was.

"She's choking!" urged Knox. "Open the door and get a goddamn medic, now!"

Emerson fumbled for his keys and quickly opened the solid metal door. Knox rushed inside. Emerson followed as the other guard, Nicholls, hurried away to find a medic.

"Get the cell open!" screamed Knox. "If she chokes, Hall is going to freakin' kill us!"

Emerson opened the door, which hissed against its hermetic seal as he pulled it toward him. He watched, dumbfounded, as Knox moved to the prisoner's side.

Knox dragged Jay to her feet and threw her on the bed, so she landed on her front. Then he stepped behind her, pulled her upright, and wrapped his arms around her waist.

"Hey, do you even know what you're doing?" asked Emerson. "Shouldn't you just wait for the medic?"

"Look at her!" said Knox, panicking. "There's no time."

He shuffled and planted his feet in a wide stance, so her legs were together in between his. He had a basic understanding of how to administer the Heimlich maneuver. Even if he didn't get it quite right and broke a rib or two, he was certain Hall would be more forgiving than if she died on his watch.

He clasped his hands together and tightened his grip around her midsection, preparing the first jolt.

Jay stopped choking.

Her gaze narrowed and focused with instant rage. She braced herself against the bed, then swung one of her legs backward, driving her calf and the crook of her knee into Knox's balls.

She spat the meat out onto the floor as he fell away, turned quickly, and sprinted toward Emerson through the open door. Before he could react, she leapt into the air and drove her elbow down into the side of his head. He crumpled to the floor.

Jay landed gracefully beside him and snatched the chain of keys from his belt. Then she took his handgun, checked the magazine, prepared it for use, and tucked it into her waistband behind her.

She walked back inside her cell and knelt beside Knox. He was rolling around in agony, both hands clutching his groin. She patted him down, taking his gun and a spare magazine from his belt.

"The hell were you trying to do?" she asked him. "Dry hump me?"

She delivered a stiff blow to his jaw, knocking him out.

"Next time, buy me a drink first."

She got to her feet. With Knox's gun held low and ready, she quickly made her way to the main door. She knew she didn't have long before every Tristar guard in the place was on her ass. The problem was, she had no idea where she was, nor how to get out.

She lingered in the doorway, glancing left and right along the corridor outside. After a moment, she shrugged to herself.

Screw it, she thought. *When it doubt, go right.*

Jay crept along the corridor, passing the unmanned security room. She paused at the end, where the corridor split into a T. She peeked to the right and saw nothing. She flashed a glance around the corner to the left and saw two men rushing toward her—one dressed like a guard, the other not.

Must've gone for the medic, she mused. *Guess I was pretty convincing.*

She glanced down at the weapon in her hand. She knew

she couldn't fire it without alerting everyone to her position. A gunfight had to be her last resort.

She rested her head back against the wall and took a deep breath, listening to the approaching footfalls, timing her attack.

She stepped out as the two men drew level with the corner, turning side-on and bracing herself. The medic ran straight into her. He bounced off her shoulder and stumbled to the floor. She then spun counterclockwise and drove the butt of the gun into the guard's temple. The impact knocked him into the far wall, then he dropped to the floor beside the medic, unconscious and bleeding.

Jay stepped over to the medic, leaned down, and grabbed his collar. He wore round glasses, which now had a small crack in one of the lenses. His skin was loose, and the thin gristle on his face was speckled gray.

"Tell me how the hell I get out of here, or I'll shoot you in the face."

The medic whimpered and cried. Sweat formed on his brow. A dark patch formed on the groin of his pants, followed by a stench that stung Jay's nostrils.

She grimaced. "Oh my God... are you *kidding* me? Did you just piss yourself? I literally threatened you *once*! Seriously, how the hell are you guys winning..." She jabbed him in the face with the barrel of the gun. "Pay attention—where is the way out?"

His heavy breathing was stuttered with fear. "Th-th-three levels up... across the c-c-courtyard."

"There you go." She smashed the butt of the gun across his face, knocking him out. She stood straight and glanced at the large stain on the medic's leg. "Jesus Christ, that's embarrassing."

Jay ran down the corridor in the direction the guard and

medic had appeared from, pausing at each turn to make sure no one was around. It all seemed quiet. She passed one room with a large window; four Tristar guards were sitting and eating together inside. She crouched out of sight and scurried past. There was no time to worry about being seen or followed.

The corridor turned right at the end. She stopped at the corner and peeked around. She saw the stairs a few feet ahead of her, on the left. She also saw the two guards standing on either side of them.

"Shit," she hissed to herself.

Her jaw clenched as she stared ahead, running through every option she had. It didn't take long—there weren't many.

She checked the magazine of Knox's borrowed gun one more time, ensuring it was full, with one in the chamber. The safety was off.

She slipped quietly around the corner, stepping softly to get as close to the two guards as she could before they saw her. On her third step, the alarm sounded. Red lights on the ceiling began to flash. The wail of the siren was deafening.

Jay froze.

The two guards looked over and saw her. They were holding submachine guns, but their surprise at seeing her standing there led them to hesitate.

Jay unfroze.

She snapped the gun level and fired twice. Two rounds. Two headshots.

She ran for the stairs and climbed them two at a time, not pausing to look around each new floor as she ascended. As she turned to head for the first sublevel, gunfire rang out to her left. She ducked instinctively as bullets ricocheted off the wall by her head. She ignored it and continued quickly up the stairs.

"Shit, shit, shit, shit!"

She reached ground level and slid to a halt. A large, mostly empty lobby spread out before her. At her one o'clock, she saw the doors leading outside. At her seven, eight, and ten o'clock, she saw men in black coveralls running toward her, holding guns.

Her eyes widened. "Shit!"

Jay bolted for the exit, firing blindly behind her, hoping to buy herself valuable seconds before they followed. The hammer clicked down on an empty chamber. Without breaking stride, she tossed the gun away and reached behind her for the other one she took. She continued firing —four, five, six rounds.

Ahead of her, the doorway was filling with more black outfits. Four, maybe five of them were filing through the entrance.

She gritted her teeth. "Oh, come on…"

Without a second thought, she dropped to a baseball slide, bringing her arm around and firing in front of her. The floor was mostly exposed concrete, so she didn't slide far. But she emptied her magazine, killing three more Tristar guards in the process.

Jay scrambled to her feet and ran at the ones still standing. She swung a wild right hook at the guard in front of her as she reached him, connecting with his jaw. She followed it up with a kick to the outside of his left knee, then slashed her elbow away from her, hitting the second guard in his face. Four more blows to the head and body, shared between them, put them both down. Once more, she scooped up the nearest discarded weapon—one of the submachine guns this time—and ran outside.

She immediately slid to a halt on the gravel.

"Holy shit…"

Winter in Nevada didn't hit quite as hard as it did elsewhere. Still far from warm, but milder than most other states. So, it wasn't the temperature that shocked her system. It was also a dull, gray afternoon. Low, thick clouds masked the setting sun. So, it wasn't the sudden influx of daylight, either.

It was the large rocket in front of her, standing on a launchpad maybe a quarter-mile away. Even though Hall had told her about it, a part of her didn't believe him. But there it was, right in front of her. Nothing could have prepared her for the sight of it. Or the size of it. It shocked her to a standstill. She stood dumbstruck and immobile, looking with fascination and fear.

Shouting and gunfire to her right yanked her from her trance.

Jay snapped her gaze right and saw a large group of Tristar guards filing out of a low building next to what she assumed was a communications tower, given the large radar dish on the roof. They were heading for her, and there were too many to fight. She fired a burst from the SMG and ran to her left. She could see the checkpoint and the barrier by the entrance. She estimated she was maybe fifty feet away from freedom. As she ran, she saw a small pool of vehicles on her right. Four dark Humvees were parked in a neat line.

I hope they have keys in them, she thought.

She changed direction and headed for them. As she did, bullets peppered the gravel in front of her. She shifted her bodyweight left, then right, zigzagging around them, trying to stay mobile enough that she was harder to hit.

She risked a glance over her shoulder and immediately wished she hadn't.

Rayne was rushing toward her, flanked by two more men she instantly identified as Nemesis assets. Their body language was unmistakable, and their tattoos were visible on their necks.

Jay felt a white-hot explosion of pain in her side. She grunted loudly as a bullet punched through her. She stumbled but stayed upright. She sucked in a deep breath and pushed the pace, aiming for the leftmost vehicle. As she passed the others, she fired a quick burst at the front tires. Each one popped with a bang. She reached the last one and dove for the driver's door. She spun around and emptied the magazine in Rayne's direction. He and the other assets scattered, sliding to the side to avoid the gunfire.

The hammer clicked on an empty chamber.

She tossed the gun and slid behind the wheel of her Humvee. She checked the ignition. Nothing. She checked the glovebox. Nothing. She looked up and pulled down the visor.

The key slid out and landed on her lap.

"Yes!" she hissed through gritted teeth.

Jay quickly fired up the engine, put it in drive, and accelerated away. The tires spun, kicking up a dust cloud behind her as she fishtailed out of the space, wrestling with the wheel as she aimed for the barrier.

A guard appeared from the security booth by the entrance. He stopped in a wide stance in front of her and took aim, firing at the vehicle. Jay ducked down as the windshield cracked and spiderwebbed from the bullets. She locked her arm, keeping the vehicle straight. She sat upright and stepped harder on the gas, plowing straight through the guard. He rolled up and over the hood of the box-like Humvee, bouncing away somewhere behind her.

She braced herself and unleashed a guttural roar of

adrenaline as she smashed through the barrier. The impact jolted her in her seat, but she maintained control of the vehicle. She quickly glanced over her shoulder, then checked the rearview mirror. Rayne was standing there, flanked by the other assets, watching her go.

She kept looking back until the entire base faded from view, making sure no one was following her. They weren't, but she knew that wouldn't be the case for long. She took a sharp right at speed, sliding out across both lanes before steering herself straight. The needle was pushing eighty.

There was no one behind her.

Jay let out a deep breath. Her hands shook as she gripped the wheel. She looked down at the blood-soaked hole in her green sweater. She winced and placed a hand over the wound, trying to focus on the road ahead. She shot past a sign that announced Heaven's Valley was eleven miles away. That didn't mean much to her. She didn't know exactly where she was, nor how long she had been there. She couldn't believe what she had just done, and she didn't understand what she had just seen. The only thing she knew for sure right now was that her plan to disappear could wait.

She had to find Julie Fisher.

Chapter Seventeen

December 12, 2020

Quincy Hall stood defiantly in the middle of his military base. The winter wind was strong, kicking up small clouds of dust and gravel and sand that surrounded him menacingly. He ignored it. He barely flinched at the uncomfortable temperature. He wore a short, navy-blue jacket over his beige suit, looking like a president who was forced to call his fishing trip short.

Hall turned a slow circle, staring with genuine awe at the world he had created hustling around him. Transport vehicles like elongated golf carts whizzed in all directions, carrying boxes and weapons and people to their destinations. Tristar mercenaries patrolled the grounds with casual routine. To his right, the large buildings stood like beacons against the mountains behind them. Some of the smaller buildings were still being painted.

Then his eyes rested on the jewel of his crown. His greatest achievement. The Orion 8 Stargazer Rocket. Like a child on Christmas morning, the sight of it never failed to fill him with a sense of joy and wonder.

Hall had worked most of his adult life to get where he was. The rocket was a technological marvel, lightyears ahead of anything ever developed before. The name wasn't exactly original, but he didn't concern himself with copyright law. Such things would soon be trivialities anyway.

He took a deep, relaxing breath, letting his gaze linger a moment longer on his creation. Then he turned to face Rayne, who was standing silently beside him. He stared patiently at the ground, watching the dust dance in the wind.

"So, tell me again how you let my prisoner escape," Hall demanded.

"We didn't let her escape, Mr. Hall," he replied. His tone was flat. Firm but lacking emotion. "She faked choking, then either disabled or killed over fifteen Tristar guards, stole a Humvee, and left."

Hall stepped closer. Rayne was a few inches taller, but that didn't faze him.

"And where were you?" he seethed.

Rayne didn't flinch. He turned his head slightly, directing his attention to Hall's increasingly red face.

"I was where you told me to be," he said calmly. "By the time the alarm sounded, she was already near the gate. Two other assets and I moved quickly to intercept. She was armed and kept us at bay long enough to get into the vehicle and leave. She shot out the tires of every other vehicle nearby. By the time we were in a position to pursue her, she was long gone."

Hall held Rayne's steely gaze for a moment, then stepped back. "Unacceptable. She is one person. A woman.

A defective, conflicted, broken woman. How in the goddamn blue hell did she escape from *here*?"

He gestured to the chaotic world around them.

Rayne turned his body to face Hall. "I admit we underestimated her abilities. It would seem she isn't as defective and broken as you think. Sir."

Hall narrowed his eyes, trying to figure out if his prized asset was being facetious or not. He concluded that Rayne's conditioning and status wouldn't allow for it.

"Have we found her, at least?" he asked.

"We have," he nodded. "She didn't disable the tracking device in the Humvee she stole. The last ping we got showed she had stopped at a hospital in New Texas, which makes sense. I know I hit her."

Hall pointed a stubby and swollen finger at Rayne's face. "Go and get her. No more screw-ups. Like it or not, that woman was the blueprint for the Nemesis program. She has valuable insight into our enemy, and I do *not* want her out in the wild. Do you understand me?"

"Yes, sir," replied Rayne.

The repeated, stuttering thump of helicopter blades grew louder. Hall looked around as the chopper approached the base from the north, aiming for the landing pad a short distance from where he and Rayne stood. The noise grew louder, drowning out the sounds around him.

He set off walking toward it as it touched down, with Rayne keeping pace two steps behind him.

The rear doors of the helicopter opened, and Gwen Parker stepped out. She wore a long, dark overcoat with a fur-lined hood tied up around her face. As the blades slowed to a stop and the sound of the base's bustle came back, she frowned and looked around. Then she pulled the hood down and unzipped the coat.

She shook her head at Hall as he approached. "What the hell is this weather? I dressed for December. It's like I landed in April."

She glanced at Rayne, who didn't acknowledge her at all.

Hall smiled as he eyed her up and down. With the coat now open, he could see the outfit she wore beneath it—a fitted pantsuit that clung to her toned, curvaceous figure. Finally, his gaze rested on her face. Her short, bleach-blonde hair was flattened more than usual from the weight of the hood.

She still looked incredible to him.

"Welcome to the desert," he said. "You get used to it."

Parker put her hands in her coat pockets and hunched it closed around her. She was uncomfortably warm, but it felt more comfortable than seeing Hall leer over her. He wasn't exactly discreet.

She stepped to the side, moving next to Hall. The two of them stared over at the rocket, towering above them.

"Well, there she is," said Parker. "Impressive."

Hall nodded. "It'll be fully operational and ready for launch in three days. Will Tristar be ready?"

Parker turned to face him. "We can have seven thousand operatives ready to deploy anywhere in the country within seventy-two hours. However, we're months away from being accepted by the public again. If you want my opinion, it's too soon to unveil Tristar as Orion's right hand again. We're unlikely to be effective against local law enforcement, let alone GlobaTech—who, by the way, has almost all of their hundred thousand soldiers back on U.S. soil now."

Hall took a deep breath. "I don't want your opinion. But seeing as you offered it anyway... GlobaTech isn't an issue. They can have all the men they want. Without real leadership and organization, they're not a threat. The Fisher woman is totally inept as the CEO. The way I hear it, she wants to shut down eighty percent of their revenue streams. Goddamn amateur. Plus, most of her elite friends are either dead or sidelined. By the time they're back up to full strength, it'll be too late. The most important thing now is securing this base. Look around, Ms. Parker."

He gestured in a slow circle, which Parker followed.

"We're bordered on the east and west by mountains no man or vehicle can easily traverse," he continued. "The seven thousand men you can provide, plus all my Nemesis assets, can form blockades to the north and south easily enough. This place will be impenetrable."

"What about attacks from the air?" she asked.

Hall shook his head. "Not an issue. Only GlobaTech and the U.S. military can even consider it, and neither will—the political ramifications will be too great."

Parker frowned. "Are you sure they know that?"

Hall smiled. "If they don't already, they soon will. Regardless… they won't risk it. They can't. Come on, I'll show you to your office."

Parker started walking toward one of the large buildings in front of her. Hall paused and looked back at Rayne.

"Get a Nemesis unit together and go get her," he said. "Don't fail me again."

Rayne's jaw muscles twitched. He nodded and walked away.

Hall caught up with Parker and placed a hand on the small of her back. She flinched but didn't say anything.

"How have you found the recruitment process?" he asked her.

Parker took a deep breath. "It's not been easy. We can't exactly take out a billboard in Times Square. But... we put the word out discreetly and got a strong response. Turns out, a lot of people are homeless and unemployed after your brief stint in office, and the issue of paying rent outweighs most people's moral concerns. We also hit up the underground fraternity. Lot of mercenaries and former Tristar operatives were more than happy to step back into their former roles."

Hall nodded along, staring at the ground ahead of them as they walked, only partially listening. "Excellent. And the training? Have the new facilities helped?"

"They have. Thank you. The idea of using abandoned hotels and homes around the country is genius. All of that... it was in place before I was given this job, right? How did you..."

Hall looked over at her and smiled wryly. "The world is a chess board, Ms. Parker, and life is but the game. Always be ten moves ahead of your opponent. What stands behind us is, and always has been, my checkmate. What you're doing for me at Tristar... it's one of many avenues of attack I thought I might need."

Parker flicked her eyebrows slightly, nodding to herself. The man made her skin crawl at times, but there was no doubt in her mind that Hall was the smartest, most ruthless, man she had ever known. She believed unequivocally that she was on the winning side. The position she currently held would yield great power and influence in the weeks and months to come. She just had to tolerate Hall's predatorial behavior.

It was still worth it.

They reached the building. It was only nine floors tall but towered over many of the others around it, which were only one or two. Hall opened the door and stepped through. Parker reached out to hold it open for herself.

The small lobby was mostly empty, and their footfalls echoed around the open space. Walls were being painted by men in white overalls. No one looked up as they walked past, heading for the elevators at the far end.

"How is the progress with the Nemesis program?" she asked. "It can't be easy funding such a valuable project with so many of your assets still frozen?"

"That's not an issue," said Hall. "I have over thirty assets on-site. There are another seventy currently being trained around the globe. There are only so many locations equipped to accommodate the program, and unfortunately, GlobaTech knows most of them. It's too much of a risk to continue the work in the States right now. Thankfully, I still have allies elsewhere who are happy to help out."

"Will thirty be enough?" she asked.

"One of them is worth fifty Tristar guards, so yes, thirty will be fine."

They reached the elevator and Hall pressed the button. The doors slid open immediately. He let Parker walk in first. He stepped in after her and hit the button for the top floor. The doors slid shut, and the mechanisms shuddered into life as they began to climb.

Hall turned to face her. She was a few inches shorter than he was, although she wore heels, which compensated a little. Her hands were still buried in her pockets, holding her open coat in place around her. He reached over and pulled it open slightly.

"You must be hot under there," he said slowly. "When we get to your office, you should take it off."

Parker tensed her body and fixed him with a hard stare. "I'm fine."

Hall's expression changed in a heartbeat. He glared over flushed cheeks. His mouth curled into a sickening sneer. With a flash of movement not befitting a man of his size and stature, he wrapped his hand around her slender throat, pinning her to the mirrored wall of the elevator.

"I'm giving you the world, Ms. Parker," he hissed. "Perhaps you should be a little more grateful."

She leaned back, trying to alleviate the pressure of his grip. She held his gaze, fighting every urge she had to defend herself.

"I'm... very grateful, Mr. Hall," she rasped calmly.

He released his grip and smiled at her. "Prove it."

He leaned close. His hot, stale breath made her flesh crawl as he licked the side of her neck.

She shuddered and took a step away, turning to face him. Every instinct she had was screaming at her to smash his nose through the back of his skull. But she refrained. It would be as easy as breathing to her, but it would cost her everything, and she had worked too hard to get to where she was.

But there was still a line she wouldn't let him cross.

"I'm proving it by doing my job better than anyone else could," she said defiantly. "I'm grateful for the opportunity, and I support what you're trying to achieve. I haven't let you down yet, and I'm not looking to start any time soon. But you need to understand, *Quincy*... it doesn't matter how rich you are. All the money in the world won't buy my body. I'm not for sale."

Hall held her gaze. He struggled to resist the urge to take her anyway. He knew she was capable physically, but that wouldn't matter. In his experience, women were all the same.

But he would let her have her moment. For now. There was work to do.

He nodded and stepped away. "Of course, Ms. Parker."

She relaxed and resumed her position facing the door. He turned at her side to face the same way.

"The vision will always come first," he continued. "But you would do well to remember that money *really* isn't an issue… and everyone has a price."

Parker stared ahead, clenching her teeth as she focused on deep, calming breaths.

It'll be worth it, she said to herself. *It'll all be worth it.*

Chapter Eighteen

The board members began filing out of the room after a long, mostly productive meeting. Julie flicked through one of the files in front of her, pretending to read, so she didn't have to speak to people as they walked past her.

She had barely slept the night before. The first chance she had, she left the office and went to sit with Jericho. He was in and out of sedation, but he was healing well. She had been reluctant to leave him. The doctor had come in to wake her up in the early hours, which was her cue to go home to bed. Five hours later, she was heading to the office to prepare for the meeting that had just finished.

Her vision blurred as she stared at the page in front of her. The low rabble of conversation around her faded as the last of the directors left the room. She looked up and sighed wearily, closing her eyes as she rested back in her seat.

"I don't remember Moses having this many goddamn meetings..." she muttered to herself.

"He actually had more," replied a voice.

Julie's eyes snapped open as she twitched upright in her

seat. Gerald Hobbs was standing a short, respectful distance away from her, smiling apologetically.

Julie relaxed as she saw him.

"I thought everyone had gone," she said.

"I'm sorry, Miss Fisher," he replied. "I didn't mean to startle you. I just... do you have a moment?"

She took a deep breath, summoning every ounce of patience left inside her. "Sure, Gerald. What's on your mind?"

She gestured to the empty seat on her left, which Hobbs took. He clasped his hands on the table in front of him.

"I just wanted to say I really admire your determination and your honorable vision for this company," he began. "You've already earned the respect of everyone on the board. Myself included. And I think you would've done that without threatening to shoot me..."

He smiled faintly.

Julie returned the gesture, tilting her head slightly as she conceded his point. "I appreciate that, Gerald. Thank you. Yet, I'm sensing a *but* coming."

He chuckled, more from awkwardness than humor. "It's more of a... *however*. Miss Fisher, I implore you to reconsider shutting down *every* research division. There is tremendous money to be made—and significant help to be given—by continuing to develop weapons and technology under the GlobaTech brand."

Julie calmly gathered her papers together into a thin, neat pile, then closed the folder on them. She clasped her hands on top of it and leaned forward, mimicking Hobbs's body language. She held his gaze for a moment as she decided how best to answer his question. On one hand, she was quickly becoming frustrated at the same concerns being voiced to her over and over. She had explained herself more times than she felt she should have to, and she had neither the time nor the patience to have this conversation again. On the other hand, she respected the fact that Hobbs hung back after the meeting to speak to her privately. He'd been respectful, and she understood his concerns were genuine and not without merit.

Finally, she decided honesty was required.

"Gerald, I've been with GlobaTech for just over nine years. The first eighteen months, I was stationed overseas. I traveled most of Asia and Africa, proudly wearing the GlobaTech colors as I was sent to client after client who wanted protection from something—civil war, rebellion, criminals… you name it."

Hobbs nodded along, listening intently.

"I guess I made a bit of a name for myself doing that," she continued. "I was brought back to the States by Robert Clark to be part of an internal taskforce, established to help flush out the corruption that almost destroyed this company. Not a great time in our history."

"Yes," said Hobbs. "Not our finest moment."

"Four years later, we were firmly in the Josh Winters and Ryan Schultz era. The glory days, right? Jericho was drafted in, and we created the D.E.A.D. unit. Jericho, Ray Collins, and I answered only to the person sitting in my chair. Between us, we commanded GlobaTech operatives and fought enemies too terrifying and complex for the government to handle. And let me tell you, Gerald, we did a damn good job. We did things only someone in my person would ever know about. We even saved the world on occasion. But do you know what I noticed during all that, Gerald? The one thing that stood out to me above all else?"

Hobbs shook his head.

"More often than not, I was on the receiving end of our weapons and technology, not the one using them."

Hobbs swallowed hard. His eyes were locked on hers, wide and unblinking.

Julie saw the shock and confliction on his face and paused. The look in his eyes told her everything she needed to know. She had finally conveyed her point in a way that superseded every business reason to the contrary.

"Times change," she said finally. "There was a period, not long ago, when the world was changing and no one but us could keep up. We did some real good for people, but we've always been a necessary evil. Do you know why the U.S. military always hated us?"

Hobbs shook his head.

"It wasn't because we're better trained and better equipped than they are. It wasn't because we earn four times as much money. It was because there was a real, genuine fight to be had... a cause worth dying for... and they weren't allowed to take part because it might offend someone politically. GlobaTech's a private entity and, as such, is not bound by the red tape that handicaps the fine men and women who signed up to serve this country. It was never about being better than them. It was about being allowed to fight at all."

Julie sat back in her seat and stretched her arms out in front of her. She picked up a pen that was resting beside her folder and began idly spinning it with her fingers.

"And now times are changing again," she said. "The battlefield shifted from the jungles to the streets, and now it's moving from the streets to the goddamn internet. Now a journalist can do more damage than a jarhead. Quincy Hall proved that this past year. Hell, so did we. We started a rebellion with Rebecca Roachford's goddamn cooking blog,

Gerald. Power... influence... it's no longer just about how many soldiers you have or how big your guns are. In post-Orion America, the people don't need us. They need the government. They need structure and security. They need to know they can trust and depend on this country again. We're an international company. Global Technology Industries. We're not U.S Technology Industries. Our weapons and research will only do more harm than good if we continue to fight this country's battles for it."

Hobbs nodded but remained silent.

Julie took a deep breath. "But that's not to say we don't still have something to contribute. We have the best scientists in the world. We recruit out of all the best colleges and universities around the world, and our research is lightyears ahead of anyone else's in every field. We also have an army that rivals that of most countries, highly trained and well equipped, which can be deployed anywhere on the planet on a moment's notice. We make a ridiculous amount of money from private contracts still, and the ongoing responsibility of being the U.N.'s peacekeeping force builds our brand better than any marketing campaign. Our medicine and our protection will do more good than selling weapons ever will. I'm a soldier, Gerald. Fundamentally, I was made to fight. It's what I'm good at. It's my first and sometimes only instinct. But even I can see that adding more weapons to this new war is unlikely to end it peacefully... if at all."

Hobbs let out a heavy sigh and shook his head. "I... I don't know what to say, Miss Fisher. That's compelling and logical, and I agree with everything you've said. You have genuinely opened my eyes. I want you to know I'm behind your decisions one hundred percent, and I'll do everything I can to make sure the board feel the same."

Julie nodded. "I appreciate that. Thank you."

"But..." The two of them shared a brief smile. "But my concerns about the new direction you want this company to steer toward are not without merit. While admirable, every division you want to close or sell collectively brings in more than eighty-five percent of our annual revenue. Lump sum injections from the sales will only last so long unless they are invested wisely or turned into profitable income streams. The two departments you want to build this company around just so happen to be negative equity assets. They don't make money, Miss Fisher. For every dollar generated by security contracts, we spend nine to actually do the work. Every medical breakthrough we make needs to make millions of dollars just to break even, because of the upfront costs to fund the research. You have to think of the business, not just the purpose. If you shut down all those divisions, you have to replace the income they generated. Otherwise, we're all going home inside six months, and we're no help to anyone."

Julie went to reply but realized she couldn't. She hadn't heard the counterargument to her plans explained to her in such a basic, blunt way before. What he said made sense to her, and she was immediately angry at herself for not seeing the bigger picture. She said it herself: she was a soldier, not a businesswoman. For a few seconds, she reverted to feeling crushed by self-doubt and imposter syndrome, questioning Buchanan's logic to give her this role.

Then she remembered how intelligent he was. How good he was at this job. She was there for a reason. She wasn't too proud and narrow-minded to not admit when she was wrong, nor when she needed help.

"You're right, Gerald," she said finally. "I do need to think about that. You're head of finance, right?"

"I am. Have been for fifteen years."

"Okay. Well, as of right now, I'm promoting you to… deputy director of operations."

Hobbs frowned. "Umm, that's not a real position here…"

She shrugged. "It is now. I'm the boss, and I just created it for you. You'll serve as my right hand in these meetings, and you'll be my chief advisor to all things business-related. Write your own ticket, give yourself a pay rise, whatever."

Hobbs smiled with confusion and disbelief. "Okay. I mean… thank you, Miss Fisher. I really appreciate it. I'm just not sure what I would do that we, as a board, don't do already."

Julie got to her feet. "Gerald, you and I have made more progress and achieved more mutual understanding in the last ten minutes than we have as a full board in the last fortnight. Do you have any idea how much I detest all these long meetings?"

He smiled sheepishly. "Yes. You… ah… you weren't blessed with a strong poker face."

Julie shrugged again. "You're not wrong, and I ain't sorry. I want this. I want real talk. No formalities. No corporate bullshit. I want real conversations and real solutions. We can work together on finding solutions, and you can help me communicate that to the board."

He stood and extended his hand, which Julie shook. "I think that can work. I won't let you down, Miss Fisher."

"I know. I don't give my trust easily. We may have gotten off on the wrong foot, but even when you disagreed with me and probably resented me, you looked me in the eye and told me straight. I admire that. I'm not after a yes man. I'm after some help."

Her phone vibrated loudly on the table. She looked down and saw it was an unknown number calling.

She reached for it. "I should take this. Gerald, thank you again. We'll get together before the next meeting."

Hobbs simply nodded and left the boardroom, shutting the door behind him. Julie watched him go, then answered the call.

"Fisher."

"Julie? It's Jay. I need your help."

Chapter Nineteen

A tense atmosphere hung over Julie's office. She sat behind her desk, leaning forward on her elbows with her hands balled into fists beneath her chin. It had been a couple of hours since Jay had called her. She still didn't know what to make of it.

In front of her, Collins paced gingerly back and forth, biting his bottom lip and flexing his hands anxiously. Kim stood by the door, watching him closely and trying to hide her concern.

"And we're sure this is legit?" he asked. "How do we know she ain't just playing ya, Jules?"

"She isn't," Ruby said. She was sitting at the back of the room, slouched in a chair with her legs crossed and her hands clasped, resting on her stomach. Collins turned to her, and she shrugged. "Look, we were all there when Rayne took her. That shocked everyone, including her. She's not the type of person to play a part in a long con like that. Hall took her, likely thinking she has information he could use. It makes no sense to let her go as part of some grand plan. There's no benefit for him."

"She's right," added Julie. "If she escaped, that means Tristar mercs are likely after her right now—corporate rebranding be damned. Probably some Nemesis assets too. We need all the help we can get, and she could have invaluable information about what we're facing here."

Collins looked back and forth between Julie and Ruby. "Okay. So, what are we waiting for? Let's go get her."

Julie got to her feet. Her expression softened. "Ray, are you sure you're up for this?"

He glanced at Kim, who gave him a faint smile. He took a deep breath and shrugged. "Maybe. Maybe not. I honestly don't know. But what I *do* know is, without the big fella, we need all the help we can get, just like ya said."

Julie smiled sympathetically. "We have a quarter of a million highly trained operatives who are more than capable, Ray. I'm sure we'll be fine if you need to sit this one out. In fact, I think—"

Collins held his hand up. "That ain't the point, Jules. This is important, and... and if there's a chance Rayne will be there, well... I gotta be there too. Whether I'm ready or not is irrelevant. I need this."

She held his gaze for a moment, then nodded. "Okay, then. It's your call."

Julie glanced over at Kim, who gave her an almost imperceptible shrug.

"I'll reach out to Link," said Julie. "No way he'll want to miss this. I'll have him meet us there. I'll organize transportation and a unit to provide us with ground support. Ray, get yourself a weapon, and we'll meet up in thirty minutes. We're using a local airfield, so we'll drive there together."

She headed for the door, with Collins close behind. Kim went to follow but stopped when she noticed Ruby lingering by Julie's desk.

"Everything okay?" she asked her.

The question prompted the others to stop and look back.

Ruby looked at everyone in turn, then rested her gaze on Julie. "I'm not coming."

Collins frowned. "Are ya serious? Figured ya'd be all over this, especially if Rayne might be there."

She smiled at him apologetically. "Look, since Adrian... my priorities have shifted. Honestly, I don't have any fight left in me. Besides, the same argument we all made for Jay applies to Adam. The man we all know is still in there somewhere, buried behind the Nemesis programming. He isn't the man we saw kill Adrian. I don't know how to avenge Adrian without killing an innocent man in the process. I... I just don't have the strength to figure that out. I'm sorry."

Julie took a deep breath and walked over to her. She placed her hand on Ruby's shoulder and smiled. "I understand and it's okay. You have nothing to apologize for. Especially not to anyone in this room. You're welcome to stay here, help run tactical from the operations room the way Josh used to, or you can go home and figure out how to move on from this shitshow. I'll support you in whatever you decide. But right now, we need to go."

Ruby placed her hand on Julie's and nodded. "Thank you. I don't really have a home, but I think it's time I went and found one. Let me know how it goes?"

"Of course."

Julie turned and left her office. Collins gave Ruby a friendly smile before following her.

Kim hovered in the doorway a moment longer,

watching Ruby with a narrowed gaze. She looked her up and down before locking eyes with her. She grinned, which made Ruby's cheeks flush with color, then she left.

Ruby stood alone by Julie's desk, staring blankly at the floor, wondering if she had made the right decision. It took her a few minutes to accept that she had. She knew she was done with this life. The killer instinct that kept her alive all this time had died with Adrian. It was time she started a new life.

But there was something she wanted to do before she disappeared.

Jericho stared up at the ceiling, breathing slowly. His mind wandered, absently counting the monotonous beeps from the machine beside him. He hated every second he spent lying there, yet it was probably the best thing for him. He couldn't remember the last time he didn't have to fight.

It had been seventy-two hours since he was attacked. He had been conscious for maybe half that time. A cocktail of rage and frustration and embarrassment bubbled beneath the surface, like a volcano waiting to erupt. Each time he closed his eyes, two images flashed into his mind, looping like a never-ending movie: the systematic beating he received from a group of enemies he was too weak to fight… and what he would do to each one of them if he ever saw them again.

The beeping next to him increased its rhythm slightly, reflecting the anger inside him. He balled his hands into fists. He was caught in a paradox of wanting to get back in the fight and wanting to avoid it at the same time.

There was a knock on his door, which distracted him

from his mental torture. He looked over as the door opened and Ruby walked in.

"Hey," she said smiling. "I was in the neighborhood, so I thought I'd check in on you."

Jericho smiled back faintly. "Thanks. Didn't expect to see you again, if I'm honest. After the funeral…"

She waved the comment away. "I figured I owed Julie at least one favor. But I'm leaving town once I know you're doing okay."

He shifted in the bed, shuffling himself a little more upright. His bare torso was littered with cuts and bruises. While still bulky and impressive, some of the definition had faded due to the reduced blood flow from lying still for three days.

"I'm fine," he said. "I'm just pissed."

"I bet." She closed the door and walked over to the bed, taking the seat at his side that Julie had occupied every chance she got. "What happened, Jericho?"

He glanced away. "Rayne and five other Nemesis assets got the drop on us. Killed everyone there except me. I held my own for about ten seconds before they overwhelmed me. Beat the hell out of me, then Rayne shot me in the arm."

Ruby looked at the bandage on his shoulder. "Is it bad?"

He shook his head. "It was a flesh wound."

"Jesus." Ruby winced with sympathy. "One hell of a message to send."

Jericho hesitated. His jaw clenched, forcing the muscles to pulse. He looked over at her, pursing his lips.

"Here's the thing: I've never been outmatched in a fight before. Even in a six-on-one, I like my chances against regular people. But these assets… they're different. The programming does something to them that normal training can't replicate. They're a split-second faster. Their technique is consistently flawless. They simply hit better and faster than anyone else, and honestly... I don't know how to beat them."

Ruby could see how uncomfortable he was, confiding in her like that. It couldn't have been easy for him to admit his vulnerability to anyone. She sympathized with him and took a moment to choose her words carefully.

"No one's unbeatable," she said finally. "Way I hear it, Ray is going through something similar. The two of you should sit down and talk about it. Sounds like you could really help each other."

"Ah, I don't know. Ray's dealing with his issues. He doesn't need the added burden of mine."

"We're all dealing with stuff, Jericho. That doesn't stop anyone from being able to listen to other people. Especially those closest to you."

"Yeah, maybe." He smiled weakly. "Thanks, Ruby."

She smiled back. "Any time. You guys will figure this all out, I'm sure. Hopefully, sooner rather than later…"

Jericho frowned. "What do you mean?"

Ruby swallowed and winced to herself. She shook her head. "Nothing. I just mean it's only a matter of time before—"

"No, something's happened. I can see it in your eyes." He sat upright in bed. "What aren't you telling me?"

She sighed. "Julie got a call from Jay earlier. She managed to escape from Hall, and she's on the run. She asked if they could go and get her."

Jericho stared at her, processing what she had told him. Then his instincts took over. He pulled the IV from his arm. He detached the wires linking him to the heart monitor, causing it to flatline. He threw the covers off him and swung his legs over the side of the bed, putting his back to Ruby.

Before he could stand, the door burst open. A team of doctors and nurses rushed in, reacting to the alarm triggered by the machine disconnecting.

The doctor moved in front of him. "Mr. Stone, you can't be out of bed. You need to rest. Please."

Jericho shook his head. "Not a chance."

The doctor placed a hand on his chest. "Miss Fisher left clear instructions. I can't let you leave until you're fully healed."

Jericho looked down at the doctor's hand, then slowly rose to his feet. He towered over the doctor. He narrowed his gaze, glaring down at him.

"You can't stop me," he said.

The doctor backed away. Ruby stepped around the bed and placed a hand on Jericho's arm.

"Jericho, are you sure you're ready for this?" she asked him.

He looked back at her. "No… but I'm going anyway. Are you coming?"

She stepped back and shook her head. Jericho held her gaze for a moment, then nodded.

"Okay," he said. "Can you do me a favor? GlobaTech is using a private airfield in the city."

She nodded. "I know. Julie mentioned it."

"I need you to call them. Tell them I'm coming and to have a team, a chopper, weapons, and a change of clothes waiting for me."

Ruby took a deep breath, then shook her head. "Sure."

"Thanks." He looked turned to the doctor. "Give me the largest pair of scrubs you have."

The doctor sighed and beckoned him to follow as he headed for the door.

Jericho glanced back at Ruby. "Take care of yourself."

"I will," she replied. "I'll give the location to the team. Julie has an hour head-start."

"Don't worry. I'll catch them."

Chapter Twenty

The three SUVs blasted across the Texas wasteland, heading toward Dallas. The sun peeked through the gray clouds hanging ominously low overhead. There was no hint of snow, yet the temperature still reflected the season.

The convoy had been waiting for Julie and Collins when they landed. The three-hour flight had dropped them at a military base roughly ten miles outside the city limits, thanks to pre-approved clearance from the White House. They had traveled with a five-man unit of GlobaTech operatives. Link was waiting for them when they landed with another unit, all kitted out and ready to move.

Julie drove the lead vehicle, with Collins at her side. Link was squashed in the back beside Stevens, a senior operative who had fought beside Julie many times before, including during their rescue of President Schultz in Wyoming. He was one of the few people Julie trusted.

As they entered Dallas, everything around them changed. Collins was absently staring out of the window, his mind wandering, but his attention was quickly drawn to the world outside.

"Jesus, would ya look at this place..." he said absently.

None of them had been to Texas since 4/17, even during the rebellion. None of them had seen first-hand the devastation the state had suffered because of tyranny and terrorism.

Julie glanced at the skyline. Tremendous progress had been made to rebuild in relatively short time, but that progress was sporadic. Pockets of shiny, tall, new buildings rose from the ashes, surrounded by rolling hills of rubble and decay. For the most part, people seemed to be living normal lives. Traffic was light but steady. The sidewalks were busy without being crowded. A functional society was still just beginning to rebuild itself.

"It'll take decades to get this state back to what it was," said Julie. "But I'm telling you now, in generations to come, New Texas will be a beacon of hope for this country."

"That's if we don't blow it to hell again first," said Link from the back.

Julie glanced at him in the rear view. "Yeah, let's try and avoid that, eh? Which reminds me..."

She activated her comms unit and placed the bud in her ear, so she could speak to everyone across all three vehicles.

"This is Fisher," she began. "We're about a half-mile out from the hospital where Jay is holed up. I highly doubt we're the only people coming for her, so stay alert and watch out for hostiles. Forget what you read in the papers—Tristar is still your enemy, and this time they're not alone. Nemesis assets are dangerous and should not be engaged unless absolutely necessary. If we encounter any hostile force, we defend ourselves long enough to complete the mission, then we run. We do *not* stand and trade in a firefight. Especially not here. This place has seen enough blood to last a lifetime."

Crackles of static and murmurs of acknowledgement flooded in.

"My team and I will head inside to secure Jay," she continued. "We scouted the hospital using our satellites. It's set back from the main street and surrounded by construction sites. There are only two ways in: each side of the main driveway. I want a team stationed at each one. Our presence will likely cause concern for the locals, so be respectful and as discreet as you can. I want this done quick and clean, understand?"

More confirmations came in.

Julie nodded to herself. "Good. Now, get ready. We're here."

The hospital loomed into view on their right, popping up from behind a tall building wrapped with scaffolding. It was only three stories high and looked brand-new. Hospitals and schools were prioritized when rebuilding began across the state. Most people living in New Texas now moved there from other states. They needed the incentive of a functional way of life. There was also a recent influx of people who had been homeless during Orion's occupation, so the local economy was quickly bouncing back.

Julie stopped, then reversed the SUV into a space by the main doors. The other two did the same beside her. Everyone stepped out, adjusting themselves and stretching before taking up their allotted positions. Julie watched as the operatives from the other vehicles split in two and headed toward each entrance. Weapons were ready but held low.

The four of them huddled near the entrance. Julie looked around the group.

"Link, you and Stevens head inside and secure the entrance," she said.

He nodded and walked off, with Stevens following close behind.

She then turned to Collins. "Last chance, Ray. You sure you're up to this?"

He smiled and shrugged. "It's just a regular pick-up, right? I'm fine."

"Uh-huh. And if it becomes more than just a regular pick-up?"

He shrugged again. "Then I'll get to shoot at some bad guys... work off a little tension." He grinned, but he wasn't sure Julie was buying it. He sighed. "Jules, I'm fine. Honest. Let's just get her and get out of here, yeah?"

Julie let out a long, resigned breath. "Okay."

They walked together and headed inside the hospital. The stinging odor of disinfectant hit their nostrils. Everything inside looked the same as the exterior—new and shiny. Nurses in neat, new uniforms bustled around them. A handful of patients sat quietly in the waiting area away to the left. Julie looked around and saw Link standing close to the front desk. Stevens was off to the right, watching the entrance.

With Collins in tow, she headed over, making eye contact with the first receptionist she could.

"Excuse me?" she said formally.

The nurse looked up. She had a friendly face and tired eyes. "Can I help you?"

Julie flashed her credentials. "I'm here with GlobaTech Industries."

The nurse's eyes widened slightly. Her lips pursed as she swallowed with concern.

Julie smiled. "There's nothing to worry about. We're

here to protect one of your patients. Female, early-forties, brown hair... came in yesterday with a gunshot wound to the body, likely using a false name. Can you tell me where she is please?"

The nurse took a deep breath. Her hands trembled slightly. "C-can I see your I.D. again?"

Julie nodded patiently. "Of course."

She handed the small black, leather wallet to the nurse, who examined it closely.

"You're Julie Fisher?" she said finally.

"I am."

"But... you're the one who... you're in charge now, right? After the rebellion that you..."

Julie shifted awkwardly on the spot, feeling her cheeks flush. "I am. I'm also running a little short on time, so if you could just..."

"Oh, yes, of course. Sorry." She handed Julie her I.D. back. "I won't be a moment."

Collins stepped close and nudged her arm playfully. "Check out the celebrity..."

She shot him a hard glare. "You want a bed in here too? Keep talking."

He smiled and stepped away. She rolled her eyes and looked back at the nurse, who was hunched over the keyboard in front of her, searching their computer systems.

"Someone matching your friend's description and injuries checked in yesterday under the name Elle Hunter," said the nurse. "She's recuperating in a ward on the second floor. Room C6."

Julie nodded. "Thank you."

She headed for the stairs with Collins a step behind. They climbed two at a time, quickly reaching the second floor. They followed the signs leading to room C6. Their heels clacked and squeaked on the floor, echoing around the quiet corridor. When they reached the door, Julie knocked once, then opened it.

Jay was sitting on the bed, dressed in clothes she had taken from another patient's room: jeans and a sweater, both dark gray, like slate. She was nursing a polystyrene cup with black coffee inside it. She looked up with weary yet determined eyes.

"You took your time," she said flatly.

Julie raised an eyebrow. "Oh, I'm sorry. See, I still have to rely on aircraft to fly me places. But I'm here now. You're welcome."

The two women held each other's gaze for a moment, then shared a respectful smile. They weren't friends, but they no longer saw each other as enemies either.

"Yeah, thanks," said Jay. "Can we go now? This place is depressing, and the coffee sucks."

"Yeah, I have people waiting," replied Julie. "You good?"

"Good enough to get the hell out of here."

Jay stood and headed out of the room, coming face to face with Collins. The two of them shifted awkwardly in front of each other.

"It's been a minute," she said with a weak smile.

Collins nodded. "Aye. It has."

"You good?"

He shrugged. "Been better. You?"

She shrugged back. "Had my ups and downs."

Julie moved to her side. "And you can tell us all about them when we're back in Washington. Right now, we need to move. I suspect you didn't make any new friends on your way out of wherever you were, so we can only assume they—"

An explosion outside cut her off.

The three of them exchanged looks of concern.

"Never mind…"

Julie set off sprinting toward the stairs. Both Jay and Collins followed her. They were greeted by chaos when they reached the reception lobby. Screaming was audible over the wailing alarms. Nurses and security guards were ushering patients to the back of the building. Julie scanned the sea of bodies to find Link and Stevens. Through the crowd, Link locked eyes with her and gestured to her with a flick of his head. She made a beeline for him.

"What happened?" she asked urgently.

"We have hostiles," he replied. "Two vehicles approached from the west. Didn't see them until they started throwing grenades."

Julie winced. "Shit. Any casualties?"

"A couple of our guys are down and not moving. Not sure about civilians yet. Stevens is out there coordinating our defense."

"Tristar?"

"I assume so."

Link looked past Julie and stared at Jay. His eyes twitched. He didn't say anything to her, and she made no effort to break the ice herself. She just nudged Julie's arm with hers.

"Seeing as shit just went sideways, any chance I can have a gun?" she said.

Without looking around, Julie reached behind her, drew a handgun from her waistband, and held it out.

Jay took it with a smile. "Hmm, peachy."

Julie glanced over her shoulder, back at the waiting area. Most patients were gone now, and the staff who remained were clearly preparing to follow them. Security guards were standing with them.

"It looks secure enough in here," she said. "When we get outside, stay low, find cover, and work on getting our guys to safety. I'm not leaving anyone behind, dead or otherwise. We do only what we need to, so we can get out of here. I have a meeting tomorrow, and I don't want to miss it because I've been shot. Everyone ready?"

Jay held her gun with both hands, taking slow breaths. "Yup."

Link held his own weapon up to his face. It looked like a cannon. A bulky piece with an oversized barrel—GlobaTech's own variation of the Desert Eagle. He set his jaw and stared out through the doors.

Julie glanced at Collins, who had yet to draw his *Negotiator*. "Ray?"

He didn't respond. His gaze was locked on the carnage outside.

Julie sighed. "Ray!"

"Huh?" He looked over at her. "Aye, I'm ready. I just… well… take a look for yaself."

He nodded through the glass doors at the small parking lot out front. The west entrance was farthest away from them. The two enemy vehicles were parked haphazardly across the street, blocking it off. Fanned out in front of it were five men dressed in Tristar black, all holding machine guns level at their hips, firing relentlessly at the hospital entrance. Just behind them, the face of Adam Rayne stood watching.

Collins let out a short huff. "This just became more than a regular pick-up…"

Julie stared over at Rayne, grinding her teeth to suppress the justifiable rage she felt burning inside her.

"You know the plan," she said. "Let's move."

The four of them stepped out. The sound of gunfire immediately grew louder. They rushed for cover behind their SUVs, returning intermittent fire to buy themselves valuable heartbeats of reprieve. Julie and Link pushed on, heading for a low concrete wall across from where the vehicles were parked. Stevens was already there, popping up to return fire every few seconds. Beside him, lying motionless on the ground, was one of their operatives.

"You good?" shouted Julie over the noise.

Stevens growled through gritted teeth. "We've lost half our guys already. We can't sustain this much longer."

They paused to shoot back. Each time Link fired, it sounded like an explosion. He clipped one of the Tristar men in the shoulder, the impact of which knocked him clear off his feet.

Julie looked around. Jay and Collins were behind their SUV to the left of the entrance. Behind them, another two of their guys were taking cover behind the third vehicle, closest to the west entrance. The remaining three operatives were pinned down opposite the east entrance, where Tristar had appeared. They were crowded behind two civilian cars parked there, too close to the hostiles to survive trying to move.

Julie ran through all the options she saw open to her in her mind. She kept coming back to wishing Jericho was there with her. He was the battlefield general, not her.

What would Jericho do? she asked herself.

Across from her, Jay took out two more Tristar men with accurate headshots from behind cover. Beside her, Collins squatted against the wheel arch, holding his gun and staring ahead with unblinking eyes.

She frowned at him. "Hey, any time you wanna help…"

Automatic gunfire peppered the hood, forcing Jay to duck for cover. Collins twitched and flinched on his haunches, bringing his hands up over his head.

"I... I... I can't," he muttered. "I can't."

Jay cursed to herself, then leaned over to him.

"Hey." He looked at her, and she slapped him across the face. "Get it together, numbnuts, or we're not making it out of here."

He slid his legs out in front of him, sitting heavily on the cold, damp concrete, transfixed on the open door of the vehicle ahead of him.

He shook his head rapidly. "Don't... please... don't close it. Don't close it!"

Jay looked at him with wide, concerned eyes. "Oh, shit..."

She popped up to return fire, then glanced over at Julie.

"Hey!" she shouted. When Julie looked over, she gestured to Collins with a nod. "I think I just broke your boy."

Julie frowned, then looked at Collins. She immediately rolled her eyes and grimaced. "Ah, shit..."

She started to shout something, but Jay held up a hand.

"I've got him," she yelled. "Just get us out of here."

She then knelt by his side and rested a hand on his shoulder. "Ray, we're gonna get out of here, okay? Just... follow my voice."

Collins twitched from her touch and looked at her. His eyes were filled with tears. "I can't... I can't..."

"I know." She sighed, closing her eyes. "I know."

Julie watched them for a moment, angry at herself for listening to Collins in the first place. Of course, he would say he was fine. She knew he wasn't, and now his life was in danger. As far as she was concerned, that was on her.

"To hell with this..." she hissed.

She popped up to her feet and emptied her *Negotiator* at the two remaining Tristar guys, forcing them to retreat behind their own vehicles. As they did, she locked eyes with Rayne, who smiled at her before raising his own gun and returning fire.

She dove to her right to avoid the onslaught, rolling behind another vehicle. The three GlobaTech operatives pinned to Rayne's left took the opportunity to start shooting back, but as they moved out of cover, Rayne turned and dropped all three of them with headshots.

"No!" shouted Julie as she watched in horror.

"You're running out of fodder," Rayne called out in the brief silence. "You have... what? Six left? Seven?"

Julie stared at the ground; her expression narrowed into a point with anger. Her jaw ached from clenching.

"You ain't doing so well yourself," she shouted back. "Walk away, Adam."

He started laughing. "You might want to count again, Miss Fisher."

She frowned, then glanced around the side of the vehicle. Over Rayne's shoulder, approaching from the east, were two more Humvees. The first slid to a halt, and two people got out. A man and a woman dressed in olive-green fatigues. They walked calmly to Rayne's side, preparing their handguns.

"Shit," she muttered.

They were Nemesis assets. No doubt.

The second Humvee stopped a few feet behind the first. Six more Tristar mercenaries climbed out, armed with the same machine guns as the others.

Julie glanced across the small parking lot at Link and Stevens. Link gave her a discreet shake of his head.

This wasn't a fight they were going to walk away from.

"It pays to have friends," said Rayne. "Shame most of yours are dead now. Give us Jay, and I'll make it quick for you. But this isn't your rebellion, Miss Fisher. There are no bonus points for tenacity here. Resist, and this ends bloody and painful for a lot of innocent people."

Julie took a deep breath, then looked back over at Link. Using hand signals, she instructed him and Stevens to run for the last SUV. He nodded.

Link then looked over at Jay, who was holding Collins's head to her chest to comfort him. With a subtle nod, he gestured toward the last vehicle. Jay nodded back, then looked at Collins.

"Hey, we're gonna get out of here, okay?" she said softly.

He shook his head. "I can't. It hurts... I can't..."

Jay winced. "Look, Ray... I'm not good at this caring thing, all right? We ain't got the time for you to lose your mind. Just... do what I tell you. Be crazy later."

Julie looked at her weapon. The *Negotiator* was a rare piece. Only three were ever made, and they were locked to the user by a thumbprint scanner on the grip. It fired a variety of ammo types, in additional to standard bullets. She switched to armor piercing rounds. She knew it carried three shots. She had to make them count.

She took a breath, then stood and walked out of cover. It was the first proper look at Rayne she had gotten since seeing him activate. She eyed him up and down. It was him but... it wasn't at the same time. There was someone else behind those dark eyes of his.

The two assets on either side of him tensed at the sight

of her. Behind him, the six Tristar men formed a loose line, weapons raised.

Julie knew they couldn't win here. But she needed to buy Jay and Collins enough time to escape. She raised her gun and took aim at Rayne. In response, the two assets took aim at her, as did the six Tristar mercenaries.

She swallowed hard.

"Maybe this all ends right here, right now," she said to Rayne.

He simply smiled at her. "It doesn't. You pull that trigger, we pull ours, what's left of your team pull theirs... everyone dies. But that doesn't stop anything. All that will do is give GlobaTech a public relations nightmare to deal with, which means Mr. Hall can continue without distractions. Honestly, you'll be doing him a favor."

The male asset on Rayne's right shifted his gaze slightly, staring over Julie's shoulder. She saw his mouth curl slightly at one side. Then he adjusted his aim and fired three times past her. She flinched and looked around in time to see the two GlobaTech operatives behind the farthest SUV disappear out of sight, dropped by headshots. Then she saw the front end of the vehicle jolt and dip forward. The third bullet must have taken out a tire.

Rayne grinned and looked around. "And then there were five. Who dies next, Miss Fisher?"

Julie nodded to the asset next to him. "That guy."

She snapped her aim and fired once, putting one of the armor piercing rounds squarely in his chest. The asset dropped instantly. Blood bubbled up from the wound and began pumping out onto the ground around him. The armor he wore counted for nothing.

Rayne stared in shock at his fallen brother, then directed his venomous gaze at Julie. He unleashed a nerve-shredding growl and opened fire. Julie, who had anticipated his reaction, was already sprinting back to cover.

"Kill them!" yelled Rayne. "Kill them all!"

In an instant, the air was filled once again by the staccato roar of gunfire. Julie slid back behind the vehicle near the entrance. She looked over to see Link and Stevens pinned down. Small clouds of dust and brick puffed up around them as the hail of bullets chipped away at the wall they were hiding behind.

"Shit," she hissed.

Jay knew she and Collins couldn't stay where they were. It was only a matter of time before Tristar began walking them down, emptying their guns until everyone was dead. If she were in their position, that's exactly what she would do.

She looked at Collins. His gaze was still wide and vacant. He was no use to her.

The time for being gentle had long gone.

She grabbed a handful of clothing at the back of his neck and stood, dragging him up and along with her.

"Come on," she urged. "We're leaving."

He was too spaced to resist. Keeping pressure on him to force him low, the two of them hustled out from cover and moved around to hide behind the last vehicle, putting more distance between them and their enemy.

Collins whimpered and moaned at the sight of the two dead GlobaTech operatives, but Jay ignored him. She forced him to sit directly behind one of the wheels.

"Wait there. Say nothing." She reached over to retrieve a weapon from one of the fallen operatives, checked the magazine, then prepared to return fire. "Ray. Ray? Look at me."

Hesitantly, he did.

She leaned forward slightly. "You're gonna be okay. I promise."

She turned away and refocused on the fight. She saw Link reloading. Julie was out of sight.

As she took aim, she saw a third Humvee arrive from the east.

"Oh, come on..." she muttered.

She glanced at Collins. He was hugging his knees and rocking back and forth, shaking his head. He was muttering inaudibly to himself. Then she looked back across the parking lot as six more Tristar men climbed out of the vehicle and—

—disappeared in a thunderous explosion, consumed by fire.

She frowned. "What the hell?"

She looked left, toward the west entrance. A black SUV braked hard; its tires screeched as it turned a one-eighty and slid to a stop.

Rayne and what was left of his Tristar force had scattered from the explosion. He looked over, angered and confused.

The door of the SUV opened, and Jericho stepped out, reloading a large cartridge into his *Negotiator*. He strode purposefully into the parking lot, took aim, and fired another explosive round in Rayne's direction. Another Humvee exploded. The blast shattered the glass in the hospital's entrance doors.

Julie seized the opportunity and ran, ducking against the flying shards and heading for Link and Stevens. As she reached them, they all stood and walked backwards, firing everything they had left at Rayne.

Jericho switched his weapon to standard bullets and

started shooting. He hit the female asset twice, but she was still moving when she hit the ground. He stepped over to Jay and Collins.

"Go," he barked. "Now."

Jay didn't need to be told twice. She reached over and dragged Collins to his feet by his collar, then ushered him along beside her as they sprinted for the SUV. They dove through the open rear door. One of the operatives standing beside it slammed it closed behind her and slammed his palm against the roof. The SUV sped away again.

Jericho looked around, noting the middle of the three SUVs was the only one still roadworthy. He moved to the driver's door and climbed inside. He gunned the engine and sounded the horn.

Julie, Link, and Stevens looked over, then sprinted toward it. They all clambered inside—Julie in the front, Link and Stevens in the back—then Jericho slammed his foot to the floor. The tires spun and screeched as he fishtailed out of the parking lot.

Link looked behind him and saw Rayne pacing across the lot, firing blindly in their direction. Only one person wearing Tristar black was standing with him. Two vehicles were engulfed in flames, with thick, dark smoke billowing to the sky.

He looked back around and fist-bumped Stevens with relief.

Julie sat back in the seat and took a deep breath. Then she glanced over at Jericho. He was staring intently ahead, his gaze flicking between the road and the rearview.

"You're supposed to be in bed," she said.

Chapter Twenty-One

December 13, 2020

The mood in Julie's office was somber. It had been a long night with little sleep for anyone, and today wasn't going to be much easier.

Jericho paced around the room like a caged animal. Whatever pain he still felt in the aftermath of his attack was nulled by the anger that consumed him now. He wore a T-shirt that looked too small for him, on account of his enormous frame. Any definition he had lost in the hospital bed had been replaced and seemingly improved upon. His arms pulsed with adrenaline. His expression was hardened with focus. His jaw was set with determination.

Link sat quietly in the corner, leaning back in his chair with his feet resting on another chair in front of him. He watched Jericho, looking without really seeing. After yesterday, his mind was struggling to focus on much of anything. His role in what came next was now without question. His initial reluctance to commit fully to another big fight had been replaced with a renewed thirst for revenge and justice. Seeing Rayne outside that hospital... seeing his complete disregard for innocent life... it was hard for him to comprehend. It looked like the man he had considered a brother, but he knew it wasn't. Not really. It made the fight a little harder but no less important.

Julie stared at both men in turn. Both giants. Both warriors. Both itching for a fight. Yet each one looked lost. She understood that. There was a time yesterday, standing in that parking lot, staring down Rayne and the other assets, when she had accepted her time was up. She was beaten, and she had cost good men their lives in the process. Had it not been for Jericho arriving when he did, she knew unequivocally that she would be dead. Her night had been spent tossing and turning in bed. Any sleep she managed was brief, cut short by nightmares that forced her to wake up screaming, sheathed in cold sweat. Jericho didn't stir once beside her, and she didn't wake him. He had enough on his mind without her troubles.

She just hoped it was all worth it.

She turned to look at Jay, who was standing next to her desk, patient and a little awkward. She had stayed in GlobaTech's headquarters overnight. There were guest quarters and shower facilities. She looked rested and clean. Her hair was tied back, similar to Julie's. Her dark eyes were back to being a choice, rather than a consequence.

"Okay, look," said Julie. "Yesterday was rough, but the mission was a success. We can grieve and feel bad later. Right now..." She looked at Jay. "...we need you to debrief everyone in here about what happened to you. Make the sacrifices that were made yesterday worth it."

Jay opened her mouth to speak but never got the chance. The door to Julie's office burst open, and Ruby rushed in, looking red-faced and disheveled. All eyes turned to her. She ignored them. She kicked the door closed and stepped to Julie's desk, looking her in the eyes.

"I heard about Ray," she said, slightly out of breath. "I got here as fast as I could. Is he okay?"

Julie pursed her lips with a faint smile, touched by her concern. "He'll be fine. He's mildly sedated. We're keeping him in a psych ward for observation. Yesterday was a shitshow for all of us. It must've triggered something inside of him that he wasn't ready to deal with."

Ruby put her hand to her mouth. Her eyes were wide with regret. "Oh my God…"

"He'll be okay, Ruby. We're flying his therapist over to see him. They've been working via video calls so far, and according to Kim, it's been going well. I think he needs the personal touch right now."

Ruby shook her head. "I should've been there. I could've helped. This is—"

"It's no one's fault," said Julie, cutting her off. "Especially not yours. If you *had* been there, you would've been one more person who felt like they weren't going to walk away from it. That's all. No one is putting any of this on you, okay?"

Ruby refocused and stared at Julie. She simply nodded and flashed a quick smile.

Then she noticed Jay.

The two women locked eyes. Jericho stopped his pacing. Everyone tensed, like all air had been sucked from the room.

Ruby stepped over to her. "Hey."

Jay nodded, making no effort to move. "Hey."

"You okay?"

Jay shrugged. "Better than I have been recently. You?"

"Not even a little bit."

"Yeah…"

They fell silent. Ruby took a few deep breaths, finally calming herself. She turned back to Julie, but Jay stepped forward, keeping her attention. She reached out hesitantly, then decided against it and placed both hands in the pockets of her jeans.

"Hey, I, ah… I just wanna say…" She glanced away, as if searching for the words. "I'm sorry about Adrian."

Ruby said nothing. She watched Jay, noting how uncomfortable she looked.

"I don't fully remember who he was to me before all *this*," continued Jay, tapping her temple. "But he fought for me more than once when he had every reason not to, and I was grateful for that."

Ruby took a slow breath and nodded. "I appreciate you saying that. Thank you."

Jay shrugged humbly. "How it all went down that day… he deserved better. I hope you can put all this right, so it wasn't for nothing, y'know."

Julie leaned forward, resting her palms flat on her desk. "I'm glad we're all on the same page. Last thing we need right now is any issues between us. But we're running out of time." She looked directly at Jay. "We need to know where Quincy Hall is and what he's doing. We need to know how Tristar is involved, and we need to know how to stop this before it gets even more out of control. That piece of shit has our soul drive, and without it, GlobaTech has no safety net. We have no second chances. We lose here… we're dust. We can't sustain another long-term fight against Hall. Not with the Nemesis assets in play. Right now, you're all we've got."

Ruby stepped away and took a seat near the door, close to where Jericho was standing. She nodded to him, which he returned. Link sat forward in his chair, resting his forearms on his knees.

Jay looked around the room. "I'll tell you what I know, which admittedly isn't much. After your boy Rayne was activated and... did what he did, they took me to a military compound where Hall's been hiding out. I woke up in a holding cell, so I don't know how I got there."

"Any clue where it is?" asked Jericho flatly.

Jay nodded. "I know it's in Nevada. I'm not sure where. Hall said, during one of the times he tortured me by talking for an hour about how great he is, that he bought the base years ago, after Adrian destroyed it."

Ruby frowned. "What?"

"Yeah, he said Adrian was there once, and he blew it up for some reason. The location was perfect for Hall, so he snapped it up for a bargain."

"Wait a minute..." Julie shook her finger in the air as she searched the depths of her memories. Then she looked at the room. "Heaven's Valley."

"Yes!" exclaimed Jay. "That sounds familiar. I was in a bit of a rush on my way out of there, but I saw a sign for that place. Does it mean something to you?"

Julie nodded. "When I was initially recruited to GlobaTech, it was by Robert Clark."

Jericho tilted his head slightly. "That's the guy who recruited Josh Winters, right?"

"And Ryan Schultz, yeah. See, at the time, GlobaTech wasn't exactly doing everything above board. A corrupt element within was making all kinds of shitty deals with bad people, then skimming money off the top. Clark was hired to clean house, and he wanted my help doing it."

"How does Adrian fit into all this?" asked Link.

Julie looked at him. "One of those shitty deals was with a Russian extremist group called Dark Rain, who were operating out of the military base that Hall now owns. Adrian was in Heaven's Valley working a contract that tied into that deal. He ended up fighting the local mob *and* the terrorists, the result of which was him blowing that base sky-high, despite Clark begging him not to."

Ruby smiled to herself. "Sounds about right."

Julie rolled her eyes with a wry smile. "So, Hall bought the crater Adrian created and rebuilt the base... okay. We know where he is. That's a good start." She looked back at Jay. "Now, we need to know why."

Jay shook her head with disbelief. "I'm pretty sure it involves him going into space."

Once again, total silence enveloped the room. Everyone exchanged looks of incredulity.

Link chuckled nervously. "Ah... say again?"

Jay looked over at him. "Space. You know... the big, black thing we're all floating in."

Link raised an eyebrow.

Jericho stepped forward. "What makes you so sure? Did he say anything?"

"The first clue I had was when I finally made it outside, during my escape, and saw a big-ass spaceship."

Julie's mouth fell open. "You saw *what*?"

Jay looked at her. "A massive NASA-looking rocket... ship... thing, like you see in movies. It's standing on a launchpad about a quarter-mile out west of the compound."

"And Hall made no mention of it to you?" asked Julie.

"He talked a lot of bullshit while I was there. Really likes the sound of his own voice. He mentioned it briefly, but I didn't really pay attention. Kept going on about how money isn't an issue anymore, which made no sense to me. I thought the fat prick was rich anyway."

Jericho nodded. "He is. Tristar was shifting large amounts of cash around for him. It's how he's funding the new-and-improved Tristar now all of Orion's assets are frozen."

Jay shrugged. "Yeah, maybe. But he didn't mention the rocket. He just kept trying to get me to tell him everything I know about you guys."

"Did you?" asked Link.

She stared into his eyes. "No."

"How come?" asked Ruby. When Jay turned her attention to her, she shrugged. "Just curious."

Jay sighed. "I made a deal with the boss lady here that if I helped you, I would get to disappear. I just want to walk away, and I knew that wouldn't happen if I rolled over on GlobaTech."

"And here's me thinking it was because you liked us," said Link sarcastically.

Jay smiled at him. "Don't take it personally. I don't like anyone."

"So, that's it?" asked Julie. "There's nothing else you can tell us that might help?"

Jay shrugged. "Rayne was there the whole time, at Hall's side like a personal bodyguard. But that's all I know. Sorry." She paused. "Look, that compound... it's huge. Kinda looked like your old digs, to be honest. Surrounded by mountains on three sides. Maybe a bit smaller but no less impressive. It was also crawling with Tristar guys. He has a stockpile of weapons. There's only one way in or out. No way you're getting in there."

Jericho shrugged. "You managed to get out on your own..."

"Yeah, but I took them by surprise. After yesterday, you think Hall's not expecting the red and black cavalry to come marching over the hills any day now?" She looked at Julie. "You attack that place, you're leading your people to a slaughter."

Julie didn't respond. She knew Jay was probably right. Instead, she looked over at Jericho, silently imploring him to give her the solution she was missing.

Jericho stared at the floor for a moment, deep in thought. His arms were folded across his chest, forcing his biceps to bulge against the tight seams of his shirt.

"It doesn't matter how impenetrable this base seems," he said finally. "It doesn't change the fact that we need to take it offline as soon as possible. We're still rebuilding ourselves. We probably couldn't sustain another rebellion against Orion, Tristar, *and* Nemesis. Honestly, even if we could... this country, the *world*... people deserve peace. We can't let this become another war."

"I agree," said Julie. "But we can't do that until we know what Hall's endgame is here. What, is he going to lay claim to the moon now because it didn't work out in the States? What?"

Link nodded. "Also, how long has he been planning this? I mean, rocket ships aren't exactly like Lego sets, are they? It must've taken him years to build that thing, which means it was potentially around before his brief stint in the White House. Was conquering the country his master plan, or was that always meant to be a stepping stone to whatever this is?"

Julie nodded. "That's a damn good point."

Ruby bolted upright in her chair and began waving her arms urgently in front of her. "Oh... oh... oh!"

Everyone turned to her, confused.

She looked at Julie. "Josh's files. Josh's files! Where are they?"

Julie glanced down at her desk and pointed to a pile of thick files in front of her. "Right here. Why?"

Ruby rushed over to the desk. "Gimme!"

She began scrambling through the mountain of paperwork, feverishly scanning each page.

"What is it?" asked Julie. "Talk to us, Ruby. What did—"

"Here!" she exclaimed.

She quickly looked over the page in her hands. Her lips moved almost imperceptibly as she read to herself. Her expression morphed from focus to fear. Her eyes went wide.

"Oh my God..." she whispered.

"Ruby, what is it?" asked Jericho.

She turned to face the room and began to read aloud from Josh's notes. "He says here, 'I don't think it's possible yet, but the reports of asteroid 16 Psyche are starting to worry me. The raw metal that thing contains is currently estimated to be worth upwards of ten... *quintillion* dollars.'" She looked up. "That's more zeroes than will ever make sense to me."

She looked back at the paper.

"He goes on to say, 'That's enough to make every man, woman, and child living on this planet a billionaire overnight. The technology isn't where it needs to be for NASA to effectively reach it, but there's nothing stopping private companies like JPL and GlobaTech from trying. Especially the latter. Some of the experimental propulsion technology they're working on is borderline *Star Trek* fodder. If anyone ever laid claim to that thing, they would literally rule the world... simply because they could buy it.'"

Ruby looked up again, greeted by stunned, blank expressions from everyone in the room. She nodded slowly. "Yeah... pretty much."

The silence hung over them for a solid minute.

"This can't be it," said Link finally. "I mean... this is some crazy, science fiction shit, right? It's not *actually* possible."

Jericho shrugged. "If it is, I would bet my last dollar it's Hall's real endgame. Think about it. A tyrannical billionaire who invaded the country with a private army buys a military base in the desert and builds a rocket there. It has to be what he's planning."

Jay shook her head. "But why? Your notes just said the technology isn't there yet."

Julie slammed her hand down on the desk. "Oh, shit!"

She took her seat and began typing urgently on her laptop, searching GlobaTech's extensive database of files.

Jay sighed. "What now?"

Julie stopped typing and sat back in her chair, pushing herself away from the desk and clasping her hands behind her head. She stared at the screen for a moment before looking at the room.

"The technology might not have been there when Josh wrote those notes," she said. "But it's there now."

"What?" asked Jericho. "How do you know?"

Julie looked at him. "Because we made it..." Then she turned to Jay. "...and you've already used it."

Ruby shook her head. "I don't follow."

"Last September, Tristar hit a GlobaTech transport in Cambodia. William Roachford was involved. It was the day they betrayed him and left him for dead. But the tech they stole from us… it was this. The propulsion technology. They reverse-engineered what we had already designed, then perfected it." She looked at Jay again. "The bullet you fired in Paluga… no one had ever seen anything like it. That was the first application of the technology. You said yourself, Paluga was a practice run for Hall, right?"

Jay shrugged sheepishly. "Yeah."

"We all assumed he was testing GlobaTech's capabilities in the field. But what if he was testing the final piece of his rocket as well?"

Ruby returned to her seat and sat heavily, letting out a long sigh. "So, if we hadn't stopped Hall when we did, he might already be up there right now, mining this… this asteroid?"

Julie nodded. "I think so, yeah."

"Then Link was right," said Jericho. "Taking over the country wasn't Hall's grand plan—this is. Maybe he figured doing it from a position of power like the White House would make his claim more valid."

"Or more intimidating," said Link. "Like, *this is what I'm doing, and all you other countries better sit back and mind your business because I control America.*"

Julie shrugged. "Makes more sense than, *I own a news channel—please don't shoot me.*"

"We have to stop him," said Jericho. "No matter what."

Julie nodded. "Agreed. We have to prevent the launch of that rocket. If Hall gets ahold of that much money, the world will change forever. No rebellion's going to fix that."

"But like Jay said, we can't just attack the base. Regardless of how many Tristar personnel they have on-site, they have Nemesis assets."

Jay nodded. "Yeah, at least ten of them. Probably

more. Hall's kept the program busy this whole time too. As long as the assets are in play, you don't stand a chance."

"What about the U.N.?" asked Ruby. "You're still their peacekeeping force, right? Can they not sanction something?"

Julie shook her head. "That isn't what the peacekeeping initiative is there for. It isn't an army. When we wear the U.N. colors, we keep the peace... we don't wage wars. However... I think this is something I can take to the president. The U.S. military is almost back to full strength too. If they can help, this will be a cakewalk."

Link got to his feet. "Hey, yeah... that could work. Just carpet-bomb the crap out of it, and we can all go home."

"You think Schultz will help?" asked Jay.

"We can only ask," said Julie. She looked around the room. "Okay. Here's where we're at, people. We have three objectives: stop Hall from launching that rocket... take out the Nemesis assets so we stand a fighting chance... and get our goddamn soul drive back, so we can get on with our lives. I'm going to put a formal mission briefing together to take to Schultz. With his help, maybe... *maybe* we can stop Hall for good."

Jericho, Link, and Ruby all murmured their agreement. But Jay stepped forward, raising her hand slightly.

"Actually, you have four objectives," she said.

Julie looked at her, frowning.

Jay shrugged. "Tristar. They have a new Brandon Crow, right? This Gwen Parker woman? She's trying to rebrand Tristar and change public opinion."

"So the story goes, yeah," said Jericho. "I know firsthand that their employees don't even make the association between Tristar and Orion."

"Exactly. Just like you said GlobaTech rebranded itself, back in the day."

Julie scoffed. "The difference is we meant it."

"Right. Tristar doesn't and we know that. But you need to deal with them because they still account for almost all of Hall's defense. If you can lift the lid on their bullshit, maybe it helps your case with the president."

Julie stared at Jay, thinking. Eventually, she nodded. "Fair point. Okay... four objectives."

Jay raised her hand again. "Let me do it."

"What?"

"Let me deal with Tristar and go after Gwen Parker. For better or worse, I owe Brandon a lot. Her replacing him, trying to do what he did... that's personal to me. Let me do this."

Julie glanced at Jericho, who gave her the slightest of shrugs. Then she looked back at Jay and sighed. "If you do, understand this is an investigation, not an assassination. By all means, use our resources, but you're looking for evidence we can legally use to prove they're full of shit. You're not looking to leave a trail of bodies behind you on a revenge mission. Understood?"

Jay saluted. "Scout's honor."

"Don't make me regret this..."

"It's the least I can do."

Julie nodded. "Okay. Jericho and I will prepare for the meeting with Schultz. Jay, you head to New York and get me something that brings Tristar tumbling down. Link, Ruby... sit tight for now. There's plenty of fighting still to be had." She focused on Ruby. "If you want it..."

Ruby got to her feet. "I'll set about reading Josh's files again. Now that we have an idea what's going on, maybe there's something helpful that we dismissed the first time."

"Go for it. You're welcome to my desk."

Julie walked around it, placing a hand on Ruby's shoulder as she headed for Jericho. She stood in front of him, looking up into his eyes. They were cold and unblinking. Focused. They always were, to an extent. But she saw the warmth behind them that few others ever could.

"You ready?" she asked him.

Jericho cracked his neck. "Like you wouldn't believe."

Chapter Twenty-Two

President Schultz sat behind the Resolute deck, stunned silent. He rested his elbow on the arm of his chair and leaned on it, clasping his hand over his mouth. His eyes stared blindly at a paperweight next to his phone, wide and unblinking.

Sitting across from him, Julie and Jericho watched patiently as the president processed everything they had just spent an hour telling him. They both felt sympathetic toward him. It was a lot to take in, and they had barely had enough time to wrap their own heads around it.

"Mother of God..." muttered Schultz absently.

Julie cleared her throat. "That's pretty much where the rest of us are at, sir, yes."

He refocused and stared over at her. She had hastily thrown on a business suit and tied her hair up. She looked smart. But she also looked uncomfortable. She was sitting rigid and upright, hands clasped on her lap. She shuffled in her seat every couple of minutes, awkward and restless.

"How in the holiest of hells did that son'bitch build a

goddamn rocket ship without anyone noticing?" he asked. His voice rose with each word, until he was almost shouting.

"To be fair, sir," said Jericho, "we've been a little busy lately."

Schultz's gaze snapped to him. They locked eyes for a moment, then the president looked him up and down. The man was the polar opposite to his girlfriend and boss. He wore a T-shirt, stretched over his hulking frame, and Globa-Tech's black and red camo combat pants.

Never been one to stand on ceremony, mused Schultz.

"Haven't we all?" replied Schultz. "But even so... by all accounts, it's a pretty big rocket. You'd think someone might have seen something before now."

Julie sighed. "Sir, it's in the middle of the desert. We stayed mobile during the rebellion, but we stayed as near to civilization as was safe. Hall was also sitting in your chair, which meant every satellite network in the country was under his control. There was simply no one around who would think to look, sir. And there was no way to see, even if there was."

"Almost like he had this whole thing planned out from the start," added Jericho. His flippant tone didn't go unnoticed, as evidenced by the glance both Julie and the president cast his way.

Schultz got to his feet gingerly. He reached for his cane, then limped over to the large window to the left of President Lincoln's portrait, which hung on the wall behind his chair. He stared out across the Rose Garden in silence.

Despite the limp, Julie thought he looked well. He had already regained some of the weight he had lost in captivity. His pressed, navy suit jacket strained across his chest and gut. The cane worked for him. She thought it made him look more distinguished and less like a Texan redneck. She let slip a small smile to herself.

Finally, he turned to face them both. He let out a deep, tired sigh, which rumbled up from his stomach and shook his jowls.

"Okay," he said with a resolved nod. "So, what are you doing about it?"

Julie and Jericho exchanged an uncertain look.

"Well, sir, that's why we're here…" Julie began, sounding confused. "We need your help to stop him."

Schultz nodded slowly. "I see."

"Logistically and tactically, that base is near-impregnable. Any force launching an attack will be bottle-necked into a kill zone before they even reach the front gate. The mountains surrounding it make any other approach completely impossible. The only move that makes sense is from the air."

Jericho nodded. "She's right, sir. You said all branches of the military are almost back to full strength. We propose a targeted air strike. First pass with a high-altitude strike from the B-52. Take out the rocket, any air defense, and as many strategic buildings as we can. Follow that up with a second pass. Low-level flyover from a couple of F-16s to sweep up the bulk of the manpower and any vehicles. This could all be over in ten minutes, and it would make what Adrian did to that place back in the day look like a fireworks display."

Schultz stared at him. He paid attention in his security briefings. He knew what the USAF had at their disposal. Everything Jericho just said made perfect sense. It was a sound strategy and likely what any of his own military advisors would have suggested to him. He was impressed.

"I have no doubt that if I took your plan to the Joint

Chiefs, they would say the same thing," said Schultz. "Damn fine idea, son."

Julie narrowed her eyes. "But…"

Schultz looked at her and smiled. No humor. Only regret. "But… I can't involve the United States military. I'm sorry."

"What?" yelled Julie, forgetting herself. "Were you not listening? Hall is going to own the world! How the hell can you justify sitting back and doing nothing?"

Schultz stared at her calmly. If anyone else spoke to him like that, he would throw them in prison for treason. But he had a soft spot for GlobaTech, and for these two in particular. They were Josh Winters's recruits and Moses Buchanan's right hand. They also saved his life and prevented full-scale war more times than he could count. Julie, especially. She was a hothead, but he liked that about her. She was one of the most capable women he had ever met. He could see why Buchanan was so fond of her. He knew that wasn't what she wanted to hear and saw no harm in letting her vent her frustrations. If anyone had earned the right do that, it was Julie Fisher.

Julie leapt to her feet and slammed her hands down on the desk. "Damn it, sir, answer me! This will be the end for *all of us*. How can you do nothing?"

Jericho got to his feet and placed a hand on her shoulder. She snapped her head around to stare at him. He saw the fire in her eyes. He admired it. He loved it. But he also knew there was a time and a place for her passion, and this was neither. He set his jaw, flashing a half-smile laced with regret. He realized the moment the president spoke that his attack plan couldn't work. Begrudgingly, he also understood why.

"Julie," he said softly.

She brushed his hand away and continued glaring at the president.

Schultz sucked in a deep breath. "Miss Fisher, if the U.S. military gets involved and launches any kind of attack on its own soil, folks are going to notice. Saying it's a training exercise is a tired cliché that no one believes anymore, so questions will immediately be asked. The people of this country have been through enough. Having me back in this room is supposed to usher in a new peace. If I'm seen to be the one throwing the first punch here, I lose all public support."

Julie scoffed and shook her head. "I don't care about the next election, sir. No offense, but this fight is more important than your polling data."

"Julie, stand down," said Jericho.

"No!" she snapped as she turned to him. "How can you be so calm? I thought you, of all people, would be pissed. It's your plan he's ignoring."

"I know it is, but... he's right."

His admission took Julie by surprise, and her body relaxed a little.

Jericho cast a glance at the president, who was stood watching them, silent and patient. Then he looked back at Julie.

"This isn't just about what people in this country will think," he explained. "After what we've all just been through, an airstrike on U.S. soil will garner worldwide attention. Other nations will start asking what we were doing. How long do you think it'll be before someone somewhere figures it out? Suddenly, the power to control the entire world will be on everyone's radar. There are still a lot of countries standing tall post-4/17. You think Hall is bad? What do we do when Russia or China start fighting to lay claim to that asteroid? Or worse... what about our allies? That kind of power is more appealing than loyalty. We'll have no choice but to get involved, and we can't fight everyone."

Julie's shoulders slumped forward as she sighed. "But... we have to do *something*, Jericho."

He nodded. "I know. And we will. But we gotta do it alone. From the president's point of view, it's safer to risk Hall winning. If GlobaTech can stop him, great. But if we can't, the White House can unite the world against Orion. Together, we *will* win that fight, and at that point, talks can be held to distribute that wealth to everyone... peacefully." He looked at Schultz. "Isn't that right, sir?"

Schultz nodded. "You're right on the money, son."

He moved back over to his chair and sank heavily into it. The hinges squeaked and protested under the weight.

He looked at Jericho. "You might not be one for formalities anymore, given how you dress to meet your president, but there's no denying you have a general's mind, son."

Jericho took a deep breath, his chest swelling slightly with pride.

Schultz turned to Julie. "Miss Fisher... let me give you some advice. Whatever battle lies ahead of you, there's always a bigger war behind it. You're more than just a soldier now. You understand? You're a CEO. You're a businesswoman. And you have the world's largest company *and* the world's largest private army at your disposal. Attacking this bastard head-on, on his own doorstep, is unlikely to be the only course of action available to you."

Julie stepped back and took her seat again. She was breathing heavily, trying to manage the flow of adrenaline. She stared blankly ahead. She closed her hands into fists to stop them shaking. She was still angry, but as seconds ticked by, more of that anger redirected to herself.

She should have thought of all that before they even got here.

Buchanan would have.

Schultz saw the turmoil in her expression and smiled sympathetically. "Miss Fisher, I understand your frustration. You think I don't miss the days of sitting in your chair, not worrying about politics and red tape and public opinion? But I sit in *this* chair now, and all those things take precedence over any action."

Julie looked up at him. Her body began to relax. Her shoulders dropped slightly. Her breathing slowed.

"Stop thinking like a soldier, and start thinking like *his* boss," continued Schultz, casually nodding at Jericho. "I will do whatever I can to help you. But that cannot include direct military involvement. The world stage is too fragile. Even our allies are thinking twice about admitting we're friends nowadays, and I honestly can't blame them. Except France. To hell with those onion-smelling yellowbacks..."

Jericho suppressed a small smile.

"I have every faith in you, Miss Fisher. Just like Moses did." Schultz sat back in his chair and took a deep breath. "Now, go away. You have work to do, and I have a call with the British Prime Minister, which is always tedious."

Julie and Jericho got to their feet.

"Thank you, sir," said Julie, heading for the door.

"Sir," said Jericho with a curt nod.

As he turned to follow Julie, Schultz held out a hand to get his attention.

Jericho looked back, frowning. "Sir?"

"I know this ain't the first time I ever extended this offer to you, Jericho," said Schultz. "But when this latest shitshow is over… if you ever want a change of scenery, I got two stars with your name on 'em. After pulling my ass out of Wyoming, I could even stretch it to three."

Jericho simply nodded. "Thank you, sir. I appreciate that, and I'll bear it in mind."

"Good man." He waved toward the door. "Now, get out of here. You have a world to save."

Jericho turned and walked over to Julie, who was waiting by the door, smiling at him.

"Should I salute you now?" she asked quietly, smiling. "Or wait until the eight-year-old boy inside you has stopped going red?"

Jericho rolled his eyes. "Shut up."

Chapter Twenty-Three

A couple of hours later, Jay stood across the street from Tristar's office building in New York City. The sidewalk was crammed with people. She leaned against the wall of a coffee shop, hands plunged into the pockets of her thick, fur-lined coat, hunched against the temperature.

Seeing the building again was more difficult than she thought it would be. She had a lot of memories there. Or did she? Sometimes she wasn't sure who she even was anymore. Janine remembered flashes of Jay's life, and vice versa. She tried to keep a clear head, but it wasn't always that easy.

Suddenly, a memory flooded into her mind. Police. Sirens. Crowds. Like a shadow in darkness, she moved through the chaos, supporting Brandon Crow's injured body. The aftermath of Roach's one-man assault. It felt like a million years ago. It also felt like yesterday.

As the memory faded, Jay looked up, following the building to the sky until her gaze rested where Crow's office used to be. She set her jaw, determined to not let her past get in the way.

She was armed. She felt the reassuring bulge of her gun holstered to her side beneath her coat, pressing against her arm as she sheltered against the wind.

No shooting. Just be a goody-two-shoes like GlobaTech wants, then you can disappear.

She knew she couldn't just walk in there and ask for Gwen Parker. If Tristar's new approach was a lie, there was no doubt they would recognize her. She needed a way to—

"You're not thinking of applying for a job there, are you?"

Jay frowned at the strange voice and looked to her left to see a young man standing there. He was thin and timid, shivering as he clutched a cup of coffee. He was fresh-faced. His cheeks were red from the cold.

"Are you talking to me?" she asked.

The young man smiled and shrugged. "Sorry. I didn't mean to disturb you. I just saw you looking over *there* and figured it was my duty to save you." He laughed awkwardly.

"I'm not looking for a job," Jay said. "But I do have business there."

The man scoffed. "If I were you, I wouldn't bother. That place is toxic."

Jay turned to face him. "Who are you, exactly?"

He smiled apologetically. "Sorry. I'm Kyle. Kyle Vaughn."

She nodded. "Hi, Kyle. I'm Ja... Julie. Julie Hughes."

They shook hands.

"So, what do you have against Tristar?" she asked him. "Aren't they going through some big rebrand at the moment?"

Kyle scoffed again. "Ain't nothing changed in that place. Three days ago, they fired me for literally no reason. It's complete bullshit."

Jay narrowed her gaze. "You must've done something?"

He shook his head. "Not a damn thing, I swear. I was an intern. I'd only been there two weeks. Joined the day after GlobaTech helped take back the White House, caught up by their marketing. My job was to make coffee and photocopy papers. Then, out of nowhere, the big boss called me into her office and fired me. It seemed like she did it to make herself feel better. Total crap. I should sue them for unfair dismissal. I'm sure that would look great in the papers."

Jay shrugged. "Why don't you?"

"Are you kidding me? I was an intern for two weeks. You think I can afford a lawyer in this town? I just... I want to march back over there, tell them they were wrong, and... and *demand* my job back. Otherwise, I'll... I'll tell the media and ruin their image all over again."

"Okay. So, why haven't you?"

Kyle glanced away. "Because... I'm too afraid to. I wouldn't know what to say, and I'd end up looking like an idiot. So, I've just stood here every day since, drinking overpriced coffee and staring at the place, wishing I could do more than I can." He sighed. "Sorry. That must sound kinda silly to you, huh?"

Jay struggled to think of a more pathetic person, but his story had given her an idea.

She smiled. "Kyle, I think you and I can help each other."

Kyle frowned. "Y-you do? What do you mean?"

"How much money do you have?"

"Um... a couple of hundred bucks in my account. Maybe ten dollars in my wallet. Why?"

"I need to be discreet, and I'm not exactly dressed for a meeting."

He looked her up and down. The large coat covered most of her body. Flat boots poked out from beneath. He shrugged.

"You look fine to me." Then his eyes went wide. "Oh... God... I'm sorry. I didn't mean... I just meant..."

Jay smiled. "Relax, kid. I know what you meant. But look..."

She opened her coat, revealing her outfit underneath. She wore tight leggings tucked into her boots, which ran up to just below her knees. Her sweater was white and thick and fitted, hanging off one shoulder. There was no bra strap visible. But her tattoo was. She cocked her hip to one side, posing slightly.

"... not exactly ready for the boardroom, am I?"

Kyle's eyes bulged in their sockets. His mouth fell open, and he dropped his coffee.

Jay watched it hit the ground, then looked back at him, pulling her coat back around her. "Let's get you a new drink, hmm?"

Kyle said nothing. He just nodded and murmured his incoherent agreement, then followed her into the coffee shop.

Less than an hour later, Jay and Kyle marched across the street, heading for the entrance to Tristar's office building. She was wearing a new pantsuit, which Kyle's life savings had purchased. She also carried a small, leather briefcase, which contained her gun and holster.

Kyle struggled to keep pace with her as they climbed the steps that led to the revolving door. "Listen, ah, Julie... you don't have to do this, okay? I appreciate it and everything, but won't I get in trouble?"

She shook her head. "Not while you're with me, you won't."

They paused outside the doors. Jay glanced through the glass, quickly scanning the lobby. The layout had changed since she was last there. Unsurprising. Roach left it in need of a little remodeling.

"All right. Listen to me, Kyle. We get in there, you leave the talking to me. If anyone asks you a direct question, you look at me like I'm your lawyer, and I won't let you answer. Got it?"

He nodded. "I mean, yeah, but... why are you helping me?"

"I need a word with your old boss, and she's unlikely to want to see me. This way, we can get in a room with her before she realizes it's me, and I can talk to her. And you never know... we might actually get you your old job back."

"Really?"

Jay shrugged. "Sure. Although, I gotta tell you... whatever you think you know about this place, you're wrong. They're still the bad guys. And Gwen Parker? She's the worst of them all."

"H-how do you know?"

She sighed. "Because I worked for her predecessor. Now, come on."

She pushed the large revolving door and stepped inside the cylindrical doorway.

Kyle hurried after her. "Wait... you what?"

The front desk was away to the left of the new lobby. The walkway that had once looked down over the entrance was gone. A new ceiling had been fitted, and the bank of elevators now stood on the first floor. The waiting area was over to the right now. She caught herself staring at the floor where she had wrestled Roach to a stalemate before disappearing with Crow.

Good times, she thought.

Jay refocused and moved for the front desk. It was a flat, waist-high counter with two cardboard triangles, standing one at each end, sporting graphics of happy employees and promoting their current recruitment drive.

Two male security guards stood behind it, wearing dark suits, flanking a female secretary sat typing at a computer. She wore glasses with pointed frames and a dress suit. Jay ignored the guards and spoke directly to her.

"I'm here to see Gwen Parker," she announced.

The secretary stared over the rims of her glasses. "Do you have an appointment?"

Jay shook her head casually, trying to ignore the sharp, condescending tone. "No. But my client here is looking to file a lawsuit against her for unfair dismissal. I wanted to give Ms. Parker the opportunity to make things right before she gets dragged into a very public court battle."

The secretary raised a curious eyebrow, then turned her attention to Kyle. He stood straight and awkward at Jay's side, holding his coat over his arm. His gray suit was ill-fitted and crumpled.

The secretary looked back at Jay. "Right. Well, I'm afraid Ms. Parker isn't in the office today. She's away on business."

Jay narrowed her eyes. "If you knew she wasn't here, why would it matter if I had an appointment?" She went to reply, but Jay held up a hand to cut her off. "It doesn't matter. I'm sure we can see whoever is in charge in her absence." She smiled spitefully. "We're happy to wait."

The secretary held her gaze for a moment, then looked away and began dialing a number on the desk phone beside her. She spoke mutedly into it for a moment, then hung up and looked at Jay.

"Mr. Connor can spare five minutes for you," she said begrudgingly. "Ninth floor. Elevators are over there."

She pointed to the far wall, but Jay didn't look over. She stared blankly at the secretary, looking through her as her mind wandered.

The ninth floor.

Parker must be in Crow's old office, she mused.

She snapped out of her trance and thanked the secretary, then walked away. Kyle kept pace with her.

"Is everything okay?" he asked.

Jay let out a terse breath. "Peachy."

Minutes later, the doors slid open with a gentle ping, revealing the ninth-floor lobby and the man standing ready to greet them. His suit was dark and pinstriped, pressed almost into a point. A maroon and sky-blue tie was fastened neatly around his neck and clipped in place by a gold pin. His skin was artificially tanned and looked like plastic. His hair was long on top and styled to the side. His smile and his teeth were as fake as his tan. Jay noticed the glint in his eyes as he saw her.

"Kyle!" he called out with exaggerated politeness. "I'm glad you wanted this meeting, truly."

He extended his hand, which Kyle reached for, quickly finding his arm almost yanked from its socket.

The man turned to Jay. "And you must be the lawyer. Welcome, Miss…"

"Hughes," she replied flatly. "*Mrs.* Hughes."

He didn't offer a handshake, and she wouldn't have accepted it if he had. For a heartbeat, he was thrown off his game, but he recovered like a professional.

"Excellent. My name's Greg Connor. I'm the Deputy Executive Officer here at Tristar Security. I'm afraid Miss Parker isn't in the office today. She's—"

"Out on business," said Jay. "Yes, your receptionist told me. I guess you'll have to do."

Connor swallowed. "I will certainly do what I can to help." He turned to head left, away from the elevators. "Please. This way. We'll use Gwen's office."

Jay followed him, taking in the new look of the building. She resented how the place had changed. The walls were a burnt orange. Fake walls had been installed to create a narrow maze of corridors with rooms shooting off in all directions.

Kyle trailed behind her, staring at the floor as he walked, as if paranoid people were staring at him.

They reached the corner of the floor, and Connor pushed open the door to Parker's office. Jay clenched her jaw, forcing herself through the hesitation she felt toward stepping over the threshold and into Crow's old office.

Once inside, she took a discreet breath and glanced around, keen to keep up appearances with Connor. She had been in this room many times before. Compared to the rest of the building, it remained largely unchanged from its original design. Jay felt a little more comfortable in familiar surroundings, yet at the same time, the tide of memories crashing into her mind was overwhelming.

Connor moved comfortably across the room and took a seat behind the large desk that dominated the room. Behind him, the fading light outside shadowed his features.

Jay cleared her throat, eager to distract herself. "This should be a quick meeting, Mr. Connor. My client believes that he was fired from his internship unfairly and is seeking re-employment and financial reparation."

She sat in one of the chairs opposite him and rested her briefcase on the floor by her feet. Kyle sat beside her.

"I see." Connor nodded. "Kyle, I'm sorry you feel the way you do. Truly. But the terms of your internship include a one-month probationary period, during which you can be let go without notice or explanation, at the company's discretion. If you felt this was handled… poorly, you have my sincerest apologies. But Tristar only did what it was legally entitled to do. I don't know what your *lawyer* has told you, but you have no basis for a legal case here. I'm sorry you wasted your time."

Jay stared at Connor. She genuinely had no idea if he was telling the truth. Ultimately, she had no interest in Kyle's situation at all. She had her own mission here, and thanks to a helpful coincidence, she could now ask the questions she really wanted to.

She turned to Kyle and leaned over slightly. "Kyle, would you do me a favor and go lock the door?"

He frowned. "W-what?"

Jay simply nodded reassuringly. Kyle hesitated, then got to his feet and walked over to the door. He turned the latch just below the handle until it clicked.

Connor got to his feet. "Excuse me… what the hell do you think you're doing?"

Jay leaned forward quickly, raising herself out of her chair just enough to reach for Connor's tie. She grabbed a handful of it and yanked it down hard, smashing his face into the desk. She then hustled around to his side and placed her hand on the side of his face, pinning him to the spot.

Connor grunted. "Are you insane? What the hell is this?"

Over by the door, Kyle gasped, covering his mouth with his hands.

Jay leaned forward, her mouth mere inches from Connor's ear. "Listen carefully, you goddamn Ken doll. I want Gwen Parker. Tell me where she is, or I'm going to lobotomize you with that stapler."

Connor's eyes flicked to his right, resting on the shiny, seven-inch stapler resting beside a neat stack of papers. His mouth opened with fear. Jay simply increased the pressure on his head, squishing his cheeks together and forcing his lips to pucker like a goldfish's mouth.

"Go ahead," she said quietly. "Make a noise. See what happens."

He did his best to nod.

Kyle shook his head. "Oh my God... oh my God... what is happening right now?"

Jay glanced up at him. "Kyle, take a breath and shut up. I'm working." She turned her attention back to Connor. "Where's your boss?"

"I don't know, I swear," he managed. "She didn't say where she was going. I just know she left last night. Why... why do you want to know?"

Jay eased her grip on his face and took a deep breath. "Tristar is full of shit. You can put out all the ads you want. You can hire all the blind idiots you want. You're full of shit. You know how I know? Because I used to work here. I spent a lot of time in this very office, as a matter of fact." She nodded toward the other window, away to her right. "The desk used to be over there. It looked better."

Connor swallowed hard. Spittle was beginning to drop from his mouth onto the desk. "Who are you?"

"I used to work for Brandon Crow. I was his bodyguard. I don't know, nor do I care, how much you really know about what's going on here. But I can guarantee Gwen Parker knows everything. See, everything she's trying to rebrand, Brandon created. Quincy Hall did him dirty, just like he'll do to her once she's served her purpose. You're working in a real bad place, Greg, and I aim to stop Tristar before they can do something stupid. Now, for the last time, where is your boss?"

He moved to speak, but Jay pressed his face harder.

"Please bear in mind, before you consider lying to me, I have no issue with throwing you head-first out of the window. The landing won't be pretty, Greg. Your head will explode on impact. Whole thing will look like a goddamn pizza."

Kyle idled toward the desk and took his seat again. His eyes were wide and unblinking. He shook his head slowly in disbelief.

"Please..." begged Connor. "I don't know where she went. She didn't say and I didn't ask. I think maybe it was somewhere in Nevada. She was boarding the company jet last night, and I'm sure her assistant mentioned it. But that's it. I swear to God!"

Jay released her grip and stepped away from the desk. She let out a heavy sigh and rolled her eyes. She knew exactly where Parker was. Unfortunately, it was the same place she just moved heaven and earth to escape from.

Connor immediately stood and straightened his suit, eager to regain a modicum of dignity. Jay walked back around the desk and stood behind Kyle. She placed a hand on his shoulder.

"We're done here," she said.

"No, you're not," said Connor, still sounding flustered. He fussed over his hair for a moment, then pointed at Jay. "I'll have security in here before you can blink. You hear me? You're done!"

Jay sighed. "Sit down, Greg, before you hurt yourself. Or, more importantly, before I do. No one's doing anything. I'm here doing GlobaTech a favor. You want them up your ass right now? Forget me. Forget this meeting. And, if I were you, I'd distance myself from Gwen Parker too. This place is gonna burn, and I'm gonna be standing with the people holding the match. Kyle and I are leaving. Quietly and with no fuss."

Kyle got to his feet slowly, staring regrettably at Connor.

Jay looked at him and frowned. "Hey..."

"Hmm?" He turned her. "What?"

She saw the fear in his eyes. A part of her felt sorry for him. It was a strange sensation. She had used him and, consequently, felt like she owed him something.

"You still want to work in a place like this?" she asked him.

He shook his head.

"Probably a smart career move. But, hey, after three days of freezing your balls off and getting angry, you're finally here." She pointed at Connor. "There's the face of the people you feel wronged you. Anything you want to say and get off your chest, now's the time, slugger."

Kyle looked at her. He stared into her dark eyes, and with each breath he took, he found himself standing taller. He had no idea who this Julie Hughes was, and she scared the hell out of him, but being near her gave him confidence.

He swallowed hard, took a final, deep breath, then

looked over at Connor. He stepped in front of him, moving central to the desk, and jabbed the air in front of him.

"What you did to me was... was wrong," he said. "The people here are horrible, and you... Mr. Connor... you're an asshole!"

He leaned forward and shoved the stack of papers onto the floor. Seething with adrenaline, he turned away, then immediately looked back over his shoulder at a shocked Connor.

"And I'm not here anymore to clean that up. *Asshole!*"

He marched toward the door and went to yank it open, only to fail because it was still locked. He fiddled with the latch, then tried again, pulling it with such force that it slammed into the wall next to him. He then stormed off toward the elevators.

Jay laughed. "Holy shit. Go, Kyle!"

Then her smile faded. She looked around at Connor, who was still standing completely still, shocked. "And you... you're lucky. If I really *was* his lawyer, I'd have shot you."

She picked up her briefcase and left the office gracefully, without looking back. She walked through the maze of corridors without paying attention to the new layout, nor the looks from people around her who had clearly heard some of the commotion coming from the office. She reached the elevators to find Kyle standing patiently, watching the light flash as it counted up to nine.

"So... you feel better?" she asked him.

Kyle's gaze was focused in front of him. "I think I just peed my pants."

She failed to suppress a small smile. "Atta boy, Kyle."

The elevator arrived with a ping, and the doors opened smoothly. They both stepped inside, and Jay hit the button for the first floor. The doors closed again, and the carriage jolted into life.

Kyle glanced sideways at her. "So, um, Julie… do you maybe wanna grab a drink or something?"

Jay stared ahead. "Not even a little bit, Kyle."

"Oh. Okay. No problem."

His shoulders slumped as he focused on the floor.

Jay tensed her jaw as another small smile graced her lips.

Chapter Twenty-Four

Collins stared at the air in front of him, his eyes slightly glazed over. He rested back against the soft, thick cushions of the armchair. His face held no expression. His mind focused on nothing except his breathing and the rise and fall of his chest.

He was sitting in a private consultation room. He didn't know which hospital he was in, but he assumed he was in D.C. Five armchairs formed a loose circle in one half of the room, with a small coffee table in the middle. The other half was mostly empty, save for a noticeboard that dominated the far wall, with posters and leaflets about mental health pinned to it. There were no windows.

Beside him, Kim sat quietly, leaning toward him a little, so she could hold his hand. She hadn't left his side in twenty-four hours. It broke her heart to see him in such pain.

She watched him as he zoned out, happy he was calm at last. He was fully cognizant, but he had been given something to relax him. He was also given a change of clothes and told to rest.

She squeezed his hand gently, and he turned to her. She smiled, and he smiled back.

"Ya okay, love?" he asked softly.

Kim smiled wider, shaking her head. "I'm fine. It's you we need to worry about."

"Ah, I'm all right. Just enjoying the silence."

She squeezed his hand again. "Me too."

There was a knock on the door. When it opened, Kim caught a glimpse of the one of the GlobaTech operatives who were standing guard outside. Two women walked in. One of them was an orderly. She was young, dressed in navy scrubs. She simply gestured to the room and left again, clearly showing the other woman where it was.

The second woman stepped inside. The door was closed behind her by one of the guards. She wore long, loose-fitting pants and flat shoes. Her jacket was open, revealing a thin sweater beneath. She had a small bag resting on her shoulder, and she carried another in her hand—a larger overnight bag. Her mousy brown hair was scraped back into a tight ponytail, revealing her high cheekbones.

Collins looked over at her, then turned to Kim, his eyes wide with surprise.

"What is this?" he asked, looking back at the new arrival. "What are ya doing here, Doc?"

Dr. Kaitlyn Moss smiled warmly. "What can I say? Sometimes a video call just doesn't cut it."

Kim stood and walked over to greet her. Dr. Moss placed her bag on the floor and shook her hand.

"How was your flight?" asked Kim.

Dr. Moss smiled and rolled her eyes. "Long. I landed in Dulles about an hour ago and came straight here. If you get the chance, please pass on my thanks to Miss Fisher. I assume it was her influence that allowed me to skip through security?"

Kim grinned. "Most likely. I will."

Dr. Moss then looked over at Collins, who still looked on with disbelief.

"So..." she said. "Sounds like we've both had an eventful twenty-four hours, eh?"

He felt his cheeks flush with color. "Aye. Something like that. Listen, Doc... ya didn't have to fly all the way out here to see me. I'm fine, honestly."

Dr. Moss carried her bag over to the circle of chairs. She rested it against one directly opposite Collins, then dropped her other bag and her jacket onto it.

"I'm sure you are," she said. "I saw what they gave you when you got here."

Collins looked back and forth between Kim and Dr. Moss. "Wait, they weren't vitamins?"

He smiled, prompting both women to roll their eyes at his poor attempt at humor.

"No, Ray," said Dr. Moss. "It was a significant dose of Zoloft."

He nodded slowly. "Aye. Well, I was close."

She took a seat beside him. "How about you tell me what happened?"

Kim hovered just outside the seating area. "I'll leave you two to talk."

She turned to head for the door, but Collins sat upright in his chair and reached out to her. "No, stay. Please. It's okay." He glanced at Dr. Moss. "If that's okay with you?"

Kaitlyn smiled. "This is your time, Ray. It's your decision."

He looked back at Kim. "Please, love."

Kim nodded. "Of course."

She took her seat on the other side of him.

Collins looked at Dr. Moss. "What do ya know already?"

"Nothing, honestly," she replied. "Miss Fisher called and asked me to come see you. She said you were on a mission, and something triggered a PTSD episode."

Collins shifted in his seat, suddenly uncomfortable. "Aye, well, I don't know about that myself. It all got a bit... hazy for a time there."

"That's okay. Just... take your time. Tell me what you remember. As much detail as you can."

She sat back and crossed her legs, settling into her professionally patient demeanor.

Collins took a deep breath and turned slightly to face her. He reached behind him without looking, searching for Kim's hand with his own. Kim took it, gently rubbing her thumb over the course skin on the back of his palm to let him know she was there.

"We got a call from someone asking for help. It's all a bit complicated, but... it was one of those *enemy of my enemy* kind of deals, ya know? Anyway, she was in trouble, and we were going to get her, keep her safe, see if she could help us out."

Dr. Moss nodded along.

"Turns out, we weren't the only ones after her. We kinda figured... but we weren't prepared for who came looking."

Dr. Moss frowned. "Who was it?"

Collins grimaced as he recalled. "A bunch of real bad people. Including the fella who killed Adrian."

She failed to hide her shock. Her jaw fell open slightly. "Oh my God..."

"Aye. Worst part of all that is, he was Adrian's friend. He fought beside all of us during the rebellion."

"Do you know what made him turn on you?"

He chuckled. "I do. Sort of. Long story for another time, but basically, he was brainwashed by the same people Jay used to work for."

"Okay. And Jay is…"

"The woman we were there to rescue. Adrian's wife. Or ex-wife. I don't know."

Dr. Moss listened patiently, studying his body language and making mental notes as he spoke.

"It didn't exactly take long for shit to go sideways. Explosions. Big gunfight. The whole shebang."

"I see," said Dr. Moss, nodding. "Well, Ray, as you know, I'm an accomplished professional with years of experience in psychology and psychiatry. But frankly, and with no disrespect to Miss Fisher, a child could figure out what happened to you yesterday…"

Collins smiled with embarrassment. "Aye."

"You've been making great progress, Ray, but what possessed you to put yourself in that situation?"

He glanced around at Kim, who simply shrugged.

He sighed and looked back at Dr. Moss. "Look, in my defense, we all kinda thought we would be in and out before shit hit the fan."

"And what made you feel like you had to go along?" asked Dr. Moss. "If it was so straightforward, did Globa-Tech need you there?"

Collins winced and sucked in a short breath through clenched teeth. "It's not as easy as that, Doc. Jericho was out of action. He got beat down badly by these guys. Jules was running low on people she could trust. All our operatives are world-class, but few have the experience with something this big and this delicate. She needed people to watch her back, and I felt I had to step in. If I had to do it all over again, I would."

Dr. Moss sighed, relaxing slightly in her seat. "I know you would. And as admirable as that is, Ray, you're no use to anyone unless you're truly recovered... as evidenced yesterday."

He nodded slowly, gazing at the floor as he pursed his lips together. He suddenly found it difficult to look her in the eyes.

She leaned forward in her chair, clasping her hands on her knees. "PTSD is a deceptive medical condition. People discount it because it's not visible, like a broken bone. But that doesn't mean it shouldn't be taken seriously and treated. Now, in some cases, what triggers an episode can be hard to distinguish. It can be subtle, like a spoken phrase or a passive sound, which is hard to pinpoint. Other times, it can be big and obvious, like being in a gunfight after suffering a terrible assault. Do you remember the coping mechanism we worked on in our first session together?"

Collins held his hand up, lightly pressing the tip of his middle finger to the tip of his thumb.

Dr. Moss nodded. "We conditioned your mind to think of a happy memory whenever you do that, to help calm you. I'm not expecting you to remember to stop and do that when you're being shot at, and in such dire circumstances, it would be unlikely to make a notable difference anyway. But that's one example of the types of tools that can help you manage this going forward. But this is a team effort, Ray, and I really need you to avoid gunfights for a while, okay?"

He huffed and grinned, finally looking back up at her. "I'll do what I can, Doc."

She held his gaze. "I'm going to need you to try really hard on this one, Ray."

"Aye. Sadly, it isn't as easy that." His smile faded. "See, the problem is—and I can't overstate this enough—there is a *lot* of shit about to hit the biggest fan. Kinda one of those *all hands on deck* situations, ya know? Truth be told, I ain't got time to be crazy."

"You're not crazy. You're suffering through the effects of a significant trauma."

Collins held a hand up. "Aye, I know, I know. It was a figure of speech. Look, the whole Orion invasion pales in comparison to what GlobaTech is facing right now. I need to find a way to be useful because there's no sitting this one out, Doc. Not this time."

Dr. Moss narrowed her gaze. She glanced over at Kim, who nodded discreetly. She took a deep breath. "How long is this unavoidable fight going to take?"

Collins shrugged. "No idea. But I suspect, one way or another, it'll all be over in a few days, at this rate."

Dr. Moss nodded. "Okay. I'll arrange to stay here in D.C. for a week or so. I have to be honest, Ray... I'm not happy about the situation. You shouldn't be anywhere near a battlefield right now, and I don't agree with GlobaTech putting you in a position where you feel you can't stay away. This isn't how you get better."

"I appreciate that, Doc, but this isn't GlobaTech's fault. Jules ain't telling me to just get back on the horse or whatever. This is literal world-ending shit that only GlobaTech can stop. This has been coming for a long time. Quincy Hall... taking over the White House wasn't his grand plan. It was a stepping stone. What's coming now... *that's* his endgame. If we don't fight, it's all over. Then it won't matter whether I have PTSD or not. Do ya understand? Losing this will change everything forever. I can't rock up to the debrief with a doctor's note saying I'm not allowed to play."

Dr. Moss swallowed hard. She saw the fear in his eyes. It wasn't the fear of a victim or a patient. It was the fear in a soldier's eyes when they're faced with a war they don't know they can win. Right then, she knew her work with him couldn't take priority.

"I understand," she said. "I'm sorry this is happening and that you have to be involved. Honestly, it's... it's a little terrifying." She flashed a momentary, nervous smile. "But the moment... and I mean the very *second* this fight is over, you call me. We'll sit down and we start working on getting you better. Deal?"

He let out a short, focused breath. "Aye. Deal."

"Good. In the meantime, you're going to have to go without any medication if you want to be medically cleared. I want you to use the techniques you've learned so far at all times. I want you walking around with your finger and thumb glued together. You understand me?"

"Yes, ma'am."

"I appreciate this might not always be possible, but if you feel yourself slipping into a panic attack, do whatever you can to find some distance. Take as long as you can to breathe and stay calm."

Collins smiled patiently. "Never been in a gunfight, have you, Doc?"

Dr. Moss smiled back, without humor. "Actually, yes, I have. I've been shot at, and I've seen people tortured and killed in front of me. Perhaps not to the scope of what you have faced, but I have a better understanding than most people in my line of work."

Collins shuffled awkwardly in his seat. He let go of

Kim's hand and ran his fingers over his head. "Ah, right. The time ya spent with Adrian. Shite. Sorry, Doc."

She held up a hand. "It's okay. Just... find a way, as best you can, okay?"

"I'll give it a damn good go, I promise."

She got to her feet. Both Collins and Kim did the same. She exchanged handshakes with both of them, then retrieved her jacket and bags.

"I have a hotel booked," she announced. "I'm sure they will be able to extend my stay without fuss. It's getting late, and I think we both need some rest. Ray, stay here tonight. Let the doctors here monitor you as long as they can. Tomorrow, you go and do whatever it is you have to do to keep us all safe. I'll see you when it's over."

"Thanks for coming, Doc. I really appreciate it."

She smiled. "Are you kidding me? GlobaTech's paying me a fortune to fix you."

They shared a laugh, and she left the room.

"How are you feeling?" Kim asked him.

He shrugged. "Doing better than I was. Ya can go on home and get some sleep, love. Ya been here long enough. They're gonna start thinking ya crazy too."

She smiled. "I go when you go."

They shared a quiet moment, staring into each other's eyes with real affection.

"Come on," Kim said finally. "Let's get you to bed. You can be a badass tomorrow."

Collins grinned. "Yes, ma'am."

Chapter Twenty-Five

December 14, 2020

The sky was clear and almost cloudless, glistening in the sunlight like an ice-cold crystal. Hall stood in front of the large, wide window and gazed out, hands clasped behind his back. He stared ahead to where the winter sky met the jagged teeth of the western mountains. His cream suit jacket was open, hanging slightly off his bloated shoulders.

His office was a circular dome atop the smaller of the two towers that dominated the base's skyline. The window ran down to his waist but stretched a full semicircle around, offering a stunning panoramic view of the complex.

Away to his left, his rocket stood tall and proud, pointing to the heavens he was preparing to conquer. He took a deep, almost meditative breath as he stared at it. His mouth twisted into a loving smile. He had worked his entire life for this, and now here he stood, less than twenty-four hours away from fulfilling his dream.

A sharp knock on the door distracted him. He glanced

over his shoulder as Parker strode in. Hall looked her up and down as she ended a call on her cell phone. She approached the desk behind him. There was urgency in her every step.

He turned to face her and nodded at the phone in her hand. "That damn thing is practically glued to your ear. I never see you without it."

Parker shrugged. "It's the job. You get used to it."

He straightened, forcing his shoulders back, then took his seat. It was a high-backed leather chair, custom-made to be wider than normal, to accommodate his girth. He shuffled toward his desk until the edge stopped his body, then rested his elbows on the surface. He bridged his fingers together and looked over them, staring Parker straight in her eyes.

"Well, if you want to keep that job, you're going to fix this," he said bluntly.

Parker frowned and shook her head. "Fix what?"

He scoffed. "All those phone calls, and no one's told you? A piece of advice, Gwen—it's all well and good putting the fear of God into your subordinates, but they still need to know they can come to you with bad news without fearing for their job... or their life. Otherwise, you'll never know anything."

She ran a hand over her short, smooth blonde hair and sat opposite him. "Mr. Hall, what's happened?"

He leaned back and sighed. "Yesterday, an unidentified woman walked into Tristar's New York office posing as a lawyer for someone you fired a few days ago. She made her way into your office, then assaulted your Number Two and demanded to know where you were. We believe she found out."

Parker hid her shock well behind her professionalism.

She shook her head. "That's not possible. Other than the state, no one knew where I was going. Not even my assistant, who arranged the trip. No one could know—"

Hall held up his hand. "Given who this fake lawyer was, I'm pretty sure she knows *exactly* where you are, Gwen."

Her eyes narrowed. "Who was it?"

"Jay. Which means—"

"The defective asset?" She shook her head again. "Then we're fine. Even if she figured out I was here, she'll never come back looking for revenge. Especially given the trouble she had escaping in the first place. It would be suicide."

Hall leaned forward and jabbed a swollen finger inches from Parker's face. "If you ever interrupt me again, you'll be strapped to the outside of that rocket when it takes off. Do you understand me?"

Parker held his gaze defiantly and nodded.

"I'm not concerned about her coming back here looking for revenge," he continued. "I'm concerned about her coming back here with all her friends dressed in black and red."

Parker frowned. "From what you told me, she wanted to disappear off everyone's radar. Would she choose to get involved by running to GlobaTech?"

"She can only disappear if GlobaTech lets her. But I know she reached out to them, because they rescued her from a hospital in New Texas two days ago, killing one of my assets and several of your men in the process."

"Oh. I see."

"All those phone calls, yet you're still so out of touch. I hope I didn't make a mistake bringing you in."

Parker shook her head. "You didn't, I promise. Just tell me how I can help. I'm assuming you have, like, eight contingencies in place?"

Hall smiled. "Eleven, actually. I underestimated Globa-Tech's tenacity once before. I don't intend making the same mistake again. The solution to each one of their problems lies in this compound, so they will come at us with everything they have. I'm sure by now they have some idea of what I'm planning. Plus, they will want their precious soul drive back. We all know how vulnerable they are without it. That's why I want you to send twenty of your best men to guard the underground vault."

Parker frowned. "Why not just send a couple of your Nemesis assets to do it?"

Hall leaned forward. "Because I want my assets protecting me and my rocket."

"But surely it makes more sense to—"

"Gwen, do we have a problem here?"

She swallowed. "No, Mr. Hall."

"They want that drive back, but it won't be their priority. Their primary objective will be going after the rocket, which is why I'll have all my assets standing by the front gate, waiting to greet them."

"Should I station some of my people at the launch site, just in case they break through?"

Hall smirked. "They won't. But even if they did, do you think I made it that simple to disable my baby? See, Globa-Tech's problem has always been that they try to look ten moves ahead, so they can focus on the next battle and do the most amount of good in the world. It's pathetic. It also means they can sometimes lose sight of the war that's right in front of them. Just like when Santa Clarita fell. I mean, that was so easy to do, it was almost embarrassing."

Parker flicked her eyebrows with a gentle shrug. "Fair point."

"The Nemesis assets are too skilled. Each time Globa-

Tech has come up against them, they've lost. Badly. Putting that steroid freak in the hospital was a message to hammer that point home and prove they're outmatched. Plus, with Rayne leading the Nemesis presence on-site, the psychological damage that will do to them is enough to neuter any attempt at an attack until it's too late."

Parker nodded slowly. Hall was a detestable human being who made her flesh crawl, but he was also brilliant.

"I'll give the order to move my men into position at the vault now," she said, getting to her feet. "Once I'm back in New York, I'll move ahead with the marketing campaign and press tour. If you're planning the launch for tomorrow, we need as many people as possible believing Tristar will protect them when GlobaTech implodes. I'll—"

Hall held up his hand once again, shaking his head. "Until further notice, I want you to stay here on base. You'll be given secure quarters to sleep and work in, with a nice view of the launch, obviously."

"But sir… I have no luggage, and I have a business to run. I can't just—"

"Gwen, it's only going to be for a few days. Once the launch is complete, I'm going to need you in New York, as you have said. After this, you can rule the city with an iron fist, if you wish. But until then, I need my key people here, where it's safe."

She let out a heavy sigh.

"That's my girl." Hall grinned. "There's an asset waiting for you outside. She'll show you to your room."

Parker simply nodded. "Thank you."

She turned and headed for the door.

Hall tilted his head slightly, watching her walk away with a lecherous smile. Once she had left, he spun around in his chair and stood, resuming his appreciation of the gorgeous sights before him.

"Soon," he whispered to himself, "I'll control the world from this very spot."

Chapter Twenty-Six

Julie's head rested in her hands as she stared at the surface of her desk. Hobbs had left a few minutes ago. Their meeting had gone on longer than either had intended, and it was intensive. She was relieved to not have any vocal opposition in the boardroom anymore. She could deal with it, but it was a problem she could happily do without. But now, with Hobbs on board, her vision for GlobaTech was coming to life, and the enormity of what she had to deal with was becoming clear.

It was a lot to handle.

On top of that, there was Quincy Hall to deal with. Everyone was due in for a debrief any time now, and her head just wasn't in it.

There was a single knock on the door, then Jericho opened it and stepped inside. He looked over and smiled, but his expression changed to one of concern when Julie barely registered that he was there.

"Hey," he said. "What's wrong?"

She looked over at him. "Hmm? Hi."

He shut the door and approached the desk. "Everything okay?"

Julie sat back in her chair and sighed. "I really, *genuinely* have no goddamn clue how Moses did this job."

Jericho gave her a small, sympathetic smile and rested against the edge of the desk.

"I couldn't even begin to explain all the shit that has to happen now. You need business degrees coming out of your ass to understand all this. Thank God for Hobbs. And I never thought I'd say that."

Jericho nodded. "Yeah, I saw him leaving as I got here. You both on the same page now?"

"We are. I even promoted him. Pretty sure I can do that, right?"

Jericho smiled. "You sure can."

"He's been great, and he believes in what I want to achieve here."

"Well, there you go. Use him as much as you need to. Let him do the heavy lifting in terms of the boardroom and business stuff. Just because you're in charge, it doesn't mean you have to do everything yourself."

Julie smiled and shook her head. "You know, considering your skillset, you always seem to be able to kick my ass and make it sound like you're hugging me."

He smiled and felt his cheeks flush a little with color. "Glad I can help. Look, you think what you're about to do is the right way to go, yeah?"

She nodded without hesitation. "I do. It won't be easy, which is where Hobbs comes in, but it's what our next step needs to be. GlobaTech has done incredible things for this world. But there's only so much you can do when you're simultaneously starting the wars you fight to end."

"That's a fair point. I agree with you. This is worth

doing, Julie. I know you don't care about such things, but when this happens, it'll be *your* legacy. It'll be *your* name in the history books. That's not nothing, y'know? In my experience, the right thing to do is rarely the easiest. But you'll find a way. You always do. I know it, Buchanan knew it... and I think, deep down, you know it too."

Julie got to her feet and embraced him, throwing her arms around his neck and pulling herself into his massive chest. He held her close, relishing the feeling of her being next to him. They rarely had the opportunity to sleep at the same time lately. The job kept them busy and separated during the day. It felt like an age since the two of them had shared a moment that was just theirs.

Julie stepped back, admiring his body as she rubbed her hands over his shoulders, smiling to herself. Then she looked up at him.

"So, how are you doing?" she asked.

"Me?" He shrugged. "I'm fine."

She tilted her head slightly and looked into his eyes, searching for the truth. "You sure?"

"Yeah. I'm a little sore still, but I'm fine." He smiled. "Itching for a fight."

Julie didn't smile back. She nodded slowly, then turned away.

"Okay..." she said tersely, sitting back behind her desk.

Jericho frowned. "What's wrong?"

She sighed, impatient and frustrated. "We're supposed to talk to each other. I know we haven't had a lot of time recently, but we're here now. I just... I don't understand why you won't tell me how you're really doing."

Jericho folded his arms across his chest. "What are you talking about? Where's this coming from?"

Julie spun slightly in her chair to face him. "All this time... everything we've been through... you think I don't know when you're hiding something? We've barely spoken about anything other than work since the funerals. You haven't uttered two words to anyone since Rayne attacked you. Admittedly, your actions spoke volumes in Texas, and I'm grateful for that. But I know something's wrong, Jericho. Right here, right now, it's just me and you. I'm not your boss. You're not the invincible soldier. It's just us. Why won't you talk to me?"

He shook his head. "Julie, seriously, I'm fine," he insisted.

She got to her feet again, tensing as she moved in front of him. "Okay. If you're fine... roll up your sleeves."

She reached out and plucked the fabric of his thin sweater on his shoulder.

Jericho flinched. He caught his words before he could speak. He couldn't lie to her. His jaw muscles pulsed with contemplation. His eyes became focused and unblinking.

"How did you know?" he asked eventually, his words reluctantly spilling out on a resigned sigh.

Her body relaxed. Her expression softened. "I saw them, when you were in the hospital."

Jericho grimaced, cursing to himself.

Julie shook her head. "I just... I wish I'd noticed sooner. We haven't had the chance to see each other much at night, or... be with each other. And that's no one's fault. But I should be there for you. Be more attentive. We all need someone we can turn to. Even you."

"Julie, you don't—"

"No, Jericho. This job is important. What we're all about to face could change the world. But I'm your girlfriend and I love you. And I was doing that long before all this shit happened. I haven't been there for you. Not the way you are for me. Even after everything you've been through lately, the first thing you do when you see me is ask how I am. I've let you down. That's on me. But I'm here now, so please… talk to me, Jericho. Show me your arms."

Jericho held her gaze. He saw everything in her eyes. Anger. Sadness. Sympathy. Pain. He knew there was no sense in keeping anything from her now.

He wrapped his right hand around his left wrist and slid the sleeve of his sweater up. Etched into the outside of his forearm were several cuts. Thin, neat lines. Some had already scarred. Others were fresh and recent.

Julie moved a hand to her mouth. Seeing the full extent of his wounds for the first time both shocked and confused her.

"Jericho, what… what is this?"

He pulled the sleeve back down and glanced away. "Nothing."

His response angered her. She took a deep breath and momentarily closed her eyes, summoning the strength to remain calm.

"Please, tell me. Is this a cry for help? Are you… I mean, do you feel like you… I don't know. Talk to me, Jericho. Please. Help me understand what you're going through, so I can help."

Julie reached out to him, but he stepped back, snapping his arm away from her. "Don't. Just… leave it, okay? I'll figure it out."

Again, she felt anger boil inside of her. The man she loved was suffering, more than she had ever realized. All she wanted to do was help, and she couldn't understand why he wouldn't let her.

She waved her arms incredulously. "Are you... *fucking* kidding me? This is *me*, Jericho. You have to tell me, so I can help you. You can't just—"

"It's penance!" he snapped.

The volume and intensity of his voice made her jump, and she skipped backward until she was sitting on the edge of her desk. Her eyes were wide, instantly misting over with tears.

Jericho breathed heavily through clenched teeth. "God... *damn it*! It's my punishment, Julie. It's a reminder of the people we've lost. It's a reminder that I'm still capable of feeling something... *anything*... because right now, this life we're living... the never-ending cycle of bullshit we have to fight through... I'm just numb. Do you understand? I feel nothing." He lashed out, slamming a fist into the wall next to him. "Nothing!"

He paced away from her. Julie watched him, clasping a hand over her mouth to mute her cries. Tears silently streamed down her face.

He stopped in the middle of the room and turned back to her. "I've never been scared of anything in my life, Julie. And I'm not just saying that. Even as a kid, I ran head-first into trouble, each time it found me. Every fight, every battle, every war... I've never been afraid. I just do what needs to be done. Even when Rayne had me surrounded. All those Nemesis assets... I believed I was going to die. I still wasn't afraid. All I could think was, I'm going to take at least one of these bastards with me. But this..." He held up his arm and pointed to his forearm. "... feeling like this. Feeling like I'm already dead inside. Like I'm not even human anymore. Like I'm losing sense of who I am. I swear to God, Julie... it fucking terrifies me."

Julie stared at him. She had no words. She had never

seen that side of him before. Not angry or frustrated or even scared.

He was vulnerable.

She wiped her eyes, walked over to him, and simply held him. She wrapped her hands around his waist, rested her head against his chest, and held him tight, as if the winter winds would carry him away from her forever if she let go.

For a moment, Jericho stood still. His hands were shaking. His breathing was deep and labored. He was confused by how many emotions he felt at the same time. But then he felt her. He could feel her heart beating against him. He could smell her hair. Slowly, he brought his arms around her and embraced her, as if shielding her from the world.

The two of them stood there, locked in the moment, for several minutes.

When they finally parted, they walked back over to her desk and sat side by side in front of it, leaning forward, close to each other, holding each other's hands.

"Why didn't you say something?" asked Julie quietly.

Jericho shrugged. "Honestly? You have enough on your plate right now. I wasn't looking to add to your problems."

She rolled her eyes. "You're not a problem, you big idiot. Me and you… we're the comfort zone, understand? No matter what else we're dealing with, us together, like this… like right now… this is our safe zone, okay? It always has been, and that shouldn't change just because of what's happening."

Jericho nodded silently.

"How can I help?" she asked. "What do you need from me that can help you to not feel like this?"

He swallowed his nerves. "Honestly, there isn't anything you can do. There's nothing anyone can do. I'm the problem here. You can argue all day and night that the people we've lost aren't on me, but it wouldn't make a difference. It's how I'm wired, Julie. This is what I do. It's *all* I do. If I can't do it anymore, what the hell is left? Who am I without the fight?"

She smiled weakly, causing a stray tear to escape down her cheek. "Maybe when all this is over, you should sit down with Kaitlyn Moss."

Jericho frowned. "Ray's therapist?"

Julie nodded. "She's staying in town on GlobaTech's dime until we're done with Hall. It couldn't hurt."

"Yeah. Maybe I will." He took a deep breath. "Because I've been thinking about it, Julie, and... when all this is over —assuming we manage to stop Hall and Orion again—I reckon I'm done."

She tensed and frowned. Her grip of his hand tightened. "Done? Done with what?"

Jericho sensed her tone and smiled. "Not with you. *Idiot.*"

She visibly relaxed again, smiling slightly with embarrassment.

"I mean with all this," he continued. "With GlobaTech. With the fight. It's demanding more from me that I'm prepared to give anymore. I think I need to walk away."

Her grip tightened once again, but this time with a smile. "I understand that. Maybe more than you think. You've seen how difficult the transition to the boardroom has been for me, but a part of me is glad Buchanan chose me for this. As stressful as it is, it's a nice change from being shot at every ten minutes. Now, it's closer to every half-hour..."

They shared a gentle laugh.

"But I don't think being a CEO is a long-term thing for me," she continued. "It isn't who I am."

Jericho nodded slowly. "Then maybe it's time we both let GlobaTech go. I mean, you can't deny we've given everything for this place. It sounds like we're both approaching the same place. Honestly, it kinda makes me feel stupid for not talking to you earlier."

Julie rubbed her thumb lovingly over the back of his hand and smiled.

He smiled back. "Maybe it's time we think about *our* future for once, instead of everyone else's. I reckon Ray would agree with us right now too. Maybe he'll settle down with Kim. We can be neighbors in some quiet, suburban cul-de-sac, away from all this shit."

Julie smiled warmly. "I never thought that life would sound appealing, but I reckon you're onto something there. I can step down as CEO, take a position on the board. I'll have stock options, show up to a meeting once a month... nice and easy."

"Maybe you and I can get married, start a family."

She lifted her head slightly, her eyes wide, smiling like a seven-year-old girl who always dreamed of being a princess. "Why, Mr. Stone... are you asking to make an honest woman of me?"

He laughed. "I'm saying I want to, when the time's right."

She leaned over, placed her hands on his face, and kissed him. When they parted, she looked deep into his eyes. "Well, just know that, when you do, I'm going to say yes."

He took a deep breath and grinned. "Good to know."

Julie kissed him again, then got to her feet. "Come on, we can retire later. We still have work to do, and the others will be here any minute."

Jericho placed his hands on his knees and sighed as he reluctantly got to his feet. "Yeah… there'll always be another war waiting for us, right?"

She sat behind her desk and opened her laptop. Then she peered over the lid at him.

"That's right," she said. "But this one's our last."

Chapter Twenty-Seven

Link and Ruby were the first to arrive. They hurried into the office, shrugging their winter coats off as the heaters welcomed them inside. Hugs and handshakes and pleasantries were exchanged.

"It's arctic out there today," said Ruby. She moved over to one of the heaters built into the wall beneath the window and huddled beside it. "Do you think Hall would mind waiting until the spring before he tries to conquer the world?"

Julie smiled briefly.

"How's Ray doing?" Link asked Jericho.

Before he could answer, Collins and Kim walked in through the open door.

"I'm fine, big fella," he said with a smile. "Thanks for asking."

The others surrounded them, offering more hugs and handshakes, which were gratefully received. Kim closed the door behind her as they moved into the middle of the room.

Julie moved over to her desk, leaned against the front of it, and faced the room. The others formed a loose semicircle in front of her. She looked at each of them in turn: Ruby, Link, Jericho, Kim, and Collins.

This is it, she thought. *We're either going to save the world or watch it burn.*

The talk with Jericho had helped her. She was thinking more clearly. She was more focused. She had her priorities straight. She knew it wasn't the time for being nice. That ship had sailed. Now was the time to make sure they won.

"Okay, first thing's first," Julie began, her voice firm and authoritative. She looked at Collins. "Ray, are you sure you're up for this?"

He nodded. "Aye, I am, Jules. Don't worry."

"You're among friends here. Among family. This is a safe space, and it's perfectly okay to say you're not. I ask because, as sorry as I was about what happened to you in Texas, you shouldn't have been there, and we both know it. You have nothing to prove to anyone, Ray. My concern is that if that happens again, we might not be so lucky."

Collins held her gaze, his jaw set, his body tensed. "Don't worry about me, pet. I promise ya, I'll make it through this fight. Plenty of time to heal afterward. Scout's honor."

Julie watched him for a moment, then nodded. "Good enough for me. Now, I was hoping we would have an update from Jay, but—"

The door burst open. Jay stood motionless in the doorway, staring at everyone.

"You really need to add me to your little WhatsApp group," she said. "I'm beginning to think you don't like inviting me to things."

She kicked the door shut behind her and moved to Julie's side. She glanced quickly around the room.

"We have a problem," she stated.

"No shit…" said Link, rolling his eyes.

Jay looked over at him and raised an eyebrow. "A *new* problem, asshole."

"What is it?" asked Julie.

"I found Gwen Parker. She's at the base in Nevada. Been there for a couple of days now. No one at Tristar knew where she was going when she left. No indication when she'll be back."

Julie nodded. "Good work. Thank you." She addressed everyone. "If Hall's brought Parker to Heaven's Valley, there's a good chance he's gathering all his key people together now, which means he's preparing to launch. That means we're out of time. We're on our own, and whatever we're going to do to stop him, we need to act now. Suggestions?"

"A frontal assault on the base isn't an option," said Jericho. "With Tristar rebuilding, we don't know exactly how many people they have on-site."

"It's a big place," said Jay. "Best guess would be a couple of thousand, easily."

Link shrugged. "That's not a big deal, is it? We've taken on more than that before. GlobaTech can win a straight-up fight against those pricks every time."

"Not on that scale," countered Julie. "Only time we've fought that many at once before was during the fall of Santa Clarita, and we all know how that went."

"Aye, but they caught us with our pants down then, didn't they?" said Collins. "This time, we're ready for the bastards. Big difference."

"That may be," said Jericho, "But Tristar isn't the problem. We can't effectively fight Nemesis assets for long, and everyone knows it. Including Hall. Jay, how many would you say were on the base?"

Jay shrugged. "I saw three—Rayne and two others. But Hall told me he has a small army of them, so Christ knows how many that means."

"I know of at least three more," said Jericho bitterly. "More, if they weren't the same guys you fought."

"Let's not forget the team of those bastards that hit us when they killed Jessie and took your hard drive," added Link through gritted teeth.

"Okay," said Julie. "The key to victory here is disabling Nemesis somehow. We might not have the Air Force's help, but I agree with Link: we can hit them head-on and win if we're only dealing with Tristar." She looked at Jay. "Do you have any insight into how we can stop the Nemesis assets?"

Jay sighed. "Why does everyone think I have all the answers? No, I have no clue. We're programmed and conditioned and trained to be unstoppable. That's the point."

"We stopped you," mused Link.

Jay shot him a vicious glare. "Only because I was broken before you started. Pretty sure I've kicked most of the asses in this room. Watch your mouth."

Link took a step forward, but so did Julie. She pointed a finger at him. "Hey, stand down." Then she turned to Jay. "We're all on the same side here, like it or not. You have your way out, once this fight is over. But you would still be wise to avoid pissing anyone off. Understand?"

Jay held her hands up and nodded an apology. "Old habits." She looked at Link. "My bad."

Link didn't say anything. He just huffed and stepped back in line.

"Josh!" shouted Ruby.

Everyone turned to her, surprised and confused.

"Josh's files," she continued. "There was something... I think. Do you have them?"

Julie reached behind and lifted a thick folder off her desk. She held it out toward Ruby, who strode forward to take it. She opened it in her hands and began flipping through the pages.

"What is it, love?" asked Collins. "Got us all on tenterhooks..."

"I don't know," she said absently. "Something he mentioned about what he and Adrian did once. Something... ah! Where is it?"

The room watched her, patient and curious, as she muttered to herself, quietly reading snippets of notes, desperately searching for what she wanted before the thought evaporated from her mind.

"Got it!" she exclaimed. She took the sheet of paper and tossed the folder back onto the desk. Then she turned and faced the room, standing beside Julie. "Six years ago, Adrian killed a crime boss called Wilson Trent. He was the guy who..."

She trailed off, suddenly realizing who was in the room. She looked over at Jay.

"Um... Trent was the one who... who killed your daughter and left you for dead," she explained.

Jay rocked on her heels, like a strong wind had blown her off-balance. Everyone turned to look at her, watching as her eyes glazed over and she became lost inside a whirlwind, surrounded by memories she wasn't sure she could believe.

"I don't... I mean, I can't..." She sighed and shook her head, refocusing on Ruby. "You say Adrian killed him?"

Ruby nodded. "He did."

"How?"

Ruby checked the notes. "He... curb-stomped him in the middle of the crowd at a Steelers game."

Link shook his head quietly with disbelief.

Jay thought for a moment, then shrugged. "Good. Carry on."

"Okay," said Ruby. "Well, when he did, he took out five of Trent's security guards using technology I think he got from you guys."

"From GlobaTech?" asked Julie.

"Yeah. Some experimental, miniaturized EMP thing. It was a super short-range blast that was set to..." She paused to read the notes. "'...disrupt the electrical frequency of a human heartbeat.'"

Jericho looked at Julie with concern. "We can do that?"

Julie shrugged. "I have no idea..."

"Apparently, you can," said Ruby. "So, here's my thinking." She pointed at Jay. "Your tattoo has nanotechnology in the ink that permanently transmits an electrical signal, right? That frequency is what activates you, and your codewords just tell your brain when to ignore it."

Jay nodded. "Basically."

Ruby looked at Julie. "What if we can use this EMP thing to disrupt that signal, instead of the heartbeat? If you can expand the range, could it, theoretically, disable all Nemesis assets in range?"

Julie raised her eyebrows and blew out an uncertain breath. "I don't know. I mean... I didn't even know the tech existed. If it does, it was buried by either Josh or Moses long ago. I can ask Dev, our weapons expert. Logically, what you're suggesting makes sense. But in reality, I don't know."

Ruby looked around the room. "I think it's worth asking, right? It worked for Adrian."

Collins raised his hand. "This might sound like overkill,

but why not just leave the frequency as it is and kill the bastards?"

Jay looked at him. "Because we *all* have heartbeats, dumbass."

"Oh. Aye. Fair point."

Kim, who had been quiet so far, placed a hand on his shoulder, then looked at Julie. "Let's not forget, these assets are innocent people when they're not... activated. Right?"

Julie nodded. "There is that, yes. Which leads to another issue: what do we do about Rayne? Let's say this idea works, and he becomes Adam again. What do we do with him?"

The room fell silent. No one had an answer.

Julie let the question stew for a moment. "Okay. One step at a time. Let's assume this EMP thing will work... you guys start thinking on how to execute the plan. I'll go and make a call, see if this is even possible."

She reached behind her to retrieve her cell phone, then started dialing as she headed for the door. She placed it to her ear as she stepped outside.

The others all looked at each other blankly.

"That thing sounds like some crazy-ass sci-fi shit," observed Link.

"Right now, I'll take anything that gives us an edge," said Jericho.

Ruby nodded. "According to Josh, he slipped these tiny discs into the pockets of the guards, so they were close enough to work. Adrian pressed the button that sent the signal. Killed them all."

Collins nodded. "Okay. Well, if this gonna work for us, we would need to find a way of boosting the signal somehow, right? We can't exactly go around asking everyone to hold one of these things while we zap 'em like bugs."

Silence fell again. It was broken by Julie walking back in, holding her cell phone ceremoniously in the air.

"Okay, that was Dev," she said. "Yes, that tech is definitely ours. Yes, it still exists. Yes, it could be used how we want to…"

Everyone looked around at each other, a wave of excitement enveloping them.

"That's awesome," said Link.

Julie nodded. "In theory. There are some things we have to figure out first."

"Such as?" asked Jericho.

"First, we need to identify the signal. We can't do anything unless we know what frequency to zero in on. Then we need to find a way to increase the range."

Collins nodded. "I just said about that, but no ideas. Sorry, boss."

"I can help," said Jay quietly.

Everyone turned to her. She looked up at each of them in turn.

"I can help," she said again.

"How?" asked Julie.

"Your guy can analyze my signal. It'll be the same for all of us. It's the activation phrase that's unique. As for the range…" She looked at Collins. "…the whole place is one big launch site for a spaceship. It has a communications tower. I saw a big-ass radar dish on its roof. That would do it, right?"

Collins nodded. "Aye. Aye… it might just. If I calibrated their system to recognize our signal, then broadcast it, in theory, it could go around the world. It would definitely deactivate every asset on the base."

"Including me…" whispered Jay.

Everyone's breath caught in their throats. They knew,

given her condition, deactivating Jay could leave her brain-dead... or simply kill her.

Julie turned to Jay and hesitantly placed a hand on her shoulder. "I'm sure we can adjust the range to only cover the base." She glanced back at Collins. "Right?"

He nodded. "Aye. Easy-peasy."

She looked back at Jay. "You just need to wait out of range until it's done, then you can join us."

Jay nodded absently, distracted.

Julie looked back at the group. "Okay. So, *potentially*, that's the assets taken care of. Jericho, how do we do this?"

Jericho stepped forward, turning to face everyone from the side of the room. "The way I see it, there are two primary objectives: stopping the rocket from launching and getting our soul drive back. A small team could theoretically approach through the mountains. If we can drop the Nemesis assets remotely, we could sneak in and do what we need to before anyone notices."

"That sounds risky, Jerry," said Collins. "What are the odds no one sees us?"

"That's why we create a distraction. Link, you pointed out we can handle Tristar in a straight fight. Without Nemesis, we could attack them head-on. A big show of force should aim for the main entrance, nice and loud."

"Hall will be expecting that," said Jay.

Jericho nodded. "Good. I'd hate to disappoint him. Send a few thousand operatives to knock on his front door, give everyone there plenty to think about. If we can sneak inside and prepare the signal blocker, we can hit it just before our operatives reach the main gate. Shock and awe. The assets drop, everyone's confused, our guys hit them hard and fast. Meanwhile, we can use the chaos as cover, find the drive, and stop the rocket."

Julie nodded, allowing herself a small smile. Listening to Jericho... watching him formulate military strategy on the spot like that... it was impressive. The president saw the potential in him. She caught herself wondering how much day-to-day work was involved in being a three-star general. If he took to retirement as badly as she figured he would, perhaps he could stay busy without fighting?

Jericho looked around the room.

"Kim, I'm assuming you won't be joining us?" he asked with a wry smile.

She laughed. "No, I'm... I'm good."

"Okay. So, that leaves six of us. Ray, you and Link head for the comms tower. You always say you're our tech guy. Now's your chance to prove it. Get there, calibrate their systems, get that signal ready to transmit. Julie, you and I will try to find Hall. We get him, chances are we get our soul drive. Ruby, you and Jay hang back outside the perimeter of the EMP blast. You'll have the activation switch. You get the go-ahead from Ray, you hit the button, drop the assets, then head inside with the main GlobaTech force. The six of us link up and head for the rocket, shut it down before it can launch."

Collins chuckled. "Damn, Jerry... that's just crazy enough to work."

He nodded his gratitude, then looked over at Julie. "Well? What do you think?"

Julie took a deep breath and stepped forward. "I think we have a solid plan. Ray, you and Jay go and see Devon Green right away. Tell him what you need and don't leave his side until you have it. Jericho, you have two hours to organize as many operatives as you can and get them prepped for battle." She checked her watch. "It's just after eleven. I want two thousand of our best operatives mobile and en route to Nevada by seventeen hundred. It's a long trip. We have any people who are closer, arrange a link-up point and have them join the party."

"Mind if I join him?" asked Link. "I wanna stay useful."

"Go for it." She looked at everyone in turn. "This is it, folks. Hall is bound to know we're coming. But he's unlikely to know how we're about to hit him, so we have the element of surprise. We make this count. He launches that rocket, it's game over. We have a plan. Do what you gotta do, then get some rest. Tomorrow, we end this. Move out."

Julie walked behind her desk and sat heavily in her chair. Jay was the first to leave the office, followed a moment later by Collins, then Kim. Link paused in the doorway and looked back, waiting for Jericho.

Jericho stood in front of the desk. "What are you going to do?"

Julie looked up at him. "I'm going to give the president a head's up. Figured he would want to know we're fixing to tear a new hole in Nevada."

He nodded, smiled faintly, then headed for the door, following Link outside.

Ruby lingered in the corner. Realizing she hadn't moved, Julie looked over.

"You okay?" she asked.

Ruby took a deep, tired breath. "Yeah."

"Look, I know you've been hesitant to get back into the fight, and you know I understand why. I get Jericho kinda jumped the gun just then and presumed your involvement, but we really need you on this one, Ruby. This is the fight that matters."

"I know, I know." She sighed again. "I'm happy to back Jay up while she takes out the assets, but when it comes to storming the gates, I'm out. I'll either hang back, be your eyes on the ground from a distance, or I'll drive away completely if you don't need me."

Julie sat back and frowned. "Okay. What's going on with you? Honestly, I figured you would be the first to sign on for this. This is how we win, Ruby. This is how we avenge those we've lost."

Ruby stepped in front of her. "Maybe for you, it is. But I'm not looking to avenge anyone. Not anymore."

"You're gonna have to help me out here…"

She took a seat in front of Julie and leaned forward on the desk. "There's something I have to tell you."

Devon Green's workshop occupied the floor three levels below Julie's office. Collins and Jay stepped out of the elevator and were greeted by stacks of boxes and crates. A host of GlobaTech personnel hustled around them, unpacking and installing their contents.

Collins scanned the open floor and spotted Devon Green on the other side, hunched over a large table. He pointed, and the two of them headed over to him.

"Dev," Collins called out as they approached, "are ya busy?"

Green looked over in the direction of the distinctive voice. His dark skin resembled leather, slightly cracked and creased with time. His face had flecks of stubble along the jaw, and he wore his baseball cap backwards. His eyes lit up with his smile, and he straightened to greet them.

"Ray… my man!" He held out his hand, which Collins shook. His smile faded to a sincere line. "How are you keeping, brother? You doing okay?"

Collins smiled gratefully. "Aye. Ya know me. I'm all good, Dev."

Green nodded. "I *do* know you… that's why I'm asking."

The two men shared a brief laugh. Then Collins stepped aside and gestured to Jay.

"Dev, this is Jay," he said.

Green nodded a courteous greeting. "Pleasure."

Jay returned the gesture but said nothing.

"Dev, the boss lady sent me," said Collins.

Green narrowed his gaze, noting the seriousness of his tone. "Is this about the EMP device?"

"Aye. We need you to repurpose it."

"Yeah, her theoretical application was a little out there, but it's definitely possible. How soon do you need it?"

"Right now. We can't leave here without it."

Green sucked in a deep breath. He took his cap off, ran a hand over his short hair, then replaced it again. "Ray, I gotta tell you, this might take some time."

"I know, and I'm sorry to do this to ya, buddy. I know ya got a lot going on down here, but this is real *fate of the world* stuff."

Green sighed, then stepped away to a small stack of boxes next to the table. He rummaged inside the top one for a few moments, then moved back toward them holding a small disc in his hand. He held it out for them to see.

"Is that the gadget Adrian used back in the day?" asked Collins, pointing to the device. "It's tiny."

Green nodded. "It's not an EMP in the traditional sense. Typically, you get a blast… a *pulse*, right? Well, this here converted that pulse into a radio wave, then transmitted a signal to small receivers over short distances. No more than a few feet. Its original function was to safely disable electronics and bombs in close-quarters situations. Mr. Winters helped reconfigure it so it would short the electrical frequency of the human heart, then... um... *borrowed* it."

Jay's mouth curled into a subtle smile. "Yeah, we heard."

Green looked at Collins. "Tell me *exactly* what you want to make it do instead?"

"We need it to go back to being a blast," explained Collins, "but in a way that only affects a very specific frequency. We also want to amplify its signal by linking it to a broadcast system."

"Huh. You don't want much, do you? Anything else?"

"Aye. We need to be able to set it off remotely."

"Jesus. Okay. I'm gonna need to isolate the frequency you want to target."

Collins nodded, then looked back at Jay. She stepped forward and tugged the neck of her sweater down, exposing her neck.

"Go for it," she said.

Green frowned, then turned to Collins. "What's this?"

Collins smiled sheepishly. "The signal is built into nanotechnology inside the ink of her tattoo."

Green's mouth slowly fell open. "Come again?"

Collins sighed. "Long story. Jay here is part of the Nemesis program. There's a signal being transmitted at all times from the ink of her tattoo, which kinda reconfigures her brain to make her a deadly killing machine. There's a whole bunch of people just like her, and they're too strong for us to fight. We want to disrupt this signal to disable them."

Green nodded. "Okay. I hate that that makes sense to me, but it does." He looked at Jay. "But won't it take you out as well?"

Jay smiled humorlessly. "That's why we want to do it

remotely. I'll be standing outside the blast radius of the EMP when it goes off. Hopefully."

"Okay. Okay. This is doable." He looked at Collins. "Give me ten minutes to gather what I need, then we'll get to work."

Collins smiled. "Ya the best, Dev."

He shrugged. "I know."

Green set to work. Two solid hours passed as he hunched over his workstation, surrounded by laptops, soldering irons, and a whole host of other tools. Collins and Jay sat quietly and watched. Finally, he turned to face them, his hand held out to them. In his palm was the disc, which was now a little thicker and wider than before.

"I reckon I'll call this the One-Inch Punch," he announced, smiling.

Collins and Jay moved to stand in front of him.

"Have ya done it?" asked Collins excitedly.

Green nodded. "I have. On its own, this bad boy will unleash a pulse with a twenty-foot radius. It'll shut down any example of your frequency it finds."

He reached behind him and retrieved a piece of paper from beside one of the laptops, which he presented to Collins.

"What's this?" asked Collins, taking the paper from him.

"Those are the configuration options you'll need to calibrate your system to the blast signal," explained Green. "Once you're done, the pulse won't come from the device when you hit the button. It'll transmit the signal to your system, then broadcast across the range you input."

"Holy shit…" said Collins, marveling at the device. "This is awesome."

Green held it out to Jay. "I'm guessing you'll be doing the honors?"

Jay reached out and took the device from him. She held it up between her finger and thumb, studying it.

"So, this is the Nemesis Killer?" she asked rhetorically. "Shame Marshall couldn't be here to see this…"

Collins turned to Green and leaned close.

"I think her name for it is better," he whispered.

Chapter Twenty-Eight

December 15, 2020

The pale, winter sun began to crest over the mountains. A sliver of light peered over the peaks, casting pink streaks across the dawn sky before climbing higher. The dull stutter of helicopter blades cut through the silence that covered the dark, barren desert below.

Six bodies sat quietly, focused and alert, staring at the riveted metal floor. Julie, Jericho, and Collins had their backs to the pilot, facing Jay, Link, and Ruby. Each of them was dressed for combat. Head to toe in black, armed with as much as they could carry, bulked with armor and technology. They all wore headsets, clamped over their ears, for communication during the flight, although most of the trip had been spent in silence.

The previous day had been an unrelenting exercise in chaos and stress. What each of them had managed to achieve in such a short space of time was nothing less than a miracle.

Julie's conversation with President Schultz proved more fruitful than she had hoped. Despite his inability to become directly involved in what was about to unfold, the president still helped by securing military transport for GlobaTech operatives. Thanks to Jericho's logistical prowess, close to two thousand men and women would arrive at Hall's compound in Heaven's Valley inside the next two hours. GlobaTech had small bases and training facilities all over the country. Small pockets of operatives had been traveling via trains and planes non-stop since yesterday afternoon—moving out on a moment's notice and slowly merging into one dominating force along the way.

Julie and the others had set off later but traveled faster. They had hitched a ride on a routine flight to Edwards Air Force Base. From there, they transferred to the stealth gunship currently blasting them across Nevada.

Julie adjusted the mic of her headset, so it was directly over her mouth.

"Okay, everyone, listen up," she said. The others looked over at her. "We're about five minutes out from Heaven's Valley. We're landing by a gas station near the city limits. We have two vehicles waiting for us. Each one has a local operative behind the wheel. It's a thirty-minute drive until we clear the city, hit the desert, and reach Hall's base."

She looked over at Jay. "You got the device?"

Jay nodded.

"When you get the all-clear from Ray, you hit that button. Understand?"

"No problem," replied Jay, with a sigh that blew static into everyone's ears.

Julie turned to Ruby. "You'll be with her, watching her back. Anything goes wrong, you get her out of there. Don't hesitate. Don't worry about us. Just go. Okay?"

Ruby gave her a thumb's up. "You got it."

The two of them locked eyes for a moment, then gave each other the same small, restrained smile.

Julie then turned to her right to look at Collins. "It's your job to make sure nothing goes wrong. You and Link get to that comms tower, configure the signal, and activate the link to the trigger. You set the range to a thousand feet. That should encompass most of the base. Jay will be a quarter-mile away, which is outside of that blast radius. Be specific. We don't want to take her out too."

"Ya got it, boss," said Collins. "I know what I'm doing. Don't worry."

Julie looked over at Link, sitting directly across from her, his giant frame squashed between Jay and Ruby. "Make sure you know what he's doing too, understand? If something goes wrong, you need to finish the job."

Link's deep, graveled voice boomed through the mic, naturally distorting. "He's walked me through it. But I'll make sure he gets the job done."

She nodded. "Good. I don't need to tell you all how important this is. Hall *cannot* be allowed to launch that rocket. If he does, it's game over."

She glanced left at Jericho, who gently nudged her arm with his, offering her a reassuring smile. He looked deep into her eyes. He saw conviction. He knew she believed they were going to win, and that's all he needed to believe the same.

Just under forty minutes later, the journey was done. The vehicles and drivers had stayed behind, parked on the main highway by the exit that led out into the desert. The six of them stood in a line on an elevated outcrop that overlooked

Hall's compound from the southwest, about a half-mile out. The wind whipped around them, biting at any exposed flesh it could find. They were dressed for war, not comfort. The local climate helped take the edge off, certainly compared to Washington, but it was still cold.

They each took turns looking through field binoculars at the empire Hall had secretly been building for the last seven years. The base was tucked into a horseshoe of mountains, still shrouded in dawn's shadow as the sun continued to climb. Buildings dominated the right side of it, varying in height as they ran along and across at the back, in a large, inverted L-shape. The comms tower and control center stood out like beacons in the top right corner, distinctive and obvious.

But that's not where their collective attention was ultimately drawn.

Away to the west, up on a plateau linked to the compound's expansive courtyard via a narrow, winding road, was a launchpad. Standing on it, resting against a tower of scaffolding, was the rocket.

Upon seeing it for the first time, the group fell into a stunned, overwhelming silence.

It was Collins who finally broke it.

"That's a big-ass rocket," he said. "Like, a real-life spaceship."

"It sure is," said Link quietly.

"Six-year-old me is freaking out right now."

Link huffed. "Thirty-seven-year-old me is freaking out right now."

Julie took a deep breath. "Okay. Now that it's out of your system, we have work to do." She pointed to a section of fencing along the eastern border, which disappeared behind the first building. "That's our entry point. Jay,

Ruby… you head down, but stay low and hidden. Watch your range. The rest of us, we're going to circle counter-clockwise from here, make our way around to that southeast corner, and sneak inside. Be mindful of security cameras. Ray and Link, you head for that massive radar dish in the north-east corner. You encounter anyone, you drop them quietly. The longer we can go without being noticed, the better this will be."

Jericho pointed at another building along the right side, which was not as tall as the two towers. It resembled an office block, yet the top floor was mostly glass.

"That looks like an observatory," he said. "If Hall is intending to launch today, I'm guessing he'll be there, for the view."

Julie nodded. "Agreed. You and I will start there."

Silence fell once more.

The enormity of what they were facing was sinking in.

"So, this is it, huh?" mused Link.

"It is," replied Julie. "The cavalry should be just over an hour away now. If this goes to plan, we may find ourselves under fire without back-up for a little while. Be prepared."

Jericho drew his *Negotiator* and checked the magazine. "We are."

"All right. Good luck, everyone. Let's move."

Chapter Twenty-Nine

The four of them approached the compound in a slow, wide arc, keeping low and using the rocky surroundings to their advantage. After heading up a slight rise, they came to the edge of the cliffs along the east side of the compound. The perimeter fence was only twenty feet in front of them, but they were easily ten feet above it. The way down wasn't a sheer drop; there was a distinct pathway to the ground. However, on a steep and uneven slope and in limited daylight, it was treacherously thin. One wrong step and it would be game over.

With weapons stowed, they descended one by one, measuring each step carefully until they reached solid ground. The pathway was mostly dirt, littered with small pockets of dead grass. They regrouped and crouched close to the fence, comfortably behind one of the first buildings. There was no guard patrol, but there were cameras, which they made sure to avoid.

"Okay," whispered Julie. "We have maybe thirty minutes before the sun's high enough to shine a spotlight on this place. We need to move quickly. You all know where you're going. Only engage if you have to. Quick, clean kills. Hide the bodies. We need to stay hidden for as long as possible. Questions?"

The others all shook their heads.

Julie nodded. "Let's go. Ray?"

Collins shuffled forward and retrieved a small pair of wire cutters from one of his pockets. He set about clipping a hole in the chain-link fence.

Jericho looked back and forth along the perimeter. The distance between the fence and the buildings wasn't big—no more than ten feet. Enough room to move but not enough to justify patrolling it. He was happy that they wouldn't encounter anyone until they reached their target buildings, at least.

Collins worked quickly and quietly, and it only took a couple of minutes to create a hole large enough for them all to shuffle through. Once inside, they drew their weapons and moved single file toward the northeast corner. Jericho took point. Julie was behind him, then Link and Collins brought up the rear.

The walk took a few minutes. They had to occasionally stop while a camera completed its sweep, and moving across a gap between buildings required good timing, but they soon reached the first building they wanted: the offices with the glass penthouse.

"This is us," said Jericho, stopping in a crouch. "The comms tower is just up ahead."

Collins turned back to Link and held out a fist, which he bumped. "Ya ready, big fella?"

Link nodded.

Collins looked at Julie. "Good luck."

She smiled. "You too."

Jericho moved to the corner of the building and peered around. Julie moved close behind him, watching as Collins and Link moved on.

Once they were clear, she touched Jericho's arm gently to get his attention.

"You think they'll be okay?" she asked him.

He took a deep, contemplative breath. "Under any other circumstances, I would've made Ray sit this one out. But there's no one else I'd rather have here."

Julie nodded. "Same. I'm just worried about him."

"Link's there to watch his back. Come on. We have our own shit to worry about."

Julie refocused, subconsciously adjusting her grip on her weapon. "What are we looking at?"

Jericho glanced around the corner again. The gap between buildings was narrow. There was a door in the side of the office tower. Ahead, he could see the expanse of the courtyard, already teeming with activity.

"Side entrance, maybe twelve away," he said. "It's busy out there. No time to pick a lock if it's not open."

Julie's lips twisted with concern. "What do you think?"

Jericho shrugged. "No other way inside. Only other option is to wait until—hold up…"

The side door swung open, and a man dressed in janitor's coveralls stepped out. He paused to turn his collar up against the early chill, then rummaged in his pockets for a cigarette. He trapped it between his lips, then held a lighter to it with cupped hands. Once lit, he took a long drag, gazed to the sky, and blew out the smoke with a long breath.

Looks like he was on a long night shift, thought Jericho.

He reached behind him with one hand and gestured to Julie, telling her there was one hostile approaching and to hold her position.

The door was left open. Which way was the janitor going to walk?

The man paced back and forth, then turned his back on the base and headed for the perimeter fence.

Jericho held his breath. The man was six or seven steps away. If he looked to his right, he would stare straight at them.

Quietly, Jericho holstered his *Negotiator*, trying to keep his movements to a minimum, to reduce the risk of being seen in the janitor's periphery. He watched the janitor's movements, tracking his steps, calculating the distance between them and how quickly he would need to move to disable him.

He held his breath.

The janitor reached the end of the small alley, drawing level with the edges of the buildings.

He took another long, satisfying drag on his cigarette, once again staring up at the dawn sky. He was older. Thin hair and thick stubble covered his head. He had a hand in his pocket.

Jericho lunged forward, springing up and reaching with both hands. The janitor turned, but he saw him far too late. Jericho clamped one giant hand over the janitor's mouth. The other wrapped around his throat. Pulling him close, he spun them both around with a swiftness and grace not befitting a man of his size. He whisked them both back out of sight, behind the opposite building. Jericho was positioned behind the janitor. He quickly adjusted his arms, hooking one under the jaw and around the throat, and the other around the back of the head. He pulled him close as he puffed out his chest. The choke took less than five seconds to send the janitor unconscious.

Jericho lowered him to the ground gently, lying him as

close to the building as he could. Then he stepped to the edge and peered around. The door was still open. There was no sign of any movement. He glanced across at Julie and nodded.

She nodded back and quickly stepped out from behind cover. Jericho followed her inside and closed the door gently behind him.

They were standing in a small maintenance corridor. The concrete floor was bare and patchy with damp. Julie moved ahead, checking corners for security cameras as she approached another door. Jericho was behind, making sure no one tried coming in after them.

"Jericho, check this out," hissed Julie.

He caught up to her and stared at a small, plastic sign stuck to the cinderblock wall beside the door.

"Looks like a map of the building," she said. "Mapping out fire exits."

He studied it closely. It showed ten floors. The top one was listed as an observatory. The first few had generic labels, such as accounting and personnel. His eyes settled on the eighth floor, which he tapped with a finger.

"Accommodation," he said. "If Hall's been staying here since the rebellion, he'll be there, right?"

Julie nodded. "I think it's a safe assumption, yeah. We just need to make it up eight flights of stairs without being seen."

"We should stick to the emergency stairwell. The central one will have more foot traffic. We take out anyone we see quietly and leave them there. Less chance of them being found."

Julie raised an eyebrow. "Still a fairly strong chance, though."

Jericho shrugged. "We only need to stay hidden until the

reinforcements arrive and cause chaos at the main gate. It'll be fine."

"Okay." She tapped a spot on the map. "This looks like the maintenance stairwell here. Let's go."

She edged her way out through the door, checking left and right. There were no signs of life. She saw one camera high up on the left, but from the angle, it was unlikely it could see that far along. She headed right, with Jericho close behind. The corridor was short, with two doors on either side of a dead end. The right door was a storage room, labeled as such. The left had a picture of stairs on it. She pushed the door open gently and moved to the center of the wide stairwell, looking up through the gap at the floors above.

Still no sign of life.

"Come on," she called back quietly.

Their footfalls made a dull echo in the hollow, square column as they climbed, two steps at a time. As they reached the third floor, the door opened in front of them, swinging inward and partially blocking their path to the fourth. Julie skidded to a halt. A man stood in the doorway, dressed all in black. A visible weapon was strapped to his thigh. He stared into Julie's eyes, his mouth open with shock and confusion.

He hesitated, but Julie didn't.

She rushed forward and slammed her *Negotiator* into the side of his head, then stepped away. The impact stunned him and sent him flying into the door. As he rebounded off it, Jericho moved past Julie and grabbed him with a steady hand, planting a forearm into his temple. Julie quickly closed the door. Jericho guided the unconscious guard into the opposite corner and dumped him. The body was out of sight of anyone looking down the stairwell, and it would be temporarily blocked from view by anyone opening the door.

They looked at each other and sighed.

"So far, so good, right?" asked Jericho.

Julie raised an eyebrow. "If you say so…"

They pressed on, making it to the eighth floor without further interruption. Julie paused at the door, looked back at Jericho, then nodded to his weapon.

"Suppressors," she said. "Just in case."

He nodded, and the two of them took a moment to screw their silencing attachments into place. Their weapons were unique, and the suppressor only worked so long as they fired regular rounds. As tempting as it may have been, it wasn't the time for explosive-tipped bullets.

Julie turned the handle slowly and opened the door an inch. She peered through the gap, staring ahead to the left of the door. There were no signs of movement. She opened it further and peeked her head around the corner to look right.

The whole floor resembled a hotel. The carpet looked brand-new and clean. The walls were cream with a walnut trim. Numbered doors lined the wall in front of her, spaced generously, suggesting large rooms or apartments within.

At the end of the corridor, up a few steps, was a large door with two armed guards outside it. There was no number visible.

Julie ducked back into the stairwell and looked back at Jericho.

"Room at the end," she whispered. "Two guards posted outside. That's gotta be it."

He nodded. "What's the approach?"

She shook her head. "There isn't one. It's a straight run

to the door from here. No cover. No way to reach them unseen."

"How far?"

"From here to there?" She shrugged. "Maybe thirty feet."

"We're both pretty good shots…"

Julie thought about it. The gunshots, no matter how suppressed, would likely attract attention. It would leave two bodies and a fair amount of blood. Assuming Hall was even in there, it would make getting out again even more difficult. However, she was unable to come up with a better plan in that moment.

She shrugged and nodded. Jericho moved to her side.

"I'll move across, take out the guy on the left," he said. "You take the one on the right."

"Works for me," said Julie.

"Ready?"

"On three."

He paused and smiled at her. "Be honest… would you really choose this over the boardroom?"

She looked him in the eyes and nodded. "Every goddamn time."

He winked at her. "Three."

They stepped out in unison, aimed their weapons, and fired at the two guards with fluid movement and synchronicity.

The muted whispers still sounded like thunderclaps in the deserted hallway. Both shots found their mark. The Tristar guards dropped like stones, leaving light sprays of blood on the wall behind them.

Jericho and Julie rushed forward, not waiting to see if they had been heard. They cleared the three steps with a single leap and took up position on either side of the door.

Julie's hand moved to the handle. There was no sign of a lock or swipe card entry system. It was just a door. Even if it was locked from the inside, she knew Jericho could kick it clean off its hinges if needed.

They exchanged a nod, holding their weapons low and ready. Julie tried the handle. It turned. The door wasn't locked.

Jericho counted silently, mouthing the numbers. On three, Julie burst through the door. She dropped to one knee and aimed into the room. Jericho followed, remaining upright, covering her.

The room was exquisite and spacious. Wide open, save for the bathroom in the far-right corner. A minimalistic office area stood central, with a barren desk standing in front of a large, wide window that overlooked the compound. There was a chair behind it and a closed laptop resting on its surface.

Away to the left was a king-sized bed on a raised platform, with red silk sheets draped over it. The wall behind it was adorned with artwork. Standing in front of it, putting an earring in, was a woman. She was bare-footed, wearing a suit dress and a loose-fitting white blouse that was only half-fastened. She looked back over her shoulder at the disturbance, frozen with surprise.

Julie stood and relaxed, lowering her gun. Jericho shut the door behind them and lingered there.

The woman slowly turned to face them, abandoning the effort to put her earring in. She toyed with it in her hand as she looked at each of them in turn. Then she smiled.

"Let me guess..." she said calmly. "Julie Fisher and Jericho Stone, right?"

Julie narrowed her gaze. "And you are?"

The woman approached her and extended a hand.

"Gwen Parker. Director of Operations at Tristar Security. And you two are trespassing."

Julie ignored the offer of a handshake, instead leveling her weapon at Parker's chest. "So, call the cops. What are you doing here?"

"Well..." She made a show of glancing at her watch. "I was going to get some breakfast before starting work, but I guess that's off the table now."

"Good guess."

Parker looked over at Jericho, who hadn't moved. "I expected you to look worse, given what those assets did to you. Impressive." She looked him up and down exaggeratedly. "*Very* impressive."

Julie huffed impatiently. "I was expecting more from you. You look... irrelevant."

Parker grinned. "You wish."

"I don't have the time or the patience for this. Where's the soul drive?"

"The what?"

Julie held her gaze. "Where's Hall?"

Parker shrugged. "No idea. Thankfully, not here."

"Thankfully?"

"Brilliant though he may be, that man is a cretinous, horrible creature. Makes my goddamn skin crawl."

Julie flicked her eyebrows with agreement. "Well, no arguments there. Here's where we're at, Gwen. My team is on-site right now, working to disable the launch of that rocket. In about thirty minutes, this entire compound will be swarming with GlobaTech troops. It's over. We want Hall, and we want the drive back that he stole from us."

Parker ignored her. "Tell me, Julie, as one female CEO leader to another... aren't you tired of constantly fighting uphill? Struggling against the odds to see even an ounce of success?"

Julie shook her head. "It's not a struggle. I'm really good at what I do."

"Right. You're on the wrong side of this, you know. You're too late to stop Orion. Your men won't make it through the front gate. If you step down now, maybe we can find a place for you. I'm sure we would work well together."

Julie glared at her, setting her jaw as she tightened her grip on the gun.

Parker grinned. "Of course, there will have to be some sacrifices. Not everyone is as valuable as you, after all."

Jericho stepped forward, letting out a long sigh. "Quit stalling. Your guards outside are dead. No one's coming to save you. Tell us what we want to know, and maybe we'll just turn you over to the FBI when this is all over."

Parker looked over at him. "Oh, how generous of you. But tell me, Mr. Stone... what makes you think I need to be saved?"

She tossed the earring at Julie, who instinctively swatted it away. In that moment of distraction, Parker charged her, delivering a flurry of well-placed punches before Julie even realized what was happening.

Her gun was knocked from her grip in the melee. She recovered long enough to step back into a fighting stance, bringing up both arms in a tight guard. Parker continued the assault, connecting with almost every strike she threw.

Julie staggered to the side under the impact of a kick that caught her in the gut. Sensing the follow-up, she ducked under Parker's incoming punch, rolling toward her and swinging a right hook to the body. The blow landed, and Parker grunted as the air was pushed from her lungs.

She toppled back against the step leading up to the bed but retained her balance.

Julie moved forward with renewed focus, pressing the attack. She threw a couple of combinations, varying the punches between head and body shots. Parker weaved like a boxer, deflecting or avoiding nearly all of them. She then countered with a stiff straight right of her own, which caught Julie flush on her chin.

The shot dazed her, forcing her to stumble backward. Parker seized the opportunity, thrusting her leg out and burying her foot deep into Julie's stomach. Winded, Julie dropped to one knee, doubling over and leaving her head exposed. Parker wound up to deliver an elbow that would undoubtedly knock her out. But she never got the chance.

Jericho stepped forward, aiming his gun at Parker. "Don't do it."

Parker froze and looked over at him. He could see her analyzing him with her eyes, watching his body language, trying to determine if he would shoot her.

She lowered her arm and walked away from Julie, padding barefoot across the polished, wooden floor to confront him. She stopped a few feet away and stared up. The height difference was significant.

"You won't shoot me," she said confidently.

Jericho's mouth curled in a subtle smile. "Yeah? And why's that?"

"Because you don't know how useful I can be to you. I'm your best bet of getting out of here alive."

He holstered his gun and stared at her. "Perhaps you're right."

"Then again... maybe I'll kill your girlfriend back there. Force you to give up and leave."

Jericho's body twitched.

Parker smirked. "What's the matter? Too afraid to hit a woman?"

"No."

"Hmm. Let's see, shall we?"

She feinted left, then moved right, closing the gap between them, and threw a left haymaker. She swung from the hip, aiming right for Jericho's throat.

With the slightest of movements, he caught her hand in one of his giant fists. The dull slap of her knuckles against his palm reverberated around the apartment. He didn't register the impact. Gwen's eyes bulged in their sockets. She tugged at her hand to break free, but Jericho tightened his grip and held her in place.

"It's not that I'm reluctant to hit you," he said quietly. "I'm simply trying to work out exactly how useful you can still be to me."

"Very," she replied. Her voice quaked with fear. "Let me go and we can talk."

Jericho frowned. "But... you already said you don't know where Hall or our soul drive is."

"Yes, but—"

"But that's all I want to know. So, how can you help me?"

Parker swallowed hard. Panic was setting in, and she was struggling to hide it. Her legs trembled. Her hand was cramping in Jericho's vise-like grip. A thin film of sweat made her brow glisten. She thought quickly, desperate to buy herself some time.

"What about the rocket?" she offered. "Don't you want to know what it's for, or how we built it?"

Jericho shrugged. "You built it using propulsion technology Tristar stole from GlobaTech in Cambodia two years ago. You're going to use the rocket to mine an asteroid that's worth more money than I can pronounce."

Her eyes grew even wider. "How did you…"

"We're GlobaTech. We're really good at what we do. Like Julie told you—it's over. This place is going to be shut down within the hour. Either help us now, or face the same consequences as everyone else."

Parker shook her head defiantly as she continued to pull against his grip. Eventually, he relented and let go. She stumbled backward, then unleashed a gut-wrenching scream and charged toward him, hands raised. As she reached him and swung for his face, Jericho side-stepped and drove his fist into her head as hard as he could.

Her grunt was cut short by a loud crack. She stopped immediately in her tracks and fell to the floor, landing awkwardly. Her jaw was completely dislocated, one of her cheeks had caved in, and her head was turned a full one-eighty degrees. Her eyes were wide and lifeless, forever frozen in the shock that consumed her final seconds.

Jericho stared down at her impassively for a moment, then moved over to Julie. He helped her to her feet and clamped a hand on her shoulder to steady her as she recuperated.

"You okay?" he asked her.

She nodded. "Yeah. For a director, that woman can sure pack a punch. Where is she?"

Jericho nodded behind her. "Over there."

Julie turned and saw Parker's body.

"Holy shit!" she yelled as her mouth fell open with shock. She looked at Jericho. "What the hell did you do to her?"

He shrugged. "She charged me. I defended myself."

"Yeah, but… Jesus… how many times did you hit her?"

"Just once."

Julie shook her head with disbelief and looked back at Parker's mangled body.

"My hand's a little sore," said Jericho, "if that helps?"

She stared up at him with wide eyes but said nothing.

He flexed his hand. "She didn't know anything that could help us, anyway. It's her own fault. We should go. We have a lot of ground still to cover, and our element of surprise isn't likely to last much longer."

Julie nodded slowly, unable to tear her gaze from the disfigured corpse on the floor in front of her. "Right…"

Jericho scooped up her gun and handed it to her, then headed for the door. She followed a moment later. However, before they could reach it, it burst open. Jericho froze. Julie leveled with him. They both stared as two Nemesis assets and a group of five Tristar guards filed into the room and spread out before them. All were armed and aiming guns at them.

One of the assets casually glanced past them and stared at Parker's body, then raised an eyebrow at Jericho.

He ignored him and looked at Julie. "See?"

Chapter Thirty

Collins and Link reached the comms tower without issue. The entrance faced the compound's expansive courtyard, but the discarded crates surrounding its circular base provided enough cover to get inside unseen.

The layout inside wasn't what either of them had expected. Most of the floors were used for storage. Each level was spacious, filled with racks of large shelving, which held wooden crates and cardboard boxes. They were linked by a wide, winding staircase attached to the outer wall. Every ten or fifteen feet was a flat walkway, which flowed into the access point of a floor. In the center of the column was a bank of elevators—four in total, one on each compass point.

Pressed against the outer wall, Collins and Link moved quickly up the stairs. They had seen a few people on each floor as they passed, but they were always far enough away that they remained undetected.

"This place is bloody weird," observed Collins.

"I imagine it's busier during the day," replied Link. "Shouldn't be much farther now."

"Good. My calves are killing me."

Link was in front. He glanced back at Collins and frowned. "How are you this unfit?"

Collins looked up at him. "I got the shit kicked outta me not so long ago, remember? Tends to affect your cardio."

"Oh, yeah. Sorry. Well…" He increased his pace, taking the steps three at a time. "…try to keep up."

Collins watched with dismay as Link peeled away from him. "Oh, piss off."

They continued and eventually reached the top level. It resembled a boiler room. Exposed piping and HVAC units lined the ceiling. The bare concrete was cracked and stained. The area was a hollow square, and in the middle was a staircase carved into a solid concrete block. Both men completed a circuit of the area in opposite directions, reconvening at the foot of the stairs, resting against the wall on either side of them.

"I'm guessing we go up," said Collins.

"You mean like we've been doing this whole time?" replied Link with a raised eyebrow.

"All right, no need for sarcasm."

Collins peered around the corner and looked up the stairs. Link stared back at where they came from, aiming his rifle in the direction of the spiral staircase, covering their backs.

"What do you see?" he asked.

Collins moved back and looked over at him. "Not much from down here. As far as I can tell, it's like a control tower at an airport. The stairs lead up through the floor. Computers and whatnot all around. I saw at least three people moving around up there. They were dressed like nerds, so I'm not sure if there are any guards."

Link nodded. "And you're feeling okay? You're up for this?"

"Aye. I'm fine. Let's just get this done, so we can all go home, eh?"

Link moved around the corner and headed up the stairs. The second his head breached floor-level, he quickly looked all around him. Collins was right—it looked exactly like an air traffic control tower. Thick, dirty windows offered a three-sixty view of the compound and mountains. Beneath them were banks of computers and consoles and screens. There were six men moving around, wearing white lab coats. No sign of any weapons.

Link hustled into the room. "All right, nobody move!"

The six guys froze with shock. Their eyes were collectively drawn to his assault rifle. One of the lab coats at the back took a small step to the side and began to reach for the console next to him.

"Hey!" hissed Link. "You press anything, I'll blow your goddamn head off. Understand me?"

The color drained from the man's face as he slowly withdrew his hand.

Another man, who was standing next to the staircase, suddenly bolted, jumping down the small ledge to land a few steps down. But he ran straight into the barrel of Collins's *Negotiator*.

Collins tilted his head to the side, looking past the weapon, and narrowed his eyes. "Are ya deaf, buddy? He literally just said don't move. Up ya go."

He walked the lab coat back up into the control room, then moved to the left.

"I want all of you in the corner opposite me," instructed

Link. "Hands behind your head, fingers interlocked. I won't tell you twice."

The men did, huddling together, sharing looks of fear and confusion.

Link pointed to the guy who had tried running. "You. Come over here."

Reluctantly, the man obeyed. The man walked across the room, past the opening to the stairs, and over toward Link. Once he was close enough, Link smashed the butt of his rifle into the man's jaw. The man fell backward, sprawled out unconscious on the floor.

"That's what happens if you try to run," said Link calmly. "You stay still and quiet, and you all get to go home to your families when this is over. You don't... I start collecting kneecaps. Any questions?"

Each man shook his head enthusiastically.

Link nodded at Collins. "Get to work."

Collins smiled. "Nice."

He then turned to face the bank of consoles in front of him, scanning each one until he identified the one controlling the huge radar dish mounted on the roof of the tower. Once he had, he began entering the frequency and reconfiguring the broadcast range.

Link kept his eyes locked on the group of lab coats. His rifle was leveled steadily at them. His breathing was measured and calm.

So far, so good, he thought. *I hope the others are having as easy a time.*

Minutes ticked by. The only sound in the room was the tapping of keys as Collins worked, occasionally accompanied by the rattle of the air conditioning.

Link became anxious.

"Hey, what's taking so long?" he called over.

Collins shook his head. "I don't know. The system won't let me synchronize to the trigger. The frequency's keyed in, but there's no way to broadcast it."

One of the lab coats tentatively raised a hand.

"Um... wh-what exactly are you trying t-to do?" he asked weakly.

Collins looked back at him. "I want to broadcast a signal that will be transmitted remotely, but it isn't recognizing the trigger frequency."

The man went to say something, but one of his colleagues tugged his coat urgently in protest.

"Hey," said Link, noticing. "Come here."

The man looked back at his colleague apologetically, then walked toward Link. He stepped over the unconscious body and stood in front of him.

"P-please don't hit me," he stammered.

Link rolled his eyes. "I won't if you can help. What's your name?"

"Harry."

"Okay, Harry. Do you know why my friend can't do what he's trying to do?"

He nodded. "I think so, yeah."

Link gestured with the rifle. "Then go and help him."

Collins side-stepped as Harry moved next to him.

"What's wrong with this thing?" asked Collins.

Harry took a deep breath. His hands were shaking. "The system isn't designed to track external signals. It was built to broadcast purely from this location. You need to reconfigure part of the operating system, so it will recognize the... the trigger you have."

"Can ya do it?"

"Maybe, yeah."

"Well, chop, chop, ya goofy bastard. Time's a-wasting."

"Do you have the frequency you want to send?"

"Aye. That's already keyed in. The range is locked to a thousand feet. It can't be any more than that."

Harry frowned. "Why? What signal are you sending?"

"Mind ya business. Just do what I'm telling ya." Collins placed the barrel of his gun against the side of Harry's head. "And if ya try anything smart, I'll turn ya noodle into pâté. We clear?"

Beads of sweat formed instantly on Harry's forehead. He swallowed hard and nodded, then set to work. Collins watched him closely.

Another couple of minutes ticked by.

"Ray, what's happening over there?" asked Link.

Collins sighed and used his gun to tap Harry on his shoulder. "Tick-tock, Harry. What's taking so—"

The piercing wail of an alarm siren burst into life. Red lights affixed high up on the walls began to flash.

Collins's eyes went wide. "What in the deep-fried hell did ya do?"

Harry held his hands up. "N-nothing, I swear! The system, it—"

Collins slammed his gun in the side of Harry's head, knocking him out. "Aye, well, *that's* bullshit."

He shoved Harry's body away from the computer with his foot, then moved in front of the console once more.

"Ray, shut that damn thing off!" barked Link.

"What do ya think I'm trying to do?" shouted Collins. "Order an Uber?"

He worked quickly, grunting with frustration each time he hit a dead end. Eventually, he slammed his fist down on the console.

"Bollocks!" he shouted.

"What?" asked Link.

Collins turned to him. "The system's locked me out. I can't configure it."

"What does that mean?"

"It means we're boned, all right?"

"So, now what?"

Collins tensed his jaw and stared blankly at the floor, playing out the consequences of the setback over in his mind, searching for another way to do what they wanted to do. But there wasn't one.

He sighed. "Now, I gotta make a really shitty phone call."

He took out a cell phone and hit one of the speed dial buttons, then pressed the phone to his ear. A moment later, it was answered.

"I'm guessing that alarm isn't a good sign?" asked Jay.

Collins put a finger in his other ear and squinted against the background noise. "Ah... no. Listen, I can't boost the signal. The system locked me out. The trigger you have is all we've got. That means we only have twenty feet to play with."

Jay sighed heavily down the line. "Yeah, I know what that means."

The call ended.

Collins looked back around at Link. "Well, this sucks."

Suddenly, gunfire erupted below them. Bullets sparked and pinged off the metal flooring and staircase around them. Collins had enough time to see several Tristar guards filing into the holding area just below them before he dove away.

"Look out!" yelled Link.

He leaned out and returned fire, shooting blindly down the stairs, forcing the new arrivals to step back and find cover.

"We're pinned down!" he shouted.

The remaining lab coats dropped to their knees, using their arms to shield their heads.

Link fired another short burst, just enough to deter the guards from rushing them.

"Ray, we need a plan," he called over.

There was no reply.

"Ray?"

He looked across the circular room. Collins was sitting on the floor, hugging his knees, squashed as far as he could fit underneath one of the desks. His eyes were wide. His gaze distant. His lips were moving silently, and he was rocking gently from side to side.

Link sighed, momentarily closing his eyes as his shoulders slumped forward with involuntary resignation.

"Ah, shit…"

Chapter Thirty-One

Despite the early sun shining into her eyes, Ruby shivered as she crouched, resting against the cold rocks on the outskirts of the compound. Her legs ached with the onset of cramp.

The alarm had burst into life moments earlier, and despite being muted slightly by distance, its wail still carried on the wind, enveloping the world around them.

She looked up at Jay, who was staring at the cell phone in her hand.

"Was that Ray?" asked Ruby.

Jay nodded absently. "Yeah."

Ruby frowned and got to her feet. "What is it? What's wrong?"

Jay turned to face her and let out a resigned sigh. "The system tripped the alarm and locked them out. He wasn't able to link the trigger's frequency, which means the EMP can't be transmitted."

She stared at the small disc in her hand, tossing it gently up and down, lost in thought.

Ruby looked at it too. She swallowed hard, her lips pursed together. They both knew what this meant.

"How do you want to play this?" she asked finally.

Jay looked away to her left, down the slight angle, across roughly a hundred and fifty feet of dust and desert, toward the compound's main gate. Even from their vantage point, the chaos was clear. Dozens of pockets of black shapes moved quickly back and forth. Red lights blinked with urgency on the sides of buildings. She thought about Julie and Jericho. About Ray and Link. She wondered if they were okay, or if they were already dead.

She let out a long sigh, then turned back to Ruby. "I'm gonna go cause a ruckus."

Ruby stared at her with something akin to admiration. They both knew the range of that device. They both knew there was a significant chance of Jay suffering permanent mental injury or death if she pressed it. Yet, she was prepared to run head-first into the belly of the beast and cause as much carnage as she could anyway.

Ruby flashed a half-smile. "That's exactly what Adrian would've done."

Jay nodded, returning the smile. She drew her handgun, checked the magazine, and racked the slide to chamber a round. She held it up next to her face, admiring it for a moment. Then she looked into Ruby's sparkling green eyes and arched a brow.

"You coming?" she asked seductively.

Ruby reached inside her thick jacket and grabbed one of Adrian's Raptors, which were both holstered under her arms by a shoulder strap. She could barely bring herself to look at the weapon as she prepped it, the way Jay had done seconds before.

She took a deep, hesitant breath, then smiled. "No. It's how I'm stood."

Jay slid the EMP device into her pocket, then the two women set off running. They quickly scrambled down the shallow slope of the rock face and headed for the main gate.

The banshee cry of the alarm grew louder with each stride. As they closed the gap, they could see the men stationed on either side of the barrier that blocked the road leading into the compound. There were two of them. Both dressed in black, both standing with their backs to the world, looking with uncertain fascination at the base, likely trying to figure out what was happening. Beyond them, more and more Tristar mercenaries were appearing from the buildings, flooding the courtyard.

Ruby peeled away slightly, moving around in a sweeping arc to come up directly behind her target. Jay ran straight for her guy, like an arrow cutting through the air with deadly intent. With instinctive synchronicity, they took aim and fired once. Both guards dropped like stones, chunks of their heads unceremoniously removed.

Neither woman broke their step, and they burst through the gate.

Ruby quickly scanned their immediate vicinity. Dozens of Tristar guards rushed around them, but they all seemed to be heading for the far end of the compound, paying little-to-no attention to their presence. She looked ahead. The communications tower loomed over the northeast corner. Link and Collins were inside, likely pinned at the top.

Did Tristar know Julie and Jericho were also there? Chances are, if they didn't already, they soon would. Ruby glanced to her left. Jay was already taking aim at the next group of enemies in front of her. Past her, away to the left, was the vehicle pool. Beyond that, the dirt road led out to the west, toward the rocket.

Her gaze was momentarily dragged toward the rocket. The huge feat of engineering looming over her was intimidating. Even from a quarter-mile away, she still felt like a goldfish staring down a blue whale.

Gunfire pulled her from her musings. She slid to a halt on the gravel, kicking up small clouds of dust around her feet. Jay was shooting, sending an unprepared group of Tristar guards scattering for cover.

There was movement on her right. Ruby snapped her head around to see another group heading toward her. Four men. No... five. All were armed and preparing to fire. She reacted on instinct, squeezing off a handful of rounds as she darted away to seek cover behind the Humvees parked haphazardly to the left of the entrance. Three men dropped as if they had suddenly run into a stone wall.

Ruby reloaded as she ran. She slid to a crouched stop behind the hood of the nearest vehicle. As she looked around it and took aim once more at her remaining pursuers, she saw Jay in her periphery. She had dropped her group and was already moving onto the next one. She was a force of nature. Ruby caught herself transfixed for a moment, wondering how the killing machine in front of her could ever have lived a normal life of suburban, domesticated bliss with Adrian...

More movement distracted her.

There was another group approaching Jay. They were directly behind her. No way she had seen them.

"Shit..." hissed Ruby to herself.

She went to stand but found herself hesitating, as if her feet were buried in concrete. She had cover. She was protected. She could help from here, right? She could take out a few guys and buy Jay the time she needed. The two of them could hold this position and wait for reinforcements. An entire company of GlobaTech operatives was speeding toward their location right now. It wouldn't be long. She would be fine where she was. She would be safe.

Ruby closed her eyes.

No. She wouldn't be fine. None of them would if they didn't stop Hall.

That's all that mattered.

She gritted her teeth, clamping her mouth shut until her jaw ached. She glared at the air in front of her, allowing an impossible rage to consume her. Then she stepped out and fired twice, taking out the last two Tristar guys who were chasing her.

"Jay, behind you!" she called out.

She began firing at the new arrivals. Jay dropped to one knee and turned. She got a couple of shots off before having to roll backward out of the firing line. The two of them regrouped and stood shoulder to shoulder, firing as they walked slowly backward. More and more Tristar guards were heading for them, approaching from seemingly every direction, closing them down and pinning them into the corner with only the vehicles for cover.

Jay looked around at the wide, spaced-out semicircle of black outfits surrounding them.

"Well, this is going well…" she said.

Ruby quickly reloaded again. "How are you doing for ammo?"

"I'm trying not to think about it."

"Yeah… I'm running out too. We need to find a way to—"

"Look!" shouted Jay, cutting her off.

A gap had formed in the middle. One by one, the

Tristar guards stopped shooting. The ones on the edges of the semicircle began to peel away, joining their colleagues as they sprinted to the far side of the compound. Those who remained were looking behind them.

A man appeared between them, walking calmly into the middle of the battlefield. He was dressed in slate-gray fatigues, with a black bulletproof vest fastened over them. The eagle tattoo on his neck protruded from beneath the collar.

Adam Rayne.

Jay snapped her aim onto him, ignoring everyone else. Ruby didn't. Her body relaxed involuntarily. Holding her gun by her side, she took a step forward, hypnotized by the sight of her former colleague. By the sight of the man who killed Adrian.

"Ruby!" hissed Jay. "Focus! That isn't him. You understand?"

Rayne had stopped roughly twenty feet away. He looked back and forth between the two women, then smiled. "It's over. Your friends are likely already dead. Both of you are coming with me." He focused on Ruby. "I know Mr. Hall will want to talk to you." Then he turned to Jay. "And you... I understand Mr. Hall made you a promise."

He took a small step to the side. More people appeared through the gap, filing through in a tight line. Eight men. Nine. Ten. They kept coming, perhaps twenty in total. All dressed similar to Rayne. All with visible tattoos.

All Nemesis assets.

Rayne grinned as the new arrivals fanned out around him. "Time to see just how defective you are."

"What's he talking about?" asked Ruby. "What promise?"

"It doesn't matter. I'm not going with them." She looked

at Ruby. "Understand? I'm not going back. You can't let them take me alive. If that's what it comes down to, you don't let them take me. Do you hear me?"

Ruby searched Jay's eyes and saw only resignation.

"What do we do?" she asked. "It's like Hall sent every asset he has! There are too many of them."

Jay shook her head. "No. This is perfect."

She glanced down at her pocket. Ruby understood.

"Twenty feet, right?" she said.

Jay nodded, then looked back over at Rayne. "I'll show you defective, you sonofabitch. Me and you. No weapons. Let's finish this."

Rayne burst out laughing, then holstered his gun. "I'll take you both out."

He turned his back on them and looked around, following the line of Tristar guards. There were fifteen of them stood watching.

"Mr. Hall will want these two alive," he said. "So, I'll show you what we do with traitors and rebels. Watch and learn."

He looked back at Jay and Ruby. He held out a hand and beckoned them toward him with his fingers. "Come on. I always wanted two women at once."

Jay tossed her gun aside and rushed toward him. Ruby tucked her Raptor behind her and followed. Rayne stepped to meet them. He threw a combination of strong punches, which Jay was able to either dodge or block. She countered with a couple of her own. One landed, but if it did anything, Rayne didn't show it.

Ruby circled to his right and swung a stiff hook at his body. He dropped his left arm to parry the shot, then countered by slashing the back of his hand quickly across her face. It caught her flush, and she stumbled away. The

Raptor flew from her back as she landed, sliding out of reach.

He delivered the same shot to Jay, mirroring the movement with his right. She leaned back to avoid it, but in doing so, left her body exposed. Rayne stepped through and thrust his leg into her gut. She creased over and fell, rolling back a few feet but coming to a stop on one knee.

Rayne paced back and forth, grinning with confidence and menace. Then he walked away casually, dismissing them as any kind of threat. He rolled his shoulders and cracked his neck, as if he was simply warming up.

Jay glared at him, snarling with frustration as she held her stomach and caught her breath. He was fast and strong. She glanced over at Ruby, who had landed a couple of feet to her right. She knew they needed to coordinate their attack if they were going to beat him. If they could—

She frowned. Ruby was lying on her side, her arms up, protecting her head, with her knees brought up to protect her body. She had seen the shot that caught her. It didn't look that bad...

"Hey," she said. "Get it together, will you?"

Ruby unfurled herself and stared at Jay. "He clipped me pretty good, that's all. I'm fine."

"No, he didn't. Christ, what is wrong with you? Do you not understand what happens if we lose? We need to work together to take him down. Now, I know you're tougher than this, so get your goddamn head in the game."

Ruby looked at the ground and nodded slowly, as if ashamed. "I know. He caught me off-guard, okay? I'm fine."

Jay shook her head with disbelief as she watched her sit upright. "I hope so. Jesus, Ruby. The way you dropped and went all crash position, you'd think you were scared, or..."

Her eyes went wide. Ruby looked over at her, meeting her gaze. She swallowed her fear and took a deep breath.

Jay's mouth fell open. "Holy shit. You're—"

"Look out!" shouted Ruby, pointing behind her.

Jay turned a split-second too late and was met with a stiff knee to the side of her face. Ruby scurried backward as Rayne reached down and grabbed Jay's throat. He hauled her upright and buried four punches into her stomach and ribs. Jay winced as she felt something break under the last one. He tossed her aside, sending her rolling away on the cold, unforgiving ground.

Rayne lashed out with a kick like he was punting a field goal, and it connected with Jay's face. She grunted and rolled away a few more feet, coming to rest on her front. She spat a thick globule of blood onto the sand next to her face. Her vision lost focus, and her head rang like a church bell.

He stared down at her, smirking with disdain. Then he turned and locked eyes with Ruby. A menacing grin crept across his face. He reached slowly for his gun and took aim as he stalked toward her.

With her arms outstretched behind her, Ruby kicked out with her legs, desperately trying to gain some traction on the ground and shuffle some more distance between them. Rayne stared down the barrel and into her eyes.

"You're the one who held the assassin in her arms as he died, aren't you?" he observed. "You cried as he bled out. It was touching. Well, you're about to be reunited."

Ruby's eyes immediately filled with tears. She looked at the face of the man she fought beside for so long and saw a stranger looking back at her.

"Adam, p-please," she said. "Don't do this. This isn't you. I know you. You would *never* have betrayed Adrian willingly. I understand, okay? It'll be okay. Just stop this. Please."

Rayne's finger slid inside the trigger guard.

"The briefing said you were dangerous," he said. "That you were a deadly assassin and should be treated as a serious threat." He paused, then shook his head. "I don't see it. You're nothing. It's embarrassing, really. At least *she* has an excuse. But you... I guess I expected more."

"Adam, please! Don't do this!"

He took a step forward. "Any last words?"

Tears flowed freely down her face, warming her cheeks. Ruby sobbed, struggling to remember a time when she felt more afraid.

"Please." She looked him in the eye and took a deep, quivering breath. "Please, Adam. Don't. I'm—"

A gunshot rang out, making her twitch with surprise. Rayne sank to his knees. His eyes were still locked onto hers. She stared as blood trickled from the fresh hole between them. Then he fell forward, landing awkwardly on the ground in front of her, his head resting between her feet. Ruby looked up to see Jay standing there, still holding the Raptor out in front of her. A whisper of smoke danced from its barrel.

Despite the alarms, a silence seemed to blanket the world around them in the wake of the gunshot. The semi-circle of Tristar guards shifted nervously on the spot, exchanging looks of uncertainty.

Jay ignored them. She didn't worry about the assets behind her. They wouldn't shoot her. Rayne said Hall wanted them alive. She walked over to Ruby and extended a hand. Ruby took it gratefully and was hoisted to her feet. She dusted herself off and looked at Jay.

"Thanks," she said.

Jay held out the Raptor. "Don't mention it."

Ruby nodded and took her gun. Jay then retrieved her own, and the two of them turned to face the compound. The guards weren't moving. The large group of Nemesis assets stared at them, seemingly unsure how to proceed.

Ruby turned to Jay. "I can't tell if your plan worked, or if it just went to shit."

Jay shrugged, subtly tilting her head. "Guess we're about to find out."

Chapter Thirty-Two

Julie and Jericho were frog-marched up two flights of stairs by a Nemesis asset each. Five Tristar guards surrounded them: two in front, three behind. Jericho grimaced as they passed under an alarm. Being a little over six-five, his head was closer to it than most other people, and the loud shrill pierced his eardrums.

The stairs led directly into the observatory on the top level of the building, coming up through the center of the floor. Julie looked around as they stepped up into the room. It was a near-perfect square, with the walls on either side and behind her made entirely of glass. The sound of the alarm seemed quieter now, as if the room was soundproofed.

Directly ahead of her, sitting behind a large desk, was Quincy Hall. He cradled a tumbler in one hand, filled with a dark amber liquid. In the other, a large cigar balanced between two fingers, with thick smoke swirling from the tip.

The two assets yanked them to a stop in front of the

desk, then stepped away to the side, standing casually. The Tristar guards fanned out around the stairwell behind them.

The contempt Julie felt toward the man in front of her was rivaled only by her frustration. After everything *they* had been through... after everything *he* had done... she was finally within six feet of him again, and she was powerless. She may as well have been standing six miles away.

Hall rested back in his chair, smiling. His light gray suit was stretched over his robust frame. His jowls sagged with age and spilled over the lip of his collar. He alternated his gaze between Julie and Jericho, exuding arrogance.

He took a long, satisfying drag of his cigar. "Well. It's so nice to see you again, Miss Fisher. What's it been? Two weeks? And Mr. Stone... you look well, considering."

Julie glared daggers, grinding her teeth and clenching her fists. She willed herself to stay still, resisting the urge to leap over the desk and choke him.

Jericho remained calm. He was watching Hall, studying his demeanor. His body language. His mannerisms. He found himself repeatedly drawn to a memory of Adrian Hell. Something the assassin had once said to him during a rare moment of peace between the two of them.

Antagonize and capitalize.

He smiled to himself. A minute twitch in one corner of his mouth.

Sometimes, you have to do things the wrong way.

Jericho nodded at Hall's hand. "Is that whiskey?"

Hall frowned for a moment, then chuckled. "It is. A twenty-one-year-old Glenfiddich."

"It's, like, eight-thirty in the morning..."

Hall shrugged. "It's always happy hour somewhere, right? Besides, today is a big day. A *glorious* day. A day to celebrate."

He raised his glass and tipped it toward them both, then took a hearty swig. He winced and sucked in a breath through gritted teeth as he swallowed, relishing the burn as the scotch made its way down his throat.

Jericho rolled his eyes. "Right. So, what are we celebrating?"

Hall grinned. "Oh, I think you know perfectly well what's going to happen today."

He nodded. "You're right. I do. I'm not sure you do, though."

"And why's that?"

"Because if you did, you wouldn't be drinking whiskey for breakfast. You'd be praying."

"Is that a fact?" He leaned forward and tilted his head. "You hear that? That alarm blaring across my entire base? That's the sound of whatever plan you had failing miserably. You do understand that, right?"

Jericho narrowed his gaze. "It is? Huh. And here's me thinking I'd won a prize."

Hall laughed. "You're trying to be funny. That's good. A sense of humor always helps in the face of defeat."

"And let me guess: a cigar and a whiskey helps in the face of victory, right?"

Hall leaned back and took another drag of his cigar. "It sure as shit does, boy."

"You should pour us both a glass, then."

Hall frowned. "I'm... I'm sorry—am I missing something here?"

Jericho nodded. "Yes."

Beside him, he saw Julie cast him a glance of confusion, but he ignored it.

"Please, enlighten me," said Hall. "Do you mean the thousands of GlobaTech soldiers marching, flying, and driving across Nevada right now, heading for my little ol' slice of Heaven? Because, if you do, they ain't exactly hard to miss."

Jericho didn't say anything.

Hall shook his head. "No. See, you ain't smart enough to play this game with me, Jericho. Truth be told, neither is your girlfriend." He looked at Julie. "I can't tell you how much I hated your old boss. Best part of being in the White House was killing that black bastard."

Julie lurched forward with venom in her eyes. Jericho quickly shot his arm out in front of her, holding her back. She reluctantly stood down.

Hall chuckled. "Typical woman. Too goddamn emotional. Too quick to react. Yes, I hated Buchanan. But I still respected him. He was a smart man and a worthy adversary." He leaned forward and used his cigar to point at Julie. "But you… you're nothing but a little girl trying to sit at the grown-up table. And let me tell you, Miss Fisher, the only way you would belong at that table is if you were bent over it."

A burst of rage exploded inside Jericho, which he struggled to suppress. Only the subtle movement of the asset beside him taking aim with his gun stopped him from vaulting over the desk.

Hall smiled, happy to have gotten the reaction. "Now, as fun as this has been, I still have a little business to attend to."

He nodded past them, toward the window. They both glanced back to see the rocket standing proudly on its launch pad.

"There she is. The Stargazer. My pride and joy." Hall beamed. "And in just under thirty-five minutes, she's going to climb into the heavens and make me richer than God."

He leaned back and gulped what was left of his whiskey.

He slammed the glass down onto a coaster beside him, took a final drag of his cigar, then stubbed it out in a large, crystal ashtray.

"If you're lucky, your little army might arrive just in time to see it."

Jericho took a deep breath. He wasn't as good at pissing people off as Adrian was—a trait he never thought he would be jealous of. He turned to Julie and stared into her eyes, silently asking if she had any ideas.

She pursed her lips together and swallowed her regret.

She didn't.

Link roared with adrenaline as he emptied another clip down the staircase. Directly across from him, the small group of lab coats huddled together, visibly shaking with fear.

Away to his right, Collins continued to shelter beneath the desk, rocking back and forth, muttering incoherently to himself.

Link began reloading his final magazine. "Ray... you gotta snap out of this, man! I need your help here. You understand? Can you hear me? Ray! Shit!"

He chambered a round and continued firing, picking his shots while trying to stay out of sight of the Tristar guards beneath them.

Collins stared vacantly ahead, fixated on one of the rivets in the metal floor. Each breath he took quivered with fear. The noise around him was unbearable. The wail of the alarm. The cacophony of gunshots. The muted whimpering of the people opposite him.

It was too much.

The chaos was overwhelming his senses. He felt trapped, like he was locked in a box too small to move around in. Darkness was creeping toward him, surrounding him like a prison.

He held his hand up to his face. It was shaking beyond his control. With wide, misty eyes, he looked past it and saw Link, firing down into the stairwell, at the source of all the noise.

Come... on... Ray...

He closed his eyes and slowly pressed the tip of his middle finger against the tip of his thumb. He took a deep breath. And another. But nothing changed.

Get ya head out of ya ass, will ya!

He took a third breath. And a fourth. And a fifth.

And then it hit him. Light and color rushed toward him in his mind, swirling behind his eyes like a tornado. When it settled, the image he saw was crystal-clear. He was sitting in a bar. He had a beer in his hand. He was laughing. Opposite him, Jericho was laughing with him. Between them, Julie had just spat beer out onto the table in front of her as she shared the joke.

He felt his breathing become steadier. He felt his hand shake less and less.

He wanted nothing more than to have a drink with his friends right now. He knew if that was ever going to happen again, he needed to get out of that tower. To do that, he knew he needed to ignore the fear and the panic he was feeling.

Collins opened his eyes. His vision was clear. His breathing was calm. He looked at his finger and thumb and smiled.

"Sonofabitch..."

He clambered to his feet and drew his *Negotiator*, prepping it as he moved to the side of the stairwell across from Link.

Link looked at him. "You good?"

Collins smiled. "Aye. What say we finish this and go home, eh?"

"Sounds good to me. But I'm running out of bullets faster than they're running out of bad guys."

Collins held up his gun. "Allow me."

He leaned forward enough to aim down the stairwell. He fired a single round into the darkness below. A heartbeat later, an explosion rang out, shaking the floor beneath their feet.

Link fell backward. "Holy shit!"

Collins moved to the top of the stairs and looked back at him. "Shall we?"

Link stood and collected himself. "Jesus Christ. Yeah, man. After you."

Collins set off down the stairs. Link followed.

"Run out of things to say?" asked Hall. "Finally accepting the fact that you've lost?"

Jericho shook his head. "We haven't lost yet. You underestimated us once before, asshole."

Hall took a patient breath. "Your reinforcements are miles away. No one's coming to save you, Mr. Stone. My Tristar security force outnumbers you five hundred to one. And we all know you're no match for my assets."

Julie looked at him. "Oh, so you're finally admitting you're still running Tristar? I bet the press would love that."

Hall smiled. "Well, I guess someone has to, now that their CEO is dead. Such a waste. Gwen was one of my favorites. But no matter. To be honest, I'll probably shut Tristar down completely first thing tomorrow morning. I won't need them anymore once I reach that asteroid." He checked his watch. "Just over thirty minutes before I can buy GlobaTech three times over for every man, woman, and child on this planet. We all know you're superior to Tristar anyway. Perhaps I'll just use you to build my own personal army. Or… maybe I'll destroy you too. Tear everything down and start from scratch."

"You won't get the chance," said Jericho.

"Oh, of course, I will."

Slowly, Hall reached inside his suit jacket and took out a small box. It was thin and fit comfortably in the palm of his hand. He held it up between his finger and thumb, as if he were about to reveal a winning poker hand.

"The soul drive," said Julie. "You've had it on you this whole time?"

Hall nodded. "Yes, not that anyone knew that. I made the mistake once before of trusting people with the whole story. But Brandon Crow was proof that didn't work. So, this time around, I didn't tell anyone everything. Not even Gwen. I made her believe I was keeping it in a vault in one of the sublevels." He chuckled to himself. "I even instructed her to send a detachment of Tristar personnel to stand outside it, just to keep up appearances."

Jericho frowned. "Why?"

"Because I didn't trust her not to cave under pressure, should you get a hold of her."

Julie and Jericho exchanged a look of frustration and desperation. They both knew they were in a no-win situation. But the heart and soul of GlobaTech was finally within reach. They had to do something…

"Which reminds me," continued Hall, looking past Julie

at the men guarding the stairwell, "you lot, head down to the vault, get your friends, then take up position outside. I want every man we have pointing their guns at the goddamn entrance. Understand me? Give those GlobaTech bastards a proper welcome when they come rolling over the hill."

Neither Julie nor Jericho looked around, but they heard the movement as the men left the room as instructed. They were alone with Hall and two Nemesis assets.

Still holding the drive, Hall took out a cell phone and began dialing.

"I thought you might like your friend, Mr. Rayne, to join us," he said. "We can watch the launch together before he executes you both."

He placed the phone to his ear and flashed them an arrogant smile.

Once more, Julie looked at Jericho. With just her eyes, she gestured to the asset on her right. Jericho sighed reluctantly and responded with a near-imperceptible shake of his head. He wasn't sure they could take on two assets in a straight up fight, and it wasn't the time to die swinging. Julie's jaw pulsed with frustration.

Jericho hated how helpless he felt right now. Despite the alarm, he had to believe the others were having more success than they were.

Ruby and Jay stood and watched as the Tristar guards surrounding them began backing away, as if acknowledging this was no longer their problem to deal with.

"You think this is everyone?" asked Jay as she moved her hand to her pocket.

Ruby shrugged. "God help us if it isn't."

"There's... what? Twenty assets here?"

"Looks like it."

"I reckon they're maybe twenty feet away." She nodded at the group. "How far would you say the buildings are from them?"

Ruby shook her head. "I don't know. Eighty feet? Ninety, maybe? Why?"

"Because I'd bet my last dollar there are way more than twenty Nemesis assets in this place. If I can get close enough to the buildings, maybe I can take out a few more of them."

"And how do you intend to reach them? In case you hadn't noticed, we're kinda surrounded."

"Yeah, I had spotted that..."

Jay glanced to her left and right. There were six Tristar guards in total. The four to the right were currently standing between them and the entrance to the compound. She then looked at the line of assets in front of them. She tried to motivate herself, to stay positive about what needed to happen next.

It's only fifty feet, she said to herself. *Just get yourself within range of the building, hit the button, and we can all go home. And if it doesn't work, you won't know about it anyway. Win-win.*

"I need you to do me a favor," she said finally.

Ruby turned to her and frowned. "What?"

Inside her pocket, her hand wrapped around the EMP device.

She took a deep breath and looked at Ruby. "I need you to run."

"You what?"

"As soon as I hit this, there will be chaos and confusion all around. I need you to run as fast as you can, as far away from here as possible. Keep running until you reach GlobaTech's reinforcements. Can you do that for me?"

Ruby turned her body to face Jay. Her face was contorted with disbelief and offense.

"Are you kidding me?" she hissed. "I'm not leaving you! The moment you hit that, everyone here will start shooting. It isn't going to affect the Tristar guards. Someone needs to protect you!"

Jay shook her head. "I'll be dead."

"You don't *know* that!"

"No, but when has Lady Luck ever glanced my way, hmm?" She placed her hands on Ruby's shoulders. "I have a plan, okay? It should buy you enough time to shoot a couple of bad guys and get your ass out of here."

Ruby went to protest, but Jay cut her off.

"You need to stop thinking like an assassin and start thinking about the future, okay? Your priority needs to be tomorrow. Just... let me do this. Please. If this is when I punch my ticket, let me go doing something good for once. Let me protect you."

A single tear crept down Ruby's face. She nodded and stepped back.

Jay smiled. "Thank you." She then turned to face the mob of assets. "I'll come quietly," she shouted out. "But just me. You let her go, and I'll give you GlobaTech."

Two of the assets began walking toward her, weapons drawn and held low. Both men were roughly the same height and build. One had a tattoo of a horse visible on his neck. The other had a koi.

Jay's hand quickly disappeared into her pocket. Then she took it out and held her arms up casually. She watched the assets approach.

"If I don't get the chance to tell you, I just want you to

know…" She took a breath and looked over at Ruby. "I never liked you."

She smiled. It was a gesture Ruby struggled to return.

The assets moved so that Jay was between them. Each put a hand on her shoulder and shoved her forward. She walked away without looking back, her arms down by her sides, fists clenched. As she reached the group of assets, they formed a circle around her. She watched them impassively, allowing herself to be taken. She was ushered away to her left, heading for the far end of the compound. All around them, Tristar guards continued to appear, moving with organized urgency.

Jay glanced over her left shoulder. Ruby was still standing there, watching her. The guards nearby hadn't moved. She took a deep breath and looked to her right, at the line of buildings that peaked against the mountain background. Beyond them, the sky was turning blue, with sporadic clouds floating overhead. The sun was bright but cold, and it did little to warm the world below it.

She was perhaps forty feet away from the nearest building. She wanted to be as close as possible. Assuming there were more assets indoors, she wanted the blast to take out as many of them as she could.

It was now or never.

She pivoted clockwise and smashed her fist into the asset walking beside her. The shot connected flush, momentarily stunning him. It was enough to buy her the small window she needed. She dropped her shoulder and charged through the narrow gap she had created. She burst out of the group and sprinted toward the low building in front of her.

Thirty feet.

Twenty-five.

"Ugh!" she grunted as she lost her balance.

One of the assets had been quick to react, giving chase and lashing out with a kick that caught the back of Jay's ankle. She fell forward hard, and the impact jolted her enough to release her grip of the EMP device. It flew from her hand, landing a few feet away in front of her.

"Shit!" she hissed.

She scrambled to her feet, struggling for purchase on the dusty ground. But she fell flat again as a stiff kick buried itself into her ribcage. Suddenly, her world darkened, and as she rolled over enough to look up, she saw the group of assets swarm around her like a plague. A flurry of punches and kicks rained down on her, yet she didn't bother to try and protect herself. Instead, she reached out, stretching as far as she could, desperate to lay just one finger on the small disc that could change everything. Millimeter by millimeter, she scratched and crawled along the desert floor, willing herself to remain conscious long enough to reach it.

She felt a crushing weight on top of her that flattened her out. Her hand couldn't have been more than three inches from the device. The asset who was kneeling on her back delivered a hammer blow to her middle of her spine. Her back arched involuntarily, and she let out a yelp of pain.

"Nice try, bitch," said the asset.

The man with the koi tattoo dragged her upright, then knocked her back down to the ground with a hard left hook.

Jay's head bounced off the gravel, splitting her forehead open. Her eyes rolled back in her head. She refocused long enough to register the small pool of blood around her face.

But the punch had knocked her forward a few feet.

Surrounded by the dark liquid seeping from her temple, inches from her face, was the EMP device.

Over by the entrance, Ruby watched Jay's unsuccessful attempt to escape the assets. She saw them attack her as one. She couldn't even see her any more beneath the gang of bodies.

She looked past the guards on her right and stared at the entrance. The barrier was raised, as if inviting her to safety. But she stared back across the compound at the huddle of violence consuming Jay and stubbornly set her jaw.

"Screw this," she muttered.

Ruby drew the second Raptor from her shoulder holster and snapped her arms out to the sides. She fired repeatedly, riddling all six guards around her with bullets before any of them knew what was happening.

She didn't wait for them to drop. She holstered one of the Raptors and reloaded the other as she set off sprinting toward Jay.

Another kick buried itself into Jay's side. Her hands were covering her head, desperately trying to avoid any more damage, but she couldn't move her legs enough to protect her body.

The asset grabbed a handful of her jacket and threw her over onto her back. Squinting through the blood in her eyes, Jay looked up at the ring of faces staring down at her. Agents of death, circling her like a clock face, reminding her that her time was up.

The man with the koi tattoo sneered at her.

"Hall wants you alive. Didn't say anything about conscious." He pulled his arm back, preparing to deliver a knockout blow. "Sweet dreams, *Defect*."

Jay opened her right hand, revealing the EMP device.

Her thumb moved over the button in the middle of it. The asset looked at it, confused. She had just enough energy left inside her to smile. In that split-second, snippets of her life began to flash before her eyes. She saw herself standing beside Brandon Crow, looking out over an underground base filled with Tristar mercenaries. Then a cloud of static floated across her mind, wiping away the image as it moved, and revealing another in its wake. She was standing on the driveway of a large house, holding a little girl's hand. It was summertime. The two of them were waving at a car as it reversed away from them. She couldn't see the driver, but she instinctively knew who it was. The memory felt unfamiliar to her, yet it offered her comfort all the same.

She locked eyes with the asset and smiled. "You first, shithead."

Jay pressed the button.

The world was filled with a blinding flash of blue light, and then...

Darkness.

Chapter Thirty-Three

Hall was unable to hide his shock as he listened intently to the voice on the other end of the phone. He glared through a deep frown at the air in front of him, his mouth hanging slightly ajar.

"He's what?" he asked. "How?"

Julie and Jericho glanced at each other. She flicked an eyebrow up with silent inquiry. He responded with a gentle shrug.

The Nemesis assets on either side of them took a step toward the desk, sensing the concern in Hall's voice.

"Just bring her to me," said Hall firmly, then he ended the call. He looked at Julie and Jericho in turn. "Well, it seems—"

He was cut short by the piercing screams unleashed by both assets. They dropped to their knees, clutching the sides of their heads.

Hall was as equally stunned as Julie and Jericho were. The three of them watched with confusion as the assets fell to the floor, writhing in agony until…

Silence.

Julie and Jericho looked at each other, then at Hall.

Hall stared back with panic-filled eyes.

Then the world began to move faster.

Hall fumbled hopelessly behind his desk, trying to shuffle his bloated frame out from under it in an effort to escape. But Julie and Jericho moved much more gracefully. Each of them dove to the prone assets at their feet and retrieved their *Negotiators*, which had been taken from them earlier. Then they both stood, turned, and took aim at Hall.

He froze, like a deer caught in headlights.

"You shouldn't have sent your guards away," said Julie.

Hall held the soul drive above his head, as if intending to drop it. "Let me go, or…"

His words trailed off as Jericho calmly walked around the desk and slowly plucked it from his swollen fingers.

"I'll take that," said Jericho.

He slid it into one of the many pockets in his pants and rejoined Julie.

"For the record," he said. "That drive is shatterproof and can stop a bullet. You think you were going to break it by dropping it five feet? It's not a smartphone, dumbass."

Hall swallowed. Beads of sweat glistened on his brow. He looked around the room, searching for another move to make. He snatched up his crystal tumbler and launched it toward Julie's head. Jericho snapped his arm up and caught it one-handed, a couple of inches in front of her face. He looked at her and winked.

"Thanks," she said, smiling.

"Don't mention it." Jericho looked at Hall and held the glass up like a trophy. "I'm keeping this."

Hall spat across the desk at them. "Go to Hell!"

"Not yet," said Julie, taking a step forward. "First, you're going to abort the launch of your little rocket."

Hall stared at her and let out a deep, menacing cackle. "You're too late. The launch sequence is already underway. It can't be stopped now. In just over thirty minutes, that will take off, and there's nothing you can do about it. The world is mine now. You understand? You've lost!"

"What if I shoot your astronauts?" said Jericho. "No pilots, no launch, right? Simple."

Hall shot him a glance, screwing his face up with disbelief. "The only thing that's simple around here is you. It's an unmanned rocket. It will be remotely controlled from the ground. Once it reaches the asteroid, it will begin mining, filling its cargo holds with raw materials before making the flight home."

"Then we shoot the guy with the joysticks," said Julie, shrugging. "Where is he?"

Hall rolled his eyes. "Not here. You think I'm an idiot? I told you. There's nothing you can do to stop this. Even if you kill every man and woman on this base. The rocket will launch, and it will buy me the world."

"Not if you're dead."

Hall grinned. "You think I don't have contingencies for that? You think I don't have a whole network of people ready to carry on Orion's legacy when I'm gone? How disappointingly arrogant of you."

Jericho shook his head, frustrated. They were running out of time.

"How is any of this even possible?" he asked. "How could you do this in such a short time?"

Hall shrugged. "I didn't. I bought this place when it was just a crater, about three months after the dead assassin blew it to kingdom come. That was seven years ago, and

I've been working on this ever since. The only thing stopping me was the propulsion technology, which I secured from you a couple of years ago. It was a little rudimentary for what I wanted, but our engineers were able to improve it. Once we had tested it in Paluga, we retrofitted the rocket and began preparing for the launch. If you hadn't managed to take back the White House, my baby would already be heading back to Earth full of money."

"There has to be a way to stop it," urged Julie. "Some kind of failsafe. Tell us how to prevent the launch!"

He smirked at her. "Or what? You'll kill me? Please. You're going to do that anyway. At least I got to see that look of defeat in your eyes. GlobaTech has been a thorn in my side for too long, and I can't tell you how happy it makes me, knowing you lost." He glanced at Jericho. "Keep your little hard drive. You think a bunch of computer files can save you now?"

Jericho frowned. "What are you talking about?"

Hall shook his head. "Still playing checkers against a Grandmaster. Pathetic." He leaned forward. "You think I didn't plan for this? For this exact scenario. You ordered a sizeable chunk of your people—presumably with the president's blessing—to attack this base head-on, causing a distraction that would allow you and your friends to sneak in and stop me. Well, the alarm's still going, you musclebound *freak*! Your friends failed!"

"Did they?" said Julie. She nodded toward the assets. "In case you hadn't noticed, we found a way to disable all your Nemesis soldiers. And judging by the conversation you just had, I'm going to assume someone has killed Adam Rayne. Without them, we all know we can take down your Tristar forces. Looks to me like we're winning."

Hall slammed his fists down on the desk. "Of course, it

does, you arrogant whore! You can barely see your own hand in front of your face, let alone two, three, four steps ahead. How do you think it's going to look when GlobaTech attacks Tristar, so soon after fighting the rebellion against them? Parker made them legit again, remember?"

"That little PR stunt was bullshit," said Jericho. "Everyone could see that."

"You know what else it was?" countered Hall. "Subtle. No one knew she was working for me. All the world saw was a security company quietly trying to make amends. We did polls. We did focus groups. We did press releases. Like it or not, it was working. So, how do you think people will react when it comes to light that GlobaTech launched a large-scale, unprovoked attack on them? That little rebellion is the only reason people forgave you for letting the Palugan president die on your watch. And for letting me take over the entire country. Surely, the mighty GlobaTech should've seen *that* coming?" He spat at them again. "Considering you act like the champions of the people, you don't really understand them, do you? People always want someone to blame. They need to be able to point the finger when something goes wrong. And in case you hadn't noticed, I'm very good at making sure they point it at you. Even if you manage to walk out of here, GlobaTech's finished."

Julie looked across at Jericho. He was staring ahead, trying to determine if Hall was telling the truth or just stalling. But she had already figured out that Hall was right. He was too smart not to be, and he was too arrogant to lie about it.

They were wasting time.

She lowered her gun and looked at Jericho. "Come on. We have work to do."

"We're just going to leave him here?" he asked, frowning.

She shrugged. "Where's he gonna go? Come on."

She turned and began walking toward the staircase. Jericho's gaze lingered on Hall for a moment, then he reluctantly followed her.

Hall smiled to himself. "You know, maybe I had you all wrong, Miss Fisher."

Julie stopped and looked back at him, narrowing her eyes. "What?"

Hall leaned forward on the desk. The sweat from his palms stained the wood. "Maybe you *are* smarter than your predecessor. He didn't know when to walk away. If he had, maybe he would still be alive."

Her jaw muscles tensed.

"Don't rise to him," whispered Jericho. "He's trying to bait you into wasting time we don't have."

Julie ignored him and turned around to face Hall again. They were standing roughly halfway between the stairs and the desk.

"Say what you want," she said to Hall. "You're going to face justice for everything you've done."

Hall ignored her. "I honestly can't tell you how satisfying it was to put a bullet in his head. He was in the middle of celebrating his victory too. It was… *delicious*. Just a shame I didn't get chance to shoot your friend as well. Roach, was it? He caused nothing but problems for Crow. But no matter. At least I got the one that mattered."

Julie took a deep breath, trying to quell the fire raging inside her.

Hall grinned. "It was wonderful seeing his blood stain the floor of the Oval Office. Honestly, I was just surprised it was the same color as mine."

Jericho's shoulders slumped forward. His eyes closed.

"Shit..." he muttered.

A wave of calm washed over Julie. She looked over at Hall, tilting her head as she examined him. The smug smile. The confidence, despite his position. He was detestable. In all her years of combat with the military, with GlobaTech... she had never truly hated anyone. Conflict was never personal. It was just a job. But in that moment, she experienced true, genuine, heartfelt hatred toward Hall.

She looked down at her gun. Her thumb danced absently over the buttons on the grip. She knew she was going to shoot him. She could tell Jericho did too. Hall perhaps thought she wouldn't, but that was his mistake and not her problem. Part of her thought that was too good for him. Maybe he deserved to live... to suffer until his last day, imprisoned. But that was too good for him too.

She turned and continued walking toward the stairs.

Jericho frowned. He glanced back at Hall, who had started laughing. Then he followed her.

"Hey, what are you doing?" he asked. "I thought you—"

As he reached her side, Julie spun around on the spot, raised her gun, and fired an explosive-tipped bullet directly at Hall's chest. Almost instantly, Hall evaporated with a loud bang. The wave of heat from the explosion rushed toward them, like an oven door opening. Julie closed her eyes and embraced it, feeling it wash over her.

A large, crimson cloud splashed across the windows behind the desk, darkening the room. A combination of white globules of bone and sickly, yellow fat slid down the glass. There was no sign a human had ever been there.

Jericho turned to her, wide-eyed and dumbstruck. "What the hell was that?"

Julie holstered her gun to her thigh and looked back at

him. There was nothing in her eyes. No emotion. No remorse. No humanity.

"Justice," she said.

Then she turned and made her way down the stairs.

Jericho watched her for a moment, then looked back over his shoulder at the carnage she had caused. He didn't think she was capable of such malice, yet a part of him wasn't surprised, given how far Hall had pushed her. He found it hard to argue that he didn't deserve it.

Jericho looked at the crystal tumbler in his hand, then tossed it over toward the desk.

"Celebrate that, asshole."

Minutes later, the two of them burst out through the entrance of the tower and slid to a stop on the gravel. All around them, Tristar guards were rushing toward the main gate, completely ignoring them as they ran past. They looked over to see the first wave of GlobaTech operatives swarming inside.

"Looks like the cavalry's here," said Jericho. "Right on time."

Julie took a deep breath. "That should keep Tristar occupied. Now we just have to find a way to stop that thing." She nodded toward the rocket.

"The launch control room is at the far end, right?" said Jericho. "Any chance we have of preventing it from taking off must be there."

"Agreed. We should—Ray!"

She held a hand up as she saw Link and Collins running toward them. She and Jericho moved to meet them. Fist-bumps were exchanged all around.

"You two okay?" asked Jericho.

Collins nodded. "Just about, aye. You?"

"Still standing."

"So, you did it?" asked Julie. "We saw a couple of assets drop."

Link stared at the ground for a moment. When he looked back up at her, his expression was one of regret. "That... wasn't us."

Julie frowned. "What do you mean?"

Collins pointed to the sky, gesturing to the persistent scream of the alarm that filled the air around them. "*That* was us. System locked us out. We couldn't boost the EMP blast."

"So, how did we take them out?"

"Whoever dropped was within the twenty-foot blast radius of the actual device when it went off. That's it."

Jericho took a deep breath. "Jay. She detonated it manually?"

Collins nodded. "Aye. She must've done."

"Where is she?" asked Julie. "And where's Ruby?"

The four of them turned and quickly scanned the crowd. The entire base was a flurry of movement as black shapes raced around, standing out against the pale ground and the cold sun.

It wasn't difficult to see the shapes that were motionless.

"There!" shouted Link.

Halfway between them and the entrance, Ruby was crouching beside a prone body, next to a large pile of more prone bodies. They all set off running toward her, shooting at anyone in a black uniform who happened to look at them as they crossed the courtyard. Thankfully, most of them were too distracted by the arrival of the GlobaTech forces.

They reached Ruby and quickly moved to form a loose perimeter around her. She was resting on one knee, holding her gun up and aiming all around her, as if daring anyone to approach. She momentarily pointed her gun in their direction before she realized they were on her side.

Julie noted the fraught look in her eyes. "Are you okay?"

Ruby didn't reply. She just nodded hurriedly.

Collins glanced down at Jay's body. "What about her? Is she…"

"I don't know," said Ruby. "She was already down when she hit the button, surrounded by all those bastards." She pointed at the pile of Nemesis assets a few feet away. "I dragged her out from under them. She's breathing, but she's not moving."

"Ah, shite…"

Ruby looked up at Julie. "Is it over? Please tell me this is over."

Julie sighed. "Not yet. Hall's dead, and we have our soul drive back, but we have to stop that rocket from launching."

"Does it really matter now?" asked Link. "If Hall's gone…"

"It matters. If Orion gets a hold of the materials on that asteroid, they control everything. Hall said there are contingences. There are people ready to step up and take over. The threat is still there, even if he's gone."

"You believe him?"

"I do."

"Then how do we stop it?"

"I… I don't know."

"How long before it launches?" asked Collins.

Jericho checked his watch. "Twenty minutes. Maybe less."

"We figure the best place to start is the launch control tower at the far end," added Julie. "We gotta move. Ruby,

I'll make sure a unit comes to get you to safety. Stevens is here. He's one of us. He'll get you both out of here, okay?"

Ruby stood and looked at Link. "Will you stay with us until he gets here? Please. Just in case."

He stared at her, confused by how vulnerable she sounded. He looked over at Julie for clarification.

Julie didn't hesitate. "Of course. Link, help her get Jay's body off the battlefield and out of the firing line, then find Stevens."

He nodded, then turned back to Ruby.

"Let's go, Boss Lady," he said.

He crouched and effortlessly scooped Jay's body up into his arms.

Julie, Jericho, and Collins huddled together.

"Here's the plan," said Julie. "We have to reach that control tower. We'll be running against the tide here, so eyes open. Once inside, we get to the top ASAP and disable that launch by any means necessary. Understand?"

The others nodded, and they set off running together. Collins glanced to his left, staring up at the rocket in the distance. As they drew level with the western path that led from the compound to the launch site, he slid to a stop.

"Hey, guys, hold up," he called out.

Julie and Jericho stopped and looked at him.

"What is it?" asked Jericho. "You okay?"

"Huh? Aye, I'm fine. It's just… maybe there's another way to stop it."

Julie shook her head. "There isn't. The launch is automated. The answer must lie with the launch control."

"Or on the rocket itself…" countered Collins. "If I can get over there, maybe get on board, there might be a way to disable it from the inside. Disconnect the thrusters, shut down its systems… something. Some way of sabotaging it."

"That's too risky," said Jericho. "We don't have the time."

Collins smiled at him. "Hey, I'm the tech guy, remember? Besides... look... let's be honest here, folks. We're dealing with the longest of long shots, no matter how we play this. We need a plan B. This way, we double our chances of stopping it, right?"

Julie and Jericho exchanged a look.

"Fine," said Julie. "Go. We both have our cells, right? Keep in touch."

Collins fist-bumped them both and grinned. "Best of luck, ya crazy bastards."

"You too," said Jericho.

Collins watched as they continued toward the tower, then he turned and ran as fast as he could toward the access road. He ducked slightly and held an arm up to his head as bullets started flying around him.

A small pool of transport vehicles that resembled golf carts was parked next to the road. They were four-seater buggies with no roof or windows. He headed for the one closest to the west exit. Just beside it was the body of a Tristar guard. As he passed, Collins noticed a belt of grenades around the man's waist.

"Huh..."

He quickly crouched, unfastened the belt, and removed it from the body. He held it up, inspecting it.

"We'll call ya plan C, yeah?" he said to himself.

He jumped in behind the wheel of the nearest cart, rested the grenades on the seat beside him, then gunned the engine. It was electric but still packed a punch, despite its size. With a gun in hand, he sped toward the exit. He fired a few rounds at any guards he passed who were blocking his path and soon cleared the compound. The road wound loosely up the shallow side of the mountain, toward the large plateau at the top. The closer he got, the higher the rocket seemed to stretch up to the sky.

Collins kept glancing at it as he drove.

"Just us now, ya big bastard," he said quietly. "And ya ain't going nowhere."

Chapter Thirty-Four

Julie and Jericho sprinted as fast as they could toward the launch control tower in the northeast corner of the compound. It was a straight column of brick and glass, which loomed over the other buildings like a king surveying his kingdom. Far behind them, a full-scale skirmish had erupted between GlobaTech and Tristar forces. The chaos had provided them with all the distraction they had needed. Aside from the odd Tristar guard who had recognized them, whom they had put down without breaking stride, they arrived at the tower unhindered.

The east side of the tower was covered by scaffolding. It stretched all the way up to just below the top, which was easily fifteen floors high, if not more.

"How long do we have?" panted Julie.

Jericho winced as he desperately sucked in heavy breaths.

"If Hall was telling the truth," he said, checking his watch, "then... sixteen minutes."

"Shit. Come on."

They pushed through the main entrance and were greeted by a steady blast of cool air—refreshing but warmer than outside. There were no guards around them.

Julie pointed ahead. "Elevators."

They ran toward them and hit the button for the top floor. They stepped inside a moment later and began their ascent.

"You think Hall *was* telling the truth?" asked Julie. "About there being no way to stop the launch now?"

Jericho shook his head. "There must be a failsafe or security protocols in place. I'm sure there are a billion things that could go wrong when you're launching a ship into outer space."

"I hope you're right. You got a plan for what we do when we get up there?"

He shrugged. "Ask nicely?"

She raised an eyebrow, unconvinced, but said nothing.

The doors pinged and slid open, revealing the control room spread out before them. They stepped out into a short corridor, which led onto a raised platform overlooking the room.

"Holy shit…" whispered Julie.

Rows of computers ran almost the full width of the room, which was teeming with life and activity. There were easily thirty men and women working there. A loud babble of voices, all having multiple conversations, filled the air.

Directly ahead of them, running floor to ceiling and wall to wall, was the largest display screen either of them had ever seen. It was split into various sections, showing charts and readouts, but the largest one showed what appeared to be a live feed of the rocket.

On the wall to their left was a digital clock, counting down from fourteen minutes.

Jericho took a step forward and placed a hand on the guardrail in front of him. Four steps led down from the platform on his right. He raised his gun and fired twice at the high ceiling.

The individual conversations merged into a collective scream, followed by a deathly silence as everyone turned to face him.

"Mission's over," he shouted. "Stop the launch, right now."

Everyone exchanged looks of confusion and panic.

Jericho fired again, prompting another round of screaming to rise and crash back down into silence like a tidal wave.

"I don't know if you've looked out the window in a while, but you've lost," he said. "GlobaTech forces are storming the gates as we speak. This is over. You understand? I'm standing here with the CEO of GlobaTech Industries, with the backing of President Schultz, and I am *ordering* you to abort this launch immediately!"

Below him, a man stepped forward. He wore thin-framed glasses and a tie, which was pulled loose around his neck. He glanced behind at his colleagues, then looked up at Jericho.

"Umm... we can't," he said quietly. "*Sir.* Sorry... I—*we* can't stop the launch now. It's too late."

Jericho snapped his aim down, lining the barrel of his Negotiator up with the man's forehead. "Who are you?"

"Leo Kowalski. I'm... I'm overseeing the launch."

"Okay, Leo, you sweaty little goblin, listen to me—if that rocket launches, the world changes forever. And not in a good way. You understand? You can't all be drinking from Hall's Kool-Aid, surely?"

Kowalski held his hands up and yelped, then shook his

head. "We're not. I swear to God, sir, we're all here under duress. None of us have been here longer than six months. Mr. Hall said the launch has to go ahead, or…"

"Or what?"

"Or he destroys this entire base and everyone in it."

Jericho shook his head. "That's over now. Hall's dead. Like, *really* dead. You're safe, I promise. But if that rocket takes off, it could trigger a global war that no country on Earth is equipped to fight. The rebellion will look like a schoolyard scrap. 4/17 will look insignificant to the shitshow that will ensue if Orion takes control of that asteroid."

The color drained from Kowalski's face. "W-wait… what? Mr. Hall is dead?"

Jericho shrugged. "Yeah."

"Oh my God…"

He clasped a hand to his mouth. His face fell with shock. The people around him reacted the same way. Jericho and Julie exchanged a confused and concerned look.

"What's wrong?" asked Julie.

"What have you done?" said Kowalski, absently staring at the floor.

"Leo, talk to me," urged Jericho.

Kowalski looked up at him, eyes wide and fearful. "We're all going to die."

"No, we're not…'

"We are!" he screamed. "The rocket locks itself and begins its own prelaunch diagnostics." He glanced over at the clock. There were twelve minutes left. "That's in two minutes. When that happens, Mr. Hall has to make a call. He… he has to cancel the airstrike before…"

Jericho's eyes went wide. "What airstrike?"

"In case something went wrong, he had a contingency in place. A helicopter will launch an airstrike on the entire base if he doesn't call it off when the rocket enters the prelaunch phase. If he's dead, he can't..." He paced back and forth in front of the platform. "Oh, God!"

Jericho looked over at Julie. "Call Ray, now. Get him the hell out of there!"

She took out her cell phone and started dialing.

Jericho turned back to Kowalski. "We need to stop the launch. Isn't there some way to remotely destroy the rocket? Some kind of safeguard?"

Kowalski shook his head. "No. Once the rocket locks itself down, the self-destruct protocol is disabled. There's no going back."

Jericho grunted. "Shit."

He looked up at the clock, which had just ticked below eleven minutes, then spun around to face Julie. "We're running out of time, Julie..."

She glared at him, frustrated. "I know! It's ringing..."

She paced away, pressing the phone harder against her ear, as if it would help establish the call.

Come on, Ray, she said to herself. *Pick up. Please.*

Collins slammed on the brakes as he approached the base of the rocket. The launchpad was a massive square of blacktop hastily laid over the desert dust on the mountain plateau. He grabbed the grenade belt and sprinted toward the rocket, fastening it around his waist as he ran.

There were workers all around, rushing as the countdown to launch ticked ever closer. Collins figured he had about fifteen minutes.

Framework made of thick, red, steel girders surrounded the rocket, stretching up almost as far as the rocket itself.

Beside it, attached to an enormous crane by a winch, was a makeshift elevator. It ran all the way to the short walkway that connected the elevator to the rocket.

Collins ran toward it, ignoring anyone he passed. He reached the crane and stepped inside the elevator. Like on a construction site, the barriers were barely higher than his waist. He slammed the gate closed and stared at the small control panel in front of him. It had two large buttons—one red, one green—and a lever.

"Green means go, right?" he said to himself.

He hit the green button with his fist, then pushed the lever forward gently. The mechanisms rumbled into life. The cables whined and creaked as they began turning. The elevator jolted and began its climb.

He gripped the railings with both hands. He had little issue with heights, but it was difficult to ignore the ground racing away from him.

As he got higher, more and more of the compound revealed itself to him. The distant blare of the alarm carried on the wind. He could see the two factions of soldiers clashing by the entrance. People wearing Tristar black swarmed across the base's courtyard like a shadow. Away to the right, a long line of GlobaTech operatives and vehicles continued to file in on the desert road.

Collins shook his head. "Sweet Jesus... what a bloody mess."

He looked up as he approached the top. He reached for the lever and eased it back again, timing the speed reduction so that he ended level with the platform. The elevator jolted again as it came to a stop. Collins threw the gate open and sprinted along the short walkway. Thankfully, the barriers along the sides were much higher. He didn't want to risk looking down.

Ahead of him, stepping out of the rocket's only door, was a man dressed in a long, black coat with neon strips sewn into it. He turned as he heard Collins approaching and stared at him with confusion.

"Hey, who are you?" he called out. "You shouldn't be up here."

Collins didn't hesitate. He drew his *Negotiator* and took aim. "No arguments from me, buddy, but here I am all the same. Leave."

The man's eyes bulged in their sockets, and he sprinted past Collins, toward the elevator.

Collins stepped over the threshold of the small, metal door and inside the rocket. The cockpit was little more than a narrow circle. Every surface was a different type of computer. A series of screens above panels of flashing lights and various buttons with little-to-no labeling.

There was a single chair in the middle, which Collins moved to sit in. He looked around him, overwhelmed by the sensation of drowning.

He had no idea what he was doing.

"Ah, shite…"

His phone rang, echoing around the metal chamber. He fumbled in his pocket for it, then answered by putting it on speaker.

"Yeah?"

"Ray? Thank God! It's Julie. You gotta get out of there!"

"Huh? What? Why? I just got here."

Her breathing was hurried and shallow. "You cannot be inside that thing when the countdown hits T-minus ten minutes, do you understand me?

"Hey, slow down. It'll be fine. I'm… trying to figure this

out, okay? But I need time. What happens at T-minus ten minutes?"

As the words left his lips, the room darkened. Red lights flashed into life all around, and the door began to swing close. Realizing what was happening, Collins leapt from his seat, but the door hissed closed and clicked into place.

He banged his fist on it in frustration, desperately searching for a handle.

There wasn't one.

He sat back in his seat and picked up the phone. He took it off speaker and held it to his ear.

"Ray? Ray? Are you there?"

"Aye." He sighed. "I, ah... I just figured out what happens when we hit ten minutes."

"You have to get out of there!" implored Julie.

"Yeah... probably not, Jules. I'm locked in."

"Goddammit!"

"Hey, hey, it's okay. I have ten minutes, right? Plenty of time to work my magic. But just in case, you and the big fella keep working on a way to stop this thing from taking off, yeah? Us Irish fellas aren't meant for orbit, ya know."

Julie sighed, sending a burst of static down the line. "There's something else."

Collins closed his eyes. "What?"

"Hall left us a final *fuck you*. An airstrike is scheduled for when the rocket locks itself down. A contingency in case something went wrong, I guess. Apparently, only a call from him will stop it."

"Shite. How long?"

There was a pause. "I don't know. Presumably any minute now."

"Jules..."

"It's unlikely to target the launch site, but it will definitely level the compound. You might be the only chance we have, Ray. I'm sorry."

Collins looked around him. The panels still blinked with importance. He still didn't understand any of it.

He took a deep breath. "Look, you and Jerry find cover. Do whatever ya can, okay? Are ya hearing me, Jules? We gotta win this. We gotta stop this rocket, no matter what."

"I know."

"No matter what, Jules."

There was a heartbeat of silence.

"It isn't gonna come to that, Ray," said Julie. "I promise. We'll figure something out, get you outta there, and then it's beers on me tomorrow, yeah?"

Collins smiled, which sent a single tear rolling down his cheek. He nodded to himself.

"Aye. That sounds grand, love."

"Just hold on, yeah? I'll see you—"

The line clicked dead.

Collins stared at the phone for a moment. Then he looked at his hand and pressed his middle finger to this thumb. He closed his eyes and took a deep breath. He felt the weight of pressure wash over him like a waterfall, then away, leaving his mind clear.

He opened his eyes, clenched his jaw, and stared at the console in front of him.

"Here we go…"

Jericho knew they were running out of time. He stared at Julie, studying the range of emotions that played out on her face as she spoke to Collins.

He looked around at Kowalski and the rest of the room.

"You need to find a way to stop the launch. Is there some way to override the lockdown procedure from here?"

Kowalski shook his head. "The system was designed to protect the launch at this stage. It can't be shut down now."

A woman moved to Kowalski's side and looked up at Jericho. "I... I might have an idea."

Jericho looked down at her. She was a thin, timid woman. Probably in her forties. Her short hair had flecks of gray in it.

He nodded to her. "Talk to me."

"Well... um... we can't disable the launch sequence, but we might be able to reenable the self-destruct protocol. It'll take time, but... it's possible."

Jericho shook his head. "Negative. I have a man inside that thing. Likely trapped, now. We can't blow it with him still inside. You need to shut down the launch."

Kowalski took a heavy breath. "Sir, we can't. This... might be the only way."

Jericho held his gaze as he processed the gravity of the choice that lay before him. He said nothing for several seconds, struggling to ignore the human voice in his mind and focus solely on the soldier's logic.

Finally, he swallowed and nodded. "Do it. Get to work."

Jericho moved back to stand with Julie and listened to her conversation.

"I know," she said. "It isn't gonna come to that, Ray, I promise. We'll stop the launch, get you outta there, and then it's beers on me tomorrow, yeah?"

Jericho smiled at her. She smiled back as she looked into his eyes. They both saw the regret.

"Just hold on, yeah?" she said to Collins. "I'll see you—"

The call dropped. She stared at her phone, confused.

"What?" asked Jericho.

She held the phone up to him. "Service dropped. Did we..." Her words trailed off as she looked at big screen behind Jericho. "What's that?"

Jericho looked around. The image on the screen had changed. It no longer showed the launch site. There were no charts or countdowns. The whole screen was a real-time feed from a camera inside the cockpit of an aircraft, moving quickly. In the bottom corner of the screen, a thin tower stood aflame in the middle of the desert.

It was a cell tower.

More people in the room were drawn to the screen, until everyone had stopped to stare. An eerie silence had fallen.

"That's a gunship," Jericho whispered to Julie. "Stealth, probably."

"Where is it?" she whispered back.

They watched the screen intently as the landscape whizzed past the camera. Then they saw it. At the top of the screen, ahead of the helicopter, they saw the outline of the compound appear. As it grew closer, white crosshairs appeared, dancing around the screen until they locked onto a building and turned red.

"Oh, shit..." murmured Julie.

The helicopter had locked onto the launch control tower.

Jericho stepped forward. "Everyone, hold onto something!" he shouted. "We're about to be—"

A series of thunderous explosions erupted all around them, shaking the foundations of the tower. Jericho stumbled backward, grabbing one of the nearby handrails to steady himself. Julie fell the opposite way and landed awkwardly on the floor, close to the steps leading down from the platform.

Everyone in the room shrieked and screamed, frozen to the spot.

An unearthly calm fell upon the room in the aftermath of deafening destruction. Julie and Jericho locked eyes, staring with concern. He extended his arm, offering her a helping hand. She went to move for it, but a loud, creaking sound pierced the silence, causing her to hold still. The uncertain groan grew in a crescendo before abruptly dropping off into nothingness.

"What... was that?" whispered Julie, as if the volume of her voice might cause it to return.

"I don't know," replied Jericho. "But I think we should—"

The world exploded into noise and chaos. Somewhere beneath them, the building began to crumble. The structure fell away, raining down debris on the compound below. A large fissure tore down the center of the room, running vertically from the large display screen, all the way to Jericho.

There was a disastrous implosion as the right side of the room collapsed and fell away, hanging at a forty-five-degree angle by strands of metal and cable and chunks of concrete. The screen crackled and fizzed as it split in two. Gravity's cruel grip pulled desks and chairs down the slope and out through the large holes that had once been windows. Many of the workers on that side of the room followed, screaming as they plunged from sight.

Jericho instinctively grabbed the handrail again, hoping he was far enough left of center that it would hold his weight.

Julie reached out, clutching helplessly at the air between them before sliding away.

"Julie!" shouted Jericho.

He looked ahead of her, toward the drop. She couldn't see what she was hurtling toward. Her arms flailed desperately for something to grab but missed everything she passed, on account of her speed.

"No!" he called out.

He let go and dove head-first down the slope after her. His body skated over the broken surface. He had one arm outstretched in front of him, the other out to the side.

Julie looked back and saw him. She used her legs and hips to twist her body, so she was moving feet-first. Then she reached up for Jericho's hand. He was moving faster than she was, due to his additional size and weight working with gravity.

He unleashed a guttural roar as he closed in on her, keeping one eye on the hole in the building she was heading toward. He strained against his own shoulder joint, desperate to gain an extra inch of reach. Julie did the same.

"Jericho!" she screamed.

Their fingertips were a hair's breadth from each other.

Jericho moved his other arm ahead of him, making himself more streamlined. Their hands met. He wrapped his around her wrist and forearm, gripping her so tight, his knuckles lost their color. She did the best she could to do the same.

He immediately snapped his other arm back out to the side as they reached the edge of the room. A long piece of electrical wiring was hanging from what remained of the ceiling, dancing as sparks fired from the exposed end. Jericho grabbed the insulated cable and came to an abrupt stop.

"Got you!" he called out.

His body was being pulled to its extremes. He was almost standing again, albeit on a steep slope. His left leg was bent at the knee; his right was straight out in front of him. His arms were stretched out to their full span. His right was holding Julie's body weight as she rested precariously on the edge, teetering over the broken window frame. His left arm was pulled taut behind him, holding onto the cable, trying to avoid the stray current pulsating from the end. His muscles bulged and strained against his clothes. So much blood was bumping around his body, even his thick, winter clothing looked painted onto his physique.

Julie stared up at him. Her eyes were wide, misted with tears and brimming with fear. Her body was against the broken tiled floor. Her legs dangled over the chasm outside —a fifteen-story sheer drop into the cloud of rubble, dust, and fire below that masked the ground.

Above him, Kowalski peered over the edge of the floor.

"Oh my God!" he shouted.

Straining with effort, Jericho turned his head to look up at him.

"A... little... help..."

"Oh, God... right... just... hang on!" He winced. "Sorry!"

He disappeared again.

Jericho looked down at Julie. "Just try to keep still, okay? I'm gonna pull you up."

She tried to throw her legs up and over the lip of the building, to relieve some of the weight Jericho was holding.

Kowalski appeared again. "I can't find anything to pass you! There's just... oh, God... there's just bodies and fire up here. I'm sorry!"

Jericho ground his teeth together, growling at the effort.

"But we did it," said Kowalski.

Jericho glared at him. "Did... what?"

"What you wanted. We were able to reenable the

rocket's self-destruct protocol. It can be activated from here. You just gotta hit this button next to me."

Jericho looked down at Julie. She stared back up at him. The fear had gone from her face. Her eyes streamed with tears. She nodded up to him.

"Jericho, you have to let me go," she called out. "You have to get Ray off that rocket and destroy it before it takes off. That's all that matters, you hear me?"

"No!" he shouted. "I'm getting you out of here first."

"I'm giving you an order, Jericho!"

"I don't care!"

He unleashed a primal howl as he began to lift her up toward him. The wind rushed in around them, carrying with it the sounds of carnage and destruction from the battlefield outside. The heat from the fires beneath them countered the icy winter air.

His palms were sweaty, and his grip on the cable was weakening. He glanced down and could see that Julie's feet were almost inside the room again. That would take some pressure off him, perhaps allowing him to pull them both up to the section of the room above them that was still level.

Then a frighteningly familiar sound flooded in from outside. A muted roar of engines, rushing toward them and getting louder with every heartbeat.

Jericho caught his breath.

The airstrike was making its second pass.

"Shit…" he hissed.

Another round of explosions rained down on the world outside. The symphony of destruction was building to its glorious finale.

The tower shook. The side of the building already hanging off broke even more, dropping to create a ninety-degree angle to the floor above it.

Jericho screamed as the cable was torn from his grip. He fell straight down, pulled by Julie's weight below him. He reached out desperately and felt his hand connect with an exposed steel girder, which now protruded from what remained of the tower's east wall. He gripped it, grunting as their rapid descent came to an abrupt halt.

Kowalski screamed as he flew past him, uprooted from safety and plummeting to his death.

Jericho's eyes bulged in their sockets as he was forced to watch. There was nowhere else to look but down.

Once again, his body was stretched in opposite directions. He hung by his left arm, which supported not only his body weight but also Julie's. She now held onto his right arm with both hands as she swung precariously over the fiery abyss created by the airstrike.

Jericho tried to look up but couldn't move his neck enough to see if there was any path he could take to get them both to safety. He had to settle for looking to the side. A thin column of window frame remained intact, perhaps four feet to his left. He couldn't tell how sturdy it still was, but if he could swing Julie over toward it, she had a better chance of hanging onto it than he would.

He looked down at her. "I'm gonna move you to my left, your right. The metal frame. You see it? I want you to reach for it, okay?"

She looked over, then back at him. He could see the terror in her eyes. The defeat, drowning in tears.

"Come on, Julie," he shouted. "You got this. On three. Ready?"

She glanced down and screamed. Then she looked back up and nodded.

He smiled at her. "One. Two. Thr—"

Part of the tower crumbled away below them, causing

the whole right side of the structure to shift and slide down. The shock jolted Jericho's body. His left hand slid a few inches along the girder, toward the edge of it. He tensed every fiber of his being to reinforce his grip.

When he felt steady, he looked back down at Julie.

"I've got you!" he shouted. "I promise!"

He glanced back over at the frame. It had gone. There was nothing.

He looked around, desperately searching for an alternative.

Another loud creak echoed around them as the building strained against itself to stay together. There was another tremor. More of the building fell away beneath them. Once again, the building shifted. Jericho's grip remained steadfast on the girder, keeping them both rigidly in place.

But Julie's grip didn't.

Her hands slid from around Jericho's forearm.

Jericho felt the weight lift from his grip. He looked down to see Julie's face, contorted in a silent, horrified scream, staring up at him. He unleashed an otherworldly howl of anguish as her final, wide-eyed expression burned into his mind forever. He was forced to watch her shrink as she fell away, reaching up to him until she disappeared, consumed by the fire and dust below.

Jericho screamed.

He had lost her.

For what felt like an eternity, Jericho hung over the chasm, numb to the chaos around him. He questioned whether his instinct to simply let go was genuine. But a strong gust of cold air punched into him, waking him from his daze.

He glared ahead at the mountains, remembering the mission... and the consequences if he failed. He looked up and threw his right arm above his head, gripping the girder with both hands. He tested its stability, then began to hoist himself up.

There was still a world that needed to be saved.

Now that he was able to look above him, he could see a clear path of debris he could navigate through. From the girder, he reached up for the corner of a desk, still attached to the floor. He clambered up onto it and jumped to the right, reaching for another desk a few feet away. From there, he could reach the cables hanging from between the exposed concrete flooring. He shimmied up it with ease, finally placing a hand on the flat, more stable floor.

Jericho heaved himself up and over the ledge, standing sure-footed in what was left of the control room. More of the floor had cracked and fallen away. He quickly scanned the remaining banks of computers and screens for the self-destruct button Kowalski had mentioned, but there was no sign. Nothing left looked remotely operational.

"Fuck!" he yelled out.

He had no move left to make. The clock had gone, so he had no idea how long was left until blast-off. His only hope now was that Collins had managed to disable the rocket from the inside.

Collins pressed his face against the glass of the porthole in the rocket's door, staring back at the base as fire rained down on it.

"Holy shit..." he muttered.

He was concerned for the fate of his friends, but he did his best to push those thoughts aside. He knew he was unlikely to get any help from the ground now. He moved back to his seat and set to work on the console, desperately searching for a way to override its systems.

Every attempt he made was met with a resounding beep as the system remained stubbornly active.

"Ah, bollocks to ya!" he shouted out, slamming his fists down on the console.

He looked all around him, cursing himself for having so drastically underestimated the complexity of the system. He shook his head.

He didn't know what to do.

Suddenly, the whole rocket began to shake. He reached out and grabbed the sides to steady himself. The entire cockpit vibrated around him. He heard the rushing of fuel and the mechanical roar of powerful engines as they started their ignition sequence.

"Oh, no, no, no, no…"

He leapt to his feet and reached for the door, wrestling with the handle and slamming his shoulder into it.

But he knew it was futile.

He unleashed a frustrated scream and slumped back into the chair, staring at the floor with defeat.

"Shite."

The noise around him grew louder, which further clouded his mind.

Then his gaze came to rest on the grenade belt beside him.

"No matter what…" he said to himself.

He got to his feet and began opening all the maintenance panels he could find, searching for one that looked more important than the rest. He settled for the one beneath the console, by his feet. Inside it was a huge space he probably could have fit in, had it not been for the sea of wiring in there.

"You'll do."

He sat down heavily in the seat and spun around to face the console. His legs rested on either side of the open maintenance panel.

The noise around him was deafening now. Everything shook. He fastened the seatbelt around his waist.

"Best get a bit of distance first, eh?" he said to himself with a resigned smile. "Give six-year-old me something to remember."

With the grenade belt laid across his lap, he leaned back in his seat and braced himself. There was an earth-shattering crash outside as the scaffolding fell away. The roar of the engines consumed his world. He looked over at the porthole and watched with morbid fascination as the mountains disappeared from view, replaced with clear sky.

Pinned back against his seat, he fought to lift his arms. He grabbed the belt of grenades and held it up in front of him. Then he hooked his middle finger through one of the pins and pressed it against his thumb. He sat back and closed his eyes.

Collins saw himself sitting with Julie and Jericho, sharing a beer and laughing together. He smiled.

Then he saw another image. One that made him even happier. He was standing with Kim. They were slow dancing in her kitchen, moving around the island where their glasses of red wine stood, half-empty.

A tear rolled down his cheek.

He sniffed back the emotion and opened his eyes. He stared at the grenade pin. There was no doubt about what needed to happen now. There was no fear. He felt nothing except calm and acceptance.

He yanked his hand away, removing the pin. Then he

threw the belt of grenades inside the panel, sat back, and closed his eyes again.

He pressed his middle finger to his thumb once more and smiled as he resumed his dance with Kim.

"I'll see ya soon, baby. Gotta go be a hero."

Jericho rushed toward the elevators. The wall to his right had fallen away, revealing glimpses of the world below. He could see rivers of bodies and columns of fire.

The airstrike had done its job.

The doors stood open in front of him. There was no sign of the carriage. He didn't have the energy for more problems. Without a second thought, he stepped out into the dark shaft and grabbed one of the two cables before him. He drew his gun, took aim at the winch above his head, and fired once. The cabling began unraveling from the mechanism. The other cable screamed as it was pulled upward with great force. The one he held was dragged along for the ride, running counterclockwise. He quickly descended the shaft, doing his best to count the floors as he passed them. He had no real idea how he was going to stop.

He waited until he saw a set of open doors below him. Timing it as best he could, he let go as he approached and dove through them on the way down. He landed hard and rolled away to a stop, several feet from the elevator shaft. He scrambled to his feet and quickly looked around. The lights were out. He could make out the shapes of bodies scattered around him. The structure appeared mostly intact. He sprinted for the stairwell and cleared the last three floors as quickly as he could.

Jericho burst through what was left of the entrance and

out into the courtyard, sliding to a stop on the gravel. He squinted against the influx of light. His eyes stung as the wind blew away his tears. He looked all around him but saw no one he recognized.

Just a lot of bodies.

He moved out into the center of the courtyard and looked to the sky. It was dark gray and shrouded in thick smoke. He couldn't hear any planes overheard. He looked over at the entrance. Vehicles burned. Bodies were strewn all over the ground, as far as he could see. It was impossible to tell his allies from his enemies.

He turned his attention to the launch site. It was a quarter-mile away. If he could get there... if there was still time... maybe he could—

A sonic boom thundered from beyond the mountains, and a bright light filled the sky. A moment later, clouds of fresh smoke billowed up over the peaks, followed by a plume of fire.

Jericho put his hands to his head and watched helplessly as the rocket ascended toward the heavens to a deafening ovation of burning fuel.

He was too late. Collins was too late. He mustn't have been able to—

The rocket exploded.

A horizontal shockwave silently raced away from the ball of fire that consumed the ship, transforming from orange to red, then eventually to a white light that scorched the sky.

Jericho gasped.

A second later, the sound of the blast hit him, and he was knocked off his feet as the shockwave passed him by.

He lay still, staring up at the dark clouds above him, shivering on the ground as tears flowed down his cheeks and dripped onto the dust around him. He roared with sadness, placing his hands over his face as he wept.

Part of him... the instinctual soldier he had always been... knew the fight was over. Orion was finished. The rocket had been destroyed. The asteroid would remain estranged from the grip of humanity, and the world would have no reason to go to war.

They had won.

But as he lay there, he realized none of that mattered to him. Not anymore. The soldier in him had fallen into the abyss alongside the woman he loved. It exploded in that rocket along with his best friend. All that remained was a stranger who begrudged the victory. Who couldn't fathom the cost of it. Who, despite knowing what winning this fight meant, could only focus on one thing:

He had lost everything.

Epilogue

December 31, 2020

A heavy snow had fallen overnight. The sky was now a pale gray, harboring low clouds and even lower temperatures as it blocked the sun from casting any light on the world below.

Jericho Stone stood silently by the graveside. He wore a black suit and tie. There was no military dress. No medals. No pride. No fight. Not anymore. His hulking frame was like a giant shadow against the brilliant white earth.

Beside him, equally imposing, was Link. He wore a black turtleneck sweater beneath his suit, with a flat cap and scarf to protect his shaved head from the elements. His hands were clasped in front of him as he stared down at the coffin, resting peacefully in the fresh grave.

Finally, Ruby DeSouza and Kim Mitchell huddled together, arms linked, wearing respectful black dresses beneath long, thick coats fastened at the waist by belts.

The service was beautiful. A fitting tribute to both Julie Fisher and Ray Collins, who would come to rest side by side in Arlington, one row removed from Adrian Hell, Josh Winters, Moses Buchanan, and Jessie Vickers. They deserved the comfort of friends as they rested.

The wind picked up, and the first flecks of snow began to flutter down around them. Instinctively, the four of them turned to form a small circle, hunching against the approaching snowstorm.

"What will you do now?" Ruby asked Jericho.

He shook his head as he stared vacantly at his shoes. "I don't know. I really... don't know."

His voice cracked as another swell of emotion rushed forth. Link placed a hand on his shoulder and squeezed gently. A gesture of brotherly support.

Jericho smiled faintly. "If... if you'll all excuse me."

He turned and walked away, stepping respectfully between two headstones and pausing by another grave. Ruby watched him go. She knew he was standing with Adrian.

Link turned to Kim and extended a hand. She took it and he shook it gently. He then looked at Ruby and held out his massive arms. Ruby gratefully accepted the embrace.

"Are you leaving?" she asked him as they parted.

He nodded. "I am. We've all fought for other people for so long, and we have nothing to show for it except a collection of graves. I'm done. I need to find my own cause. Fight on my own terms for once."

Ruby smiled. "You look after yourself, Link. You have my number, don't you?"

"I do."

"Good. Make sure you use it from time to time. Me and you... we're all that's left of Blackstar. We should stick together."

Link grinned. "You know it, Boss Lady. I'm gonna go check on the big guy before I go. Take care. Both of you."

"And you."

He moved to join Jericho. Kim stepped in front of Ruby and looked at her, smiling in the way she always did when she saw things everyone else had missed.

Ruby frowned. "What?"

"Do they know?"

"Know what?"

Kim raised an eyebrow. "About the baby."

Ruby was momentarily taken aback but soon recovered. She knew better than to be shocked that Kim had figured it out.

"No. I haven't told them," she said. "It's never felt like the right time, y'know? When did you figure it out?"

Kim shrugged. "When you got back from Missouri."

Ruby laughed. "Jesus. You're something else, you know that?"

"I do."

They shared another smile.

"So, does *anyone* know?" asked Kim.

Ruby nodded. "Julie did. I told her, so she wouldn't think bad of me for wanting to sit out the fight. Not that I did, in the end. And Jay. She figured it out right before she hit the EMP that dropped Nemesis."

Kim took a deep breath. "How is she?"

"Jay? Well, she *was* recovering in a GlobaTech medical facility and doing fine. Doctors who were briefed on the Nemesis program suspected enough of her subconscious conditioning had unraveled and that any danger from being deactivated had passed. But a couple of days ago, I got a call to say she had checked herself out and disappeared."

"Do you think we'll ever see her again?" asked Kim.

Ruby thought for a moment, then shook her head. "Probably not. Which is a shame. I would've liked the opportunity to square things with her. She was our enemy for so long, yet when it all came down to it, in that final fight... in those last critical moments... she put herself on the line to save as many of us as she could. I feel like I owe her for that."

Kim nodded. "I get that. I'm sure, if you wanted to, you could find her. But I reckon you have more pressing matters now, don't you?" She smiled at her and nodded to her belly. "What about you and your little jellybean?"

Ruby felt her cheeks fill with color. "Honestly?" She smiled. "The shit I've done in my life... being a single mother doesn't feel all that intimidating. I have money. Adrian left me everything. My baby and I will have a good life. A *safe* life."

Kim grinned. "God help anyone who incurs the wrath of this mama bear!"

"Damn straight!" she said, laughing. Then she took a breath and tilted her head slightly. "What about you, Kim? Any plans?"

She flicked her eyebrows and shrugged. "Well, Ray and I intended to retire somewhere quiet, but that stubborn man had to go and be all heroic, so... here I am, without the first clue what the future holds."

Ruby smiled warmly. "Maybe that's okay. Maybe we all need a clean slate now. No plans. No script to follow. Just... tomorrow."

Kim smiled back. "Take care, Ruby."

The two women embraced like the sisters they had become, and then walked away from the graves in opposite directions.

Link heard the movement and watched them go. Then

he turned back to Jericho, who hadn't moved since standing in front of Adrian Hell's final resting place.

"Sure could've used that crazy bastard in Nevada, huh?" said Link.

Jericho didn't react. He simply nodded.

Link turned to him. "Look, man... nothing I can say is gonna make dealing with what you lost any easier. I know that. I can't even imagine what it was like for you... Well, anyway, the way I see it, those of us lucky enough to walk away from the desert should stick together. You need someone to watch your back. And who knows, when you're feeling up to it, there's always freelance work. Me and you... man, we're warriors. We could do some real damage together, y'know. What do you say?"

Jericho looked up at him. "I appreciate what you're trying to do, Link. But I'm done fighting." He paused to take a deep breath. "Julie and I, we... we were gonna leave this all behind. We were gonna get married, start a family, have a house in the suburbs with a grill out back... the whole nine. I even joked that Ray and Kim could move in next-door. I was done, Link. Even before Nevada, I knew this was gonna be my last fight. I just... never thought it would end up being Julie's too."

"Oh, man..." Link took a breath. "You know, I just got through telling the ladies the same thing. That I felt it was time to walk away, stop fighting for someone else. I had no idea you and Julie had the talk. I... I know this might sound strange, but honestly, I'm happy for you, Jericho. I'm happy that you found someone you could picture having that life with. Guys like us, we're hard men to love. But you found that little slice of happiness in spite of the life we led. You both did. Not many people can say that. I know it was taken away from you, but still... you should hold onto that. When times get tough."

Jericho's mouth curled into the smallest of smiles. "Thanks."

Link went to walk away but stopped himself. When he turned back around, his expression was one of reluctance.

"Listen. I'm... I'm sorry, but I gotta ask you." He tapped his own forearm with two fingers, then nodded to Jericho's. "I know what you were doing."

Jericho's body tensed, and he took a step back. Link placed a hand on his shoulder.

"Hey, I get it, okay? I understand it. Honestly. There's no judgment from me. No lectures. I got nothing but love, brother. But if I'm gonna be leaving you to your own life, I gotta know you intend to live one. We both know Julie would kick my ass if she thought I was leaving you high and dry."

They shared a quiet moment and a half-smile.

Jericho patted Link's hand. "I'm fine. I promise. I'll admit there are... a couple of fresh ones there. But they're the last ones. Like I said, I'm done fighting, and... well... I'm running out of people to lose. I need some time to process everything. Julie's family is staying in town. One of her brothers invited me to stay with them for a few days."

"You going to?"

"I haven't decided yet. I feel like she would want me to. Perhaps my urge to be alone can wait for now."

"That sounds like a plan."

The two of them walked back to stand in front of Julie and Collins's graves.

"You have my number," said Link. "So does Ruby. You use it any time you need to, you hear me?"

Jericho nodded silently, as his gaze was drawn to the ground.

"I'm serious, Jericho," continued Link. "We've been through too much together for you to pull that stubborn, masculine pride crap with me. You're not alone, brother. As long as I'm okay, you're okay. Understand me?"

Jericho turned to him and offered his hand. Link clasped it with his, and the two men embraced. As Link stepped back, he nodded toward the graves.

"I'll leave you to it," he said.

With a final pat on the shoulder, Link turned and walked away.

Jericho was alone.

He stared blankly at the coffins of his lover and his best friend. Julie's body was eventually recovered from the ruins of Hall's Nevada compound. But for Collins, it was more symbolic.

His lips pursed together as he tried to make sense of all the emotions vying for prominence inside him. He was angry at himself for being unable to save them. He was afraid of who he would become without them in his life. He was also afraid of being alone. Ultimately, he felt sadness, which crushed him like an ocean—vast and infinite.

He moved a hand to his face as the emotions spilled out of him. Warm tears rushed from his eyes, burning his cheeks in the cold air. His shoulders moved as he sobbed. He didn't know what to do, and he had no one who knew him well enough to offer comfort.

After a few minutes, he heard someone close by clear their throat. He took a deep breath and hurriedly wiped his face before looking around. A groundskeeper was smiling apologetically from a respectful distance.

"I'm sorry," he said. "I didn't mean to intrude. I... I

need to start preparing the graves, but if you need more time, I can—"

"No, it's fine," said Jericho, flashing a gentle smile. "I'm sorry for keeping you waiting."

"Hey, don't worry about it. Take all the time you need."

"It's okay. I was just leaving anyway."

He began walking away, but the groundskeeper called after him.

"Hey… ah… look, I'll be done by the end of the day," he said softly. "You can always come back tomorrow, if you'd like."

Jericho glanced back over his shoulder and nodded. Then he left.

He looked up to the sky as he walked, embracing the cold, feeling the snowflakes land on his face. He took a deep breath as he contemplated the unknown future that was now laid out before him. The corner of his mouth twitched into a small smile.

"Yeah," he whispered to himself. "Tomorrow…"

Post-Credits Scene

The two women sat beside each other quietly. On the wall behind the bar, the television continued its coverage of the first commemorative event, which marked one year since Quincy Hall's occupation of the White House ended. The president was walking onto the stage, about to deliver his speech.

But neither woman paid any attention.

"You're a hard woman to find," said Ruby, swirling the whiskey around the glass in her hand.

"Not hard enough, apparently," replied Jay. "What do you want?"

"We need to talk."

"About what?"

Ruby downed her drink, then spun in her seat to face her. "About the man we loved."

Jay didn't look around. She stared ahead, signaling to the barman to bring her another drink.

"That's in the past," she said. "I've moved on. You should too."

"Right." Ruby watched her throw back her whiskey. "How are the headaches?"

Jay sighed and finally looked over at her. "Every day feels like my skull is splitting open. You happy?"

"Not about that, no. Is it the Nemesis programming wearing off, like the doctors said?"

Jay nodded solemnly. "I assume so."

"Well... maybe I can help." She gestured to a small booth across the room from the bar. "Please."

She walked over to it and slid into the seat facing the door. Reluctantly, Jay followed and took the seat opposite her.

She rested her hands on the table. "How could you possibly help me, Ruby?"

Without a word, Ruby produced a folder from inside her coat and pushed it across the table toward her.

Jay frowned. "What's this?"

"That," explained Ruby, "is a file I retrieved from Josh's secret Winnebago last year. GlobaTech kept everything that was relevant to them. I kept everything else. That's Adrian's entire life story, from the moment he met Josh when he was eighteen years old. That means it's all the stuff he did when you were married... as well as the things he did after he thought you were dead. It's every key moment from his life that Josh was around to witness."

Jay moved the folder so it was in front of her, but she felt inexplicably hesitant to open it.

"Why would you give this to me?" she asked.

"Because I don't need it," replied Ruby. "I've read it, although Adrian told me a lot of it himself during our time together. But everything in there that's relevant to me, I was there for at the time. I know the man he was, and I'll never forget who he was to me. So, I figured you might find use for it. Maybe catching up on everything you missed might make the pain of Janine and Jay merging a little easier to bear."

Jay opened the folder and skimmed the first couple of pages. Her eyes filled with tears. She quickly swallowed her emotion and closed the folder again.

"Thank you, Ruby," she said. "I really appreciate this."

Ruby smiled. "You're welcome. There's... one more thing."

She reached behind her, drew both of Adrian's Raptors, and laid them on the table between them.

Jay shifted in her seat, visibly tensing at the sight of them. She looked around the bar. There was no one there except the barman, and he had his back to them, cleaning glasses.

Ruby smiled again, amused by her apprehension, then slid one of them toward her.

Jay frowned. "What are you doing?"

"These meant the world to Adrian," said Ruby. "They were a posthumous gift from Josh, and they got him... and me... and *you*, on occasion... through some pretty scary times. Me and you... we're the only two women on Earth who know what it was like to love that man. I think he would want us each to have one."

Jay didn't reach for it. She clasped her hands together and held them close to her body.

Ruby reached across the table and placed a friendly hand down in front of her. "Honestly, Jay... I want that too. Please. It would mean a lot to me if you took one. Keep his memory alive."

Jay took a deep breath, then nodded. She picked up the Raptor in front of her and tucked it into her belt beneath her jacket. Then she gathered the folder up and got to her feet. Ruby did the same and stood in front of her. The two women regarded each other silently for a moment, then embraced.

"What will you do now?" asked Ruby.

Jay shrugged. "Same thing I've been doing for the last year—try to stay hidden and build a new life. Preferably somewhere no one knows me."

Ruby nodded. "I hope it works out for you. Sincerely."

"Thanks."

Jay smiled, then moved to walk past her, toward the rear entrance of the bar. As she drew level, Ruby held out a hand to stop her.

Jay frowned.

Ruby grinned. "Do you want to meet him?"

They held each other's gaze for a moment, then Jay's expression softened.

"Sure," she said with a warm smile.

They walked out the front door and stood on the sidewalk. It was cold, but the air was mostly still. In front of them, standing beside a white SUV with a stroller in front of her, was a full-figured woman with bright red hair and three nose piercings. She wore jet-black lipstick and matching eyeliner. Her colorful dress blew lazily in the breeze.

"This is my friend, Veronica," said Ruby.

Jay nodded a polite greeting. Veronica waved enthusiastically.

Ruby walked over to the stroller and leaned over it. She stood straight a moment later, holding a nine-month-old baby boy. She moved back over to Jay, who had lingered by the door to the bar, bouncing him in her arm.

"And this," said Ruby, "is David Joshua DeSouza."

Jay stared at the baby and waved awkwardly. His eyes

were only half-open, having been roused from a nap moments earlier. He managed a small grin, which created a spit bubble on his lips.

"David?" asked Jay.

Ruby nodded. "It was Adrian's father's name, and his middle name. I felt calling him Adrian was a little too on the nose."

"Fair point." Jay held out a hand, inviting Ruby's son to grab her finger, which he did. "So, this is what the offspring of two of the world's deadliest assassins looks like, eh? He looks slightly less threatening than I imagined."

Ruby smiled as she handed him back to Veronica, who took him with feigned effort.

"Ooo, come to Aunty Veronica," she said loudly. "That's it. Who's my gorgeous little murder baby? You are! Yes, you are!"

Jay frowned and smiled, looking questioningly at Ruby.

Ruby laughed. "Ronny knows what I used to do, and she had the pleasure of meeting Adrian once."

Veronica nodded. "I gave him a fake nose right before he killed the president. Lovely man."

Jay shook her head, smiling with disbelief. "He's really great. I'm happy for you both."

"Thank you," said Ruby.

"I know I don't need to tell you, but make sure he grows up knowing who his father was. Perhaps skip over the violence and murder and borderline insanity... but definitely mention the heroic stuff."

"You know I will."

The two of them embraced again. When they parted, Jay nodded to Veronica, then held the folder up in her hand. "Well, I guess I have some reading to do, so I'm probably gonna keep drinking. You all take care of yourselves."

"You too," said Ruby.

Jay turned and walked away.

"Will you stay in touch?" she called after her.

Jay spun around and walked backward as she smiled at them. "Probably not."

She turned once again, then rounded a corner, disappearing from view.

Ruby took her son from Veronica and kissed his cheek. "Let's get you home, little man."

More by James P. Sumner

vinci-books.com/hardtokill

They left him for dead. They should have made sure.

Unwillingly thrust into a world of high stakes industrial espionage, the man known as Roach must fight back against the people who betrayed him and left him for dead. But when his crusade for vengeance starts putting those he cares about at risk, he is forced to question who the real enemy is: the people trying to kill him… or the man in the mirror?

Turn the page for a free preview…

Hard To Kill: Prologue

The world burned before his eyes. Flames sprouted around him, forming walls that stretched up to the sky, igniting the clouds that darkened it.

He rested on all fours. His hands melted into the ground. His gaze darted frantically in all directions, searching for help or an escape. Embedded in the flames that confined him were the tortured faces of a million dead souls. They stared at him with empty eyes and shrieked with pain he instinctively knew he was responsible for.

He opened his mouth, anxious to unleash his own screams. To release the fear inside. To cry for help. But there was only silence. Yet, something caught in his throat, choking him. Not words. Not guilt. Something else. Something primal.

He looked down at the liquifying concrete beneath him. He wretched and gagged and watched in horror as cockroaches spewed forth from deep inside. His eyes bulged, threatening to burst from his head. He looked on helplessly as the creatures surrounded him, further encasing him in this inexplicable prison.

He looked ahead, searching the everlasting expanse for a sign of hope.

Cry Havoc

A child approached him. A young boy. His clothes were torn and stained, and his eyes glistened with tears. Slowly, he reached out. He saw the boy's mouth moving, yet he made no sound. He strained against the roar of the flames, against the restraints of the earth, silently imploring the child to talk louder.

No words came.

Instead, the child unleashed a howl that melted the skin from his bones. He looked on, helpless, as the small body crumbled to dust before him, trapped inside the echo of the ungodly cry.

In that moment, he realized the dead still scream long after they're gone.

Hard To Kill: Chapter One

OCTOBER 27, 2019

The man's body lay motionless. A barely perceptible rise and fall of his chest was the only sign that life still resided within. Slow, rhythmic breaths settled in time with the ticking of the broken air conditioning.

A steady trickle of saline traveled along an IV line, dripping into his bloodstream via the cannula inserted into the back of his hand. Fresh bandages covered almost every inch of skin. Only his eyes and mouth were exposed.

It wasn't much of a life, but it was a life nevertheless.

A nurse entered, looking weary and uncomfortable as she began another long shift at the end of another long week. Her uniform hung shapelessly on her body. It was spotted with dark patches of unavoidable sweat—a consequence of the oppressive heat.

She wasn't young but had aged well. The few lines on her face betrayed her years and told a story of dedication, rather than strife. However, today, she was tired and disinclined to hide it.

She moved to the bedside, expertly checking the

machines that hummed and clicked, exactly as she had done three times a day for the past month.

Nothing had changed.

She couldn't help asking herself if this seemingly futile exercise was worth it. No one knew who the man was. It was unlikely anyone knew he was there. It appeared he was clinging to life for no other reason besides habit.

As she switched out a fresh bag of solution for the IV, she looked down at the body and let out a tired sigh. She followed it up a moment later with an apologetic smile, as if he could hear her thoughts.

"Good morning, you stubborn bastard," she said.

Her voice was friendly. She spoke quietly, despite the mystery man being the only patient in the small room.

She adjusted the pillow beneath his head, fluffing it to remove the dent in the middle where he had been resting.

"There you go. Nice and comfortable. You're healing well, y'know? Those bandages should be coming off in the next day or two. Then we can finally look at that handsome face of yours."

"Has he talked back yet?"

The nurse turned, catching her breath. Then she rolled her eyes and smiled through mild embarrassment.

"Doctor Monroe, I didn't hear you come in," she said.

He smiled, friendly and warm. "Clearly."

Monroe idled into the room, walking with effortless and patient steps. A man who understood there was no reason to rush anywhere. He wore a yellow shirt, paled with age, beneath an open white coat. Also, black pants and shoes. There was no tie around his neck. His collar was unfastened, revealing more of the coarse bristle that coated his face and throat. His eyes were soft and kind, almost out of place on his otherwise hardened face.

"Any change?" he asked, retrieving the medical chart that hung over the bottom railing of the bed.

The nurse shook her head. "No. Same as always."

Monroe sighed. "Well, no news is good news in his case."

"Doctor, do we..." She hesitated. "Is there a way to find out—"

"Who he is?" Monroe nodded. His smile was one of understanding. "Probably. But it's not our place to find answers to those questions. We're here to keep him alive and help him heal. That's it."

She turned to face him. "I know. I'm sorry. But what if he doesn't wake up?"

Monroe placed a friendly hand on her shoulder. "Then we will never know who he was or where he came from, and we will carry on regardless. We provide discreet healthcare to a... *niche* clientele. The people who pay us for this service do so because they trust us. We never ask questions, and nothing good will come from starting now."

"I just feel bad for him. No one's come looking for him."

Monroe shrugged. "Maybe that's for the best. While we have a good idea *what* happened to him, we don't know how or why. Perhaps it should remain that way, hmm?"

The nurse nodded.

"Come on," he said. "We have work to do, and your friend still has healing to do."

The pair of them left the room, disappearing along the corridor outside.

The man in the bed remained still as always, save for his stubborn, shallow breathing. His arms lay exposed on top of the bedsheet. Natural muscle strained against the bandages. On his right hand, as fresh saline dripped into him, his index finger twitched. A tenacious tremor, barely visible—the sign of a fight not yet lost.

The nurse returned later to repeat her routine of checking the machines and topping up the IV. The air inside the room was stifling, which meant she needed to change the bedsheets every day.

She negotiated the fresh bedding around the man's solid frame on autopilot, having faced that challenge countless times before. As she pulled the clean blanket over the body's feet, she saw one of them twitch. A movement so small it wouldn't have registered in her periphery.

Her brow furrowed with confusion when it twitched again a moment later.

Perhaps a subconscious tick of a restless nerve, she thought. *It happens.*

She glanced up and saw a pair of unblinking brown eyes staring back at her.

The nurse shrieked, clasping her hands to her mouth.

A monotonous moan escaped his dry lips in response.

"You're awake!" she exclaimed.

Her words barely registered over the perpetual echo of a dying scream inside his head. Consciousness washed over him, tugging him awake like a lazy tide trying to drag him out to sea.

A gradual awareness of discomfort and aching caused his heartbeat to quicken, amplified by a pulse of dull pain flooding his body. He instinctively tried to control his breathing, feeling overwhelmed by the rush of sensations he wasn't prepared for.

He swallowed. His throat was coarse and dry.

The world around him settled into focus. Equipment

buzzed and blipped to his right. He heard the faint rattle of a tired air conditioning unit.

He closed his eyes and let his mind wander, hoping it would stumble upon the events that had brought him to wherever he was. But the more he tried to remember, the more he came up empty. There was a gaping hole where his memories should be, as if someone had deleted a file from a hard drive but left the folder in place.

His eyes opened again. He took a deep breath to subdue the rising panic inside him.

"Where am I?" he asked.

His question seemed to fall on deaf ears. The nurse gazed at him with wide eyes, frozen to the spot. The only movement was from her mouth.

"You're... you're awake?" she repeated.

The man shifted in his bed, shuffling to sit upright and find a modicum of relief for his aching body. "Yeah. Apparently."

He tried to smile but found he couldn't. It was as if the muscles required hadn't been used in so long, they had forgotten what a smile was. Instead, he felt he simply looked bewildered.

"Please, where am I?" he asked. "What... what is this place?"

His own voice felt foreign to him. The unfamiliar sound, tone, and accent further added to his disorientation.

"I can't believe you're awake," muttered the nurse, mostly to herself.

She shifted her gaze between the man and the door, caught between the urge to run and the urge to stay where she was. The result was a visible hesitation. She simply rocked her weight from one foot to the other.

Finally, her instincts took over.

"I should get Doctor Monroe," she said, her voice still little more than a vacant whisper.

She paced quickly out of the room. The man reached out in a futile gesture to stop her.

"Wait! Don't…" He paused to let out a sigh of defeat and frustration. "…go."

He slouched against the soft pillows behind him, searching for the right position to alleviate the soreness he felt in every inch of his body. He eventually settled for everywhere simply hurting a little bit.

He closed his eyes again and let out a heavy breath.

"Great."

Hard To Kill: Chapter Two

He awoke with no sense of how much time had elapsed since the nurse ran out on him. Consequently, it wasn't clear to him how long the man had been standing in his doorway.

He sat up again, wincing first with frustration at having fallen asleep, then as an acknowledgement of the fresh bolt of pain that plunged through his chest. His body tensed with instinctive caution. The new arrival approached the bed with idle steps. He had his hands clasped behind his back and a practiced smile on his face.

"I'm Doctor Monroe," he said after a moment. His voice sounded whiskey-rough, like the bark of an old dog. "How are you feeling?"

"I'm fine," he replied with a poor attempt at stoicism.

"That's encouraging to hear."

The man shifted in his bed, searching for comfort as he sat upright.

"Where am I? How did I get here? And why am I…" He looked down at his arms and body. "Mummified?"

Monroe's smile softened and grew wider. "One thing at

a time. Let's start with something simple. Can you tell me your name?"

The man frowned as he searched the clouded recesses of his mind for the answer.

After a moment, he gave up.

"No, I... I don't know," he said regrettably.

Monroe nodded. "That's okay. I expected as much. What's the last thing you *do* remember?"

The man leaned back against the pillow, allowing his head to loll to the side. His gaze drifted to a random point on the ceiling, away to his left. His vision blurred as he fought against his own mind to recall something—*anything*—of any substance.

He looked back at Monroe. "Nothing. I can't remember anything."

The doctor nodded once more. "That's fine. Don't worry, okay? Post-traumatic amnesia is a relatively common side effect. Now you're awake, most of your blanks should fill themselves in over the next few days. Just try to relax and let it happen."

The man furrowed his brow. "A common side effect of what?"

Monroe took a deep breath. "You've been in a coma for the last month."

"Seriously?"

"You arrived here in one of the worst states I've seen in a long time. First- and second-degree burns covered most of your body. There was a bullet in your left thigh. Another in your chest. You had cuts and bruises all over. You also suffered a head injury, resulting in a severe concussion. You looked as if you'd been hit by a train."

The man let out a heavy sigh. "I sure as hell feel like it right now, let me tell you."

He took a moment to let the doctor's words sink in.

"Burns and bullet wounds?" he said eventually. "What the hell happened to me?"

"I honestly don't know," replied Monroe. "But the surgery to remove the bullets was successful. You were fortunate. They didn't cause any permanent damage to the muscle or bone. Most of the lacerations healed on their own. A couple needed stitching, but that was it. The burns were mostly treated with ointments and antibiotics. You had one that was a little more severe, on your left shoulder. That required a simple skin graft to prevent too much scarring. We kept you bandaged longer because you were comatose, but by all accounts, you were quite lucky."

The man rolled his eyes. "Yeah, real lucky. So, what is this place?"

"This," he explained, gesturing to the room, "is a privately funded medical facility roughly twenty-five miles off the coast of Pattani."

The man stared blankly.

"Thailand," Monroe continued. "This hospital isn't open to the public. Our patients are... not typically fans of law enforcement, shall we say."

The man did not understand, and the struggle to do so gave him a headache.

"How did I get here?" he asked. "And why would I be brought somewhere like this? What the hell did I do?"

Monroe took a heavy breath. "Private security is big business in this part of the world. A couple of contractors happened across your body just outside a forest in Cambodia. They dropped you off on our doorstep. My guess was they assumed you were one of their own. Maybe they felt honor-bound to help a fallen brother. I don't know. They didn't say, and I didn't ask. But that was a little over four weeks ago, and you've been here ever since."

"Huh."

"As for what you did, or how you came to be lying unconscious and on fire in Southeast Asia, I honestly couldn't tell you."

The man nodded slowly. "I see."

"I appreciate this is a lot to take in," offered Monroe.

"You think?"

Monroe took his sharp tone as a sign their conversation had lasted as long as it needed to for now.

"Try to relax and rest up," he said, getting to his feet. "Tomorrow, we'll get those bandages off you, maybe look at starting some basic physical therapy."

"Therapy?" His eyes bulged in their sockets with instant panic. "What, am I paralyzed or something?"

Monroe flashed a comforting smile. "Not at all. But your muscles haven't been used in a month. You need to warm up a little before you go running any triathlons."

The man nodded, relaxing. "Ah, yeah. Makes sense."

"The nurse will be in soon with some food for you. Try to take it easy, okay?"

As Monroe turned to leave, the man called after him.

"Hey, Doc, you said this place was privately funded. Who by, exactly?"

Monroe smiled. Polite and professional with no humor. "Honestly? I don't know and I don't ask. Probably best you don't either."

He rolled his eyes again. "Yeah. Right."

He sank back into the pillows with a heavy sigh and stared up at the ceiling. He focused on a small stain on one of the tiles until his vision blurred. He slowly clenched both fists, fighting against a rising anxiety in his chest.

Monroe looked on, observing the struggle his unknown patient was trying to control. He found himself feeling sympathy for the man who, by all accounts, should be dead. But he would likely make a full recovery, save for some mild scarring. He was impressed by his patient's instinctive resolve. He had seen cases like this before, though not often. The adjustment period after waking from a coma was always tricky. Some people reacted with fear and uncertainty. Others with anger and frustration.

This patient was among the latter.

He couldn't imagine what must be running through his mind right now.

"Just try to relax, all right?" said Monroe finally. "Let your body and your mind rest. There's no hurry."

"Thank you," he replied with a heavy sigh. "I don't mean to sound... I don't know... ungrateful. I just—"

Monroe held up a hand, cutting him off. He smiled again, warmer this time. "Don't apologize. I'm a doctor. I'm used to patients who don't like the fact they need treatment. Trust me."

The man regarded him for a moment, then broke into a deep chuckle.

"Fair enough."

Monroe nodded and left. The man shifted until he found a position that relieved enough pain for him to relax, then closed his eyes.

Monroe sat behind his desk in the small, airless room he called his office. With the stub of a cigar clamped between his fingers, he leaned back in his chair and stared absently at the photograph beside his computer.

The wood frame had faded and chipped over the years.

The photo's color had yellowed from too much time in direct sunlight. He looked at the image of his younger self. He'd had more hair, less waist, and the enthusiasm of a man who believed he had it all figured out.

By his side in the picture was a tall woman with long, curly blonde hair that rested just below her shoulders. She wore a lab coat and a pencil skirt. They were holding hands, like the loving husband and wife they used to be.

He took a long drag of his cigar and blew the thick, blue-gray smoke up to the ceiling with a long breath. He remembered her smile. She was always a good-looking woman, but that smile could light up a room the moment she entered it.

Behind them stood the medical facility he was sitting in. The opportunity to set up their own practice overseas had been too good for either of them to pass up. They were young, idealistic, newly qualified doctors out to make a difference in the world. They were both devoted to their work.

Him more so than her.

He worked every hour he could, focused on turning their private medical practice into a profitable business. But he did so at her expense. Months of neglect turned into years. Eventually, he caught her sleeping with one of the male nurses. She cited a loveless marriage as an obvious justification for her infidelity and said their venture wasn't worth what it cost them.

She left, taking her father's money with her. With the bulk of their investment capital gone, Monroe struggled to keep the facility afloat. When the opportunity to tend the wounds of injured mercenaries off the books presented itself, he had no choice but to take it. The money was good, and as his reputation grew, he became more protected from the dangerous world in which his patients lived.

That was over fifteen years ago.

He stubbed out the remains of the cigar in the glass ashtray beside him. He caught himself thinking back to his earlier conversation with his nurse. About not intervening in their mystery patient's life. About not asking questions. Despite his experience and professionalism, he had grown fond of the mystery man. He and his nursing staff shared a hushed support for him. Seeing him now, awake and lost… he felt compelled to do something.

Being a doctor was all he had. If he were going to continue letting it consume his life, maybe it was time he found a way to help people outside of the practice too. After all, he didn't treat a global network of mercenaries without getting to know a few people.

Monroe reached for his phone and dialed a number from memory.

"Hello?" said a female voice. The tone was cautious and restrained.

Monroe smiled. "Hey, Val. It's me."

There was a low, audible sigh of relief. "Clyde, is that you? How you been, sweetie?"

"Oh, you know, I keep on keeping on. Business good?"

"You know it, sugar."

"Listen, I was hoping you could do me a favor. I need to keep this quiet, and I'd owe you."

"Clyde, honey, I'll just deduct from all the favors I owe *you*."

The pair shared a laugh.

"Fair enough," continued Monroe. "I got a patient who just woke up from a coma. Been out around a month. He's experiencing some memory loss…"

"And you want me to see if I can ID him?"

"Could you try?"

"Put everything you have into a draft e-mail on the usual account, no matter how small or insignificant. I'll pick it up and take a look. Give me twenty-four hours, okay?"

Monroe grinned. "You're the best, Val."

"I know," she replied, then hung up.

He sat back in his chair and spun around to face the window. He stared out at the dry trees and grass, baking beneath the scorching afternoon sun.

It couldn't hurt to ask. He just hoped his mystery patient could handle potentially finding out something about himself he might not like.

Grab your copy…
vinci-books.com/hardtokill

Acknowledgments

After four years, the *Thrillerverse* is over. It has been an incredible journey for me, and a truly life-changing experience to bring something so complex and original to the genre I love.

Writing Adrian Hell gave me a career, but writing GlobaTech, Roach, and crafting the underlying narrative of the *Thrillerverse* is what helped me grow into the author I am today.

Whether you've only followed Adrian's Hell path, or read everyone's part in this incredible story... thank you! Thank you for supporting this unique literary endeavor, and I sincerely hope you have enjoyed it as much as I have.

As always, I owe a huge amount of gratitude to my incredible editor, who is now also my beautiful wife, Coral. Not just because, yet again, she helped turn a good manuscript into a great novel, but also because she supported me emotionally through a difficult year that saw me make many difficult choices about my writing.

With the *Thrillerverse* completed, I'm now ready and incredibly excited to begin a new chapter of my own. Many writing projects that have taken a back seat for years because of Adrian's and GlobaTech's adventures can now be shared with the world. My audience consists of some of the most passionate and loyal readers an author could wish for, and I'm eternally grateful for their ongoing support. What comes next is for all of you.

www.ingramcontent.com/pod-product-compliance
Ingram Content Group UK Ltd.
Pitfield, Milton Keynes, MK11 3LW, UK
UKHW040638071025
463682UK00005B/170